The Man Without a Party:
The Trials of
Carl von Ossietzky

———

Richard Tres

D1572216

THE MAN WITHOUT A PARTY
THE TRIALS OF CARL VON OSSIETZKY
562
KAISERISM
MARXISM
NAZISM

This fictional narrative was inspired by the life and times of Carl von Ossietzky. I do not understand the process by which I studied the one and produced the other.

Therefore, somehow, he is and isn't "he"; we are and aren't "they."

But will you still be you?

For Janice

Chapter One
PRESENT

"Baumgarten, have you seen what the bastards are doing now?" asked the man entering the room.

The other justices and the chief prosecutor were doing their best to lounge on beautifully uncomfortable Louis XV chairs in the gilded anteroom of the German court.

"What is it now?" asked Alexander Baumgarten, wincing in anticipation of something else that could have been bad. "I haven't yet read—"

"Did Max fight again last night?" interrupted another judge in an attempt to answer the question. He perched with his legs spread out. "Last night, I was too busy to get to a wireless." He was checking his face in a pocket mirror: the forest of gray, which was better that than baldness, above the bristling eyebrows, all ready to raise or lower for full effect. But under the eyes, a puffiness…

"Last I heard, he was modeling the latest fashions in the window of some department store," added the prosecutor. While seated, he reached down the length of his leg and, with the edge of his robe, buffed a scuff near the tip of his shoe.

"No," responded the first man. Then he gave an oracular reply to his own query: "That damn Ford is building a plant in Koln!"

"You just heard that?" asked yet another judge, incredulous. "That's not news. And besides, it's nothing to get upset about. Let the Americans bring their millions. We need every penny. At least someone is putting our workers to work…"

"That's right," said the man with legs spread-eagled; now he was retying his shoes. "Ford's a hero! The more U.S. 'bucks' he spends on our dreadful economy, the better."

"All of a sudden, we have a Hilferding among us," commented Baumgarten.

"It's true! All very true. You'll see—" he remarked before interrupting himself. "Are we ready?" he asked, standing up and finishing his coffee.

"Hell, where's that Braune?"

"Probably fucking some maid in a back room."

"Who's the lucky girl? Or should I say, 'young man'?"

"I heard that," said Braune, rushing in. "No, I can manage keeping my trousers shut quite well, thank you." He was already swinging a scarlet robe over his back. "But you, you keep drinking that swill they serve you here, and you'll be calling for a recess at nine forty-five so you can go piss. I'm ready."

"What? No make-up?"

There was a snicker while Baumgarten, the head judge, grabbed the doorknob. He lowered his voice. "Gentlemen, remember what we carry on our shoulders," he advised, throwing open the door to the courtroom.

"*Sub specie aeternitatis*," Braune said under his breath as he followed the others in.

"...*teutonicae*," added the man behind him.

The bailiff leaped up at their entrance and shouted with the voice of a town crier, "All rise! All rise for the judges of the government!" and, after people took their seats again, "Now begins the trial of the German state against Walter Kreiser and Carl von Ossietzky for treason and espionage!"

It was the morning of November 17th, 1931, and the culmination of over two years of investigation was about to unfold in the Leipzig courthouse.

****

The pilot sat in the dock.

2

"Tell the judges why you thought you should betray your country and go to Mr. Ossietzky with your story."

Kreiser stared at the questioner and sniffed. The sharp smell of the overnight floor polish was still strong in the large courtroom. "After several missions in Russia, it occurred to me that something was wrong. I felt very bad."

"Tell the judges why your feelings were more important to you than your loyalty toward your fatherland."

Now the pilot was looking up into the shadows of the palatial courtroom.

"I never—"

"Oh, yes, you did. You went straight to this..." the prosecutor pointed to the grim-faced, hawk-nosed man sitting with others at a table to his right, "this conspiring publisher, and you told him what Germany was doing to defend itself against its enemies."

"But this was—"

"Too cowardly to publish it under your own name!" He looked down at a slip of paper in his hand. He spat with distaste, "'Heinz Hunter'!"

"It was recommended."

"Why did you break your sacred oath to your homeland in its hour of need?"

"I didn't think—"

"You didn't think! Precisely, young man! You..."

While the prosecutor shouted at him, his tenor bouncing off the far walls, the pilot in the dock imagined himself with the swimming motes up in the shafts of light and lofty shadows of the morning courtroom, as if he were flying again, winding his way from one corner to another under the clerestories. But then, in a dark niche, he saw the gilded statue of the imperial eagle lurking above the judges' dais, glaring angrily with its predatory eyes. And he no longer felt guilt as the prosecutor continued his rant. Fear. He only felt great fear.

"Are you listening?"

Caught. He was caught in the eagle's cutting talons.

****

After lunch they couldn't find Kreiser. He had been silent nearly all through the meal at a restaurant off Market Square while the lawyers, Rosenfeld, Alsberg, Apfel and Olden, held forth on a wide variety of matters, avoiding the case at hand. Ossietzky listened, also subdued, so he didn't think anything of it until they gathered again in the tiny anteroom and noticed the absence.

"Was he sick?"

"He was awfully quiet at luncheon."

"He had a hard time this morning, obviously."

Alsberg exhaled loudly. "How have we come to this?"

"Perhaps he's not needed this afternoon. Oss—"

But Ossietzky was already down the hall. He found the pilot in a window niche, looking out. He approached quietly, reached for a shoulder.

"We should probably go in now."

Kreiser jumped and turned to him, his face distraught. "I can't! I'm done!" He looked like he was about to break down. Ossietzky grasped his elbow, looked around, and found an open door across the hall. It was empty; they went in. Carl closed the door.

"Talk to me."

"I've made a huge mistake!" whined Walter. "My life is ruined! Even if …"

"Yes?"

"Even if I'm found not guilty, I'll be a marked man. There's no way …"

Carl squeezed his shoulder, feeling the tension of a man near the breaking point. "Walter, you've done a great thing. Focus on that, and on tomorrow only when it comes. You probably won't even be called anymore today. It's my turn. You did fine this morning!"

"I should've known! In this country ..."

"This country isn't done being made. We're making it now, and it needs people like you with great conviction and the courage to step forward and do your part by leading the way. The only salvation for Germany is to look outside itself, to develop internationally along with its neighbors. By appealing to that damned Treaty, we can strengthen our country's connections to the outside world. Only through internationalism can Germany save itself. Think about the impact this trial will have on Germany's foreign relations. Even if we lose this case, we're forcing our government toward greater accountability. And if we win ..."

The phrase hung in the air. They were quiet for a few moments. Then Kreiser took a deep breath, rubbed his face, and straightened his suitcoat.

Carl found himself reciting the lines his mother had drilled into him for years; he stifled a feeling of silliness and went on: "'Those who hope in the Lord will renew their strength. Those who hope in the Lord...'" He waited.

"'...will renew their strength.'"

"'They will soar...they will soar...'"

"'...on wings like eagles.'"

"Say it: 'Those...Those...'"

"'...who hope in the Lord will renew their strength.'"

"And...?"

"'They will soar on wings like eagles.'"

"Keep repeating it to yourself."

Krieser whispered like a monk.

"Let *Isaiah* be your mantra."

The *sotto voce* chant droned on. "Of course, you're right," he said, gathering himself together a minute later. Ossietzky sighed away his tension and was surprised when the other followed in suit. He massaged Kreiser's shoulder again, feeling it gradually relax.

"That's the spirit," he whispered. "Are we ready to go?"

Kreiser took a deep breath. "Yes. I think so." He looked up. "Thank you, Carl."

They went out back down the hall. Ossietzky, his arm over Kreiser's shoulders, thought about the things he hadn't said, the things he'd filtered out: Yes, you should have known it would be hard; that there would be no medals for this sort of heroism; that you passionately opposed these people and they almost always withered; that sometimes they play for keeps, with high stakes; that it could be dangerous to be right when one's government was wrong, and that tomorrow would only come too soon.

How did we get here? thought Ossietzky.

****

"And what did you do when this pilot, this man, Kreiser, came to you?" The prosecutor was questioning the man named Ossietzky, who now sat in the dock. It was later that same day. The afternoon sun crept up the dark wall opposite the tall west-facing windows, radiating the entire room with natural light in contrast to the morning, which had been illuminated with the electric chandeliers.

Before he answered, Ossietzky made a point of turning halfway toward the panel of judges, speaking directly to them.

"Since all the facts had already been made public, we could have printed up the story ourselves. But, as editor of *The Worldstage*, I decided that it was best to have Mr. Kreiser tell his own story."

"Which you let him do."

Ossietzky quickly shook his head twice. "Which we hired him to do. He's also a fine writer. When we saw what he had written—"

"His slanders!"

"Frankly, he had nothing new to add to the facts that had already been exposed. But his own, personal perspective was what we found so, uh, arresting." He looked directly at the judges, as if ignoring the prosecutor. "At any rate, as editor, I take full responsibility. After all, I could have rejected his piece."

"All of the secret government information!"

"But, as I say, that's what was most interesting. The basic content for all of his eyewitness details was already public. As Mr. Rosenfeld showed in the government budget commission—"

"His lies? Why would you print them again if these falsehoods had already created a public scandal for the government?"

Ossietzky squinted at the interrogator, jutted forth his chin, and said, "Why would you prosecute us for treason and the exposure of government secrets if what we printed were only lies?"

It was only a moment. But the prosecutor, whom Ossietzky had specifically addressed with his last remark, stood frozen, all except for his quivering cheeks. Ossietzky had already turned back to the judges and was pleased to note the vanishing flash of a grin on the face of one of them. He was still turned toward them when the prosecutor's rage overflowed.

"You question me? You interrogate me? How dare you? I ask the questions here!" Then, visibly controlling himself, he stopped. He glanced up sheepishly at the bank of faces staring down at him. He wrinkled the edges of his eyes as he pressed out the bitterest of smiles.

If only he could write about this in his paper! Ossietzky thought. *Shit on these secret trials!*

The prosecutor turned back toward Ossietzky and continued with a lowered, measured voice: "At this time, we will not discuss the issue of the libelous mendacity of what you printed in your scurrilous rag. We will focus, now, only on the charge of treason. Did you or did you not publish Mr. Kreiser's inflammatory myths, knowing they were damaging to the safety and defense of your country?"

Once again, the man in the dock squinted as he focused his eyes better to see his questioner, toward whom he aimed his prominent chin a second time, and said, "Did not our country sign the Treaty pledging not to participate in the operations Mr. Kreiser describes so well?"

7

When the prosecutor started to sputter incoherently, the head judge quickly intervened.

Ossietzky turned toward the bank of judges. "What are the pledges of Germany worth?"

"It is time for dinner" said the head judge quickly. "We will meet again here the day after tomorrow at nine in the morning."

As he left the courtroom with Kreiser and the lawyers, Ossietzky was careful not to turn his eyes toward the prosecutor.

****

"Have you seen the news?" asked the man hurrying into the broom closet of a room they had given to the defense for waiting. The building, it seemed, had been constructed strictly for prosecution.

Ossietzky looked up from the pad of paper on his knee. "Seen it? I'm writing it presently." He smiled briefly at the man entering, Alfred Apfel, and took a last drag on his cigarette before dropping it on the floor and crushing it out with the sole of his shoe.

"Nothing about the trial, I hope," cautioned another of the lawyers, Max Alsberg, who sat at a sofa looking over a jumble of documents on a low table before him. He talked with his head still down. "Or they'll have you back here in no time for another court date."

"And you'll be coming to us at the League for Human Rights for free lawyering again," added head defense lawyer Kurt Rosenfeld, who was bent over the same table as Alsberg, studying the spread of work before them.

"Which you'll be generous enough to donate, of course" capped Ossietzky, flashing his smile again.

"Of course, Carl, my beloved," answered Rosenfeld.

"Ha, ha, to all of you," said the first man, Apfel. "This is no joke." He swatted the paper in his hand. "Oss, the Nazis have taken the election in Hesse!"

"Yes," said 'Oss,' exhaling with a voice that suddenly sounded tired. "And Hitler's meeting tomorrow in Berlin with the Kaiser's wife. *Sic transit mundus*." He stood up, then waited for his heart to pump more blood to his head. He made sure Kreiser, sitting in the corner looking glum, caught his eye. Ossietzky winked, hoping to cheer him up.

"You should never take it for granted, what that swine will try to do," warned Apfel. "Before you know it, we'll be a blasted monarchy again!"

"I take nothing for granted since September 14th of last year," replied Ossietzky. "Where's Rudolf? I think we need him."

"I saw him talking in his car with his secretary when I came up the steps," Alsberg informed.

"What's keeping him?"

"Perhaps we should send down an officer of the court to dump a bucket of cold water on them," said Rosenfeld.

"If it's true that they're *embrassentes*, that's good," said Ossietzky. "It means he's finally getting over Hide's passing. I sincerely hope we never have to learn, through our own suffering, what he has had to go through in losing his beloved. By the way, does anyone want to see the letter I just received from Tucholsky in Sweden?" He lifted the creased sheets of paper. "He wishes us luck."

"Good," said Rosenfeld. "We'll need it a lot more than he will in Scandinavia."

"Who's Chubby screwing now?" asked Alsberg.

"No, really," Ossietzky deadpanned. "He's actually quite encouraging to us."

"He feels guilty for leaving. Let him come here to Leipzig and still be encouraging."

"Do you have your Schiller quote yet for the grand finale?" Rosenfeld asked Apfel.

"Goethe."

"What? 'First, *let's kill all the lawyers*'?"

"Hilarious. Anyway, that's Shakespeare."

"Then what is it? *'Little Meadow Rose?*'" Ossietzky asked.

Apfel blew out his trumpet laugh. "No, but I hope that it draws blood."

The tones of Ossietzky's voice rose and lengthened as he sang Schubert's ascending tune:

"Little rose, little rose, little red rose—"

"Someone throw a shoe at him," said Alsberg.

"I sang in the choir, for God's sake!"

"For the Kaiser's sake; he demanded it."

The lawyer, Rudolf Olden, finally arrived. Rosenfeld looked in mock anger at his watch. "Rudy! It's not good to upstage the judges."

"Sorry," Olden said with chagrin. "I had to go over some last-minute work with Ika."

The other men exchanged glances, saying nothing as the lawyers threw on their black silk gowns.

"Okay, gentlemen," said Rosenfeld. Let's show these deities of justice what we can do. And just remember—"

"We know," said Apfel. "'Turn every weakness into a strength.'"

"Yeah," added Alsberg. "Make like Jesus. When you're pissing in your loincloth and bleeding through all your wounds, don't forget to save this relative universe of ours."

They entered the courtroom.

****

The prosecutor stayed away from Ossietzky on the second day of the trial. In the dock, once again, the pilot Kreiser squirmed, looking up toward the ceiling from time to time.

"Tell us more of your..." the prosecutor dropped a finger on the top sheet of the stack on the table before him, then stared back at Kreiser, "operations."

Kreiser's tongue visibly twisted in his mouth, stretching his cheeks. He brought his gaze down to the wall to his left. "While in Russia, we stayed in barracks along the airfield. It was still dark when they woke us so we would be ready for take-off at dawn."

"Yes?"

"We would rev up our planes. Though German designs, they were Russian jobs, so it took some instruction and getting used to. I was third in our squadron. Usually the skies were overcast, so, at first, we stayed under the clouds. The main thing was to stay in formation."

The prosecutor paused, thinking, then asked, "And why was that the…'main thing'?"

Ossietzky noticed a slight movement of the man sitting next to him at the table, the lawyer, Apfel, to his left. He seemed suddenly to develop a rod-straight spine. Ossietzky followed Apfel's gaze up toward the dock and the dais. He thought something in the pilot's expression had triggered the change in the lawyer's posture. The pilot was pulling an ear while gathering his thoughts to answer the question posed. But Apfel wasn't looking at Kreiser; he was looking at one of the four velvet-wrapped senators of the Supreme Court—Baumgartner?—who had gathered together his red vestments and was leaning forward ever so slightly to get a better view of Kreiser's face.

Apfel coughed once. Kreiser stared at him. Ossietzky saw Apfel nod, look down his right arm to his hand where it lay palm-up on the table. The hand opened halfway. Apfel looked back up at Kreiser, who was watching Apfel's hand. The two exchanged glances. Kreiser turned his eyes back toward the prosecutor, who was impatiently crossing his arms behind his back. Kreiser exhaled slowly and began.

"We younger pilots had learned well in the classroom that one of our greatest problems during the war had been staying in formation during flight. On the ground, it was quite well they could drill us and drill us on the importance of not falling out of formation—it was our 'safety,' our 'life,' our 'only strength in formation,' we were 'a team dependent on one another for defense,'—but, when we were up in the

11

air, that all was lost as soon as we were attacked, every man was out for himself, and each went his own way. We would have to learn it all over in the air."

Now all the judges were craning their necks toward Kreiser. Time had seemed to stop. There was a creak in the floor somewhere. Ossietzky noticed the smell of his own perspiration.

"And what happened?"

"On the very first day, the Bolsh—the Russians—came after us. It was all drill, of course. They were acting as our enemies, and they were very bold. They themselves had been trained by pilots who had come over after the war from the U.S., communists, and they were quite fearless, even reckless, at dogging us, and Bauer—"

The hand had closed suddenly.

Quietly, Kreiser is urged, "Yes? Go on. Bauer?"

The hand and mouth stayed closed.

The prosecutor sensed his forced interlocutor was at a logjam. He looked back down toward the papers on his own table, shuffled through them, pulled one out of the stack, looked at it, and looked back at Kreiser.

"I...I don't remember you mentioning this Bauer in any of your articles."

Silence.

"If you tell us about this, uh, incident, the judges may take it into consideration when—" he rocked backward and forward on the balls of his feet, leaving his words hanging in the air.

"Mr. Kreiser," he said, his voice suddenly becoming stentorian again, "let me remind you that you have taken an oath in this court, and that, even if your loyalty toward your country is extremely suspect, this court is in a position to put you away and lock you behind bars for a very, very long time. Or even—" he let this, too, hang.

The hand on the table suddenly opened wider. Kreiser saw it and continued.

"Well, Bauer was no ace like Udet. When one of the Russian planes came right at him, he bolted. Broke formation. However, since Bauer had been directly in front of me, now I was exposed. And since the Russian kept on coming straight at me, we were nose to nose, and, and—"

"Go on!" Several people jumped as the prosecutor's bellow echoed throughout the room.

The pilot's eye-level was neither down nor up. As he was reliving his experience, he stared just over the heads of the men in front of him. Could he even hear the prosecutor? The Russian plane was still coming after him. Then his eyes returned to earth. He exhaled.

"At the last second," Kreiser gulped and swallowed air, "the Russian flyer peeled off and I kept on in formation."

"Yes?"

"That's all." Kreiser wanted to hurry back to his seat.

"You don't have any more to say about that day?"

He shook his head and shoulders vigorously, as if in a spasm. "No."

"You didn't encounter any more difficulty?" Silence.

"… Bauer…"

"Yes? What about him?"

"We never saw him again," the aviator whispered. "He must have had engine trouble."

****

That afternoon, the head defense lawyer, Rosenfeld, had spoken as much as he was allowed by the judges about the grave injustice he perceived in the rejection by the court of all nineteen defense witnesses on the grounds of the requirement of maintaining confidentiality about the matters involved. Convinced that he had made as much of the matter as he could, he returned to the issue of the truthfulness of Kreiser's articles.

"Whereas the defense has been regrettably unable to bring forth any witnesses in support of those charged, the prosecution's witnesses, Major Himer and Secretary Wegerdt, both confirmed the facticity, if you will, of everything under question printed in *The Worldstage*. Confirmed true! And yet, was it possible for us to use this finding in support of Mr. Kreiser and Ossietzky, or in any way to weaken the prosecution's case? No, Justices. Hard to believe, we were not allowed. And why? Because, in this case, the truth that these men should have been able to stand on confidently has been used against them! And how, Justices? Because of the supposed secrecy of the information! And how was *The Worldstage* to have known of this required secrecy, especially when it was already public knowledge, cited in reports of the congressional budget commission, that government expenditures had gone toward the payment of all costs incurred by Battalion M, Mr. Kreiser's battalion? Battalion M, a special air unit of the army, the rationale for which, as has been abundantly explained, was national defense.

"Truly a vicious circle!

"Evidently, the defendants should have known a state secret was involved because, when interviewed on this question, the Minister of Defense had declined to answer. His refusal to answer was supposed to have been sufficient to indicate to Mr. Kreiser and Mr. Ossietzky that they were in effect on the verge of breaching the Penal Code and Clause 1, Paragraph 2 of the Act against Disclosure of Military Secrets, the espionage act of June 3rd, 1914. That they were, in fact, about to draw international attention to state affairs which the state wished to keep secret. All for defensive reasons, of course!

"But did not official representatives of that same state sign the Treaty of Versailles, Article 195 of which clearly states that Germany was to have no air force whatsoever? The same state whose Constitution definitively avows in its Article Four that the rules of international law are, and throughout the life of that Constitution shall continue to be, binding for the German court?

"What, in fact, do we have here, gentlemen of the court? Is this not a double standard, which has been applied against my clients to their great disadvantage? When is it not the right of each and every citizen to know the truth about their government? Without that truth, how can the citizens of a country make informed decisions and discuss matters important to their lives with one another? How, Judges, can citizens perform their civil duties if they do not know the truth?

"And, by extension, how is the national press supposed to fulfill its obligation to those citizens, citizens who have entrusted to that press the essential, nay, the sacred duty of adequately informing the public? Finally, how is a country based on the integrity and freedom of each individual supposed to live and function if the arteries of truth are cut off by the very government they serve?"

****

On the third and last day of the trial, the lawyers finished with their concluding remarks. Lawyer Apfel started his summation of the defense: the pertinent evidence had all already been in the public domain; the government of the Republic of Germany had breached its own agreements in the Treaty of Versailles; it was up to responsible citizens to let their fellows know such important information; the prosecution had never seriously challenged the veracity of what *The Worldstage* had reported. And if the reports had been false, then the charges of treason and exposure of government secrets were certainly the wrong charges to make.

"And so, these two citizens of our country," Apfel continued, "have been summoned before you, honored Judges. And why? Because they have been untruthful? Disloyal? No, your Honors, it is we who have been deceptive and craven. Either our country should have abided by its international agreements, or it should never have made them. To love one's country and to still criticize it when it seems to have contradicted itself, this is perhaps the most difficult, and yet the most dutiful, thing for a citizen to do. Do we not want our government—the government to which you, Judges, have dedicated your careers—to be as perfect as possible? Is this not the pinnacle of patriotism? And is my patriotism to be called into question simply because I have seen my country's imperfections? Surely, one is no less patriotic toward one's fatherland than one would be loyal toward a friend one criticizes, a relative or a spouse, the inconsistency of whose actions contradicted their sworn guarantees, pledges, and promises. Surely Goethe was right about the way we should treat our country, too, when he said, 'Treat people as if they were the way they ought to be, and you help them become what they are capable of being.' Officers of the court, the true friend, the true patriot wants his country to abide by its agreements, however severe or coerced. He wants his country blameless enough to be defended in full confidence, without putting his own honesty into question.

"So these men have published writings that call into question the perfection of our country's honesty. Commend them, your Honors! Do not condemn them. How hollow would ring the accolades we extend toward that patron and father of all journalists, Guttenberg himself, if we betray the invaluable achievement of his great invention by punishing men of the press who dutifully publish the truth! Where would we be if we, citizens, were still imprisoned in the darkness of ignorance and misinformation, as we belatedly realize to our great cost we were imprisoned, both those of us on the right, left and center, during the war? If our citizens had possessed adequate knowledge before and during that war, would our country be in a better place than it is now? Would the bitter, violent splits and sects exist? And would *we* be different, perhaps better citizens toward one another? The danger, your Honors, isn't knowledge; the danger is in the withholding of knowledge from the people.

"Without adequate knowledge, are we not as our ancestors were before Johann Guttenberg set his presses to humming the truth, so that men may read it, discuss it, illuminate themselves with it, and become free? Where, finally, would we be if Luther had said that, yes, the Roman Church has propagated misdeeds, but it would not be right to criticize it, to correct it, to set the matter right before God? Where would we be, your honors, if we had failed to print on Guttenberg's presses Luther's sublime translation of Holy Scripture and disseminate it so that our souls could breathe the fresh air of spiritual freedom? I'll tell you where, Judges. On the road to hell on earth.

"No, your Honors, I know it is not your place to award these gentlemen for their courageous acts of selfless civic duty. That would be too much for me to ask. Therefore, I only request that, since you have decreed that they cannot publish anything about this trial of theirs, you set them and their reputations free once again with the acquittal these honest and brave citizens so justly deserve. Thank you."

****

"My colleague," the prosecutor began, "speaks as if today were the first day of creation, as if the slate were clean, as if the original sins of the two men accused and many unaccused had not already been committed. But we all know that is not the case. Circumstances have driven us from that Garden we once enjoyed, and our conditions are irretrievably, bitterly the ones of a fallen state. Our beloved Kaiser no longer reigns in our land; our enemies line our borders, nay, they even patrol our streets and plague our communities. Provoked, we entered into a terrible war, purely for reasons of defense; our soldiers were not defeated on the field of battle, but stabbed in the back by some at home who shirked their duty behind the lines, they were betrayed. We were betrayed by our own fellow citizens, by our leaders in government who signed the accursed Dictate and its crippling reparations, by the Entente and its starving blockade, by satanic France and its hysterical passion for revenge. It is in the context of these terrible conditions that we must understand the crimes of the men brought before the court. When our government tried to balance the unjust measures imposed upon us by training volunteers for its defense, these two men struck at the heart of our fatherland.

"Please, honored Judges, do not only condemn the one who himself composed these dangerous writings. Please include the man who published them, who, though he may not have put pen to paper, spread the evil message like a contagion. We know that Ossietzky's bias against our military, our soldiers, our officers, our commanders, stretches back for decades. Please, do not leave him out of the judgment he so deserves. Thank you."

Both men were sentenced to eighteen months in prison. Imprisonment would begin on May 10th, 1932.

In the interim, each was allowed to keep his passport.

Chapter Two
PAST

Both Rosalie and little, two-year-old Carl went to answer the knocking at their apartment door. It was Fr. Anton, the young pastor's assistant from her church. He immediately gathered Carl up in his arms and carried him down the hallway to where she directed him to sit in the parlor.

"How nice of you to come visit!" she had said over her shoulder on the way down the hall.

He sat down, propping the smiling toddler on his lap. "It's been two weeks. I know you've been to church on Sunday, but I just wanted to check up on you and the boy."

"So nice," she went on. It had been two weeks since her husband's, Carl Senior's, funeral. "We're doing fine."

"Well, Fr. Paul and I are here for you for anything," he said. "Anything. From counseling, to women on-call, to volunteer to babysit, to cash if that gets short…"

"No, nothing right now, thank you." She stood up. "I'll get us some tea." With a flash of black dress, she had left the room before he could reply. He turned the boy toward him.

"And how have *you* been, my young man?"

"Good," said Carl, looking down at the priest's cross he was holding. He examined it, turning it in every direction. "Daddy…"

"Yes?"

"Gone."

Pursing his lips, Fr. Anton hugged the boy to him, looking over his tousled flaxen hair at the phalanx of framed pictures on the tables and walls of the room, marshaled like battle-ready troops to fight against the loss, against forgetfulness, despair.

19

"You will always love your father, won't you, little Carl?"

"Yes." They hugged again. The priest stared at a photo of Carl Sr., as a young man in uniform, and recalled the story family members always told with grins. The 'von' was not an indicator of aristocracy in their case, certainly not of wealth. It had been acquired when the Elector of Brandenburg was short of cash and needed troops. Two entire regiments of cavalry lancers had been paid with that 'von,' an Ossietzky ancestor one of them. Too bad the family was not better off financially. They would be hard up until Rosalie could find work, or…

She came into the room with a tray and things for tea. Carl watched with rapt attention as she poured for Fr. Anton and herself.

"The cholera—" she started.

"It finally looks like the epidemic is subsiding," noted the priest. "We have been running ragged, especially in the poor sections."

"All the way from India!"

"Yes. That's where they say the bacillus originated. But it was certainly spread by our defective sanitation. The water pipes—"

"Oh, dear."

"—contaminated when refuse seeped in."

"My God!"

"But mainly just around St. Pauli."

They paused to sip.

"How has the boy been sleeping?"

She laughed. "Better than I have! Our roles have been reversed, it seems. At least up until…"

"Yes?"

She laughed again. "I'd been thinking about, you know, about Carl Sr.'s being a Lutheran. Worrying, I guess you could say. As soon as I closed my eyes to sleep, something clicked on in my brain and—"

"You firmly believe that the Lord will take care of things."

"Yes. I mean, intellectually…, but—"

Swirling the hot tea in his mouth, the priest waited.

Rosalie frowned. "Deep down, it was still a concern. Until …"

He waited again, rubbed the boy's back. Carl smiled and squirmed.

"Until last Sunday, because of something Fr. Paul said in his sermon." She looked up to the ceiling to remember. "Let's see. 'The outward man… is the door; the inward man…'"

"Aha! '… the hinge'!"

"That's it! After I thought awhile about that, well, I was able to fall asleep. It was as if the words had been meant for me."

"Meister Eckhart would be proud! And Fr. Paul would be glad!"

"I felt a deep sense of peace. As if Carl himself were telling me everything would be okay."

"Wonderful! And it will, Rosalie, believe me. It will." He reached over and pressed her hand.

"And then, Father, after Mass, when Carl Junior and I went up to light the votive candles under the Virgin's statue, I had the strangest feeling of peace, beyond peace, even. My inner conflict ceased, resolved. It was when Carl was lighting the lower tapers. Do you remember, Carl?"

"Lights!" the toddler exclaimed.

"Yes! You lit the lower candles."

He raised his arms above his head. "Carl dood it!"

"Yes, thanks to the long matches. You didn't want to stop! I was running out of coins! But, Father, while he was doing it, I looked up into the face of the statue, into her eyes, and I felt *she* was assuring me all would be well too."

"Yes! Wonderful!"

"And then I saw Carl, grown up. Do you remember I told you about this, Son?"

The boy put his arms back down and nodded.

"He was grown up, Fr. Anton," she said with passion. "And he was wearing a cassock, Father. Just as you are now. And it made up for everything."

Anton's face darkened; he took time to recover by raising his eyebrows and looking at the boy in mock amazement. "What do you

21

say to that, young man? Do you want to become a priest like Father Paul and Father Anton?" He mussed his hair. All three of them laughed as Carl mirrored the priest's bemused look.

Then, looking at Rosalie with eyes that tried to express too much, he said, "There will be many days before young Carl will have to make such momentous decisions. In the meantime, we can do our best by just letting him be the child he is. He and God will work it all out in time."

"But wouldn't it be wonderful, Fr. Anton?"

Looking deep in thought, the priest put his empty cup down on the tray. He set Carl on his feet.

"You know, Rosalie, Meister Eckhart said many things."

"Oh, yes, Father."

Anton chuckled. "And one of them was, 'God, I ask you to free me from God.'"

It was a few moments before Rosalie could say, "I see."

Anton wasn't so sure she did. He stayed a little longer with them, mainly playing with the boy, before saying, "Well, Rosalie, I'm glad to give you absolution before I go."

A wrinkle appeared between her eyes. "But, Father, don't you want to hear my confession first?"

"I think I already have," he replied, smiling. "That is, unless you have more to confess."

"Oh, my dear, let's see. No, I don't think so. Thank you. This will save me a trip to…"

"*Ego te absolvo a peccatis tuis*," he intoned, making the sign of the cross toward her, "*in nomine Patris, et Filii, et Spiritus Sancti. Amen.*"

He stood up, gently placed his right hand on the top of her head, and held it there for several seconds. Carl watched, took Anton's left hand and, looking up at both grown-ups, placed it on his own head.

****

Carl was now going on eight, and, for several weeks, he had been strolling into the backyard of their apartment where his stepfather, Gustav, was working on a statue in a shed there. Upon entering, he would come immediately up to wherever the piece being worked on was, a table, a pedestal, Gustav's lap, and stare at it for several minutes. After a while, he seemed to get bored and wandered elsewhere in the yard, periodically returning to check on his stepfather's progress. Oftentimes, a stray cat that was usually on the property would follow the boy in and out.

One day, when Carl first came into the shed and stood before the work, he said, "Why doesn't it change any more, Father?" Sometimes, he was surprised with how quickly he had become comfortable using the word for his stepfather.

Gustav, sprinkled with white dust, his hands with the tiny wooden hammer and fine-work chisel hanging in mid-air, looked at the boy, then back at the piece. "Why, how very perceptive you are, my son," he said. The bowl-shaped structure, tipped upward on its pedestal, was soft white plaster, about a foot round. They both continued to stare at it, a bird, with wings spread backward in swift flight, but the head off to one side rather than straight forward as one would expect. The whole thing took on the form of a heart.

"Tell, me, Carl, when did you first notice it stopped changing?"

Carl stared and pointed at a spot. "Here. The day when you did this here."

"Yes!" Gustav was excited. "You're absolutely right! You really *are* perceptive." He mussed the boy's hair. "Do you know what day that was?"

Carl twisted his face with thought. "Thursday?"

Gustav laughed and patted Carl's shoulder. "You may be right there. I myself don't remember the day of the week. But what I meant was, do you know why that day was so important to my project?"

Carl was silent for a while, then shook his head.

"That was the turning point!" Gustav sat down, collapsing with fatigue into an old wooden chair in front of the pedestal and rubbing his eyes. "I was stuck. I didn't know what to do, where to go with the piece."

"You were swearing. A little."

The man laughed again. "That's right! I sure did. And I whacked my thumb, I was so upset and angry with myself. Something like that always seems to happen when I'm at a loss in a project. I lose faith. I can't convince myself there'll be a turning point. Sometimes, not always, there is."

He got up and walked to the bird, pointing at the very spot Carl had indicated. "When this happened, I knew I was going to muddle through. I finally figured out how the wings were going to be."

They fell silent again. Then Carl asked, "Then why weren't you finished? When you 'muddled through' and the bird stopped changing?"

"No, son," he replied. "It didn't stop changing. It just stopped changing in a certain way. Look closer."

Carl moved closer to the bird. The sunlight in the shed was intermittent. Gustav saw the problem, picked up the bird, and walked over to a window. Carl followed him closely.

"There. Look again."

As Gustav turned the piece in the light, for the first time, Carl noticed an intricacy in the wings, tiny bumps which appeared better in the light and represented hundreds of feathers. Taken aback, the boy let out a quiet gasp.

"Now I see it!" he exclaimed.

"That's what I was working on. The insides of the wings."

"They look just like the feathers that I've seen!"

"That's right." Gustav patted the boy again and sat back down, sighing. "I suppose I'm about done. Do you like it? We can keep it if you like it."

"Won't you want to sell it, like you do with the others?"

"Oh, I already have a client. This project is a commission. But he'll want a much larger piece for his fountain. I'll have to do it *in situ*. And something made out of marble. This is just a plaster model to show him."

"Can I keep it in my bedroom?"

"Of course. That is, as long as your mother says yes. She's the boss, you know."

Carl went over to the chair and accepted the arm around his shoulders. After a silence, he asked, "Father, when did you decide to become a sculptor?"

"As I remember, I was around your age when I started getting interested in the arts."

More silence. "I think that's what I'll be," said Carl. "Or a writer. I always love to write stories. But don't tell anybody, please."

They watched the cat enter the shed and walk quietly around, ignoring them, exploring. When it shook its paws from time to time to dry them off, Gustav looked at Carl with a goofy expression, aping shock and befuddlement, and the latter laughed. At last, the cat was satisfied enough to settle down on its haunches and, with those eyes, as if twisted on their axis, that always startled Carl to look at, to stare up at the motionless, artificial bird. This time, they both laughed.

Gustav suddenly got an idea. "Do you know, there's a play in town I've been meaning to go to. It's written by a man who's also a sculptor." He didn't mention Hauptmann's early failure in that vocation. "Shall we go to it?"

"A play? Is it about a sculptor?"

"No, Carluccio." Gustav wiped his hands with a rag. "It's about a German patriot from long ago who becomes a soldier. And a hero. A very great man."

"What's his name?"

"Florian Geyer."

"Florian Geyer," said Carl slowly with measured syllables, as if testing out the name. "When can we go?"

25

He patted the boy's shoulder and looked out the window, up toward the house. "Let's ask the boss," he said with a sigh.

****

Sitting with Gustav in the front row of the theater, Carl could hardly contain himself. He was full of questions. He had been to puppet shows before, but nothing at all like this. A red velvet curtain hung across the stage, and Carl noticed light and shadows moving between the bottom of the curtain and the raised floor. *What was going on back there?* he wondered.

He was just glad to be there at the theater. It hadn't been easy. When they'd brought up the play to his mother, she'd immediately burst into tears, collapsed into a chair. Shocked by her reaction to the simple request, they'd gone up close to her to find out what was the matter. Had she heard some bad news? Was she not feeling well?

"There is so much at stake," she wept. "You should know this, Gustav. Given all that you've been through just for your... your... opinions."

"But, Rosalie. Be sensible, please. It's just a pl—"

"His status at the royal school hangs by a thread. We could never afford... without Carl Senior's former boss, the senator—"

"I understand, but the boy also needs horizons, dreams. *Florian Geyer*—"

"Yes, I'm well aware what your Engels has to say about that man. You've told me. An influence—"

"Mother, just this once?" Carl pleaded. "I've never been to a play. The teachers have spoken well of this Florian at school. They—"

"—a bad influence—"

"Dear, the boy expressed an interest, and, who knows, it might actually enrich what he's learning in school. Hauptmann and all that. And his birthday is approaching. I think this would be a fitting gift as he turns eight to—"

Gradually, there was a subtle softening of her features.

Carl watched as his stepfather pressed his point. "We'll make a day of it. Have lunch and go to Hayns Park. He'll love it. And you'll have a day to yourself for once."

"Well," she said, "Greta and I had been wanting to get together."

She sat back in her chair, looking down on them as they crouched around her. She dabbed at her eyes and laughed at her son. "You're right," she said. "He is growing up, right before our very eyes. Perhaps just this once." She laughed again. "I'd always fancied him a priest. My son, what is to become of you?"

And then, to top it all off, when they were leaving, "Explain the play to him so he's not confused. No, but not too much! He has his first communion in a few months!" Really!

Anyway, he was glad just to be there. But shhh! The curtain was being drawn back! There was singing! The stage was full of soldiers and peasants, marching in place, singing proudly, angrily, "*We are the black band of Florian Geyer*," raising their primitive weapons and swinging them over their heads. What were they so angry about? Entranced, Carl sat bolt upright in his seat. Gustav had a hard time focusing on both the play and the boy, who tapped his seat to the rhythm. He couldn't help but smile. *Yes!* he thought. *Let the boy feel the excitement. Let the blood of humanity and solidarity pump through his arteries!* Gustav felt his own eyes welling up. He had been right, so right, to bring the boy with him!

After the introductory song, the characters started milling about, threading between one another, mimicking private conversations. Gradually, the peasant-looking actors disappeared, replaced by ones dressed as knights. Suddenly, an ear-splitting voice from behind him made Carl jump up in his seat. A man, dressed as a herald and reading from an open scroll, was walking up the aisle between the two halves of the audience. He was vociferously reading off what appeared to be demands from the peasants, calling for an end of forced labor, tithes, closed forests, and fees for land use. As the herald approached the stage, the knights variously expressed scorn, anger, dismay and sarcasm. A knight named Sebastian, evidently Florian Geyer's brother, was the target of some of this, but when one of the knights opted to join Florian and the peasants in their uprising, Sebastian refused. At this point, the curtain was lowered. Carl stared open-mouthed at his father.

When the curtain rose again, Carl had a harder time following; there was less action than he had expected in a play, and more talking, lots and lots of talking. Gustav sensed this, and, every once in a while, he bent down to whisper into Carl's ear. "They're arguing about whether they need a leader and, if so, how they will decide on one." And: "Florian and the others stuck their knives in the church door as a pledge that they'd abide by the decision of a council of peasants." Then: "Florian is angry because the others attacked the fortress of Wurzburg without proper artillery and many peasants were killed." Also: "Jacob Kohl, a peasant leader, takes some of the blame for this and wants to atone by helping Florian retake the fortress."

During intermission, they sat on the stone steps of the theater, snacking on sandwiches.

"Go ahead and ask any questions you'd like," offered Gustav.

Carl wrinkled his face. "So…"

"Yes?"

"The peasants weren't being treated well."

"The people in power, the nobles and clergy, were taking advantage of them."

"And the peasants banded together along with some of the knights to fight back."

"That's right."

Carl chewed and swallowed. "But I thought there'd be more, more acting."

"And less talking."

"Uh-huh."

"You're on to something. A critic could say that Hauptmann should have cut a lot of dialogue."

"Do you agree?"

Gustav screwed up his face. "Yes, the play would have been more exciting if he'd concentrated the action. But as an artist, I see the author may have been more interested in other things than just excitement Have you ever watched your mother cooking dinner? She's got one pot going on the stove, and you think that's what we're eating, but then she pulls out a pan, and starts something else, and there's already something in the oven. And then, before you know it, she's frying up some fish as well. It's like she's getting distracted, but she's really kind of juggling. And then you realize she had this idea all along. Maybe Hauptmann's doing that."

"But what's he, uh, 'frying up'?"

"Well, to show what people were like back then," Gustav went on. "Or, even something better."

"What, Dad?"

"Well, we know the play's about leadership. That would be an over-riding theme. And—have you ever tried to organize something with your friends? Like picking teams for a game?"

"Oh, yes!"

"Are there problems sometimes?"

"Often!"

"Why?"

"Because!" he answered quickly, and then, thinking, "people disagree. They want to do different things. Sometimes every single one wants to have his own way. It's chaos."

"Have you ever had the feeling, Carl, that some people will disagree with an idea just because it isn't theirs?"

"I hate that!"

"I know. It seems downright perverse. But are there some people who seem to do a better job of dealing with the 'chaos' than others?"

"Uh-huh. Sometimes."

29

"I wonder what it is about those people that's different from the others."

"Me too!"

"So," continued Gustav, "maybe part of the theme Hauptmann is exploring in the play is showing how hard it is to lead, and what are the qualities of true leaders, and he can't do that without all the arguing and disagreeing. As soon as you open the door to freedom of choice, or even just ask for some input, it raises the issue of why anybody at all should do what somebody else wants them to do."

"So what is...?"

"I think we're going to find out now," said Gustav, standing up. "It looks like intermission's over."

When the curtain rose again, Geyer's badly wounded comrade, Tellermann, describes the defeat of thirty thousand peasants led by Goetz von Berlichingen. When Tellermann dies, Florian considers escaping to France, saying, "There is no end to dissension in Germany. I thought I should change this. Who am I, that I should attempt it?" But then, suddenly, he calls for his armor and claims, "I will be buried in it," and he rides off to fight again.

In the last act, which takes place in the castle of his brother-in-law, William, who has abandoned the peasant cause, Geyer asks for sanctuary. William nervously assents, but when his wife, Anna, finds out that Geyer is hidden in the building, she betrays him to the noblemen there. Geyer, though already exhausted with fighting, refuses to give up his sword. He is killed by crossbow at short range.

When this happened, the boy leapt to his feet and shouted. He turned to Gustav and whispered ecstatically, "Father, we must call a doctor!"

Gustav quietly assured him that the arrow wasn't real, that the actor playing Florian wasn't hurt at all—he was acting dead. It was as if little Carl was incapable of bringing his lips together.

Still in a state of shock, Carl mechanically applauded the actors at curtain call—he even felt a little upset that they were all smiling at the audience. Then, he stumbled hypnotically from the theater. It took several minutes before, walking next to Gustav, who had to steer him down the stairs with his hand on the boy's shoulder, his eyesight grew used to the sunshine, and he was finally able to form a question.

"Dad, why did it have to end that way?"

"I suppose that, since the play was about the peasant uprising, it had to end with either the success or failure of its leader. Also, you know the biblical saying, 'Those who live by the sword—'"

"Yes! But why did everything go bad for the peasants?"

"Perhaps it's easier to maintain power than to take it away."

"I wanted the peasants to come together and win!"

"I believe Hauptmann would be glad that he stirred you up. He might even agree with you. But here, the author couldn't change history."

"Didn't you want Florian to win?"

"Part of me, yes. But another part asks what the peasants would have done if they had. Were they ready to hold power? Hauptmann seems to go out of his way to show that they weren't."

"What did you think of Florian, Dad?"

"It was his misfortune to be the leader of a movement that had little desire for one. A great man, surely; maybe the best man of his time— well ahead of his time. But what was he up against? And how much can one man change? Remember, he was also limited by the time in which he lived, by the people he worked with, their beliefs, their values. I think Hauptmann also does a good job of showing that."

When Carl arrived home, he wrote his own version of the Florian Geyer story, with more action. And in the end, Florian and the peasants won. But in the months and even years that followed, the demise of Florian Geyer continued to trouble Carl, the problems involved in the story stayed with him. The theater-going experience had somehow rearranged not just his thoughts but his way of thinking; it filtered what he saw and how he saw it. He couldn't let it go.

Also, as a result of this excursion with Gustav, Carl decided that he wanted to become a writer.

Chapter Three
PRESENT

As the day of his imprisonment approached, neither relative nor absolute time stood still for Carl. Each day in the office, he would discuss new events with Walter, debating what might evolve into an article, and, if so, who would be best to write it. And, in Germany at that time, events followed fast upon one another; the next one shoving the last aside.

Most pressing were the rumors about the police discovery of Nazi documents in Boxheim, Hesse, planning for a possible communist takeover. Carl had heard that a National Socialist law student, a certain Werner Best, had recorded his plot for the Stormtroopers to form a provisional government, detailing the execution of resisters and anyone else with weapons, institution of courts martial, abolition of currency and suspension of property rights, annulment of interest on debts, compulsory labor, setting up of public kitchens and the distribution of food ration cards—but not to Jews, of course! This matter followed upon the April takeover by leftist Stormtroopers and their leader, Walter Stennes of the Nazi offices in Berlin, including the party newspaper, of which they printed two issues of their own. Police had been called in to free those held in the offices against their will. Hitler, calling Stennes a 'salon socialist,' a conspirator and mutineer, expelled him from the party, replacing him with one of Himmler's officers. Now, in the case of the Boxheim fiasco, those connected to the documents had been arrested. Hitler had distanced himself from Best and the entire matter, had condemned any putschist designs for Nazis, and had reiterated his pledge to a legal taking of power. Chancellor Bruning had evidently commented to the effect that Hitler's statement implied an illegal wielding of power thereafter—the man had already warned that "heads will roll"—and was considering the banning of all political uniforms. A writer had already been commissioned to work on this matter, with Walter's assistance.

In addition, on top of the obscene increases in unemployment and, in spite of the U. S. President Hoover's reparations moratorium, the German bank crisis, Hitler's 20-year-old niece—and possible mistress—Geli had either committed suicide or been murdered by a shot through the heart. Strangely—what would this maniac come up with next?—in the aftermath of her death, it was rumored Hitler had become a vegetarian. They decided to shelve this item in case it developed into something more than simply the sensational. More possibly to the interest of *The Worldstage* readership, a Catholic priest, Lichtenburg, here in Berlin, had locked horns with the Nazis for advocating that his parishioners see the new film based on Remarque's anti-war book, *All Quiet on the Western Front*. Who could he ask to follow this up? Was it the sort of thing for Kastner? Also, Nazi women had just inaugurated their own branch of the party. He had a tip to track down and interview a Gertrud Klink, its leader in Berlin. Perhaps Walter would like that project for himself...

He also had his own projects he would like to wrap up before he left: some things on the upcoming elections and the new Iron Front, which the Social Democrats were talking about forming with the Center and Democratic parties along with the confederation of trade unions, as a strategy of opposing the Nazis in next year's elections. Personally, although he was glad to see the rare politically pluralistic syncretism, he felt the opposition to the communists on the one side and the Nazis on the other was a mistake: Scylla and Charybdis. But it was all the more reason an article in the *The Worldstage*'s voice could be helpful to the commonwealth's decision-making.

And another piece he'd begun, based only on rumors so far, was about the possible misuse of secretly funneled government funds to bankrupt Prussian estates to keep the support of the Junkers for the regime and status quo, funds that ostensibly were earmarked for ameliorating the dire conditions of the poor in the area, but which in fact might have been spent on luxury items for the landowners themselves. If the rumors weren't phantoms, the scandal could possibly touch the hitherto invulnerable Hindenburg.

In addition, recently, a nocturnal image like a Freudian discharge had pulled him out of blissful sleep on several occasions, sprung him from bed beside the still sleeping, fragrant, palpable moonlight beauty of Maud his bride, and took him pattering barefoot like a gouty old man down the hallway—the image was a genie shoved back into its bottle. But now *le mauvais genie* was angry for the loss of its freedom and, like Freud's *id* itself, gnawed and champed and bit to deliver and avenge itself on its human, its German captors. Could he, in fact, work this nightmare into something printable? But what was it the genie of? And would the seal hold? Or would, instead, someone help it escape? Would some fanatic smash it on the cobbles of a street in Berlin to expand and roam and kill?

He broke from the reverie-become-daydream, looked with embarrassment at Karsch, whose head was bent back down at his work, and picked up a sheet of paper. His most pressing duty before going to jail, he knew, besides prepping Walter and Hellmut to run things here in his absence, was to spend as much time with Maud and Rosalinde as possible. In fact, he had a date with his wife that afternoon, some museum, probably. Should he feel guilty that he thought the aesthetic experience might itself serve as inspiration for writing something, since art, especially "degenerate art," had lately become such a political hot subject? No!

He read and annotated three pieces, scribbled notes to send back to the authors, and handed all of it over to Walter to type up and mail.

"Off on your date with the Mrs., Boss?" Walter asked. "Where are you two going?"

"That all depends on the whims of *my* boss," he answered, and went down to the street.

They spent an exquisite, blissful afternoon mainly in the Crown Prince's Museum. He felt a healing inside begin as soon as he saw Maud waiting for him at twelve-thirty at the agreed upon corner a few blocks from the office, and they walked down Lindens Avenue toward the Spree River. She'd heard—correctly, as it turned out—that the weather would be fine, and had fixed a picnic lunch, which he carried in a woven sack. She kissed him on the lips, put her arm through his and, bringing her mouth up to his ear, whispered, "Not a word of it! Put it all, everything, out of your mind. This afternoon is just for us."

"Where..." he started, looking around hopefully. A single street altercation—and they came often—could ruin their date.

"Museum Island," she said without hesitation, and guided him like a lead dancer.

The street and sidewalk were bustling with traffic, but, otherwise, it was quiet: no marches, brawls, or electioneering. The Boxheim scandal seemed to have muted public activity, as if everyone was waiting with baited-breath for some full-fledged catastrophe to happen. Even now, today, Berlin seemed to still be able to provide a backdrop for wonders. Crossing the river, they found a grassy spot in the sun on the museum grounds, laid out a blanket, and set out the lunch Maud had prepared. They sat facing each other and started to eat: a thermos of savory hot vegetable barley soup, crusty rye bread, thin slices of Westphalian ham, Harz and butter cheeses, Dusseldorf mustard from a tube and a half bottle of Moselle, from which Carl filled two old, chipped mugs. They clinked them, Carl saying, "To our many wonderful, happy years together, and to my ever-lovely wife. Finding you was the miracle that made all the other miracles possible."

"Thank you, my love." They smiled, sipped and tasted liquid fruit, feeling its oozing warmth permeate them like a healing balm. Carl sliced the sausage and cheeses while Maud made sandwiches. They ate, watching the shimmering sunlight on the varying shades of green of the ever-shifting grasses and leaves, the soft breeze flow through the drooping willows along the river, their pliant branches trailing on the surface of the water in the lazy current of the Spree, like the line of a fly fisher.

Maud moved closer to her husband and made him lay back against her. She cradled his head at the tops of her thighs and gently stroked his hair. Staring down into his face, his eyes closed, she was grateful for this chance, before he had to leave, to savor their relationship, this last outing to rekindle what would so soon be temporarily taken away from her.

Married since before the war, together, Carl and Maud had passed through the romantic myth and, together, had come out the other side. They were less blissful, perhaps, but they would never admit any claim that they weren't stronger, clearer, more loving, more at one with one another for the enduring, transforming, and transformative union of their loves and lives. They cherished their opportunities to come together; their still, albeit intermittently passionate relationship had weathered the devastation of much of the social reality around them and mellowed into its own unique *Geist*. Their team of two, more relaxed but more focused, with continually deepening meaning, centered on their now adolescent daughter. It was through their Rosalinde that they had been able, at a distance of years, to recover and re-experience the freshness, joy and sudden, diurnal crises of childhood and, in doing so, had cultivated a more mature, more profound bond with each other. They were thrilled with an abiding awareness of their unexpected achievement, the building of a viable life together, palpably symbolized in their blossoming daughter.

But no relationship ages without issues. Carl's times away at work had taken its toll, with Maud feeling neglected and sometimes using alcohol to cope with his absence, and Carl, feeling that he had been branded by her with an undeserved insensitivity, was doing all he could to put food on their table and keep a roof over their heads, darn it. How far things had come from the early days of their relationship, when Carl had fretted over bringing in as much as Maud did.

In her turn, Rosalinde sometimes complained that *The Worldstage* had taken both of her parents away. Since the trial, however, with the looming shadow of Carl's ever-approaching imprisonment, all three of them had pulled together in love and individually vowed to cherish the moments they would have left.

"Well, we've fed our stomachs," said Carl. "Shall we quench our thirst for the aesthetic?"

They gathered up their things, checked them at the entrance of the many-times-rebuilt baroque edifice, still pock-marked from bullet holes dating back to 1918, and started the tour of the Gallery of the Living. Though they hadn't been there for years, they found themselves hurrying back to their favorites from earlier visits. Maud especially liked the misty Monets: *Argenteuil, Summer, Vertheuil,* while Carl preferred Thoma's *Sackingen,* Leistikow's *Grunewald,* and Achenbach's *Naples.* Shoulder to shoulder, they fell in love again with Kalemorgen's *Harvest,* Kalckreuth's *Castle Kleingels,* von Uhde's *Little Princess,* and the beckoning landscapes of Ury, Slevogt, Liebermann and Vogeler, as well as the soaring architecture of the rooms.

"There's no other place like this on the earth," reflected Maud.

"Well, I heard they've built one in New York," Carl commented. "A copy."

"Good. Let's have more galleries of the living."

One man's masterpiece was another's degenerate monstrosity. Carl had the thought, here unexpressed but one he had had before, that it was a wonder German culture, with all its challenges, could produce such a fertile line of vibrant and passionate visual artists as Feininger, Marc, Kirchner, Munch, Corinth, Klee, Nolde, Kollwitz, Barlach, Kokoscka, Grosz, Beckmann, and Kandinsky.... Aesthetic miracles!

As before, there was more than they could absorb. Not bored but sated, Carl became playful. In an effort to get Maud to crack up, he quietly started imitating the ponderous, art-appreciating gestures of some of those *precieux* around them: arms crossed judgmentally, heavily nodding; meditatively massaging his chin and superciliously fluttering his eyebrows; slack-jawed, eyes gaping in a deaf look of utter shock; holding his hands up with a frown, as if to readjust a frame this way, then that. His wife, at first shaking her head to get him to stop, was soon doing it in a sequence of disapproval, embarrassment, shock, and denial. Finally, when he stood in front of a painted profile in an attempt to match its shape and the subject's severe expression, she turned away from him to look at a work on another wall, feeling she either had to break off or burst into laughter. At last, Carl stopped his clowning when he heard someone giggling behind him. Maud reprovingly clutched his hand and led him outside; head down as he trailed behind her, he emoted remorse but whispered, "At least I entertained one person."

"All of a sudden, I have Puck as a companion," she commented, not without a smile, as they stood at the top of the stairs. "If I want comedy, I can go see Karl Valentin in a burlesque show."

"*Pardon*!" he apologized. "I was done here."

Coming down the steps from which Liebknecht and Luxembourg had addressed the revolutionary crowd thirteen years before, Maud caught sight of people leaving the Pergamon Museum nearby and remarked, "Huh. I didn't know they'd finally opened the antiquities."

Carl looked at his watch. "Should we pop our heads in? Just for a peek? If we like what we see, we can bring Rosa for a full visit." Maud nodded, and they hurried over. With closing time approaching, they sped past the Miletus, Ishtar gates, and Aleppo Room to get to Messel and Hoffmann's three-winged reconstruction of the remains of the colossal Greek altar from Asia Minor. Overwhelmed by the dimensions and intricacy of the monument, the writhing reliefs and frenzied countenances, Carl and Maud walked and gawked around the friezes depicting the classic Olympians beating down the chthonic Giants. The inchoate, chaotic theomachy seemed to them an attempt to portray the genesis of terror itself, a cringing, nightmarish agony, primitive and primal. Standing under the reliefs of Dionysos and

Semele, they stared at each other in wonderment. Carl aped speechlessness; then he was done with aping; they held hands. Everyone in the room seemed to travel in a time-clogged daze.

Finally, Carl said, "Honey, have you read any Kant? Other than the peace essay?"

"No, Dear. I've tried to stay away from it, actually. Why?"

He nodded. "Well, the three critiques were drilled into us as schoolboys, you know, monuments of German thought. Quite a lot to swallow. No wonder I wanted to run away from school. But standing here makes me want, almost, to agree with him that sublime art is our direct connection to the eternal and infinite."

"Well, I'm just feeling the irony that all this fighting and all these monsters were part of the birth of humanism," she responded.

"Yes, and my rather ruthless compatriot, the magnate Schliemann, who struck gold in California and cornered the weapons market here, started all the mad searching for old stones when he used *The Odyssey* as a travel guide while sailing around the Mediterranean."

"*Le passé retrouve.* Wasn't he supposed to have been inspired by a drunk reciting Homer at the grocer's where he worked as a boy?"

They sat on the steps to the altar and caught their breath. People milled about, seemingly in a trance. Time slowed to a trickle. Late afternoon sunshine filtered mutedly down through the enormous barrel-vaulted arrangement of skylights above them. Carl yawned and stretched, turning and trying to take in the entire edifice at once.

"Freud's *ego* subjugating Freud's *id*."

"And if this is art," Maud wondered, "what were we looking at next door?"

"What art *is*," Carl replied. "This is what art *was*."

"Still," she persisted, "What did we see in the other museum? Don't parrot that pompous Spengler and say it's the wilting of the flower."

40

"You know me better than that. Mere rejection is just too easy, a form of closing your eyes. It misses the point of art. But now *I'm* sounding pompous. What would *you* say, Maud?"

She closed her eyes. "And you know *me*, Carl: Hegelian—this is the unfolding of the flower."

"'The gallery of the living' is right only by contrast. But someday they'll all be dead, those artists, and we'll all be dead; the spectators will be different. Then the name will become a misnomer. I tend to want to contextualize. What does Barlach intend in *his* context, Monet in *his*?"

"The gallery of the dead," Maud said, surveying the altar. "I wonder if people will be putting our civilization back together piece by piece someday."

"If they do," Carl reflected, "I hope we'll deserve their labors better than we've been doing up till now."

"Just absorb what's in front of you, and let the future take care of itself. This afternoon is for us, remember, Darling."

He leaned back on the steps and took a deep breath, gazing up at the ceiling. "The ancient and the modern. We've traveled a lot in a few hours."

"For all our present troubles, I'd much rather be here than there."

"You'll get no argument from me on that one, Dearest. I'm no Schliemann."

"Good, because otherwise, if we'd gotten our wishes, we should never have met, and none of these miracles would have transpired." Looking into each other's eyes, they held hands again, delighting in the undeniable here-and-now of palpable flesh against flesh, a freedom that would soon be taken from them.

Outside, walking hand-in-hand toward the underground entrance to the urban train they would take home, they dodged the sidewalk traffic. Suddenly, Maud was yanked backward when Carl halted. Letting go of his hand, she turned toward him, thinking he'd been bumped by a passerby. But he just stood there, head down, a strange look on his face. Maud stared at him in shock: What was wrong? Was he sick? God, not a heart attack! He wasn't grabbing his chest, but his upper lip was twitching. He pressed his lips together to control it.

"Carl, what is it? Are you all right?" She pushed him toward a storefront, out of the muddle of people.

"That museum!" he sputtered.

"Yes, Carl? What about it?"

"What did they want you to think about?"

Oh, God! Really, Carl? "But I thought you were dying!"

"The artworks! The ruins! What were we supposed to think about them?"

"That they were beautiful," she stated. Then, when he kept shaking his head, she went on, searching, "Primitive yet symmetrical?" No. "Wild but orderly?" No! "Massive though intricate?" NO!

"What else?"

"Oh....," she sought and sought, "monumental... all the work it must have taken to—?"

"Warmer! Whose work?"

"The archaeologists, of course! What's his name, Humann! Having the funds. Putting it all together—"

"Yes, digging it up, shipping it all to—"

"To Germany, of course!"

"Oh, Maud! Why 'of course'? Why bring it all here?"

"To preserve it. To rescue it from looters. And so people would see it, surely!"

"Yes, Germans! And why does it all belong to us?"

"Well, I suppose the Turkish government made a deal with the Kaiser."

"'A deal'! What about the people back there? Did anybody ask the Anatolians?"

Oh, my husband!

"That's what they *didn't* want you to think about! We're like your Lord Elgin and his marbles!"

The Man Without a Party

Maud remembered when, accompanied by her Aunt Mary and Uncle Hugh, she had viewed, as a child, Phidias' bas reliefs, unscrupulously taken by the Scottish nobleman from Ottoman Greece and brought after shipwreck to the British Museum: Lapiths versus Centaurs, rather than Olympians against Giants; but still, a frantic, vicious battle to the end. Her favorites had been, instead, the wonderful equestrian metopes, simultaneously and inexplicably hurried yet graceful.

"An empire, like the British," Carl went on, relentless. "But whose damn right is it to take—?"

He stopped himself, panting, staring at her. "I'll never make another classical reference!"

Maud suppressed a laugh, thinking, '*That'll solve everything!*' She said, "That is a resolution I hardly see you adhering to."

"I'm serious, Maud. What I'm talking about is the same abuse of power that's sending me to jail."

Now it was her turn to look ill. As his devastating words sank in, she looked up, saw the two of them, a frozen reflection in the display window, sandwiched between the mannequins on the other side of the glass and the reflected stream of passersby behind them. "Yes," she went on in subdued voice, "of course, you're right, Carl. Now let's go home." She took his hand, leading him, and they started walking again.

When they got home, in a defiant assertion, Rosalinde informed them that she had already been forced to see "those scary old statues" with her class on a field trip, and that she would much rather go with her parents to the Sports Palace for the skating. They planned a date.

****

Ossietzky's assistant, Walter Karsch, picked him up May 10th, 1932, in a flashy Type R to drive him to Tegel Penitentiary.

Upstairs, the three Ossietzkys heard the horn, rushed down from their apartment, and squinted at the shining, lengthy motorcar in the dazzling sunlight. Alive, it shook rhythmically as the engine purred. Walter was leaning stylishly against the machine, smoking. He opened the doors for them and loaded Carl's luggage in the trunk.

At first speechless, Carl asked, "My God, whose is this?"

"Rosenfeld said he borrowed it from a rich client," said Walter. "They wanted to surprise you."

"Daddy, you're going to prison in style!" shouted Rosalinde, now twelve, going on fifteen. She ran a hand along the sleek contour of the hood. "Oooh, the metal's hot!"

"Rosa, be careful," advised her father. "That metal's an even better conductor than Toscanini."

Maud cut her laugh short when she noticed her daughter's pout. She knew Rosalinde didn't want to be scolded in front of Walter, who she thought was cute. They piled into the automobile, with the women in the back—Carl insisted he sit in the front with Walter. And then they were off, motoring through the streets of Berlin to put their boss, husband, and father in prison on a gorgeously sunny afternoon.

"You know, Sir," Walter shouted, loud enough for Maud and Rosa to hear, "we can just keep driving right out of this damned, wretched country."

Carl was already shaking his head. He stretched his neck so Walter could hear him but not the passengers behind them. "And do what Kreiser did? The poor son of a bitch scurrying off to Paris to tattle away to a newspaper owned by an armaments factory owner? As you well know, Walter, he has not only hurt his own credibility in this country, but ours as well. I don't fault him for wanting to save his skin. He was already falling apart in a panic during the trial. But to squeal away in a country, which is still generally considered our enemy, is not only seen as betrayal of Germany by most here, but is tantamount to a betrayal of our own cause as well.

"In contrast," Carl went on, "back during the Revolution, Toller could have received pardon from his five-year sentence after just six months, but he opted to stay in jail. They were performing a play of his, and the Bavarian Minister of Justice hoped to make a *beau geste* during its run, but Ernst refused to allow the hypocrite to preen himself. Also, he didn't feel right about leaving the other prisoners in their cells to wonder what kind of information he may have given up to get out."

"Do you think he ever regretted his decision?"

Carl snorted. "I'm sure I don't know! But that's not my point, Walter. Let me tell you another tale, this one's about Quidde, a mentor of mine from very early on."

"He was tried for treason as well, wasn't he?"

"That's right! And acquitted. But I'm referring to a time before Ludwig became so famous for winning the prize in Oslo or his celebrated symbolic handshake with Passy at the Lucerne Peace Conference in '05, the sort of thing that could have kept us out of war if it had been followed upon. But this story doesn't go that far back, nor as far as his duel with a loud-mouthed anti-Semite when he was in college. No, this was right after he'd published the brilliant monograph on Caligula and imperial insanity. It was a sensation, but the Kaiser took the hint and Quidde's lawyer advised him to get on a train to Switzerland and quick. And do you know what Quidde responded?"

"Wrong time of year for a trip to the Alps?"

"'Flight is virtually evidence of guilt.'"

"What ended up happening to him?"

"Wilhelm *Imperator* actually showed some scruples for once! Or he was too embarrassed to have his counsels prosecute. But they still found a way to throw Ludwig in prison for three months a while later. *Lese-majeste*. But poor, poor Kreiser. He... he couldn't stay in formation. There's always safety in numbers, even if it's just a team of two."

45

Karsch turned off the highway. "It looks as though he's in a different formation now, sir."

The other scoffed. "For sure, Walter. An even more deadly one. *In faucibus bestiae.*"

Carl was surprised to see a crowd as they pulled up to the Tegel's entrance.

"Oh, my God," he uttered in disbelief. "What's this? Walter, what have you done here?"

"A few of your friends wanted desperately to see you before—"

"A few? You... no... it can't be—"

"A year-and-a-half is a long time for them. And even if you're let off early—"

"You can't be serious!"

There were Lion and Kurt, Alfred and Heinrich, Manfred and Max, and, oh, my God, Else and Julius and Axel—Axel, really?—Herbert and Fritz, Marie, Erich, Minna, Rudy, Arnold, Anna... All smiling and waving. Rosa squealed with excitement. They parked and got out. Hugged. Shook hands. Kissed. As far as propriety allowed, Carl chided them "for making a fuss," but, deep down, he really was moved to think these friends cared enough to, in effect, escort him to his incarceration.

When a bottle of champagne was opened, someone yelled, "Duck, everyone!" Laughter. Tears. He was handed a glass, sipped the fruitful effervescence. What to think! All this for him, an enemy of the state! All this for *Lucifer ante portas.* The thought made him wonder why his school Latin kept creeping into his afternoon: *Et tu, Patria?* After all the greetings, Carl stood in front of them. He cleared his throat.

"I must thank all of you for being here in support of our cause. But my gratitude is somewhat tempered, because, truly, it is because of people like you that I can feel it worthwhile to sacrifice a year and a half to the improvement of this increasingly justice-forsaken country. Without you, I might have caved in long ago and scuttled off for cover like my sad co-defendant. But nothing doing! If in no other way, I am wealthy in friends and loved ones, who are full of the sort of integrity that can make even the most woeful misanthrope an optimist, and the ethical invertebrate develop a little spine. I thank you all! And I promise you that you won't be able to forget me in my punitive hiatus, for I'll be plaguing you with notes, memoranda, and full-fledged letters constantly with all kinds of ideas, schemes, requests, and conundra. Nor will the officious functionaries Prussian militarism behind these dour walls have a respite in the contrition of a remorseful captive. I won't try to escape from their feudal fortress, but I do intend to show them zero regret for my misdeeds; I'll be a very grouchy inmate for as long as they see fit to keep me. And so," he finished, tossing away his last stub of a Senoussi, "I'll gather my suitcases and take my leave—"

"Not yet!" someone shouted, coming forward. It was his old friend from the failed Republican Party days in the early twenties, Manfred George. He came up to him. Although they had hugged before, they hugged again.

Carl, somewhat taken aback, joked, "Don't tell me we're going to try to start another political party, Manny."

"Heavens, no, Carl. I just have a few words to say." He smiled, pulling some papers out of his suitcoat.

"I'm worried already."

"Well, then you can just stand with them and listen. I don't need you up here anyway." He swept the back of his hand upward several times in the motion of brushing away. Telling him to hurry because he had to be inside by five o'clock or they'd come looking for him, Carl went and obediently stood between Maud and Rosalinde. They held his hands and did their best to grin at him, already keeping back tears.

As Manfred flattened out the sheets and arranged them, he started, "When you guys read *The Worldstage*, do you note the lines that especially grab your attention? I do, and I also keep old copies. So during the last few months, anticipating Carl's absence from us, I've

47

been going over his past articles. Yes, Carl! Don't shake your head. Remember, Carl is not just the chief editor of *The Worldstage*, but one of its most avidly read writers, studied regularly even by our greatest political opponents. I doubt that activity edifies them at all, in spite of all the efforts to persuade; they just want to know what we're thinking on the latest current events, how we tick. But every issue that carries one of Carl's articles is doubly his; each is his work on two levels. Anyway, while reading, it struck me that I'm not sure any of us really understand, really fathom this man. And, as I went on rereading, it occurred to me it might be beneficial to write down some of the quotes that spoke to me most significantly. And then, as I was copying, it hit me that, as I was breaking the number one rule of scholarship, never to take a person's statements out of context, I might go a step further and rearrange the quotes in a kind of history of our time, as a way to reveal both time and author, by whom, I hope, my apologies are accepted. But I feel the slight discomfort the reading of his words gives him will be more than compensated for by the pleasure it gives us. So, there. Sorry, Carl, but here we go. And I quote:

"'In November, 1918, far from our homeland, we tossed our stained forage caps in the air and cheered the Republic. The German revolution was the elemental emergency act of a greatly suffering people. Millions were united by the feeling that the slaughter had ended, that militarism had perished by its own hand, that we had become free people in a free fatherland.

"'But does not the revolutionary origin of the Republic imply also a revolutionary pledge? An election victory does not mean power; it too has its own before and after. Should the Red Flag have waved once over Germany to the end that a few lord mayors could play at being ministers, something that was even sporadically possible under the Kaiser?

"'How quickly this feeling of inner solidarity disappeared. The spirit of peace has vanished like the snows of yesteryear. Military defeat, the bad peace, price increases, decline in morals, black market—it is the fault of the Republic. Every domestic crisis brings threats of the application of Article 48, the vial of poison in the inner pocket of our Constitution.

"'The middle class, derailed and anarchistic, has evacuated one position after another, and is trying today to cling to and to stabilize the remainder of its economic substance. A shameless reversal of the simplest definitions of decency and legality is eating deeper and deeper into the German brain.

"'This is the reason for the great atmosphere of insecurity, that uncertain feeling that reaction is on the march, irresistible. The reactionaries rely on two very doubtful statements: German rulers were absolutely innocent of the outbreak of war; and the war was not lost, but the army dispersed because of fateful influences back at home: the stab in the back.

"'There is something rotten to the core in this nation that it can elect a man to Congress because he was recommended to them as a murderer. In any case, it is fascism which determines the theme and sets the *niveau*. It's an old experience that measures aimed against the extreme left quickly move to the right. The anti-communist law will soon become an anti-republic law. Today the truncheon comes down on the communist; tomorrow it will be the turn of others.

"'A trail of blood runs through the years of the Republic. There is a clear line from the Eden Hotel and Baltikum, via Kapp and the O. S. and the Ruhr struggle, and then to the election brawl. A Camorra of unemployed officers steadily and secretly attracts new recruits and involves them in its business. They have introduced trench warfare into domestic policy. 'Heads will roll.' What would the procurator of a monarchist state do to an opposition party that promised to execute the king and his ministers when it came to power?

"'All sigh at the frightful size of the military budget, but none is ready to take the first step. As it is, we can bet that each one of these gentlemen will frantically defend his own weaponry, the sailor his dreadnoughts and the cavalryman his lancers. The military experts will stifle the politics. Their task is to see that the pacifist civilians do not kick over the traces. All the politicians want to 'integrate' the Army and 'inject it with the general republic spirit'—they don't realize that they themselves have long been integrated and injected. The werewolves of the right look with laughing eyes at the worthy, who were sheep with their black-red-gold wool, and look forward to the feast. Since the battle of Sedan, it has been regarded as soft, feminine and anti-nationalist to touch upon the problem of peace; peace, the most necessary idea of our times. But, as we know and sadly rue, on related issues, even the peacemakers are unblessed.

"'But the people too have emergency rights against adventurist experiments on the part of the authorities. The patient German mare often trots ahead for a long time without asking whose knees press its flanks. But if the clique in power, which does not have two-percent of the nation behind it, should use the spurs and the whip, then even this mild mount will finally buck. Germany has suffered too much, starved too much. Most people have nothing to win, but they have a lost existence to revenge.'"

And, folding the papers and handing them to Carl, Manfred added, "Carl, thank you for your words, for the fight and commitment behind them, and don't you dare stop writing while you're in there," Manfred finished, pointing up at the dark walls. When he shook Carl's hand during some applause and cheering, the latter chided him for "going through the trouble," and turned to the group again, this time bringing his wife and daughter up to face them as well.

He waved. "I thank you all again. Please stay well, all of you, and keep an eye on these two." Hating goodbyes, he hugged and kissed Maud and Rosalinde, picked up his battered suitcases, and walked down the drive to the prison's grim medieval portal.

****

The Man Without a Party

The guards took his identification at the door, offered to carry his grips, less by request than command, and walked on either side of him through a urine-scented tunnel to the first lighted room, where waiting guards opened and checked the clothes, reading and writing material inside. Carl was told he would get the contents back soon. As they walked him to his cell, he couldn't refrain from looking at the faces of those behind the bars they passed. How many of these were political prisoners like himself? What were their sentences, their "crimes," their stories? Would he be able to learn those all-important life histories? Would he even be able to make contact?

The door of an empty cell was unlocked; he entered; it was locked behind him. He turned around and, for the first time in his life, looked through the bars from inside, watching the guards as they returned to their posts. He'd been charged with crimes before, and convicted, but fines had been paid one way or another, and he'd evaded incarceration. Now, he felt, he'd finally earned it. The seriousness of what he'd done, and the growing awareness on the part of the powers that be that he was consistently endeavoring to subvert their most important ambitions, had put him where he was now. Well, he would try to make the best of it.

And, also for the first time, he realized, hands fishing in his pockets, that he was without his beloved cigarettes. And, thus, he felt prison in his gut. When they brought his possessions, he pulled out something to read but found, instead, a photo of himself with Maud and Rosalinde and the latter's cat, all formally seated and smiling. Carl lay down on the plank bed and stared at the image as it rested on his stomach, brushing it with care. He closed his eyes.

The second time he felt an institutional shock to the system was that evening, at dinner. Bland, bland, bland. An army chef, perhaps. Oh well, complaining could come back to bite him. And, truth be told, he could stand to lose a few pounds. At least during meals, he could fraternize with his fellow prisoners somewhat. Many of them had heard in advance of his arrival, knew of him, praised him for his willingness to stand up to the military complex that, buttressed by right-wing paramilitary groups, was obviously running the marionette show over the heads of the civilian politicians.

The men were careful only to address him with heads down at table and, when he was standing, one at a time, and then obliquely. The majority of them seemed to be in for convictions of leftist-oriented violent behavior, whether deserved or on trumped-up charges, and they unanimously articulated, by word or expression, both dogged hope and aching doubt for release soon. Carl rarely felt depressed, but this painful parade disheartened him. At least there was the potential of an article or two in their tales, anonymity preserved, of course. But he was almost relieved to get back to his cell; as much as he would like to help them, the physical confines of his nine-by-nine were at least temporarily preferable to the psychological claustrophobia of the mess hall.

Anyway, he had his own matters to think about. The after-meal yen for a smoke made the insides of his throat itch. He paced back and forth until he, at last, lay down on the thin narrow cot and threw an arm over his eyes to sleep.

He found out two days later from the buzz around the latrine that Groener had been booted out by his colleagues. A sign of more to come? What next?

Over the first few weeks, he had learned of the now-unpopular Stormtroopers among the prisoners—they stayed among themselves—made some connections, enjoyed strolling around the perimeter of the grounds during exercise time, and missed Maud and Rosa and freedom and good food and cigarettes as never before, devoured and poured out letters, met with his lawyers for two more court cases in which he would soon be embroiled, and worked on articles for *The Worldstage*. His recently published pieces had included the call for the resignation of General Groener as Minister of the Interior so that there would not be "a personal union" between that ministry and the army; the comment that the ministers weren't servants of the president, a reference to Chancellor Bruning's fawning remark that he was happy to be able to serve Hindenburg; his endorsement for president of the communist candidate Thalmann against Hindenburg—not because of a change in his ideology but simply because Thalmann was the only candidate offered on the left; branding of Hindenburg's reference for "equal protection under the law" as, in fact, in the present context, aid for fascism; and an invitation, a plea to both social democrats and communists to come and sit and talk at a round table—he offered himself as an unaffiliated mediator only motivated "to save all parts of the organized working class from destruction"—finally, and at last, before it was too late, and in spite of the "walls of paper towers" that stood as barriers between them, to bury their differences and come together syncretistically to oppose the right.

But now he wanted to write something that focused on the anti-Semitism, which was so evidently on the rise. He planned to zero in on its literary manifestations, especially as seen however cryptically in the writings of Hans Bluher and Wilhelm Stapel. Bluher, one of the founders of the pre-War Wandering Bird movement, had subsequently been advocating for the segregation of Jews—the chosen people of the past—but without hatred—"*sine ira et studio*"—from Germans—the chosen people of the future—for the sake of the latter's racial purity. Stapel, on the other hand, advocated spiritual distance between Germans and Jews because, as different peoples, they were unable to get along, not just mentally but fundamentally. German anti-Semitism and Jewish anti-Germanism complemented one another. Why? Because, if one wanted peace among peoples, then symbiosis among them was *apriori* undesirable. A fact of nature. Most outrageously, one was supposed to accept Stapel's claim that no depreciation of Jews was intended by all this—a performative contradiction that stunk of the most noxious moral corruption.

At any rate, while in prison, Carl wanted to get a handle on the matter, find the words that would help him form his thoughts and the thoughts that would help him form his words. What connections could he rationally make and adequately defend between the writings of these men and others—Weininger, of course—and the anti-Semitic violence actually taking place on the streets of Germany? It was one thing to see the connections subjectively, to react to them viscerally, to condemn them—both the writings and the violence—ethically; it was quite another thing to give his opponents pause, to make them see the damning error of their ways. What rhetorical strategy would be most successful?

The buzz during the first week was General Groener's resignation from his position as Minister of Defense. Carl felt his article of January had been vindicated. But he also squirmed at being stuck in jail, unable to learn more, to discuss matters with colleagues, to better build a basis for further thought. He shook his head at himself for having remarked about his incarceration that he was no more imprisoned than anyone else in Germany. The *bon mot* was false.

Alsberg showed up one morning when he was on his stroll, and a guard led him inside to a tiny room where he could talk to his unassuming counsel. They embraced, and Max asked him how he was doing, told him he'd seen his family, who were as well as could be expected, and offered him a greedily accepted cigarette, a Batschari Mercedes. After lighting it, Carl drank the relaxing smoke deep into his lungs.

"Let's start with the Tucholsky case," Max began, "that comes up next week. Though Kurt is the author, he's out of the country, as we know. So the case really falls on your shoulders as publisher of the article, which appeared in *The Worldstage* last year. You've been charged with defamation of the German Army for the author's sentence, 'Soldiers are murderers.' In the context of the article, Kurt, or Ignaz Wrobel—his nom de plume on this occasion—was making the point that the same action of killing that a soldier commits, if performed by someone outside the war zone, could be charged as murder."

Ossietzky squirmed in his seat. "Yes. At least we're not dealing with the time he said, 'We spit on the military.'"

"Right. He can be quite the biting aphorist, can't he?"

"Words are weapons for Kurt; the sharper, the better." He recited, "'Coffins should be built well enough to last a lifetime.'"

"I like 'Public transport teaches humility.'"

"No one contributed more pieces to *The Worldstage* than Kurt. He might even be the originator of 'The death of one is tragic—'"

"'The deaths of 100,000, a statistic,'" Max finished.

"Yes," Carl chuckled. "When *Rheinsberg* became such a success, he opened a book bar in Berlin, and gave a free schnapps to everyone who purchased a copy."

"An amazing individual. Well, quite apart from any logical argument Kurt, Ignaz, or anyone else might build in court to defend the statement at issue, the strategy I propose is a legal one and has three parts. First, and most obvious: you did not write the words. It is likely that, had you rejected the article, it would have been published elsewhere. The prosecution, and the judges, will brush this point aside, of course, but it is a point that, I feel, must be made, nonetheless."

Carl was nodding, smoking and nodding.

"That brings us to the second part of your defense and, in my opinion, the strongest of the three: that neither you nor Kurt are guilty as charged. The sentence, 'Soldiers are murderers,' is a universal one; anyone is entitled to take offense. Therefore, we will argue, if you agree to this, that General Groener and the German Army cannot specifically take offence, feel slandered or defamed by the remark. In other words, it is the universality of Tucholsky's bold blanket statement, and its, uh, incommensurability, if you will, with the government's charge, that prevents a guilty verdict. For once, we are saved by the indiscriminateness of Kurt's penchant for insult."

Still nodding and smoking, Carl said, "Kurt studied law early on. It's the opposite problem of my predecessor, Jacobsohn, God rest his soul. It was his acute yen for detail that turned his career into one long, litigious nightmare. And no one could help him in this. He had his principles and stuck with them."

"I regret I never had the chance to meet him. I've heard you speak of him often so glowingly, you and others, but mainly you, that it is a particular wish I'll unfortunately never have come true."

Carl stubbed out his cigarette and declined the offer of another. "What's the last part of our defense, Max?"

"Your military career," he answered. "As uneventful and inglorious as it may have been, the undeniable fact that you served Germany in the war will, I expect, be the kiss of death for the prosecution."

"I'm not so sure I want that to come up. You know my—"

"Your long-time pacifism, yes, I know it well, and what you told me about Braune's interrogation of you prior to the last trial, that you refused to answer him when he asked if you had been a soldier in the war, that you felt that it should have nothing to do with that case or, indeed, your standing as a patriotic German—"

"It shouldn't, God dammit!"

"I know that, and you know that. But in this case, where a direct mention of the military is part of the charge, it's more *a propos* to bring up—"

"Is there anything I have to do?"

"Yes, in fact." Max paused, rubbed his nose. "I'd like you to take the stand, to give witness to your career as a soldier. You don't have to go into specific experiences, but—"

"I don't know," Carl snapped. "I'll have to think about it." A long exhale.

"That's all I can ask you, Carl."

Carl's fingers were twitching; he grabbed them and held them down. "I'm disgusted by the Social Democrats always giving into the baiting of the fascists, raising such a clamor about their own Iron

Crosses and proper discharge papers, and displaying their wounds like Coriolanus—"

Max reached across the table and grasped both his hands. "And when you decide to take the stand, as I hope you do, I want you to bring all of this passion about your convictions with you. Don't hold a thing back. It's all good, Carl."

They were done. When Max told him there were already over 40,000 signatures on the petition for his pardon for the Kreiser case, Carl said they were making "too much fuss."

"Well," Max replied, "once we get through the Tucholsky case, there'll be one more to fuss about."

"Good Lord! I've forgotten what it's about."

Max pointed to the ashtray. "You were just smoking it. It's the suit about your article concerning the government tax breaks for Philip Reemsta's cigarette empire. They took offense at your suggestion that Germany's rearmament was being paid for solely on taxes exacted from the poor, remember?"

"I knew there was something I didn't like about that cigarette."

Back in his cell, Ossietzky lay down, surprised at how exhausted he felt. He was troubled with himself for being so upset by Alsberg's request. He threw an arm over his eyes, hoping to erase the moment with a nap. Instead, he found himself thinking about his former boss, Siegfried Jacobsohn, founder not only of *The Worldstage*, but of its precursor, *The Theater Stage*. The refined, cultured man had perhaps been the greatest mentor of his life. Along with Quidde and Gerlach, who had first hired and mentored Carl, Jacobsohn had had the effect of inhabiting a higher sphere of existence from most humans, as far as Carl was concerned. Taught at university by Willamovitz-Mollendorf, Erich Schmidt and Max Herrmann, Siegfried, like Schiller, saw the stage as a moral institution, and he attacked its dilettantism, naturalism, neo-romanticism, and most expressionism. He also championed Jessner, Piscator, Reinhardt and, even early in their careers, Toller, Zuckmayer, Bronnen, and Brecht. Among critics, he had most often locked horns with Alfred Kerr.

Ossietzky had been somewhat lost when he'd first started writing for Jacobsohn's paper. Fallen through the cracks between the communists and social democrats, disillusioned with the palette of political parties and the vagaries of organized pacifism, now an unofficial member of the unofficial "homeless left," he had floundered with freelance work until he happened upon the unaffiliated weekly that had been started by Jacobsohn in 1905 under the different name as a theater magazine until its metamorphosis at the beginning of the war. Siegfried, whose politics, like that of so many, had been transformed by the war and its support coming from the Social Democratic Party, took him under wing. The elder man's abhorrence of dogmatism and party entanglements served as modeling principles for Ossietzky. However, Ossietzky's pugnacity was of a different style from Jacobsohn's: more measured and therefore less prone to petty lawsuits.

When Siegfried died suddenly in late 1926, Ossietzky was deeply affected. In the obit Carl composed for his hero, titled "The Cause," he stated, "Teutonic truncheons made of paper still batter 'Jacobsohn's *The Worldstage*' as if they would seek to prove that one honest word suffices to endanger the martial edifice of the good patriots." With Siegfried's widow now managing the paper, Tucholsky took over as editor-in-chief, a position that was, for Tucholsky, a stretch, given his temperament. In early May, 1927, Carl received a call from Jacobsohn's widow asking for a meeting. She shocked him by asking him to take over as chief editor of the weekly.

Carl still felt like a late-comer to the periodical. In a way, he was just a tag-a-long member of the third circle of evolution of Jacobsohn's creation. First, there was the pre-war group including Bab, Polgar, Feuchtwanger, Ihering and Tucholsky; second, during the war, Hiller, Goldschmidt, Reimann, and Lehmann-Russbuldt, founder of the German Peace Society; then, after the magazine's rechristening, Behne, Mehring, Lewinsohn and Seiburg, with Carl landing years later in April, 1926.

Carl was reluctant to argue with a woman who was still obviously in mourning. Nonetheless, after saying he was honored by the offer and praising Tucholsky's work, he listed his reservations about appearing as an *arriviste*, about others more qualified and experienced, and about his doubts as to whether he could approximate what his former boss had consistently been able to achieve for so many years. *The Worldstage* had a high reputation, and—

Edith finally cut him off. "I appreciate all your concerns. First of all, you must know that Siegfried was much younger than you when he founded the paper. And he was far from perfect. This paper made him a better person and an editor of the highest level. It has given us our lives."

Carl thought the "far from perfect" might be a reference to Jacobsohn's dismissal, related to a charge of plagiarism, from his prior position as writer for *The World on Monday*, but he merely nodded to Edith before she went on.

"You must also know that Kurt is many wonderful things, but even he is unsure whether one of them is being an editor. He loved doing correspondent work in Paris before coming back here when Siegfried died. He will work closely with you during the transition—"

"But—"

"Our print has plateaued at twelve thousand five." Then, she paused for effect. "You know, we don't need to continue."

Ossietzky shut his mouth.

"As papers go in this country, *The Worldstage's* longevity is greater than most. But, after all, it *is* Siegfried's legacy. It was literally his life. Especially after the Mertens articles, just before you arrived on the scene."

Carl was already nodding. Siegfried had hired Carl Mertens to research and document, as well as could be done, far right assassinations of supposed traitors—after secret trials and *in absentia* convictions—none of which had been investigated by the Weimar government, while such crimes supposedly committed on the left—communists death squads after the revolution?—had been rigorously prosecuted. In addition, these articles had followed upon *The Worldstage*'s publication of the results of the four-year study by the eminent Heidelberg statistician, E. J. Gumbel, who discovered an inordinate preponderance of government prosecution and judicial conviction of supposed perpetrators of left-wing violence over that of the right.

"Carl, at that point Siegfried knew that he could easily become the next leftist target gunned down. You tend to re-evaluate what you do when you come to that realization, and why you do it." She stopped. Carl could tell that she was not fighting tears; she was very much in control of herself, very much the responsible proprietress.

"To tell you the truth, I don't think your transition will be smooth. Not because of any fault that you may have, and not because nothing seems to go smoothly in this wretched country. But because our paper, with your help, Carl, has put itself in the position of being the one voice within our borders that exposes the wrongs, wherever they are, by whomever they are committed, courageously and without dogma. And they're going to keep coming at us for doing the right thing, Carl. Make no mistake about that.

"I'm not just calling upon you because no one has come forward. Your style will be very different from Siegfried's. As you know, he was quite a mentor. You are very quiet, except in print, where you more than make up for your natural taciturnity. But, still and all, I think you'll be a good, solid editor because you have balance and perspective, Carl. Siegfried saw this in you and often talked to me about it. And to others. You happen to be unique in having that reputation at the paper, and others respect it. You may not realize it, but they do. I'd like you to take over immediately, and your salary will reflect that. You'll decide when you want to make it official. Under the masthead, I mean."

The only thing she granted him was that they print "with consultation of Kurt Tucholsky" after his being named editor.

****

One week later, he found himself called out of his cell and hustled up into the dock of a courtroom in Berlin. Alsberg asked him to explain why he felt justified in printing the article in question in *The Worldstage* and why this case, in particular, was so important to him.

"Though, during the war, I stood in the line of fire, I have fought against war since 1912," Ossietzky thundered. "Therefore, if pacifism turns me, a war veteran, into a traitor to the country, it is inaccurate and, frankly, insulting for the prosecutor to date my crime from November, 1918. And while I did not write the words attributed to Kurt Tucholsky, they are almost a perfect expression of my deepest conviction. But Mr. Tucholsky did not take his analysis of the true situation far enough. Soldiers are murderers. But perhaps, most tragically, and certainly most ironically, soldiers are also victims, not only of other soldiers, but of society, the political and cultural context that turns men into soldiers in the first place.

"War is not an expression of something heroic; no, its legacy is horror, fear, despair, and death in many awful manifestations. It is therefore, with the greatest satisfaction I have ever felt, that I stand before you now to speak out against it.

"I first got to know Dr. Tucholsky during the 'Never Again War' movement in 1919. At that time, while we were still suffering from the fresh wounds of war, we worked together for the cause of pacifism, along with the great humanist artist Kollwitz, the eminent scientist Einstein, and many other great Germans. From Lao-tse, to the Bible, to Kant and, yes, even from President Hindenburg, we read that war is murder. If so, then who are the murderers? Soldiers are only little murderers. The big murderers are crowned with laurels.

"Should someone who walks in a peace march be put in prison? A child of peace, thrown into the penitentiary? During this trial, I'm sure we could all hear the sounds of military music playing outside. A coincidence? It doesn't matter; the point is made. But has the violent milieu of our country made us more honestly loyal, or has it rather reduced us to an abject obedience to martial authority, a self-imposed servitude that approximates that of the dog, Nipper, listening to his master's voice?"

Because Tucholsky's polemical sentiment did not specifically mention German soldiers, the court decreed that Ossietzky be acquitted of the charge of defamation of the German Army. Tucholsky had bitten his thumb, Carl reflected, but not at anyone in particular. The victorious prisoner shook hands with Max and was promptly escorted by guards back to Tegel.

Within a few days, Carl noticed a change: his acquittal was welcome and surprising news among the prisoners. If one of them could win a case against the military-political monolith, then, perhaps...

He got more smiles, nods. During exercise and time in the latrine, prisoners shared their cases: trumped up charges, convictions based on planned violence simply for leftist political activity, or political trials for simple crimes, petty theft stemming from hunger, poverty. Could Carl help? He would try. Nothing was written down, of course, lest it serve as evidence for future charges.

And the increased attention didn't just come from prisoners. Guards, wardens, janitors and clerks, all seemed to have friends or relatives in some kind of trouble. The tales seemed to be endless; endless but monotonous, always on the same theme of false charges and evidence, politicized cases, biased judges. Always the victims of justice were on the left; the further left, the harsher the sentence. Always, Carl promised he would do what he could. He sensed that a positive response was more meaningful for the suppliants than a realistic one: when supplication was the issue, everyone seemed to live for the future.

Carl learned that the manner the prisoners had for compensating for the poor food, the boiled diet and incessant turnip concoctions, was humor. As often as they could, they joked about Chef Hungerstrike and his lethal culinary inventions. The broad satire led Ossietzky to the sarcastic tone for the conclusion of his essay on anti-Semitism:

"Take your courage in your hands, and unleash the lyncher in every anti-Semite! Pick up the horse dung, throw it in the face of your Jewish co-citizen, and shout "Jew pig" at him! You will feel all the better for it, and, since we live in Germany, you will be sure of finding a court which will show understanding to your troubled soul."

And another part of the same piece developed from an afternoon talk he'd had with a fellow prisoner, a Jew who was nonetheless a strict anti-Zionist:

"Anti-Semitism is a close relative of nationalism, and its best ally," Carl wrote after talking with the man. "The two belong together. A people which has weathered two thousand years of world history without territory and without material authority is a living contradiction of nationalist ideology, which insists that the idea of 'nation' is exclusively dependent on power-political considerations. Anti-Semitism has never struck root in the working class, but it has always been something for the middle classes and the small peasantry; today, when these sections are going through their big crisis, it has become for them a sort of religion, or, at least, a religion substitute. Nationalism and anti-Semitism govern the internal political scene in Germany. They are the loud-screeching hurdy-gurdy of fascism, drowning out the softer tremolo of social reaction."

And, in a flash of inspired erudition at the service of political art that recalled his Florian Geyer days, he decided to sign the article 'Thomas Murner.' The piece was published by *The Worldstage* in July while he was still in Tegel.

Chapter Four
PAST

The day after his church group's first confession was their first communion; the first was supposed to have prepared them for the second. Like Carl, most of them were in the fourth grade. They gathered, boys and girls facing each other in single-file along the sidewalk outside the church, waiting for the others to seat themselves inside, so that they could procession in with everyone watching. It was a warm Hamburg morning, somewhat muggy, and the boys were dressed in dark slacks and white dress shirts while the girls wore white dresses and veils.

He'd seen his mother and father going up the church stairs; she'd waved to him. As with most things having to do with church, especially when he was involved, she was very excited. And although he realized he was less and less like her, and less and less moved by her enthusiasm, he'd gone out of his way to match the others' seriousness and piety about receiving the Host, the actual Body and Blood of Christ the Lord, transubstantiated. As the nun, Sr. Anna, had tried to explain to them: the outward attributes of the bread remained the same, while its essential substance was transformed by the celebrant's performance of the words and gestures of consecration. This part of the Mass was to be thoroughly distinguished from that of the Lutherans and other protestant churches, in which communion never became anything more than an earthly, symbolic act; in their misunderstanding of Jesus' power and intent during the Last Supper—and the meaning of the sacraments in general—these religions did not feel that Christ—and the Catholic priests who took his place in every Mass—could properly perform the miracle of the *panis angelicus*.

The Man Without a Party

Carl tried hard to fathom it: when the priest placed the wafer on his tongue, he, Carl, would be holding God in his mouth; they all would. That was part of the miracle. He'd heard the stories about curious children who'd removed the Host afterwards, a grave sin, and even about the boy who'd pinned it to a wall, and that it had bled. He would never do that! But God, would he really be swallowing God, just like the food he ate? And what would that mean? How would it change him? Would the effect of God ever wear off, like when he became hungry again a few hours after a meal?

Sr. Anna was walking between the two gender-based lines, her finger to her lips, shaking it at some restless children, checking on what they were wearing. Suddenly she stopped, stared at one girl, and bent over to look more closely at what she had noticed. She was whispering to herself, but Carl couldn't make out what she was saying. Whenever Sr. Anna opened her mouth, Carl had noticed on many occasions, you only saw the bottom teeth; never the top.

Carl put his fingers to his lips, checking to see whether he exposed his uppers or lowers, or both or neither. Uppers, mainly. He decided he would make an attempt, when he spoke, to reveal both rows, tops and bottoms. Then, he thought of the people he'd seen who exhibited their upper gums when smiling, like horses. Weird! He would make sure he never did that!

With all his dental musings, he failed to register Sr. Anna walking briskly away from the children.

She returned a few moments later with Mother Hermana, a short, wide, older nun who went right up to the girl, Mary, who was just a few children away from Carl. Mother Hermana whispered into the girl's ear; the latter gave a look of shock and turned pale. It was then Carl noticed that, unlike the other girls in the line, Mary was wearing a bell-shaped underskirt; it was poofing out her white exterior skirt, flouncing it like she was an *infanta*. Evidently, this expansive attire had been forbidden the girls for the First Communion ceremony.

While Sisters Hermana and Anna put their heads together to come up with a solution to the problem, Mary burst into tears.

All the other children stared at her, wondering what was the matter. One girl placed a hand on Mary's shoulder. Whispers were passed around: the nuns had considered just removing the underskirt but rejected this notion when told the offending garment was an entire slip. Carl couldn't help but become distracted; poofing slips jarred with the thoughts of Communion and the pious procession, which was already running late. Underskirts and a sobbing girl clashed with Jesus and the Host. To top it off, Mary was a very pretty girl, probably the cutest in the group; her long black hair waved and curled out from under the veil. The boys often joked about wanting to tease her, not with the intent of making her a victim, but only because it seemed like it would be more fun than teasing any of the other girls. She also was a Hildebrand, one of the wealthiest families in the parish; his mother had told him they had quite a mansion in Winterhude, with a team of servants. For her to be brought to such a pass, all because of a petticoat, well! This was really something!

Carl had never seen the Mother so angry. He couldn't tell if she was swearing under her breath because he couldn't hear her; but when he'd heard other people talking the way she was talking now, they'd been swearing; he was sure of it. Could nuns swear? And even more, would Mary have to miss her First Communion? He couldn't imagine it. Sr. Hermana, with a great struggle and much grunting, had knelt down of the pavement stones and commenced frantically to pin down the recalcitrant petticoat with straight pins she carried affixed to her habit. When she'd used these up, along with the ones Sr. Anna handed her, only a small part of Mary's outfit had been tamed, a mere section of the cone.

"If only parents would listen to directions!" Sr. Anna asserted.

"Oh, some of them think they can get away with anything!" The Mother exclaimed. "Pastor Wilhelm will be very upset that we're late." This only made Mary cry harder, her pursed eyelids squeezing out the tears, her taut fist against her gritted teeth. Her girlfriends gathered around her in support and heartfelt concern; one held onto her other hand. Some of them looked like they were ready to burst into tears as well.

Suddenly, Sr. Anna snapped her fingers. "I know where there are paper fasteners!" She ran off behind the church where there were some offices; she raced through a door, leaving it ajar. The children looked at each other. They had never seen the nuns at such a loss.

"I want all the boys to stop looking at their shoes!" the Mother snapped while they waited in the sun. Totally at a loss, all the boys looked down at their newly polished shoes; the girls looked at the boys looking at their shoes, then gave the boys' shoes a look. "No looking!" All the heads snapped up. They gawked at each other in wonder, and then they looked at Mother Hermana. A drop of sweat clung to the point of her nose.

A single cloud drifted lazily across the Hamburg sky.

The procession continued to wait. People were coming around the front doors, looking to see what was keeping them. Carl looked up at the sky; it certainly wasn't becoming any cooler or less humid. He could feel the sweat on his body sticking to his new shirt. Finally, Sr. Anna rushed back, and she and the other nun set to work attaching the binding pins to the offensive underskirt. They held extra ones dangling from their lips that were quivering with hurry. Progress was being made. One of Mary's friends jumped up in the air with excitement to cheer her up. Everything was going to be all right!

Mary dried her eyes. As Mother finished with the pins, Sr. Anna attended to the other children, angrily ordering them back into ranks. At last, the procession began, and Carl took his place. They marched up the church stairs, into the incensed shadows of the interior. People in the pews turned to look as they passed. The priest, holding a staff, flanked by the concelebrants and the altar boys, looked even more severe than usual. Were they all blaming them together for the delay?

What have you done wrong? They took their seats in the front of the church and the ceremony began.

During the service, Carl couldn't help checking on Mary, just to look and see if she was doing better. By the time Carl took communion, he had a headache and felt faint from the fumes. He was incapable of feeling a change within him, or of even feeling that he'd missed the opportunity.

He heard some weeks later that the Hildebrands had made a huge donation to the parish.

****

Gustav entered the apartment, but, when he heard the yelling, he slowed his pace, shutting the door quietly. Rosalie and Carl were shouting, that was clear. Gustav tiptoed down the hall, listening. Carl was pleading, refusing to do something; Rosalie was insisting. Her voice became ever and ever shriller, like the urgent shriek of someone in danger, in pain. Should he go into the closed room? Suddenly, the matter became clear to Gustav: Carl was fourteen, and the time for confirmation was approaching. He'd been expecting something like this.

He quietly returned to the front door, reopened it, and then shut it again louder, almost a slam. The yelling stopped. He walked normally down the hall, clearing his throat.

"Hello?" More silence. A door opened, and Carl came out, head down. He immediately went into his bedroom, shutting the door loudly. Rosalie came out of the room they'd been arguing in, arms crossed over her breast, and walked toward Gustav, collapsing in his arms.

"Rosalie, what is it? Tell me." He held her up, guided her toward a chair in the parlor.

"He won't... He won't..." She dropped into the chair.

"Carl? What's wrong?"

"He refuses to…" She wept. "His confirmation. He told me…" She halted, cried wordlessly. Gustav handed her his handkerchief.

"Sit here. I'll get you a glass of water." He went into the kitchen, came back, and raised the glass to her lips. He knelt on the floor in front of her. "Tell me."

"The confirmation classes for his age are starting," she whispered breathlessly. "He refuses to go. He says all his friends—" that was all she could get out before more tears. He dabbed at her eyes, made her drink more.

"Take a deep breath."

"Oh, Gustav! I'm so unhappy!"

"Breathe. Please."

"I feel so helpless. My child. I don't want him to…"

"It's because of your love for him that this is so important to you."

"He knows that! His soul…"

"But you also know that he needs to cut the strings for…"

"He has been! For years!"

"Yes! One by one. In order to grow and become a man."

"It's killing me! His father…"

"I want you to do one thing. How did Jesus' mother love him? Did he do what she wanted?"

"But I can't. I…"

"I'm not asking you to totally give him up. This isn't about that. It's about him taking the next step he feels he must take toward manhood. Our job is to advise and continue supporting him, yes, even when we're convinced he's making the wrong choice. Because in the long run, it's better for him to fall flat on his face than for us to catch him or, worse, not let him even take a step on his own."

"It's just so hard!"

"There was a time when he couldn't walk. He learned by falling."

He made her take another sip. She swallowed; her breathing became more regular.

"Now, Rosalie, let me ask you: Do you love him enough to accept a compromise?"

"Yes, of course, but what…?"

"That's all I need to hear. At least I have something I might be able to work with."

She finished her water. "I feel so tired."

"I can imagine. You're still giving birth to your son. Rosalie, he's fourteen years old! You must be exhausted."

She lowered her head, took in the comment.

He led her down the hall to their bedroom, helped her lie down, kissed her gently. Her eyes were already closed, her breath slowing down into a sighing exhale wrapped around a reflexive sob. He slipped off her shoes, quietly shut the door, and he went down the hall to Carl's door, knocked softly.

"Yes?"

"Can I come in?" Softly, softly.

"I'd rather you didn't."

"Just for a second?" No answer.

Gustav went in and shut the door behind him. Carl was standing, back to him, looking out the window. Gustav sat in the chair between the door and a makeshift desk piled with a mélange of books, papers and clothes to create a hodgepodge, jumbled terrain over which the plaster bird watched as over its demesne. Above it hung the crucifix; Rosalie demanded one in every room. The symbol always projected the same thing to Gustav, screaming, '*I was not made for this*!' The perfect image, he reflected, for preparing children for a future they would be overwhelmingly unprepared for. Brilliant paradox or a crucial flaw? Shrugging off the train of thought, he gathered himself for the demands of the present.

"First of all," he began quietly, "I want you to know that I am completely, totally, and utterly on your side." Carl snorted in response, shrugging his shoulders as if to say, 'What good does that do?' "Yes, I understand. Where does that get us?" He sighed.

"Secondly, I think we're both on more solid ground," here he turned his head toward the door, "if your mother never knows about my bias. It would only weaken our, uh, *your* position."

Carl turned to look at Gustav. "'Position'?" He stuffed his hands in his pockets. "She still sees me as a stupid, ignorant child," he muttered.

Gustav looked at the walls, sighing again. "Carl," he started in a confidential tone, "you've asked me more than once why I don't communicate with my father. The truth is, I had similar problems with him when I was your age. I reacted passionately to his conservatism, his intolerable chauvinism. Bismarck was his hero; Heine, mine. Starting at the middle and moving away from each other, we burned the bridge between us. There's no rebuilding it."

Carl slouched down on his bed, frowning. He shuffled his feet.

"Back then," Gustav went on, "it was either give in or leave. Rather than yield to him, I left. This made my life very difficult for a time. But," here he looked out the window at a cloud in the sky, 'if a viable alternative, some middle way had somehow been hammered out between us at the time, without either of us losing face, now, with the perspective I have at present, I would gladly go back and take it. You see, Carl, you can always burn a bridge if you want; the problem is rebuilding it when you regret what you've done and the opportunities for reconciliation have disappeared."

"But what am I going to do?"

"That's why I'm here. Do you want to hammer it out while we go for a walk?"

After a half minute of nothing, a nod was all that was returned. They went out.

The overcast had burned off, leaving a sunny day. They drifted into a busy section of Hamburg, where a system of canals linked a maze of old red-brick warehouses. To the horizon, pleasure steamers, yachts, barges, and old hulks meandered between bollards and moles. Workers tended to shipments like bees around their hives. On their stroll, Gustav discovered many things: Carl didn't believe in God, especially not the Christian one, and more especially not the Roman Catholic one.

And he certainly didn't believe in the trappings of any religion. Humans had acquired the ability to think along with other abilities in order to survive. But those abilities, including thinking, could be used for purposes they weren't meant for. The only form of thinking that should be followed was rational thought. The rest only got in the way.

Gustav made sure Carl felt supported, agreed with him on everything, praised him for his independent spirit. "As you ask," Gustav finished, "the thing is, what do you do *now*?"

More walking. "What are we doing out here?" Carl suddenly asked.

"What? Where are we?" Gustav looked around as if he were unaware where they were. "It's the warehouses! I hadn't noticed." He took a deep breath. "I love the coffee smell. There's cocoa and spices over there. And the foreign carpets—" He started to point ahead of them.

"You didn't know where we were going?" Carl scoffed. "Right. You probably had some point taking me out here."

Gustav frowned, looking at the sky. "I'll try to think one up if you insist, but actually, no, I was too focused on reliving my own youth while listening to you talk to be aware of where we were going."

"Hmmm."

At a small market, they bought things for lunch— sausage and a crusty loaf—sat on a bridge above a canal, and ate. Bulbous clouds puffed along with apparent purpose, trailing their shadows over the city. Halfway through their meal, Carl said, "I might as well also tell you I'm quitting school."

"Really!"

"Yes!"

"Now, that's more serious than confirmation."

"I can't stand the classes, and—"

Gustav waited.

"I'm stupid."

Gustav chewed. "Well, I'm not going to say that a few times over the years I haven't wondered—"

"Shut up!" Carl laughed. "I mean on the damned tests, in comparison to the others."

"Oh, that." More chewing.

"I can't take it anymore!"

"I'll admit, school's only one measure of intelligence, but an important one—"

"Well, I'm getting out of it. Maybe I'll go off to sea."

"Okay. But as far as I'm concerned, can we just focus on the first problem this afternoon?"

"I'm not asking you to focus on anything."

Silence. They watched some swallows skimming above the water that was below them.

"Have you ever wondered why your mother and I ended up together?"

"You met through some friends."

"No. I said 'ended up,' not just 'meeting up.'"

"You're both very different."

"Do you think we love one another?"

"Oh, yes!"

"Well, there it is, then. When you love, the importance of other things is… rearranged. And they don't get any say in it. It's all very strange."

Silence.

"And you love your mother."

"Of course." More silence. "That's why!" Carl exploded.

"Why what?"

"Why you brought me out here. The warehouses, these little quays, they—they're supposed to represent something, what's

73

important, our environment, context, I guess. Everything else in this city depends on them."

Gustav's jaw dropped. He looked around in mock astonishment. He sputtered, "Well, I never!"

Carl guffawed scornfully. "You 'never,' all right."

"I'm speechless. I mean, I thought your terse summation and synthesis of Kant and Darwin was brilliant. I mean, I've seen you after you've fallen asleep on your bed covered with books. I knew you were smart. But this—"

"Huh! You'll never fool me, Dad. I—"

"Well, I'll admit, you certainly have a point. Of course, these are just warehouses, not factories. Marx says everything starts with production."

"But how is your 'context' supposed to help me with my mom?"

"I tell you, it's not *my* context; it's yours. All I said was that when your mother and I fell in love, our most important beliefs suddenly lost their power; they were replaced by a merciless tyrant: Eros."

"Yeah. So?"

"And then you said you love your mother, and all of a sudden," Gustav chuckled, "it was like you were giving me a warehouse tour."

"Dad…"

"My only point is: what is the connection between confirmation and your love for your mother."

"She's using that love to get me to do something."

"And you said no."

"Right."

"But what is it that you can say yes to, out of your love for her? Think."

"Nothing."

"Hmmm. Then we're back to square one."

"Right. Thanks for all the clarification."

They gathered up the remains of their lunch and continued their walk.

"You know, your father was a Lutheran."

"You're my father."

"Thanks. I take that as a great compliment. But what I meant...I was just wondering—"

"I won't do it!"

"She just might—"

"It's garbage! If I won't allow myself to be confirmed in the Catholic Church, why would I want to be confirmed in a Lutheran one?"

"Oh, I'm not asking if you *want* to be confirmed in the Lutheran Church. I'm just wondering if you'd be willing to—"

"To make her happy!"

"Oh, she won't be happy. See, then she's giving up at least as much as you are. Neither of you are going to be happy. But there still might be a bridge between you. Unlike—"

"A bridge!"

"Yeah. They're neat little contraptions. Can you imagine what it was like around here before—"

"See? Context!"

"What a fuss it was, having to wait for ferries—"

"Dad!"

"And the fees! Cut-throat."

"Dad!"

"And you see, then she'll *have* to give you space. She's not a Lutheran, you know."

"But I'll hate it!"

"I don't see why it'll matter so much to you. *She's* the one who believes in an immortal soul, not us."

"But going through it all! The dang stupid ritual!"

"You can make it as unpleasant as you want. But the point will be—"

"I know your point! And I'm not saying yes! All I'm saying is... aw, shit! I'll think about it."

They looked quietly about them.

"But what about my other problem, Dad? It's a bigger one."

They were halfway across the Miller Bridge, facing the deteriorating structure called the Water Castle, which split the Alster River, creating a kind of moat.

"I thought you decided you were going to sea?"

"In case I don't! I thought you could help."

Reflecting, Gustav brushed his mustache. Suddenly, he smacked his lips. "Well," he said, "there I *can* finally find a connection with our walk. See the way the water splits in two directions at the castle? You could drop two sticks right here, and maybe they'd make it around the castle together, or maybe they'd be separated and never meet again."

"Dad, what are you saying?"

"It's a big decision."

"And?"

"You should have chosen a wiser father, Son. Give me some time, and this paltry old noggin might come up with something."

Carl was confirmed at the High Lutheran Church of St. Michael on March 23rd, 1904.

And with help from a tutor Gustav found him, he managed to tolerate school for three more years.

Chapter Five
PRESENT

At the end of the year, Carl was included in the much-touted holiday general amnesty, though this, in his case at least, seemed to be an undecided matter, a mere suspenseful rumor, until the very last minute when he actually appeared with his grips outside the door of the medieval fortress of Spandau Prison. As at his entry into jail, he had supporters. But, whereas the farewell had been formally planned as a surprise for Carl by the earlier well-wishers, this time an impromptu but growing crowd of friends and strangers had been waiting for his reception in the harsh November weather, some since morning. When he did finally materialize in the bone-chilling gusts, around five p.m., a victory shout shot up through the icy air and several ran toward him, led by Rosalinde, her arms outstretched. Once again astounded and chagrinned by the turnout, Carl dropped the suitcases. He was hugged and kissed—his daughter clung to him for the longest, whimpering, "Papa!" over and over—examined from head to toe—he was amazed how many comments his weight loss of about twenty pounds provoked!— handed a lit Gauloise—he gratefully smoked the inferior brand, drawing the tarry fumes deep into his lungs—and escorted to the waiting car. This time, there were no speeches, not even short ones, just a humble thank-you. The greeters waved as Walter drove him, Maud, and Rosalinde to Carl's office. There, he found his desk covered with envelopes. They stayed an hour, the four of them opening every heartfelt greeting. Then, Walter took them home.

Carl sat in the back with his longed-for wife and daughter, holding their hands and alternately smiling at them. Whenever his eyes drifted and he watched the lights of Berlin slide by, he found himself going back to his time in prison, to the men he had left behind there, both prisoners and employees. As he was leaving the prison, led by guards who carried his valises, they had waved and shouted at him in faces showing either joy or anxiety. His pockets and bags were full of slips of paper, contact information they had passed on to him against the rules, which were unenforced in his case. He would do his best.

He was surprised in thinking that he would miss the times in the prison yard when they would walk, putter in the little garden and sit together, commiserating about their particular plights. One weathered and witty prisoner, Sauer, who had worked in hotel restaurants in France, would lure their restless chatter out of the dark doldrums and fasten obsessively on the food they were made to eat. The group would latch onto the biting humor of the man, and a kind of rebellious, liberating series of snorts, chortles, and guffaws would explode over the rooftops around them.

Chef Hungerstrike's concoctions were branded with new names each day, depending on Sauer's mood; his bitter and jovial spirit induced others to join in, competing to match and overmatch Sauer's hilarious acerbity, with a veritable devil's menu of *tapenade des navets, cassoulet des navets, navet a la mode, fondue surprise des navets, salade tegeloise garni avec navets* and, branching out into a new inferno of culinary territory, *saucisse de Dr. Caligari, foie gras de Strigoi mort, tripes a la Kurten, gateau Immertrue, crepes de Chimaera* and, as last courses, *rillettes des navets tombes d'un camion,* and, to top it all off, a real *piece de resistance: ratatouille du sang des navets.*

The guards would hear the uproar and look in wonderment like uninitiates, until they caught on and, drawn like metal filings by the magnetic laughter of the circle, would listen and sometimes even take part, swearing the convicts to silence, for they too had seen and sometimes been reduced to eating the poor excuse for cuisine. At last, when the unfortunates would have blown off their steam and subsided into silence, a few final laughs popping off, they had all crept back to the wretched penal world that had been hovering over their sophomoric outburst all along, back to their troubled lives and galling problems. Were they better off for the fantastic verbal fireworks and moment of levity?

Carl gripped the hands more tightly as they rode home; it would be such a joy to get to know his girls all over again. When they arrived, they found that, in their absence, Rosalinde's cat, a spotted stray she had named *Catastrophe!* in French anapestic pronunciation and obligatory exclamation, had surprisingly ignored the Christmas decorations and, instead, in apparent anger for having been abandoned, knocked Gustav's old plaster model of the bird off its perch on a table. The ensuing crash to the floor had broken off its base. Rosalinde, wanting to ameliorate the damage *Catastrophe!* had caused, decided that the statuette had become a decorative bowl and set it horizontally upon the base on the table top it had occupied before its fall.

He had been told by his office not to come in, to take the holidays off, but, as he lay in bed later waiting for blessed sleep, he felt like his colleagues and his confines had both conspired to keep him from knowing what had happened in his absence, all that he needed to know, and he thought and rethought about the bits and pieces he'd picked up from rumors in Tegel and during the last few hours: with Groener and Bruning jettisoned by the military-dominated government, the authoritarian conservative Papen had jumped into the breach with the dubious strategy of appeasing and taming Hitler. The latter had been offered a role as vice-chancellor, but he had brought along conditions for his acceptance so outrageous even for the present adventurers that the negotiations had fallen through, along with a "Never again!" claim from the government.

Nonetheless, Papen had made the concession of lifting the ban on the Stormtroopers—Big deal: they could change back to their brown shirts from the white they'd worn during the 'ban.' After Papen had dissolved the government, both Nazis and Communists had received more votes than before in the subsequent July elections—the former for the first time passing the Social Democrats with over 37%. Bursting at the seams with its new girth, the Nazi Party teetered: left or right? Would this new creature, hitherto unseen in world history after it had first hatched in Italy, this hybrid of nationalism and socialism, chauvinism and labor, lean anti-capitalist or mainstream? Perhaps Hitler's demands had been intentionally impossible. When he followed them up by knocking the "vice" off of Papen's offer, Hindenburg himself had responded with a veto.

Ergo, another government dissolution and a November election, with a drop of two million Nazi votes and 33 delegates. The communists now had 100 delegates. Was the tide turning? With no majority possible, Schleicher replaced Papen; the "Socialist General" wanted to unite the trade unionist wings of the Christian, Social Democratic, and Nazi parties in order to achieve a legislative majority in a new labor government. Distrust all around. Unwilling bedfellows. Another failed adventure, with the clock ever ticking. Merry Christmas!

Eyes closed, he saw the Genie again, unhappily forced back into the bottle, scratching at the glass to break out. Sleepily, Carl pondered his first article in post-prison freedom. What were the themes, the motifs? Hoped-for coalitions, failing, denied. Lurking tyrannical absolutism, surely. A desperate bourgeoisie clinging to, hoping to retain the little it hadn't already lost. Much that was simply symbolic, of course: victory, triumph, the dice of the war rerolled. Turning back the clock. Placing one's boot heel on the neck of the one who has put you through hell. And what a rudderless ship of state! *"Nonne vides ut nudum remigio latus?"* Or would Horace now be shocked into silence? A protean monstrosity worthy of Homer, of Heraclitus himself!

And that *eminence marronne*. If, for Hegel, Napoleon had been history on horseback, then Hitler was a walking state of emergency for us. Our leaders! A macabre merry-go-round, each one falling and breaking his crown, a parade of hopeful, adroit jockeys, jockeys, jockeys...

Carl fell asleep at last.

****

But three days later, he couldn't stand it anymore, and he went to the office. Walter was there, of course, and scolded him for coming in.

"Just for a while," he told him. "So I don't go crazy stuck at home." He approached his desk and started sorting through the pile of well-wishing cards. "I'm not going to say it's worse than prison, but..."

"Then don't say it!" Walter warned with a smile.

"Okay, then," said Carl, his eyes working in conjunction with his hands on the mail. "Tell me."

"Tell you what?"

"What I don't know. What I've missed. What you guys have been keeping from me. Maud won't say a thing about it."

Walter set down his work. "All right. I assumed you knew everything we know, what with the lawyers allowed to see you and the prison system of communication."

"It was all very sporadic. Don't assume I know anything that's important."

Karsch stared at the ceiling. "Where to begin?"

"Last May."

81

"It all starts with Schleicher. He was really behind the whole intrigue that pushed Groener and Bruning out of power."

"So that Hindenburg would appoint Papen."

"Yes, Schleicher's puppet. To inaugurate a presidential government."

"To dissolve Parliament and end the ban on the SS and SA."

"See? You know it all already."

"No! You tell it! I have so many gaps."

"Hindenburg challenged them by demanding to know why they hadn't banned the Social Democrat paramilitary as well. Well, Schleicher really had two goals: to topple Braun's Social Democratic government in Prussia, and to split the National Socialists by making Strasser president of Prussia in the aftermath. He fabricated allegations that Braun directed his police to leave the communists alone. And he promised powerful positions in the new government to union leaders so they wouldn't call a general strike."

"Like during the Kapp putsch."

"Like what destroyed Kapp in '21. Schleicher had to make sure that didn't happen again. Moscow had called for a general strike, you know, as a way to oppose the Nazis."

"And that's probably where Strasser comes in."

"Yes. He's the Nazi with the most influence on the German worker. But Hitler complicated matters. He wanted to become chancellor, instead of Papen."

"But Hindenburg balked."

"Do you know what I heard? When Schleicher tried to get Hitler to drop his demand, Hitler threatened to commit suicide! That's what swayed the National Socialist leaders to back him with his 'all or nothing' policy."

"My head is swimming, but don't stop."

"Well, Papen knew something was up, so he wanted to call for martial law to strengthen his own position, but then

Schleicher exposed him, and Hindenburg made Schleicher chancellor."

"What a fucking mess!"

"What a way to run a country. Presidential government, indeed! Now they say Papen is plotting with old Hindenburg to bring down Schleicher."

"I heard something from my mother about trouble in Hamburg. What's the story there?"

"Yes," sighed Walter. "Bloody Sunday. Back in July. The Nazis and communists were each going to have armed parades. Only, the chief of police outlawed the latter. No reason, of course. And so the Nazis were protected by the cops with machine guns set up in wagons."

"Just like here in Berlin, May '29."

"Yes. But the repercussions were even worse for the government. And that takes us back to the situation in Prussia, because that's the alleged reason the Social Democratic government of Prussia had to be removed, Braun and Severing, because they were unable to preserve law and order. And—"

"Unconstitutional!"

"Paragraph 48, remember."

"Two thirds of the country loses democracy because—"

"—of emergency. Principally, no different from the way chancellors have been by-passing the legislature and issuing emergency decrees off and on for years. Police showed up and escorted the Social Democratic ministers from their building."

"Police! Braun and Severing had charge of over thirty thousand police officers!"

"Whom they did not call out, whatever their reasons. And the unions weren't going to strike, remember. But," he tapped on his desk for effect, "the recent irony is that both the Nazis and the communists stood shoulder-to-shoulder during the transportation strike here in early November, the day before the elections that drove Papen out and Schleicher in."

Carl exhaled. "The 'social general.' He'll bring us all together, I'm sure."

"And tame the wild beast."

Carl's desk was clear. He placed paper into his typewriter and stared at the blank sheet. "Walter, I feel like we're all in one of those Sphinx puzzles we had during the war."

"Oh, those Anchor Puzzles!"

"And no one knows what ultimate shape we're going to end up in. It's nonsense!"

"We're not only on a train that's come off the tracks, but one that continually slips off one set of tracks after another. How many atrocities have been committed over the years?"

"And will be, in the future," Carl added. "I suppose I need to be ready to go back there." Walter noticed Carl's upper lip twitching, something he'd never seen before. "It really takes something away from you. You know, Walter, I turned 43 in that hell-hole."

"Yes, sir."

"Rip Van Winkle. And I need to warn you, my friend, that I'm feeling more and more a separation between myself and what I'm doing here, the purpose of it all. If that's what prison does to you, I sincerely hope it wears away soon. I keep thinking that we've passed the point where what we're doing even makes sense anymore."

"They're still reading us, more than ever, as a matter of fact—even our enemies."

"Yes, especially them, but how are we helping anyone anymore?" he shot forth in heavy, *staccato* syllables and grabbed his scalp in his clutching fingers. "*Cui bono?*" he said in undertone.

Walter looked at his boss and took a deep breath. "If we help inform them, if we help them reach a better understanding and a more rational perspective on things, isn't that all we can set ourselves as a goal? All that we've ever been able to expect as journalists?"

Carl, his head still in his hands leaning on his desk, muttered, "But are we helping to keep the ship afloat anymore?"

"And *should* we? Is that finally our job, as journalists or even as citizens? I don't want to sound like a nihilist, but won't we be better off if this anomalous, 'in-between state,' as you yourself have called it, Carl, were to sink? If the hull is stinking rotten, unsalvageable—"

"Godammit, you're right!" he spat out. He took a deep breath and let it out slowly. He crossed his index finger under his nose once, twice, as if to stop the twitching. "Okay," he sighed, eyes closed. "Thank you, Walter. You've been helpful."

Walter stood up, looked out the window, shoved his hands in his pockets. "No, I'm not right."

"Huh?"

"Everything I've just said goes against everything you've ever taught me, Carl. I was just mimicking the deniers of democracy to see if I could get some of the old fight out of you. If you think I'm taking up with the followers of Nietzsche and Bazarov, you're very wrong. Do you think I'm a turncoat? I'd rather go down with the fighters for what little democracy we have than fall in with the fanatics. Remember Goethe's Mephistopheles: 'I am the spirit who says no.' You and the others have mentored me better than that, in spite of what Kurt Hiller might claim in his rantings."

Carl was nodding at his desk.

"You've had a rough, disorienting couple of months, Boss. But we, this scurrilous rag of a paper and our deathbed republic's cause, need you more than ever. So, back into the trenches!"

More quiet nodding. Then, looking up at him, Carl finally said, "Walter, if we taught you all that, we *have* taught you well. And our paper? What do we have to cover all this?"

"*That's* it!" encouraged Walter. "The session is open!" He walked over to Carl's desk and placed a list in front of him. It had the names of writers lined up with subjects. Carl slowly drew a finger down the page. "Very good," the editor nodded.

"And I had you down for your follow-up articles on your trial and im—"

"Yes, and put me down for another I started at home."

"About?"

"Let's just say," Carl replied, "it's about a nasty genie who's gotten terribly tired of being stuck in his lousy bottle."

"You've already piqued my interest," smiled Walter.

"Good. Now why don't I stop trying to rationalize nonsense and let both of us get back to work?"

He put in three solid hours, but, whenever his mind drifted, he thought of how Walter had grown. He recalled the time during the trial when he'd had to hunt Kreiser down and give him a pep talk in the broom closet. Here, his role had been reversed. Carl had needed the support, and Walter had more than done that. And with the work they were doing, and the situations and changes they confronted, perhaps everyone needed that kind of support from time to time.

Just as he was starting to put things away and pack up, there was a commotion at the outer door. Walter jumped up to check on the matter and returned escorting Siegfried's widow into the room. Carl jumped up at once and found a chair for her.

"I just had to see you," she said, leaning on a cane over to her seat.

"Edith! Of course!" said Carl. "I would have come to see you straightway if you'd only asked."

"Quite all right," she assured, sitting. "I have to get out sometimes." She stared conspicuously at him. "You don't look too worse for the wearing. What do you think, Walter?"

"He looks wonderful, Ma'am."

"It is wonderful to see him back, out of the clutches of those bastards."

"Oh, it wasn't so bad, Edith."

"Well, I hear they even were insulting enough to haul you back into court twice while you were, as they say, 'in the cooler.'"

"I'm afraid so."

"But you were victorious both times."

"Yes, thanks to Apfel's efforts."

"You've done a fine job, Carl, representing *The Worldstage*. Don't you think so, Walter?"

"Yes, Ma'am. A fine job."

"I'm so glad I chose you years ago. No one else would have done as well as you have, since Siegfried—"

"Yes, Ma'am. Thank you so much for the opportunity. It's been an honor."

"Not that Walter and Hellmut haven't succeeded in holding things together during your, er, hiatus."

"They have," Carl said. "Since I returned, I've just been in Walter's way."

"Don't listen to a word he says, Mrs. Jacobsohn," said Walter. "He's already done much to right the ship."

"Oh, I know," she said. "No editor of this 'rag,' as Siegfried used to call it, has accomplished what Mr. von Ossietzky has done. Our circulation has never been so great. He has given us just the right leadership and balance to roll with the times. '*O tempora*!' Right, Carl?"

"'*Nullas cordes*!' Right, Edith?"

She pressed her lower lip against the upper until they quivered. "Siegfried would be so proud of you." Her voice had suddenly become hoarse.

After she left, Carl asked Walter if he'd secretly sent for her just to cheer him up. Joking aside, the visit had been just what he needed.

Chapter Six
PAST

The office where he worked was stuffy. Light came in through windows that couldn't be opened. He had taken his coat off, but that didn't seem to help. The reflections and emanations off the wharves seemed to exude through the walls of the court office. Young Ossietzky sat at a desk and filled out a report, inserting numbers and words into the blanks. He yawned and pulled a sheet out from underneath. On it, he reread the poetic notes that he had jotted down:

> *What do eagles do? Whatever they want!*
> *So the majestic eagles think.*
> *And what do the rabbits do?*
> *What they are told! So goes the world!*
>
> *So how is it then that the little bunny*
> *snarls at the great big bird?*
> *Because Bunny's friends just lie to him*
> *and say the eagle can't be trusted.*
>
> *'I swear my heart is set on peace*
> *I'm friendly to all hares!'*
> *But when I stretch my claw to shake*
> *They scurry to their holes!*
>
> *'You make things hard for me!*
> *My eagle brood just hates you!'*
> *I tell them, 'Under fur and feathers*

we're brothers," but they laugh!'

Carl knew he was no poet, but he still couldn't keep from smiling at his creation. The mischievous attack upon the Kaiser might not be worthy of La Fontaine or even Aesop, but it gave him pleasure just as well, both to write and read. Still and all, he was having a terrible time trying to work the piece into meter and rhyme scheme.

He heard a door of his boss's office opening and quickly shoved the doggerel under the form he had been filling out. He kept his head down, but wondered if his expression was giving him away. What does Darwin say about guilt? What does it have to do with the survival of the fittest? You would think deceptiveness would be more helpful than a blush when it came to living or dying.

Mr. Petersen came over to his desk and looked over his shoulder.

"Ah!" the old man ejaculated. "You're already on the Jensen trial. Good." He laid more papers on the desk. "Here are some more for you. Keep up the good work, Carl." His boss went back to his office.

Carl sighed and thought, 'Not caught that time!' but he felt bad nonetheless. Many would love to have a job like this. He should feel more grateful to the nice man for hiring him at seventeen and without diploma. Especially after the way things had ended with his schooling. He'd dropped out, crammed for the exit exam—Prussian military history: yuck!—with the help of a tutor his father had found for him, a radical who'd been booted from the cadet academy, and proceeded to flunk the test. He still remembered staring at the list of names with passing scores and wondering if there was something wrong with his eyesight. Surely there was a mistake somewhere. No, no mistake; you just didn't cut it, in spite of the extra help. "What was going to become of him?" his mother had cried. A bad bird seemed to have landed on her son's shoulder.

At the time, he had seriously contemplated going out to sea. But then Rosalie had called upon an old friend of Carl Sr., Petersen, to hire him on probation and, seeing a concrete, if distant, path to freedom, Carl had leapt at the opportunity in spite of the deeper feeling of indebtedness to his mother that it would give him. Perhaps soon he could move out of his parents' house, go to Berlin, start his own life the way he wanted to live—by writing.

But the forms were so boring! He plowed through the one in front of him, rifled through the sheaf just dropped on his desk, and started anew with a sigh. But within ten minutes, he had pulled another sheet from under his stack, this one not a satiric attempt at poetry, but a more serious piece, an essay, something he might be able to send to a newspaper:

Why do humans kill? Why do they fight? Is this something they need to do in order to survive? Or is it because they have forgotten the unity of their ultimate source on the tree of life? If so, how can we help each other recapture that union and live it out in brotherhood and peace? What gets in the way of our attainment of this wonderful yet fully graspable, ethereal yet practical dream? What is it that leads us, as civilized as we are, into barbarism toward one another?

Man loses his way on his path along the tree of life. What was, and truly remains, one, appears as many to him. This is because he is blind to the real though sometimes hidden connections between things. And this is the value of the symbolic tree. A tree has many parts and yet it is one thing. It carries within it both life and death; it grows even as it drops its leaves; one branch withers, another blossoms. This is the truth that biology teaches us: the palpable bonding of the organic and inorganic, the material and the energetic, all together, undivided.

And does this unity vanish because man becomes social? Only apparently. We are misled by the complexity of life; the connections between things become obscure. It takes science to uncover them again for us. And so the question turns to who listens to science; who accepts scientific truth, as hard as that might have become; who allows the light of knowledge to guide them in this complex, troubled world. And so this is the wonderful promise that science offers us: from studying nature, we can learn about ourselves.

And there is a bonus: 'Every object,' as Haeckel writes, 'every blade of grass or bit of moss, every beetle or butterfly, when we examine carefully, reveals beauty. Nature, the divine artist, offers us a hand out of our vale of tears.' And then the wonders we see expand before us: the world is infinite, and everything has its part; we are creatures of that world, beautiful creatures deserving of the love of others and our own; our enlightenment leads to harmony, love, and peace.

Once again, the door opened and Petersen exited. As Carl shoved the paper away, his boss walked over to the outer door, waved, and said he had some errands. When the door closed, Carl breathed a sigh of relief and got back to work. But his thoughts kept returning to the idea of peace—how it was more than just an idea or a goal; for the enlightened people of today, it was a duty, an obligation. Everybody wanted peace, but there the quest seemed to stop; the crusade quickly became quixotic. But how to get there? Why couldn't the peacemakers come together?

He worked through the stacks of forms. When Petersen got back, he was pleased with the progress. When his boss re-entered his office, Carl pulled the satire of Kaiser Wilhelm out again and jotted down some more:

> *And when the carrots came to me*
> *to ask for my support,*
> *I sent them packing right away.*
> *No help for Carrot Republics!*
>
> *And when Grandma came complaining,*
> *I told her how to fight*
> *and beat the carrots once for all.*
> *Now don't you think that's right?*
>
> *Robert Hare knows all about it.*
> *He got my telegram! And all those ships?*
> *They're not for you, my friends.*
> *They'll fight the eastern hawk!*

Well, he shoved them away again. Back to work! But the poem was taking shape. He wanted to incorporate a French goose and Russian gander to try to goad the German eagle into conflict with the British hare. And then something about the calls for abdication, the low profile after the fiasco, the resignation of the scapegoat Bulow. Yes! This was fun! Perhaps something to send to *March* for publication. Anonymously, of course. He didn't want to make the mistake that would ruin his future. His mother already thought he was going to hell.

He picked up another form. Why did so many of the cases have to do with accusations of workers allegedly inciting trouble? Something to talk to Gustav about. And members of this German Peace Society kept cropping up in the court. Who were they? He decided he would see if they had representatives in Hamburg, and track them down, especially now that his ideas kept trending that way.

****

Carl opened the door and went inside. Two men were working at desks. He cleared his throat.

"Yes?" said the man closest to him, still looking down. "What can we do for you?"

He stepped forward. "I'm Carl Ossietzky," he said, deciding on the spur of the moment to drop the 'von.' "I think I'd like to become a member."

"Well, keep thinking about it and let us know when you've made your decision," the other snapped back. Then he looked up at Carl, a big grin on his face.

The other man looked up, shaking his head. "Please forgive my friend Otto," he apologized. "He's been demented for quite some time now. Tragically, there's nothing to be done."

As he spoke, Otto stood up, walked over to a table, picked up a sheet of paper and pencil, and handed them to Carl.

"Just fill these out, Mr. Ossietzky. We're somewhat informal here." Waving Carl toward a chair, he returned to his desk. They both sat down. Carl started filling out the form.

"You're not going to interview him first?" the other man asked Otto. "He might be a…"

Otto squinted at Carl. "Do you really think so?"

"Well, a few questions might be in order."

Looking up from the form, Carl stared at the two in confusion.

"Fire away, Fritz!"

Fritz looked up at the ceiling. "Let's see," he mused. "Carl, is it? What can you tell us about the first Hague Peace Conference?"

"Really?" commented Otto. "So general? Not what year did it take place, or why it started on the date it did?" Fritz shook his head in disfavor.

Carl lamely said, "It was very important for the peace movement."

Fritz looked at Otto. "See? I told you he might be one of the Kaiser's spies!" Carl was shaking his head vigorously in denial. Otto stared at Carl again.

"Carl," said Otto, "I was thinking of something a bit more specific. For instance, how would you contrast the first Hague conference with the second?"

Carl rolled the pencil in his fingers. "The second," he guessed, "was more successful?"

Fritz and Otto looked at each other with frowns.

"The second built on the first?"

More frowning.

"Do you want this back?" Carl held up the sheet. He was beginning to understand these two gentlemen. "Shall I leave now?" He smiled.

"That settles it," said Otto. "He's too naïve."

"Unless," Fritz offered, standing up and slapping his hands together, "he's a really good spy." He stepped between the two and leaned against a table, folding his arms. "The Second Hague Conference, Carl, in 1907, failed in just the same way as the first in 1899: the compulsory status of the permanent court of arbitration was again rejected, thanks to representatives of our fatherland. But the first accomplished much more to make the waging of war less brutal and savage: poison banned, looting banned, bombardment of the undefended banned, killing of surrendering soldiers banned, collective punishment banned, forcing people in occupied areas into military service banned—"

"Yes," Otto chimed in, "and attacking hospital ships was also banned, and—"

"They had to treat shipwrecked enemies."

"But the second conference was unique in that Germany rejected Great Britain's offer to reduce weapons—"

"Oh, England's always talking about limiting armaments!"

"My Dum-Dum colleague reminds me, Carl, that cross-tipped bullets were also banned in the first—"

"That was only a declaration, not part of a treaty, you fool."

They stopped, looked at Carl, who was trying to finish filling out the form. Contact information, then a question to answer.

"Fritz! You see?" said Otto. "You're letting your spy slip through your fingers." He gestured toward Carl, who was smiling at them.

Fritz sighed and returned to his desk. "All right," he nodded. "So you don't think he's a spy. But still, perhaps more questions are in order. The German Peace Society does have standards."

"Are you suggesting we give him an intelligence test?"

"Aren't all tests the measure of intelligence?"

"This is highly irregular, Fritz!"

"But if Carl is willing—"

"All right," agreed Otto. "Let's see. Carl, what's the significance of the Boer War?"

"War is always bad."

More stares exchanged; more frowns exchanged. Fritz started humming.

Otto tried again. "No, Carl, I was thinking more in terms of the impact of the Boer War on the peace movement in Germany."

"Oh!" Carl tried to think.

"Perhaps he's too young," offered Fritz.

"How old were you in 1900?" asked Otto.

"Ten," Carl said quickly.

"Listen!" said Otto. "I knew he was quick-witted. Just a little quiet." He sat back in his chair, tapping his fingertips together. "Did Great Britain's aggression in Africa have an impact on any

German legislation?" Now Otto moved his open hands, palms down, back and forth, obviously miming something as a hint.

"What the hell is that?" asked Fritz. "What the hell are you doing?"

"Please don't interrupt us, Dum-Dum!"

Carl, realizing he was miming deep thought, felt like a pure fool.

"Think ships," whispered Otto.

"That's cheating!" yelled Fritz.

"Ships..." wondered Carl.

"von Tirpitz..." Otto whispered lower. Fritz grunted, pulled his hair.

"Admiral von Tirpitz built the fleet," Carl stated.

"How?" asked Otto. "With his own money?"

"The legislature. They voted."

"Got it!"

"Hardly!"

But Otto persisted, "As a result of British aggression in Africa, Parliament voted in favor of Tirpitz' Second Naval Bill, authorizing up to four squadrons, each with eight dreadnought battleships, to be built over seventeen years, and thus accelerating the heinous naval arms race." At once, Otto sat back, chest thrown forward as if he had accomplished a great feat.

Fritz applauded in mock praise. "And now," he said, "we're in the midst of this Moroccan fiasco."

"Again," said Otto.

"Again," agreed Fritz. "And war with England is imminent."

Carl looked up from the form again. "Do you really think so?"

"It could happen in a heartbeat."

"I told you he was Dum-Dum," said Otto. "England would never do it. Lloyd George—"

"Oh, really?" Fritz interrupted. "You see, Carl," he explained, "one of the accursed effects of the damnable creation of a war fleet in this country is to bring England into alliance with France, with whom our country has come into conflict recently. Admiral Nelson would be turning over in his grave to see Great Britain flirting with the country of Napoleon. But it isn't England I'm worried so much about, Carl."

"The Kaiser?"

"What child wasn't happy to play with his toys?"

Carl nodded.

Fritz turned to his colleague. "Okay, Otto," he said. "I'd say he's passed the test."

Otto stood up and offered his hand. "Welcome to the club, Carl."

Carl shook it. "Thanks," he said, handing him the completed form. He then shook Fritz's hand.

"We'll be in touch with you through the mail, Carl. Who knows? With this Moroccan crisis, you may be hearing from us soon."

A few minutes after he left, Otto said, "Well, I don't think we need be concerned too much about young Ossietzky's level of intelligence."

He handed Carl's application to Fritz. Fritz read. In answer to the question, "Why are you interested in joining the German Peace Society?" Carl had filled the space given at the bottom of the front with the following:

> *If all men are brothers, why can't we all live together in peace? Our brotherhood seems to lie hidden beneath the surface. Something is needed to bring this brotherhood into the light. I feel the German Peace Society is part of that something, and that is why I want to become a member.*

And, on the blank back of the paper, Carl had continued:

Today, two movements appear to be racing toward each other. On the one hand, one sees an ever-increasing animosity between nations that only too easily finds ever-new and increasingly lethal weapons, the funds to buy them and the manufacturers to build them. Distrust, bred by the anarchy that exists between countries, motivates neighbors to prepare to defend their borders and civilians against potential belligerents even though the latter are also potential friends.

On the other hand, people from around the world are coming together for the sake of peace. They see the dangers to humanity growing like the Hydra's heads. And what they see gives them concern. And their concern leads them to act. Their task is herculean, but they are resolved to move forward, to strive to the utmost until they have reached their goal. That movement may mimic the snail in its slowness, and the threats and challenges may become ever more serious, but the peace-makers know that their labor is the greatest work we can perform on earth, the work of making all other work safe. I am joining the German Peace Society to be a fighter in the only war worth fighting, the war against war.

"You can't deny the youth has a way with words," Fritz assessed.

Chapter Seven
PRESENT

He and Maud had arrived fashionably late at Adlon for the domestic press ball, rescheduled twice, from November to December and from December to January, for various reasons, and even though the changes might result in the annual event occurring twice in the calendar year 1933. There was certainly no discussion of cancellation; the traditional get-together had been going on since the Empire. It should be noted, however, that this was the first time the foreign press year-end gala had taken place prior to the German festivity, though any discussion of combining the two events had been quickly squelched by both sides.

The January date had sufficed to effect a transformation in the mood of the evening; the pre-holiday, year-end atmosphere had metamorphosed into an outlet for long pent-up stress and anxiety, a much-needed cathartic extravaganza to release unhealthy pressures, a masked bacchanal that many hoped would allow journalists, exhausted with keeping their fingers on the pulse of the country, to let off steam at last.

Carl, no fan of such spectacles, had hoped it had taken place while he was in jail, while Maud had been delighted with the postponements, since they meant she and Carl would be able to attend. She disguised herself as Bertha von Sutter, Carl as his favorite *nom de plum*, Thomas Murner. The building was ringed with 30 of Berlin's finest.

As they filtered through the crowd, they were stopped often by people seeing Carl for the first time since his release. But there were many reasons to pause and look at the costumed folk:

clowns and mimes, princesses and princes and knights and damsels, Siegfrieds and Brunnhildas; there was a Mephisto and there a St. Walpurgis, over there Captain Kopenick, over there Iron Gustav. A Dracula chatted with a spaceman and woman— space couple? And who was that pretending to be the bloodthirsty Frtiz Haarmann?

But there were reasons to do more than just look twice, reasons to stop and gawk, disguises to ogle and incognitos to try to draw out of character and make reveal themselves. They had to stare at two partiers in straitjackets—they pretended their arms were tied behind them—aggressively arguing. Carl strained to hear their words above the din.

"Where were you the night of November 22, 1930?" one demanded of the other.

"I had nothing to do with the thugs at the beer hall!" claimed the other, who sported a toothbrush mustache.

"But you've heard of the murders at the Eden Dance Palace?"

"Self-defense! Self-defense! The Stormtroopers were being pursued! Threatened! I understand the fear of death!"

"Which Stormtroopers?"

"The ones in the brown shirts, of course!"

"So you admit being connected to the murders?"

"I admit nothing! I only say you can hardly blame a person responsible for defending himself against German Bolsheviks!"

Carl's jaw had dropped. He looked around, raised a hand as if to stop the two.

"But your party," the other continued, wagging a finger, "has many times given out the slogans, 'Beat the communists to a pulp!' and "Beat the social democrats to death!'"

"Goebbels didn't mean that literally!"

"You guys should stop," Carl cautioned. They acted deaf. He looked wide-eyed at Maud, then whispered, "There could be police spies anywhere around here." He gestured toward the costumed on-lookers. The two men ignored his warning and plunge forward in their skit.

"The whole party stands on the absolutely granite-hard basis of legality. We must be judged on our principles!"

"But what of Goebbels' program of illegality?"

Here, the man being interrogated started sputtering. He grabbed hold of Carl, who happened to be closest to him, and mimed an apoplectic fit. Then, suddenly, he stood up straight, smiled, and both men took a bow. Then they restarted their little skit. Carl and Maud at once went to find the bar. On the way they passed a trio of Charlie Chaplins standing in forlorn tableau.

The Ossietzkys gladly each took a flute of champagne from the rows set on a table against a wall. They toasted each other and sipped.

"I didn't know von Sutter was such a beautiful woman," Carl told Maud. "I can't wait to get you home."

"Yes," Maud replied. "We're quite the romantic couple."

"And who are you supposed to be?" Carl asked the person on the other side of Maud, a very tall man with a black cape and dark rings smeared around his eyes.

"'Our revels now are ended,'" he intoned, then walked off.

"Prospero?" Maud suggested, shrugging.

"I didn't know they'd begun!" Carl quipped, and then, as if to restart the revels, they clinked glasses again.

Maud nudged Carl and pointed at a couple; the man was somehow wearing a bloody plate around his neck, the woman dressed like a gypsy dancer: Salome and John the Baptist. Another man came to the champagne table made up as the Grim Reaper a la Durer. He took a goblet, smiled at them then went off.

"Can we dance a little?" Maud asked Carl.

"Yes," he said, looking deep into her eyes. "But only with you."

She laughed, making her huge hat shake. "The music sounds this way." He trailed after her.

After three dances, Schubert waltzes, they overheard someone suggesting to her partner that they have their picture taken. They followed the couple to a side room where a photographer was set up before an alpine scene. The novelty was that the photographer would take your photograph with any filter you requested: blue, purple, green orange, etc. Along mirrors affixed to the wall for the examination of vanity, they stood in line behind Old Shatterhand, the Merry Widow, someone who looked like he was a member of Amundsen's lost crew, and, right in front of Maud, a furry creature who repeatedly insisted he was Rin-Tin-Tin.

Carl and Maud debated which filter to ask for.

"Why don't they have pink?" Maud complained.

"You'd look great in green."

"Blue would echo your eyes."

"Brown would reflect the state of affairs."

When they finally reached the tripod-mounted camera, Maud asked for clear.

At some point thereafter, Maud walked off with a friend dressed as Mata Hari.

Later, much later it seemed, he saw two men in ancient Greek robes and gravitated toward them. When he was close enough, he eavesdropped.

"And when he remembered his old home," the older of the two said, his voice somewhat shaky, perhaps from drink, "would he forget his former comrades, Glaucon?"

"Not if he's a real comrade," said the other, surely intoxicated. "They are surely deserving of pity, and a true friend would not forget them in their need."

"Right you are! But going back down to the place he had left, what would happen to him?"

"His eyes would have to get used to the darkness."

"Just like when they had to get used to the light."

"When he first left the hole they were in."

Then Carl saw something he had to check out: a costumed horse—the kind made of two people. The 'horse' had just knocked someone over. Then, as Carl reached the spot, the 'horse' suddenly reared up and beat at the air: it was a real horse underneath the costume! Someone grabbed at it and yanked it down so it didn't hurt anyone else. The covering over its head was pulled off, and it looked down at them with startled brown eyes the size of billiard balls. But no one stepped forward to claim it. Where did it come from? Slowly, it was led out of the building. People joked to each other about how realistic the horse had seemed to them before the reveal.

Smiling janitors suddenly appeared and swept up the area. Were they workers or partiers? Had they brought the horse?

"Well! Look who the cat dragged in!"

Carl couldn't place the man who addressed him. He was with another man and neither wore a costume.

"Cat? Rat you mean," the other corrected. He couldn't recall their names, but knew they wrote for the official Social Democrat periodical.

"Nice costumes," Carl remarked.

"We opted to be ourselves: solid citizens of Social Democracy."

"I thought this was an event for journalists," Carl tossed off.

"I thought you were in prison."

"Precisely!" said the other. "This is not a party for criminals."

"Of the state!"

"Ah! But what state?" Carl retorted. "The military one? The state of duplicity and rotten compromise?"

"The country is rotting and crumbling because of people like you fouling the nest."

"Oh, give me patience!" Carl sighed. "Admit it: your Social Democrat bureaucracy had grown too accommodating with an imperialistic regime. It was never going to lead our country forward."

"I think it's generally agreed that, in the circumstances, it was sensible for Ebert to make an appeal to our armed forces, especially when the enemy was at the gates."

"Not just at the gates, my friend," amended the other. The Trojan Horse had already been dragged in when our soldiers returned from the east. The walls themselves had been breached—"

"The loyal troops stabbed in the back—"

"In the front, Sirs," responded Carl.

"—by its own citizens!"

"—corrupted by the Slavic menace!"

"You need more champagne, Gentlemen! Or is that too foreign for your tastes?"

"What we need is unity in the land!"

"Bubbles would serve as a fitting foundation for your crypto-Nazi worldview."

"And writers who don't foul their own nests!" added the other.

"Or divulge state secrets!"

"Or tear down what the government builds!"

Carl stopped their onrush with a wave of his hand. "What we need is true democracy, Gentlemen."

"Oh, democracy, is it? The one imposed on us by the invaders?"

"Along with the reparations?"

"Without a consensus to support it?"

"Internationalism," Carl shot back, "was the only thing that was going to save Germany. If it couldn't, then nothing could."

He turned to walk away.

"What Germany needs now is a great man!"

"Sorrier and sorrier!" Carl called out, shaking his head.

"*Tout comprendre, c'est tout pardoner!*" one yelled at his back.

'*Il leur semblait*,' Carl thought, hurrying to get away, '*impossible d'avoir le dernier mot.*' He finally found Maud sitting in the huge coatroom, chatting with some other women. They all had their shoes off.

Exhausted, he sank down in a chair next to them and started unlacing his shoes.

"You ladies have a great idea," he said, slipping off the shoes and putting his feet up on an extra chair. "My feet are killing me."

"Do you need to go home now?" asked Maud.

"Not at all! You ladies continue chatting as if I wasn't here. Just jab me if I start snoring." He rested his neck on the back of the chair, folded his arms, and closed his eyes.

After a few moments, the four women continued their discussion.

"This development of technology is unprecedented," said one, someone he knew as a journalist but didn't recognize, "because, for the first time in history, it is combined with the rise of the masses and obliterates the feudal isolation that seemed so natural before the war."

"That's so right," he heard Maud say. "Workshop to factory, carriage to train car, theater to radio, and letter to telephone."

"Don't forget the camera to the nickelodeon, silent film, talkies, and this television, they're saying, is the next wave," added the first voice. Was it Marie Gehrke? A brilliant, articulate woman! Eyes still closed, he found himself nodding rhythmically to what he was hearing. "Will it be possible" the voice went on, "to use these inventions without destroying what little is left of our privacy? Or will the observer's will continue to be subverted by the broadcaster?"

"Oh, you mean all those men like Hugenberg who promised us utopia?" This was Hilde Walter speaking, he knew without looking, one of his own contributors. "And, instead of utopia," she went on, "the right of women to employment is still being questioned. Male fear brands equal collaboration as unfair competition. Exclusion of women from the workforce would remedy mass unemployment. It doesn't take a psychologist to recognize mass psychosis here. We women, it falls to us to elucidate society by speaking out. When we are blamed for interfering in male performance, we need to blast that myth by countering that we, in fact, enhance product. But a united front of working women would be going too far; it would only provoke antagonism and inspire opposition."

Monosyllables of assent.

"What do you think, Else?"

"Well," began a new voice, "I only became a journalist by writing about my own case, but until women can gain control of their own bodies, I don't think there's much point in making other demands. It's a disgrace when a doctor from the lofty standpoint of science pontificates that a wretchedly oppressed and emaciated body must bear new life. Whoever is a doctor in the real, ethical sense should help her before she goes to a quack or lays hands on herself."

There was a pause before the voice continued at a lower pitch. "I was denounced by a colleague, my files were confiscated, and, even though I had not performed a single termination without certification from a second doctor, I was arrested for performing abortions for monetary gain. For avarice! I was taken away in the middle of the night and thrown into a damp and filthy cell. I was interrogated six to eight hours a day for weeks regarding over two hundred different cases.

"By the time I was done answering their questions, the examining magistrate had become an expert. I flattered myself with thinking that, by carefully going through each case, I was drawing forth from its formal exterior an authentic human being, who was astonished to learn his edifice of accusations was beginning to totter. But my self-flattery was vain. Even though it was clear I had only accepted modest honoraria, the prosecutors suddenly broadened the charge against me to include outpatients. I had never terminated a pregnancy on an outpatient!

"Fifty more women and girls were to be subjected to the inquisition in order to test the veracity of my defense; fifty families were to be thrown into public humiliation and anxiety about their fates. And that is when I decided to go on a hunger strike. After seven days, I lost consciousness. When they revived me, I was sent home."

"What did they say to you?"

"That my detention was being interrupted for reasons of my health. I believe I am now in what they call legal limbo."

"That is outrageous!"

"But legal. That is, until they recognize the law above all laws, Paragraph 218 included: the law that recognizes human dignity and recognizes women as human beings with the same rights as men."

Carl had fallen asleep, a burned-out cigarette hanging from the corner of his mouth.

Chapter Eight
PAST

She saw the young man again in the crowd of people straining to hear the speaker. She knew which one it was she was pursuing out of the bobbing sea of heads: the one Jane had pointed out to her the day before as the author of the article on women they'd been impressed with from *The Free People*.

"Follow me!" Sophie tossed over her shoulder.

The young woman behind her followed. '*Here I am,*' thought Maud, '*following my trouser-chasing friend. How humiliating!*'

They threaded through the audience straining to hear Fried's words. All of a sudden, Maud bumped into Sophie's back. She'd stopped abruptly, satisfied to keep close enough to the young pacifist author, without getting too close. Getting caught hunting for the youth—she'd forgotten the name printed at the end of the passionate article—could be rather embarrassing; even Sarah would admit that. They didn't want to give suffragists a bad name.

"The key to peace," boomed Alfred Fried's voice, "is the abolition of international anarchy. And the solution to international anarchy is international order. A state of nature exists between countries, even when those borders are contiguous. What Hobbes said so long ago about the *bellum omnium contra omnes,* and what Grotius said about the extra-legal conditions of the high seas, applies even today in each and every interaction between one nation and another, in spite of the most sincere yet friable treaties and agreements.

"Our peace-seeking internationalism does not preclude nationalism. In fact, it safeguards it. Nor are we idealistically taking a step into the dark. We are not talking about utopias; we are talking about greater domestic safety and healthier foreign relations. Already, the Pan-American movement illustrates this, for national identities continue not only to coexist but to thrive and flourish under the protective umbrella of that international organization.

"Your Kaiser has spoken out for peace on many occasions, but what is the next step? We must inaugurate a Pan-European organization on the model of what we have observed in the other hemisphere. We must build greater social connections between one another, stronger ties and smoother pathways of trade, transport and travel. We must find a way to settle our differences by means of a higher plane of law, something our countries can create together, something they can all approve. And, finally, to quote the great Bertha von Sutter, we must 'lay down our arms'!"

There was great cheering and waving of arms. Fried delivered his last sentence over the clamor: "These are the foundations of revolutionary pacifism! Thank you, thank you!" He stepped down from the dais and started shaking hands.

Maud watched Sophie watching the young man, von Ossietzky, she remembered now. He was writing rapidly in a small notebook. That was it! He was covering the speakers sponsored by the German Peace Society, probably working up another piece for the organ of the Democratic Union. Watching him, she felt like she was part of the news of tomorrow. But what in the world was she going to do with her friend? Poor Sophie! She was hopeless!

Though there would be more speakers later, the crowd was breaking up for lunch. Sophie and Maud faced each other, a mischievous look on the former's face. "Let's just wait," she whispered. "See what direction he takes." She was obviously forming a twisted plot.

He surprised them by not stepping into one of the more popular coffee shops like Monopol or the Café of the West. He just kept walking and finally disappeared into a small place not far from the Berlin peace convention. They saw him through the window settling down at a table and ordering coffee. "Well, what now?" Maud asked. "You've cornered your quarry. What do you intend to do now that you have him at bay?"

"Do you have a copy of his article in your bag?" Sophie asked. Maud shook her head. "Neither do I. We'll have to make do without. Let's go!"

"What?" But Sophie was already inside. Maud, at a loss, looked behind her, then hurried in before the door closed.

Inside, Sophie sat at a table near the front window, facing her prey about twenty feet distant. Carl was bent over his notes, oblivious to all else. Maud sat down facing her friend, her back to the rest of the shop. They ordered tea and Maud made a point of staying quiet: let Sophie be forced to deal with the situation she had created. '*Why should I make it easier for her to wiggle out of her impulsive choices?*'

Maud watched the sequence of facial squirms transpiring across their table. They gradually seemed to form themselves into a look of determination. Sophie jumped out of her seat. "Wish me luck," she whispered and stepped out of Maud's field of vision. Maud overcame embarrassment by forcing herself to look out the window at the passersby, the traffic, the bustle. She dare not turn her head to see what was going on behind her. When the tea came, she started sipping, and, before she knew, her cup was empty. She poured more from the small pot, then poured it back, letting it steep. Finally, she felt a hand on her shoulder; Sophie sat back down.

"He's coming over as soon as he finishes rewriting his notes." She poured herself tea. Maud's eyes went wide, then she tried to master her surprise.

"*Here?*"

"Yes, Silly. What did you think?"

"But—?"

"Just calm down!" Their traditional roles were reversed, with Maud the excited one and Sophie the tranquil.

"What in the world did you tell him?"

"Simply the truth, my dear: that we'd read his article and liked it and someone had pointed him out to us," admitted Sophie after sipping. "The unvarnished truth."

"Hello, Ladies." Carl arrived with his coffee and notebook. "It's Sophie, you said?"

"Yes," Sophie, the impromptu hostess, smiled. "And this is Maud."

She offered her hand. He seemed paler and smaller than she had thought.

"Please, make yourself comfortable, Carl," Sophie said. "It's such a pleasure to, um, come across such an eloquent man who shows sincere sensitivity to the plight of women today. Maud, I was telling him how much we enjoyed his article in the, uh, oh, wherever it was—"

"*The Free People,*" said Carl and Maud in unison, eliciting nervous laughter from all three. He stared at Maud again.

Sophie raised her eyebrows. "Well, someone remembers! Did you take notes, Maud?"

"Thank you," said Carl to Sophie, brushing the other comment away while Maud vowed to 'get back' at her friend. "I supposed it's customary for the author to say that he has a low opinion of his piece, but I'm actually quite proud of it. I think I broke some new ground, at least speaking personally."

"Well, certainly you have," said Sophie. "The very subject is new ground. How women relate to men, so important and yet so often swept under the carpet. Don't you agree, Maud?"

Maud had been studying Carl's profile, its powerful forehead and sharp nose, but, now that he turned toward her, she dropped her gaze and blushed toward her teacup. "Yes," she said finally. "Have you, uh, written much?"

"Mainly just for *The Free People*," he replied, noticing her British accent for the first time. "A few poems for *March* an—"

"Do you hear that, Maud? Our companion is a poet! We'll have to see your poems."

"Now, on that, I will be harshly critical. At first, I rather fancied myself a poet, but they're all bad, I'm afraid. I guess I'm lucky somebody publishes them at all." Then, lowering his voice, "Or maybe I'd be better off if they were rejected."

"Now, really!" Sophie continued, settling more into the persona of the older person. "We'll have none of that. Showing humility and pride together at the same time. That's too much! One at a time, please."

"You're English?" Carl asked Maud, affixing his eyes on Maud again.

"Is my accent that bad? And I've been here for months! Sophie, you must make me work harder to speak like you."

"Oh, it's not criticism," Carl answered quickly. "You speak well. They laugh at my Hamburg accent here in Berlin, so don't feel bad."

When the conversation seemed to lag, and Sophie started running out of steam—It's so taxing to have to be in charge!—Carl thought of saying goodbye and was on the verge of getting up to leave. Maud dug deep into her memory to come up with something else to say about his article.

"You wrote in your article," she said at last, "about how difficult it is for boys brought up in this country to develop a... wholesome idea of women."

"There's a dearth of healthy relating early on from adolescence," he said. "A separation of the genders just when we should be getting to know each other."

Maud was noticing a transformation going on in the young man the more he spoke. He seemed to gain power, expansiveness, life, as if speech were, for him, a kind of umbilical cord that connected what was inside him to others. He appeared to look within, and then a spontaneous fountain sprang up, and his words seemed to her all the weightier for their diminutive receptacle.

"Do you find yourself also a victim of this dilemma, Carl?" Sophie ventured to ask, fiendishly refusing to spare him any awkwardness.

Carl squirmed. "Yes and no," he thoughtfully replied. "I admittedly feel I lack experience of women my own age. But it's much worse, I fear, in the cases of my peers. From my experience, their subsequent male bonding is beyond the pale, and it sometimes—let's see; how shall I put it?—warps their view of the very women who ultimately become most important in their lives."

"Their mates," clarified Sophie.

"Their potential mates, the friends of their wives, and women in general," Carl listed.

"And you would therefore advocate more opportunities for the two sexes to grow and develop together," Sophie inferred.

"Especially in the adolescent years, the very ones when they start to keep us apart."

"I think this is a problem not only for Germany," said Maud. All three concurred on this.

"Look at the time!" said Sophie. "We'll have to hurry if we're not going to be late to Miss Pappenheim's lecture."

"I have a feeling it's going to address some of these very topics," said Maud. "Are you attending, Mr...?"

"Ossietzky. Yes. I wasn't sure before, but now I think I will. Can I escort you ladies?"

They went, but Carl had a hard time paying attention to the renowned Pappenheim's talk on the status and role of women in relation to the peace movement. He took a few desultory notes just to make it look like he was focusing.

In fact, he was thinking about other things.

****

He saw them the next day. Before parting the day before, the three had made arrangements to meet at the Tiergarten for a picnic. They threw down a blanket at the edge of some shade and set out things they'd brought. After starting to eat, Carl had asked Maud, "Can you tell me how you are here from England?"

"My father was an officer in India," Maud started.

"A very distinguished family," Sophie added.

"He married an Indian woman."

"She was related to a princess!"

"They both passed on when I was quite young."

"Simply tragic!"

Carl's head was turning like the spectators of a tennis match.

"And I was mainly brought up by Aunt and Uncle Palmer in England."

"She's loved Germanic culture since her school days."

"So I came here to really learn the language."

"I was so glad to have her come over."

"I've been here six months."

"You speak it wonderfully," Carl broke in at last.

They paused to eat. Maud looked over the shoulders of her companions and noticed a solitary child crying at the edge of the park. She jumped up and ran toward him. The other two turned and watched as Maud approach the child and, bending down to his level, comforted him, and started to look for his guardian.

Carl moved to get up and help, but Sophie held his arm.

"Everything she told you is true," she said in a confidential voice. "But, Maud came here for another reason as well, besides her sincere attraction to German *Geist*.

"She and a man back home were very serious, but it didn't work out. She decided at last that he wasn't for her and broke it off. But the man, the son of an officer who was one of her father's closest comrades, couldn't accept her refusal. Still hasn't, evidently. Anyway, he just wouldn't leave her alone, and, finally, her aunt and uncle realized she needed to escape."

Carl watched Maud. The poise and grace she exuded as she located the boy's guardian took on deeper meaning for him now that he saw her as the victim of a situation and a history that she had neither merited nor asked for. Now she was strolling back toward them across the lawn.

"So I arranged things for her to come here indefinitely," Sophie went on. "I hope I haven't been indiscreet, Mr. von Ossietzky, in disclosing this matter to you. I'm sure Maud will tell you all this and more if you, you know, but I just thought you should know what I told you for now."

"Yes, thank you, Sophie."

She turned from him and applauded as Maud, shaking her head, reached them and sat down.

"How genuinely kind of you to react so quickly!" Sophie beamed.

"Well, I had to do something."

"The poor thing! What could his guardian have been thinking?"

"That foolish girl," scolded Maud. "I gave her some choice new German expletives for becoming distracted and losing him.

She was probably flirting with some—" but she caught herself and stopped.

"I hope he'll be fine," said Carl.

"Oh, he will, as long as she doesn't lose him again before getting him home." Maud picked up a grape, put it in her mouth, and bit into it. She noticed Carl watching her, blushed and asked, "So Mr. von Ossietzky, tell us how it is that you became a pacifist."

"It was the writing of one of your compatriots," said Carl. "*The Grand Illusion.*"

"Ah!" said Sophie. "The heroic Mr. Angell."

"Yes, reading that. Also, I remember always hating it when I was growing up in Hamburg and people, anyone, argued. And, of course, the horrid militarism we're always surrounded by around here." With the last sentence, he looked meaningfully at Sophie. She nodded. "I guess one thing led to another," he finished. "How about you ladies?"

"Maud and I developed into suffragists early on when we were pen pals, she practicing her German and me my dismal English. She was an ardent follower of Emmeline Pankhurst."

"Really?"

Sophie nodded while her friend looked embarrassed. "Maud was arrested and went on hunger strike until her jailers released her."

"Really!"

"And suffragism led to pacifism."

"The two are very related," added Maud, "as we heard in the speeches yesterday."

"I'm impressed," said Carl.

The pleasant afternoon drifted along. When they parted, Carl stuttered before awkwardly uttering the suggestion that they could perhaps study Norman Angell's seminal book together,

Sophie and Carl with English editions and Maud with a German one. "I've always wanted to study it in the original," said Carl.

The ladies seemed to like the idea.

****

They met alternating Saturdays in Luneberg, on the rail line halfway between Hamburg and Karstadt, where the girls lived with Sophie's family. Carl's mother had connections with the Benedictine Cloister and was willing to arrange for Carl to use a vacant room in the accessible portion of the property. He refrained from telling her that he would be entertaining two women there, disclosing to Rosalie only that he was studying the subject of peace with some friends. After three sessions, during which they mainly focused on prickly problems of translation, they decided to spend a meeting recapping what they had covered so far.

"Angell isn't content with a one-dimensional criticism," Maud said.

"No," responded Sophie. "He takes on militarists and pacifists alike."

"In the hope that he can refute the former and convert the latter to his new perspectives on pacifism," Maud continued.

"And he refutes the former by..." Carl deliberately left this hanging.

"By showing that an arms race always leaves belligerents where they started," answered Sophie.

"And greater in debt," added Maud.

"Are we satisfied with his claim?" The ladies nodded at Carl. "Okay, so what does he have to say to the pacifists?"

"That they're self-defeating," responded Sophie, "when they make a moral argument against war and yet accept the validity of antagonism as a law of nature."

"It's the wrong strategy," Maud chimed in.

"What's the right one, then?"

Finally, he got them to pause; Carl was almost relieved to have them catch their breaths.

"It's his main idea," Sophie ventured.

More thinking. Maud said, "He makes the distinction about the modern world."

"That's it!" exclaimed Sophie. "We're too integrated for war today."

"There can't be any winners anymore."

"It's too destructive of the economic system: banks, markets, labor…"

"And the division of labor makes confiscation of land unprofitable."

"Also, neutral countries don't import from another country simply because it has more power."

"My head is swimming," said Carl. "I can't keep up with you two." Sophie and Maud grinned at each other. After another pause, Carl asked, "What about counter-examples?"

"They are all refuted because increased taxes on the population, both before and after victory, are too oppressive."

This led to the issue of indemnity, about which Angell evidently had much to say.

"The logistics involved in the transfer of funds is very problematic," said Carl. "That includes property and other resources."

"Indemnities tend to create inflation in the country of the victors," said Maud, "and deflation in the defeated countries."

"Which leads to a trade imbalance that is, ironically, detrimental to the victorious country," reflected Sophie, "as happened between France and Germany after 1870. That's why Bismarck did an about-face with his policy of tariffs in '79."

Pause to think.

"What about the seizure of colonies?" Sophie asked.

"Very problematic, especially if a different language is spoken."

"And England has shown colonial autonomy is the best policy," said Maud. "Colonies aren't owned, in the first place."

More thinking.

"Does that leave only the argument for war as a moral stimulus?" asked Carl.

"Ugh!" Sophie put in. "The worst reason of all! As if killing each other makes humans better people!"

"And it isn't supported by the bitter social divisions that cropped up in Germany after the Franco-Prussian War," included Maud.

"My stepfather always talks about that," added Carl. "He thinks the divisiveness of the time was what led to his becoming a social-democrat, even when it was still very dangerous."

"You know, Carl," said Sophie, "you've hardly mentioned your family."

"Yes!" said Maud. "Where does the 'von' come from?"

"No one knows for sure," Carl replied. "It certainly doesn't come from being an aristocrat. I'm not royalty like somebody else we know."

Sophie laughed while Maud blushed. "Do you know how many princesses there are in India?" Maud said in defense of her nobility. "It's probably as meaningless as it is in Russia."

"I can't say," said Carl. "I don't know about such 'high-falutin' matters!" He quoted one of Angell's English words that had caught his eye. The girls laughed.

****

The next time he met Maud at the Luneberg train station, she was alone; Sophie had a cold. Carl was delighted that Maud had not called the session off. They ambled to the convent in a slight falling mist, chatting pleasantly, and settled in their room off the cloister, placing their volumes on the little round table between them. Although they initially decided to focus on what they'd discussed the last meeting, they soon found their talk straying to issues that lurked behind Angell's text. It wasn't long before they were discussing religion and marveling at a few similarities among all the many differences in their upbringings, as well as how, at least as they each saw it, the halting missteps in their respective religious "trainings" had somehow led to their present political activism.

"It's not normal, I always thought," said Carl, "what I've been through. First the smothering exposure to Roman Catholicism, then my weak attempts to pull back for the sake of what I saw as my own healthy survival, along with my stepfather's secular influence, mellow yet somehow always surreptitious as it was because of my mother's pious devotion always breathing down on me. And then all of it got smashed and crammed together in a temporary Lutheran compromise. Bizarre enough. But you—"

"Yes," agreed Maud. "Even crazier, in a way. My mother grew up with Hindu beliefs, bilingual in Telugu and Urdu before learning English, and my father was Church of England, God and country all the way. And so, back in England, that's how I was brought up by Aunt and Uncle. It was only later that I tried to uncover what it must have meant for my mother to be who she was, believe what she believed. As a result, I guess I fall somewhere between the Anglican Scripture and the Four Vedas, leaning more toward the latter in my conscious thought, but still deeply conditioned by the former."

Carl had been examining her face, the depth of her expressions. Now he nodded, looked about the walls of the little room. "In my case, what I experienced from childhood taught me that there couldn't be one true religion. Otherwise, how could there be so many popular and long-standing ones?"

"And so," inquired Maud, stretching in her chair, "what does that tell us about humanity, if there are so many religions in the world yet none of them is the single true one?"

Carl's eyes wandered along the cracks in the old ceiling. "That we're pitifully desperate to believe there's more than we see. Sometimes I think we are very early on in human development, that there are whole categories of thought humans haven't even discovered yet; ones that will become indispensable for us in the future. Or, at least, ones we're barely aware of now that we'll all acknowledge and accept as true later."

"Like what?"

"Aw, that's just it!" he sighed, stretching as well. "How do you talk about things we're not cognizant of yet? I guess the best term for what I'm trying to say is 'spirituality.' I mean, look at this room, these buildings; they are all expressions of a segment of spirituality but with strings attached. They are in contrast to the visual expressions of other religions around the world, each with *their* own strings. But all of these expressions fail when they take the segment for the whole."

"But doesn't worship have to take some form, some shape?"

"I don't know if I'm even talking about worship. That seems to imply God and, while I'm more of an agnostic than an atheist, I don't think spirituality necessitates worship of God. If your man Darwin is right, then spirituality, like everything else, is the product of evolution. Whatever soul is, we have it to help us survive. But that doesn't mean it's immortal. The function for which we developed souls is entirely taken up with matters *inside* human life, not *outside* it: survival."

"I think I understand what you're saying, Carl."

"Not my idea, really. Doesn't 'survival of the fittest' show that humans who had a sense of their own soul somehow survived better than the ones who lacked it? The ones without were like clumsy goats that couldn't compete with the sure-footed ones."

"But you seem to be putting a lot of faith in evolution."

"I take that as a brilliant oxymoron."

"I didn't mean it that way. There are still plenty of creditable scientists who question Darwin's theory."

"The greater theories seem to take longer to settle in. The greater the idea, the bigger the upheaval. How long did it take heliocentrism to overcome its precursor? I wonder if this fellow Einstein's ideas will ever be accepted by most people, much less comprehended by them."

"*I* can't comprehend them."

"Me neither. But when it comes to evolution, even if we can't go as far as Haeckl with his 'ontogeny recapitulates phylogeny,' we can recognize that surely each species comprises all of the development of its precursors."

"*We* can, but that doesn't mean everyone will. Your very example of Haeckl shows how a scientist can also make mistakes."

"Certainly."

"So, that seems to put a crack, however small, in one's faith in science."

"All right!" he admitted, dropping his head. "I concede your point."

"But if you're right about the limited function of our souls," Maud speculated, "how could humans have gotten so confused with different forms of spirituality for so long? And gotten so wrong about the afterlife?"

They paused. Silence.

"Do you want to walk?" Carl offered.

"Let's!"

They took their books with them and sauntered through the cloisters.

"You were asking," Maud continued, "why so many humans have believed souls are immortal for such a long time."

"Look what culture has done to the poor caterpillar!" Carl exclaimed. "The cocoon symbolizes death; the butterfly the immortal soul. As if butterflies themselves don't die!"

"Humans are driven to think that way," explained Maud.

"The yearning for our souls to be everlasting erases the common knowledge of natural philosophy."

"That yearning is deep-seated and obvious. Isn't it also part of our evolution?"

"Which makes me feel dumb to even ask the question about religion, because the answer must be staring me in the face."

In the courtyard within the cloister, open to the sky, the nuns of the convent had cultivated a small but largely untended garden, which was full of flowers. They paused in their walk and looked in appreciation of the effusion of colorful, scented nature bounded by the high stonewalls, the geometry of the layout, its two narrow paths cut diagonally though the square to intersect in the middle and form four equal triangles.

"Carl, have you experienced the death of someone close?" she asked.

He shook his head. "I don't remember my father or his passing any more than you seem to remember your parents."

"But I'm sure, you know, you've been to some funerals."

"Yes."

"So don't you think that's the key? We believe death's not the end in order to help us through the grief."

"Yes, but look at all that has led to! Yet it's really fascinating, because you can't simply accuse those who believe in the afterlife that they're deceiving themselves. It's more complicated than that. It's not like anyone's saying, 'Okay, I'll pretend to believe my departed loved ones are in heaven,' and then, the minute they get over their grief, they start thinking sensibly again. Healing doesn't work that way. The belief is not feigned; it's a sincere one. If it were counterfeit, it wouldn't help our grieving."

"Right! It wouldn't work if it were just a phony lucky charm, a rabbit's foot that just *might* hold some power."

"But immortality is wishful thinking, nonetheless."

As they came to a corner of the cloister nearer the chapel, they could hear female singing coming from inside. A shared glance and smile showed the irony was not lost on them.

"I'll bet those women aren't faking what they believe," mused Maud. "They're living their belief. And it must all be comforting," she speculated. "I still remember that from childhood: the comfort of knowing everything would be all right."

"Yes. But isn't it still just comfort in a fiction?"
They came to the exit of the square. "Not a fiction; a possibility. Isn't there a difference? A wish, like you were saying; neither a trick of voodoo nor a claim to truth in the present."

Carl nodded tentatively, following Maud out of their path toward the road. "More like trusting in something, I suppose. If only that's as far as it all went. But..." He gestured to the buildings around them.

On their way to the station, they encountered many people on the sidewalks. Carl held her elbow and they threaded through the crowd as a unit. When he escorted her to her train, she turned toward him, and he surprised both of them by bending forward and kissing her awkwardly on the lips. Like one sparked by an electric shock, he pulled back. At the feel of each other's flesh, their scents in each other's sensation, they held each other's wide-eyed stares. When they recovered from the surprise, they smiled into each other's eyes.

Maud glanced from side to side, registering that no one seemed to be paying attention to them.

She kissed him back, smiled and, turning away, climbed up the steps into her car. When she was at the top step, she turned back toward him, noticed his second shock, and smiled. When he returned her wave, it was done mechanically, him feeling a strange sense of loss. Then she vanished into the car, leaving him suddenly feeling a new, vibrant aloneness.

****

Two Saturdays later, he found her stepping down from her train car without Sophie again.

"Is Sophie still sick?"

"No," answered Maud brazenly. "I told her not to come."

Carl looked at her in surprise.

She hooked his arm and led him briskly in the cold toward the convent. When they arrived, they found that their room was not available; the old man who let them in directed them to the empty refectory instead.

"The truth of the matter," said Maud, tossing her book on a table, "is that I'm upset with her for telling you about Allen, although I should have known she would. She's such a blabber-mouth!"

Sitting down, Carl kept quiet; he didn't know what to say.

"But it means I need to tell you all about it."

"Don't feel the need to—"

"But I must! Sophie is just as famous for her inaccuracies as she is for her candid *naivete*."

"As you wish. But she hardly told me anything. It was just during the time you were helping the little boy in the park. It's your decision."

Maud frowned. "Well, it is a long story, if I'm going to be sure you have it right. And it's also the reason I'm never going back there."

"Where?"

"To England!"

"Really?"

"Yes! Sophie doesn't know it, but my reputation's been ruined."

"Why? What did you do?"

"I didn't do anything! Oh, God!" Looking away in anguish, she massaged her forehead.

"Maud, you really don't need to tell me anything. After all, you know virtually nothing about me. I could be a criminal, a murderer, for all you know."

"Masquerading as a pacifist," she scoffed.

"Really. I care about you, not old history. Now is what's important to me." He took her hands. "We can have a clean slate."

She pulled away. "No, we can't. This," she uttered grimly, shaking her head, "this is why women must unite to advocate for themselves!"

"What do you mean, 'this'?"

"You just care about your feelings! What about mine? After what Sophie said, I feel the need to tell you everything, to set you straight about my past and why I'm here in Germany."

"Of course. I'm sorry I said anything. I should have just let you talk. But I wanted you to know that you didn't have to say anything on my account."

She sighed. "I know. I'm sorry. You were just trying to be nice, but—Oh, that damned Sophie!"

Carl got up, walked toward the kitchen area, found a glass and pitcher of water, and returned to their table. He filled the glass and handed it to her. She drank, looked at the wall behind him, then lowered her gaze to him.

"I'll start with Allen. He is the son of the man, still living, who was my father's closest friend and colleague. They grew up together, and, after I left India and came to England to live with my aunt and uncle, after my parents' deaths, Allen and I virtually grew up together as siblings. Our families were that close. It seemed natural, as we grew up, that we would always be together, so we actually grew into thinking that we would spend the rest of our lives together. Allen dreamed of following in our fathers' footsteps, dedicating his life to his country and becoming a foreign officer. Everything, well, it wasn't so much planned out as it was just assumed.

"Our guardians, his parents and my aunt and uncle, were very relaxed about it all. They just played along with what we told them, obviously thinking we'd forget all about it as we got older. You know, children playing like being adults. I suppose if they'd tried to push us together, we would've rebelled and gone our separate ways. But they didn't. They let us go on to work it all out."

She stopped, drank. Carl patted her hand.

"Take your time."

She got up and walked to the mullioned window, looking out at the rain lashing the angular panes. Her back to him, she continued, her voice seeming to bounce off the downpour itself and ricochet back to him.

"Time went on, but we never adequately revisited this... this non-decision that was and was going to go on ruling our lives. 'When we get married'... 'When we're living together'... 'When we have children of our own.' It all kept echoing through our childhood, every stage. But we never really examined what we were talking about. We were so immature!"

She turned back toward Carl, giving him a quick glance, before starting to walk back and forth along the table between them.

"Finally, my girlfriends started confronting me with what they saw. I couldn't possibly be serious, they said. Me, an officer's wife?"

"How old—?"

"Sixteen. I was already interested in the suffrage movement, the peace movement, temperance, Mrs. Pankhurst. But, if anything, Allen was more deeply as ever committed to his call to serve his country. He'd gone to cadet school and volunteered during vacations. Our ways of thinking were moving in opposite directions. But it was my friends who noticed this, not Allen and I, and they commented on it. Otherwise, we might have gone on as before. In fact, I disagreed with them. We had arguments, and I refused to see what they saw. That is, until—"

She sat down again.

"It all came to a head over education. Several of the girls were going on to nursing school. But when I told Allen what I was thinking, he threw a fit."

"What did your aunt and uncle think?"

"They were fine with my going. But as far as Allen was concerned, that was the worst choice: to go to a school with men, on an equal footing. Well, he just wouldn't hear of it."

"What happened?"

"We had the worst bloody spats. It was just terrible, what he said. 'It isn't women's place'; 'It's a waste of time, money, and effort'; 'Your place is running our home.' It was just horrible."

Carl nodded, saw her eyes were starting to fill with tears.

"And, of course, everything he did and said confirmed all that my friends had been telling me, all the things I hadn't been seeing but they had. And then—"

Carl waited silently.

"He... he gave me an ultimatum: either college or him. I couldn't have both. One or the other. It was so humiliating, having to go through it all, so I broke it off."

She emptied the glass of water. Carl poured more for her.

"But that wasn't the end of it. Allen persisted, writing letters, trying to dissuade me, saying I was betraying our love. Finally, I just had to burn them in the unopened envelopes. I couldn't read them anymore." She drew the edge of her hand along her face, catching a tear with the tip of her little finger before it fell.

"It was very hard for Aunt and Uncle. As I've said, the families were so close. I had to see Allen a few more times at family gatherings. It was so awkward! Allen just wouldn't let up. He still thought there was something he could say to convince me; he still thought he could have things his way. Yet each time he tried to persuade me, it made me more adamant. If I was on the fence about continuing school before, now it was the only thing I wanted. I couldn't believe that the person I was staring at was someone I'd grown up with, that his views had become the opposite of my own. That was shocking enough, but, in truth, it was even worse, because he discounted every opinion I had ever formed. In this, disagreement didn't simply mean agreeing to disagree yet still going on as before. It meant not only that we could love each other no longer, but…" here, her chest heaved involuntarily, she paused, controlled it with a deep breath, and went on, "but we couldn't even be friends, we couldn't even see each other anymore. I was a nervous wreck. Aunt and Uncle became concerned. Now they were just as decided as I was that I should start attending classes as soon as possible. And so, I did."

The rain had let up. Carl pulled some snacks out of his pack. They ate while strolling quietly around the room, sometimes remarking on the layout of the room and geometrical patterns of the brickwork.

Carl was thinking about what was being revealed to him, the fullness of Maud's personality as it unfolded before him. And he was very aware that everything she told him was a lesson in how she wanted to be treated.

They returned to the table.

"And so, you started nursing school."

"In Manchester. But one day, after class, I saw him, Allen, on the street. He was obviously waiting for me. I stood there in shock. All I could do was stare at him coming toward me. Then it hit me what this meant: he'd gotten my schedule, followed me. I can't tell you all I felt, Carl: anger, fear. I was indignant.

"I met him halfway down, and he proceeded to plead with me to quit school. People were passing us, going up or down, staring. I was so embarrassed! I wanted to run. In fact—"

She was squeezing her fingers, alternating one hand with the other. "This is the hardest part. This is why I can never go back."

Carl placed his hand over hers and held them reassuringly.

"Allen reached for me, and I drew back. He lost his balance and before I knew it, he was tumbling down the stone steps. He rolled all the way to the bottom. I ran down; others were converging. He was hardly conscious. There was so much blood coming from his head!"

"Was he badly hurt?"

"No, as it turns out. But what a mess! People were all over, gawking, trying to help. Some of them had seen me with him, so were looking at me, almost as if I'd pushed him. I couldn't stand it! It was the worst thing that could have happened.

"Anyway, someone found something to press against his head to stop the bleeding, got him to sit up. As he came to, he struggled, didn't want help from anybody. Carl, he wouldn't even look at me! He had someone hail down a cab, got in by himself and, waving me away when I offered to go with him, drove off."

Carl was still holding her hand, massaging the fingers. All he could do was wait, take it all in. This woman that he'd suddenly become interested in was offering her troubles to him. He was both touched and overwhelmed. But, deep down, he felt the best thing to do was just listen, become passive, show her the real concern that he had by offering back the simple, sincere expression of his face. Doing so, he sensed her increasing openness toward him, that her defenses were releasing, that she was welcoming his comfort and consolation. And, in turn, he discovered in himself a quiet strength that had been unknown to him; one that she felt in him and allowed herself to be supported by.

It was perhaps the biggest revelation of that revelatory day for Carl.

"That was the last time I saw him," she went on. "I contacted his parents, met with them, explained everything to them. They seemed understanding, but it was obvious they weren't listening to me. They were taking his side, they couldn't understand why I'd broken up with him, why I was doing this to their son. I can hardly blame them. After all, Aunt and Uncle saw everything from my point of view."

"I feel so bad for you, Maud."

"I never went back to the school. I immediately got in touch with Sophie. I knew I couldn't stay—"

"But you felt you had to leave the country."

"Allen and his friends were obviously talking about me, spreading all kinds of rumors about me. It was awful. They'd even changed my name."

"What do you mean?"

"'Mud'! Carl, they started calling me 'Mud'! Now do you understand why I can never go back?"

"Yes, of course."

"Even Allen. It was so awful, he had to leave too."

"Where did he go?"

"He joined the Royal Navy and shipped out as soon as they let him."

At the station, when Maud and Carl parted, he held her for a long time. The excitement of feeling the contours of her body against him were already grounded by the weight she leaned against him, the sense he had of a human being clinging to him, someone who had opened herself to him, someone who depended on him.

Ironically, he immediately found that the new onus he carried made everything else seem lighter.

****

For their next meeting, Maud asked if he would come as far as Sophie's home. When Carl arrived, he found the two girls united like long-lost sisters. Evidently, they had made up.

From the moment the front door had opened to him, Carl had felt the influence from Maud's beaming smiles like the warmth of the welcome sunshine. But he also felt a new strangeness in front of Sophie, especially there at her parents' home. Self-conscious, he felt he had to put on an act in front of her. His relationship with Maud had set new boundaries around his private life. And Maud's relaxed manner made him feel even more remote. She seemed oblivious to the development between them, to his unease.

It was a beautiful, sunny day, and the girls had decided they would sit in the garden. They had also decided to focus on an overview of Angell's book.

Sophie started off the discussion with a question, "So, what is 'the illusion'?"

Carl found himself exchanging embarrassing glances with Maud. She seemed to break away from him with a deliberate effort.

"Well," she answered her friend, "the author obviously feels the illusion is that war is a given for humans, that it's something that, although the opposite of good, is so integrally part of man that it's something we can't escape. Sorry about the 'obviously,' but I suppose that Angell has to assume this as a prevalent illusion because that's what he spends the rest of the book arguing against."

Sophie and Carl responded with nodding, staring at the three books on the wrought iron table between them.

"Then why 'great'?" Sophie followed up. It seemed she had taken the role of interlocutor along with that of hostess. She oversaw the maid's serving of coffee as the other two considered her question.

"Well," Carl said, "the word, I think, is used here as a pun. Angell thinks the illusion about war is so great, so pervasive and deep-seated, that it covers all earth and all our history. But, on another, less literal level, sarcastic perhaps, he considers it the very opposite of great. War is bad, evil, low, base, disgusting, a menace, and all the rest." He sipped the coffee.

"Spoken like a true writer!" Sophie patronized.

"I'm suddenly reminded," Maud interjected, "of a passage my tutor made a big deal about years ago. Aeneas is leaving the Underworld. Something about departing from the darkness and entering the light of day, leaving behind the realm of 'true visions.' I'm not sure what my point is, or the connection to Angell's title, but I still remember old Mr. Thorne was quite adamant about the importance of the phrase." She imitated an old Englishman's quavering voice, "'Is it an oxymoron? Are true visions true or false?' He said the answer impacted on the entire rest of the epic, and on Vergil's personal view of Roman *imperium*, the subjugating of the proud and all that. And I think I've come to see his point. Why are the Romans the only ones to be proud? Why is it right for any country to subjugate another? Anyway, sorry if I got off track."

Sophie said "No! That's very interesting, Maud. Let's see—" and took a sip of the coffee.

Carl found himself staring in wonder at Maud. He thought that it was no surprise that such a woman had a man in another country, a man who had gone crazy over her. Was she out of his, Carl's, element, too high of a league? A princess! What did he think he was doing? She had everything: physical beauty, grace, brilliance, intensity. What, when it came down to it, did he have to offer?

Sophie picked up the thread. "What you're saying, Maud, kind of relates to another thing I wanted to talk to you guys about. Angell has a lot to say about colonies. One of the motivations for war is taking another country's colonies away from them. But he argues against this, says it doesn't make sense, and, and..." She lost her thought.

"Right," said Carl. "I was confused by that part too. He says England was the first country to develop a correct relationship with its colonies, and it took centuries of learning from failure to do so. Since, as things turned out with England, its colonies are fundamentally autonomous, then they can't be taken away."

"Language," said Maud. "He said having the same language is the key to colonial success."

"But that doesn't mean other countries will benefit from England's colonial policies," Sophie commented. "The subjugation of other countries, as Maud mentioned, could keep going on."

"And then," added Sophie, "it could still be advantageous for one country to go to war to take away another country's colonies."

They sipped. A pleasant breeze blew through the leaves of the tall elm above them. Sophie yawned, then apologized.

"I remember, in my own case," said Maud, "when I first started reading about my mother's homeland, it was hard to accept that the presence of the British government in the subcontinent was caused by the failed administration of a British company. Yes, I know the Great Game, and that, if it hadn't been England, it would've been Russia swooping down and taking over, but, still, British colonization of India began through the naked power of a profit-seeking organization, and that led to the Raj and all it entails.

"But what really turned me off to the entire plan of digging my mother's roots was learning that the subjugation of India was just one corner in the triangle of British trade, all of it approved by the queen and her government to solve the problem of the loss of funds to China." Maud made sure she had the attention of both of them. "The illegal sale of Indian opium in China balanced the losses coming from English predilection for Chinese tea," she explained. "Tea! Britishers' penchant for the immersion of tea leaves into boiling water took precedence over the right of Indians and Chinese to live without foreign intrusions.

"Disgusting! As a result, I never learned much about the Telagana royal family, to which I'm said to be tenuously connected. I gave up. It was too dreary to go on with it."

"I wonder what Angell would have to say," Sophie offered.

"Will those countries ever be the same?"

"When autonomy is taken away by a foreign power, can it ever be regained?"

"I was told by my mother," Carl said, "that my father's people came from the Polish border because they felt the wind was blowing toward Germany. They pulled up their roots to be on the winning side, basically."

"Sad," expressed Sophie. "Why does it have to be that way?"

"Angell tries to answer that question, but—"

"I don't think he succeeds."

"No."

"I wonder if his thinking has gone beyond this book."

"That's something we could look into."

After lunch, served by the maid and supervised by Sophie's mother in the dining room, the girls escorted Carl back to the station by a circuitous route that gave them the opportunity to put the sights of the town on display. Before getting on his train back to Hamburg, he gave each girl a hearty hug. Maud managed to peck his cheek during hers.

****

The next time, Carl met them at a Hamburg station, and he took them home to meet his parents—a demand the girls had made to him. In spite of Carl's nerves, things went well enough.

Over the next few days, Carl visited the spot in the Hamburg warehouses where the river split, and he stood on the bridge and watched the current. Sometimes, he pensively dropped a leaf or twig just to see which direction it took.

Unbeknown to him, Maud, whose tutoring jobs were growing, decided to get an apartment in Hamburg; she wanted to surprise him. Suddenly, one afternoon, she took him to the furnished two-room flat. Maud had already set up the main room with four tables for her bridge lessons. Carl was dumbfounded. He sat in a chair and stared. Waiting for him to say something, she picked up a deck of cards and started turning them over one by one, sorting them in suits.

"This is amazing!" he started. "I didn't know your tutoring was enough for you to afford this."

"And now that I'm in the city, I'm sure I'll have more clients."

"I'm shocked." It was just the wrong thing to say.

"I thought you'd be proud."

"I am. Oh, I am. It's just... Maud, you might as well know, I'm not good with surprises."

"Well, Carl, just let it set in."

It started to rain. The sound gave them their first feeling of togetherness in the room. He took a seat next to her.

"Show me how to play bridge."

"What do you know about it?"

"I only remember being fascinated that one team could win or lose, but the other doesn't necessarily lose to the team that wins and doesn't necessarily beat the team that loses."

"Hmm. Who told you that?"

"Oh, someone, I can't remember."

"Well, he must have meant that the team that buys the contract wins if they make it, or loses if they don't, but the defenders don't really win or lose either way. That is, until a game is made or a rubber; then you have real winners and losers. But still, a doubled contract that goes down can mean well over a thousand points in the end for the defenders."

He took her hand before she put down the card. "Maud. I need to tell you something."

She stopped her sorting and looked into his eyes. He kissed her on the lips.

"I love you. I want to live the rest of my life with you. But I don't know what to do."

"I love you too. But what do you mean?"

"I can't expect to make enough to support a wife until I get a promotion."

"When should that be?"

"Twelve, twelve..."

"Months?"

"Years!"

"But that doesn't matter! I can help support us with the tutoring."

"But if you couldn't? If a baby came?"

"So, is what you're saying that you can't propose to me for twelve years?"

138

"I, I…"

"Well, I accept. We'll just go on like this, and consider ourselves engaged. I don't care. I love you, Carl. And… and in the meantime, you'll establish yourself as a journalist."

"No. You don't understand. That's too long. We'd be old by then. And also," he hung his head, lowering his voice and dragging a finger along the table, "I must provide for my wife."

Her head shot back, and she blinked. Immediately, she considered splitting the deck unevenly between them, giving him the less, and then having them put their cards back together in a single pile—neither would have had any cards left, but both would have had all. Would he have gotten the point? Evidently not! "In other words," she raised her voice, "you wouldn't take me if you couldn't provide for me. Is that what you're saying?"

He looked up at her. "Maud! Of course I would take you. I love you. It's just that…"

"That a man has to provide for his spouse, and not the other way around."

"Well…"

"And the man's bias not only trumps," here she slammed a card on the table, "his beloved, but it also trumps," another card slapped down on the table, "both of their feelings of love for each other. Over their happiness. That's what you mean."

He looked back down at the table and said nothing. She threw down the rest of the pack and stood up.

"That's the stupidest thing I've ever heard! Under the idealistic rationalist, you're just a chauvinist and a materialist!"

"Maud…"

"So one foolish man's bias about women gets to destroy the lives of two people!"

"Maud…"

"And you call yourself an enlightened person! Well let me tell you something, Mr. von Ossietzky. It just so happens that I can afford this apartment without tutoring. Yes, that's right, Sir! And it just so happens that I have an inheritance that would allow me, both of us, and our children, to live comfortably for the rest of our lives. But I haven't mentioned it to you because a little part of me feared you would come up with some pig-headed notion like you have. And look what happened anyway!" Here, she went to the door and opened it.

"And so I think you'd better leave, Sir, because you have some thinking to do!"

"Maud..." He followed her to the door.

"You need to decide whether your pig-headed bias against women trumps love and me!"

She slammed the door behind him.

And as soon as she heard his departing steps, she put her hand over her mouth and thought, '*Now what have I done?*'

****

It rained off and on in Hamburg for days. Carl saw Maud from afar, walking through the city blurred with precipitation. Separate, they dragged through weeks, miserably.

One afternoon, she stood on a bridge and thought, '*Would I have him any other way?*' When the doctor in the nursing school had shown her special attention, when they had gone for tea and he'd visited her home, when Aunt Mary had said that he seemed very interested in her fortune and she'd decided to break it off and even leave the school, she thought her heart had been broken. Thought! How much did she still have to learn about that fiendish organ in her chest!

And now she had a man who was not only truly in love with her, but a man who held onto his principles so tightly that he balked at proposing to her *because* of her fortune! Careful what you wish for! What were the lines of Lovelace?

"I could not love thee, Dear, so much,
Loved I not honour more."

That was the man she had now. Would she prefer the earlier over Carl? The calculating doctor over the confused clerk? Never! But where did that leave her, then? In what way could she say she *had* him, at all?

Circles started appearing in the water below her as it began to drizzle. But, thoroughly preoccupied, she stayed there on the masonry arch and watched the ripples widen. When she sighed, a slight sob caught in her throat. Slowly, the rain became harder.

Minutes went by. Then the air above her cast a penumbra over the rampart of the bridge; she sensed the presence of another. She looked up into the ribbed underside of an umbrella, then turned as Carl clutched her arm and kissed her on the cheek.

"I'm so sorry!" he said. His hair was disheveled, stubble showed on his face, and the blue eyes she could get lost in were reddened, frantic.

They hugged.

"I've been such a fool!"

She took his free hand and caressed his cheek with her other. Leaning into one another, they walked as one back to her apartment. And in their nascent love, they ceased worrying about whence the means of their life originated, neither mark nor pence nor rupee.

There would be worries enough for them.

Chapter Nine
PRESENT

There was a violent and incessant thudding on the door at 2 A.M. Maud and Carl, unable to sleep, had been sitting in the kitchen drinking coffee in their robes and pajamas, and, although both damnably insomniac, they were nonetheless startled enough to practically levitate from their seats. Maud's first thought expressed was that the pounding must be stopped before it awoke the neighbors. Too late for that, Carl commented.

"Should we open it?" she gasped.

"It's too late!" Carl yelled at the door during a brief lull.

"Open up, Mr. Ossietzky!" The banging started up with more vehemence. Would the wood split before the lock failed? Maud ran and threw the door open. Three brownshirts barged in and pushed past her.

"Where's your husband?" They trudged through the living room. Carl met them at the kitchen doorway.

"You are under arrest, Mr. Ossietzky!"

"On what grounds?"

"Arson."

"That's ridiculous!"

"You will be placed in protective custody until formal charges are made. You must come along with us at once!"

Flashing a thin-lipped smile, Carl spread his arms. "Am I allowed to dress?" Maud watched in awe as her husband seemed to grow in strength before her eyes, in dignity, in mastery over the government thugs. This was the spontaneous expansiveness that had so surprised her before, during the other trials, and even before they married, when...

"You must hurry!"

As he strolled into the bedroom, Carl tossed over his shoulder, "Maudie, offer the men coffee."

Who was this man? He wasn't even this open and relaxed when he was hosting a party with friends!

One cop told another, "Don't let him out of your sight," then followed Maud into the kitchen, where she filled cups for them. Thanking her, the men stared at the walls and sipped.

"You have heard, no doubt?"

She shook her head.

"The Parliament building has been set on fire. Our Leader has ordered the arrest of hundreds."

"Carl would never be a party to that!"

"It's worse than before," said the other policeman. "That rabbits' nest of an art colony has been cleared out at last."

"My husband is a writer, a professional journalist..."

"There are scads of those on our list. It is as simple as that." They finished drinking and set down the cups.

"But you can't arrest a man without evidence."

"It's called 'protective custody,' Ma'am."

"He was home with me all night!"

"Do you really think they'll allow the testimony of his wife?"

Maud's jaw hung open in shock.

The two men were coming from the bedroom. Maud and the policemen went out of the kitchen toward the still-open front door. Maud heard a door down the hall close quickly: curious neighbors...

Carl was throwing on his overcoat. He took Maud in his arms and whispered in her ear: "Walter. To clear out my desk." Then, breaking away, out loud: "Head up! I'll be back soon!" When he turned from her, a policeman placed handcuffs on his wrists. Then he left the apartment, two in front and one behind him.

Maud stuck her head into the hallway and watched them turn the corner, heard the steps down the stairs. She went inside, closed and locked the door, then hurried to the window. There was the police van; then Carl, between the men, was helped inside. They drove off.

And Maud, bursting into tears, slid down the wall and collapsed to the floor.

****

After Walter Karsch was telephoned by a contact and told of the Parliament fire, he called the Ossietzky apartment, where Maud told him to come quickly. On his way, he stopped by *The Worldstage* offices but, halfway up the stairs he heard voices, saw the lights were on, and froze. He peered at the backlit top step; shadows passed over the edge, to and fro. The police were already there, searching. Slowly, he tiptoed back down the stairs and, once outside the building, walked normally to the corner, then raced to the Ossietzkys'.

Maud jumped at the gentle knock. Still on the floor, she crawled toward the entry.

"Mrs. Ossietzky?" She recognized Walter's voice in the whisper and unlocked the door. He locked it behind him and crouched down to her. She clung to him, shaking.

"They took him, Walter!"

"Yes. Goebbels drew up a list when the Parliament was set on fire."

"You must get his papers…"

"Before they come back. And we need to take you away from here. Rosalinde…?"

"Away at school."

"Of course." He helped her over to the sofa. She watched him, as if hypnotized, while he opened the closet door and commenced to stuffing a satchel with Carl's work.

****

Carl sat on the floor of the van as it bumped along, racing through the dark streets of Berlin toward Spandau Prison. His head banged against the low ceiling in startled reaction to the voice coming from right next to him.

"You, Ossietzky?"

"Who…?"

"It's Renn."

"Ludwig! Fancy meeting you in a paddywagon! My God! I thought the cop was the only one in here."

"I can understand their wanting a commie like me, but you…"

"It's a wide net, evidently."

The policeman shushed them. They bounced in silence with the rolling of the vehicle. Finally, Carl said, "I want to apologize to you."

Renn snorted a laugh. "For what?"

"That review of your book."

The man shushed them again, but Renn ignored him. "And a damn nice one it was! 'Woodcut hardness.' You said I was like a Dutch painter of martyrs, that I made up new sounds for individual bits of shrapnel. Damn good for a bourgeois critic!"

Carl was trying to shake his head horizontally as the car roller-coastered toward its destination. "No, I only caught the surface qualities. The nuances you conveyed in the smells of rotting corpses."

"Well, I felt quite sophisticated, reading your review. 'The satanic orchestra of war.' Fancy!"

"Drivel. When I reread your book, I realized, in its own way, it was every bit as good as Remarque's, if not better. But that was after the review'd been printed. Too late!"

"Don't even think about it. I'm sure you sold me a lot of copies with your piece. Not that I'll be spending the royalties where I'm going."

This time, the cop barked at them in earnest, but even that seemed undercut by his intermittent levitations along with the captives: speed, potholes and gravity rendered him no less a prisoner of space than they.

Soon, the van was turning through the gates of the gothic stronghold. Carl noted, with familiarity, the stone buildings. When they pulled up to one of them, they were mustered out and into a long tunnel. Up ahead, in half-light, they could see men lined along the wall with arms raised; then he saw that they, too, were handcuffed, and that their arms were made to straddle a tall pipe that ran along the wall. Some of the men had to stand on tiptoe to accomplish this. Renn and Carl were stopped among the men, and one of their wrists was freed so they could be trussed up as well.

Renn snorted another surprised laugh.

"Torgler! Have you become a plumber?" The man he addressed looked down sheepishly.

"The piece of shit gave himself up!" shouted the man stretching his arms up on the other side of Torgler. "After the Party told all the leaders not to surrender, but to force the cops to take them in!"

"Kasper!" Renn exclaimed. "You don't say? Nice modeling for the rank and file, Torgler. They'll all know what to do at Goebbels' next roundup, and in doing so, admit guilt."

Arms thrust up, Carl found himself watching Renn assess this spat between the communists, wondering how the fellow writer would describe the experience when he had a chance. Would

Party loyalty lead him to censor himself and stifle the vindictiveness of Comrade Kasper? Already beginning to feel the ache of his joints and muscles, he was nonetheless relieved, for the umpteenth time, that his lack of party affiliation freed him to pursue the truth purely. Small blessings! Here, he was with the others, apparently holding up the damp ceiling! All cats are gray in the dark.

His head snapped back. Was that what woke him, or was it in reaction to something?

The dream! When they'd unlocked the handcuff on Renn's wrist, he'd swung the now-dangerous metal into the face of the cop, then clobbered another on the head, and smashed the third into the stone wall. Then he'd unlocked all the handcuffs and, after gathering the guns, the men had crept from the tunnel. Outside in the courtyard, they'd found the van, threatened the dozing driver, and, after piling into the back, Renn in the passenger seat with a pistol aimed at the man behind the wheel, they'd driven out of the fortress.

But, once out on the street, their chauffeur had veered straight into a building. Was it on purpose or was the man too frightened to drive?

Then he woke, back in the tunnel, painfully reaching for… nothing. He shifted his feet. Another stance to ease the strain. Somewhere nearby, there was a drip, drip, drip.

Time passes. Then, men bring out a table and chair, and an officer sits down with a satchel, from which he pulls a notebook. He waits, apparently stifling impatience, until someone brings a lantern and sets it on the table. Then the pockets of those chained to the pipe are emptied, their contents placed on the table. The officer notes down whatever he deems worthy, and the pockets' contents are stuffed into the satchel. After each man's identification is processed, he is unchained from the pipe, and his handcuffs are rejoined behind his back. Then he is led down the tunnel.

It is at this point that something happens that stirs Carl to his core, something that brings a crawling tingling to the surface of his skin. As soon as the detainee turns the corner under escort of two policemen, Carl hears a series of thuds and grunts, stumbles and shouts; cries of pain Carl seems to sense in the marrow of his bones, as if they had suddenly become receptors. It gets worse with each man. Carl feels a hollowness in his core, his innards have been reamed out, bored through, and yet no one has touched him. All is expectation. He is not feeling empathy for each victim of the violence; he is totally attuned to this new emptiness within himself.

Carl has begun a monumental journey without moving. He has embarked on a terrible trek that, by the time he has staggered, crouching from the blows, through the police gauntlet, will have taken him, still uncharged with a crime, from the fallible legality of his familiar and at least formally democratic society to the verge of a state of nature, a barbarism experienced by any Cro-Magnon or Neanderthal. The dozen policemen hit him with rubber truncheons, aim viciously for uncovered body parts, now head, now back, now knees, now shoulders; they kick him when he falls into the blood of those who went before, taunt and insult him as he tries to rise and escape, pass through the portal of torture as quickly as possible. He finishes the gauntlet on hands and knees.

Finally, he gets to his feet and, no longer escorted, turns another corner of the never-ending tunnel. A guard douses him with buckets of ice water, then pushes and kicks him reeling forward until a vacant cell is found and, drenched and shivering, nauseous and bruised and bleeding, he is shoved inside to collapse on the stone floor. The iron door to the cell is slammed shut and locked, and Carl hears the next man placed in the cell next to him, hears his cries and sees, internally, his wincings. It is some time before the last man is processed, and the wing of the prison is left pitch-black, so that the only things heard are the groans of the men lying in their blood, tears, and vomit.

In the morning, the injuries hurt more. Carl aches to move. He brings his swollen fingers to his swollen face, touches the young scabs, traces the searing skin where it is broken, the bumps, joints that refuse to move. He shocks himself by registering hunger, by heaving inside at the mere thought of a cigarette. He wishes he could focus on the significance of what has been done to him and the others, on the meaning of the violence beyond the pain he is feeling. He wants to trace what this means for his country to have done such a thing, to have become such a state, and he wants to speculate on the repercussions, the prospects for the people of Germany. What has been done? What border of civilization has been crossed? But the only thing he can trace is that jagged line of each contusion, taking stock of his bruises.

One thing he knows: he can't let Maud find out what's happened.

****

On the same day, the day after the fire at the Parliament, President Hindenburg, on Hitler's urging, issued a decree nullifying many key civil liberties, including the imprisonment of any individuals considered opponents of the National Socialist Party, in addition to the closing of any periodicals and the suppression of any publications considered anti-Nazi.

****

Rosalinde came at once from school to be with her mother. But when she arrived, Maud had a surprise.

149

"How long can you stay here?"

"Mother, I'm not going back."

"What?"

"It's terrible there."

"You don't like the teachers?"

"It's not the teachers. The teachers don't even know."

"Know what?"

"The students are terrible! When they found out that Daddy had been arrested, they wouldn't let up on me. I'm never going back to that place."

"But you can't simply stop going to school!"

"I've already applied to a Quaker school."

"A Quaker school? Where?"

"England."

"England!"

"Yes. They have a program there that looks perfect for me."

"We can't afford to send you to England! Especially now. I'm going to lose this apartment."

"That's just the point. The school is charity. And, when they find out about Daddy, that he's a victim of the National Socialists, they'll probably be willing to pay for my transportation. You should come too and get out of this disgusting country."

"We'll talk about it later."

"I have an appointment with them here in Berlin tomorrow."

Maud opened her mouth, intending to negate the plans of the willful teenager, but, seeing more than precocious determination in the set of her daughter's jaw, she brought her lips back together.

Suddenly, she saw herself at Rosalinde's age.

****

As they ran around the yard, they tried to whisper to one another. If they stopped or slowed down too much, the guards beat them with sticks or whips. It was called Sport.

Carl had been thinking that, although the Careme of Spandau still ruled the mess, somehow, as the bruises accumulated, it wasn't funny anymore to critique Chef Hungerstrike's culinary crimes.

Then Renn ran up to him. "Have you talked to Torgler?"

"About what?"

"They're charging us with the conspiracy to burn down the Parliament!"

"At least they're finally charging us with something!" Carl commented.

Renn reached down and picked up a handful of dirt. Carl noticed a guard eyeing them and kept jogging.

"But they claim," Renn hissed, catching up, "to have a photograph of the three of us from the night of the fire, planning it all out at a bar." He spat.

Carl rubbed a hand over his mouth. "But I've never had a drink with you!"

"Well, they claim to have evidence."

"I've got to get in touch with Apfel."

"Not a chance." Renn looked up into the overcast sky. "I requested to contact our party's lawyers and was lucky to get away without a beating. Besides," he added, "it's highly unlikely that any lawyer who'd defend the likes of us is both still free and still in the country." Renn ran ahead of him.

Carl swore. But then, he thought that at least he'd be able to see Maud and Rosalinde in the courtroom when he was brought in to face the charge.

But the trial was never mentioned, and Carl knew neither what the specific charges were nor how long he would be imprisoned.

One day, Carl noticed a commotion in the latrine. Guards ran in. Then, he saw them dragging a lifeless body out, a rope around its neck. Carl stared; he recognized the man. It was Hans Litten, the lawyer who had tormented Hitler on the witness stand the previous year, cross-examining him for three hours about inciting Storm Troopers to violence against anti-Nazi workers, two of whom had been stabbed to death. Contradicting himself, Hitler had later faced a perjury charge.

One of the guards was beating Litten, slapping him while another pummeled his chest. Suddenly, Litten started coughing, vomiting. The guards stopped and removed the noose. The half-dead man was quickly hurried to sick bay.

Later, Carl heard the story: the guards had been torturing Litten to get him to betray former clients, and he'd broken down, but then, in a suicide note, recanted. Now, the Storm Troopers had their man alive, back under their thumb.

Then, there seemed to be a bit of a change at Spandau Prison. Diels, the man supposed to be heading the new federal agency unifying the country's police, was asking questions of the guards and inmates. Carl, unable to stop shivering after an icy night in his frigid cell, told the concerned man, with the face carved up in student duels, that his one wish was to be freed from his body.

Some of the guards were replaced, and the brutality was lessened a bit. Some foreign correspondents were invited to tour Spandau under Storm Trooper escort, as a way to stifle the plethora of rumors published abroad about brutality in the prisons. One of them, H. R. Knickerbocker, interviewed Carl.

"How is it going for you here?"

Carl was having a particularly bad day, the kind when all seemed to be caving in on him, when he couldn't stop worrying about Maud, about Rosalinde, about Rosalie. Finally, he looked at the visitor, then the guard. The latter made a show of his scrutiny, pregnant with menacing significance.

"Good," he mumbled.

"How are you treated?"

"Good," he repeated, his voice sounding strange to him, alien, out of practice.

"How is the food?"

"Good!" Speech seemed to be coming back to him.

"Do you have things to read?"

"Yes!" Carl lied.

"You can read anything that you request?"

"Yes!"

"Can I send you any books?"

Carl stopped himself, glanced into the coarse features of the guard's face.

Something deep down in Carl suddenly bubbled up to the surface: his old self! He thought of asking for Muhsam's poems, then tried to come up with something better, both sharper and safer.

"Something about the Spanish Inquisition."

Knickerbocker drew his head back, squinted, and a smile flashing ever so briefly over his lips. He looked at the guard, then back at Carl, and nodded.

That afternoon, after the guests had departed, Carl was given extra time for Sport in the yard. Evidently, his quip to Knickerbocker had been sharper than it had been safe.

****

The Quakers placed Rosalinde's case on the fast track. She would start school in England in the fall. Funds for travel had already been granted to her. Aunt and Uncle were contacted and apprised of the news, welcoming her with open arms. On her journey, she stopped in Hamburg to visit Rosalie. Maud was alone.

She thought she would stay in the apartment until the lease ran out. After that, she had no idea what she would do. Find Sophie and beg to be taken in? The world was closing in on her. By mail, she received gifts of money from various sources, well-wishers from the most unexpected quarters, some from people she'd never heard of, checks from a Milly Zirker, from a Hilde Walter. Altogether, it amounted to an insignificant sum, and worry took hold of her. The attacks of anxiety she had been crippled by years before, the ones Carl had slowly, painfully weaned her through, returned.

She had not left the apartment for three days when, at midday, there was a clear rapping at the door. It had to be repeated before Maud roused herself from her curled-up position in the bed. She thought of the pounding during the night Carl was taken.

"Yes? Who is it?" Maud asked, her body flattened against the door. She wasn't taking any chances; they could break the damn thing down before they got in.

A voice, something indecipherable. 'Happy Hanukah?' Some kind of joke! But it was definitely a woman speaking. Maud did nothing, waited.

"Mrs. von Ossietzky? Are you all right?"

Maud interpreted the question as an offer of help, unlocked and opened the door. A small woman, pleasant of face and older than herself, stood before her.

"Mrs. von Ossietzky, I'm sorry to bother you. Mrs. Jacobsohn has hired me as managing editor of *The Worldstage* and—"

"But the paper's been banned! Carl's in jail—"

"Yes. But..." The woman looked up and down the hall. "Can I come in?" she said, lowering her voice.

"Of course!" said Maud, re-locking the door behind them. As she did so, she caught the reflection of herself in the mirror behind the door, replacing a stray curl. Perhaps they were the same age...

The Man Without a Party

The woman came into the middle of the parlor and turned toward Maud.

"I'm Hedwig Hunicke," she said. "I've been hired to draw up all the loose ends."

"Where's Edith?"

"She's left the country, Ma'am."

"Walter?"

"Mr. Karsch has also gone abroad. Unless he's in hiding somewhere in Germany. Though that would be worse for him. They're searching everywhere."

"Do sit down. Would you like some tea?"

Mrs. Hunicke sat, nodded.

"If I still have some," mumbled Maud, scratching her head on her way to the kitchen. After a moment, the woman followed her.

"What we hope," she continued, "what we have heard, is that they are both in Czechoslovakia, trying to start up *The Worldstage* there, so that we can at least disseminate it abroad, and smuggle some copies in. That's what we hope, at least." She sat at the kitchen table, dropping heavily, with a sigh.

While Maud filled the pan with water and set it on the stove above the burner, she wondered. '*What am I doing? Why should I believe anything this stranger says?*' Still, the woman had such an honest face.

"So many have left," Mrs. Hunicke went on. "It's the cultural world of Germany that has exiled itself. It's easier to name the ones who have stayed, the few Ditzens and Kastners, though many of them have gone into hiding, and more waves of artists are departing from the country every day. Benn seems to be staying, although he hardly counts."

"One can hardly blame them!" remarked Maud. Shaking her head as she thought of Carl's intransigence on this issue, she set the tea things on the table. "What is it you said your job is?"

155

"Checks are still coming in," she answered. "The police have cleared out our offices, but I have friends in the post office who hold the mail for me. I try to get some money to our writers who are still around. And now, Ma'am, that includes you, in your husband's absence."

'*Right*,' thought Maud. '*I'll believe it when I see it.*'

"I can use whatever you can spare," Maud said, sitting down. "My only family is in England, and I'm somewhat estranged from them. Besides, I would never leave Carl here by himself. Soon," she added, looking out the window, "I'll be out on the street, virtually homeless."

Hedwig rummaged around in her purse, found some bills, counted them out on the table. "This is, hopefully, just a start."

Maud's eyes opened wide, and she sat straighter, as if she had been suddenly buoyed up. Leaving the cash on the table where it lay between them, she retrieved the pan from the stove, poured the steaming water into the teapot, and sat down across from Hedwig while it steeped. After the two women sat in silence, Maud asked the all-important question.

"How will I contact you, I mean, after?" She meant after she abandoned the apartment.

Hedwig reached across the table and placed her hand over Maud's. "I'll give you a safe telephone number where you can always leave a message."

"Thank you."

****

Maud sat in the prison waiting room. When the guard brought Carl in, she surreptitiously bit her lip. She'd already braced herself —if he looked better than he ever had in his life, it would still be a shock— but seeing her husband in the drab and shabby garb of a criminal, seeing him bent, bruised, paler than usual, thin and awkwardly walking in shoes too big for him, forced her to deliberately cause herself pain in order to try to lessen the display of her sensitivity toward him. She jabbed a fingernail into the skin of her thumb. The hard look on his down-turned face as he hugged her and sat made it even more difficult for her to suppress her emotions.

The guard, staying nearby, intercepted the newspapers she tried to pass to him. As if the man were Carl's own personal torturer, Maud tapered her emotions into a withering glare the man succeeded in feigning to register, further confirming her conclusions about the inhumanity of all things having to do with the prison and the entire Hitler regime.

"He'll give them to me later, once they're checked," said Carl in a hoarse voice.

"Well, then, he'll want these." She handed a few pieces of candy to the man.

"Thank you for bringing them, Honey."

"Of course, Darling. I would have brought more, but all your favorite papers have been shut down."

"Yes."

"Those are the ones that usually just make you angry when you read them."

"Well, they'll be better than trying to make sense out of the news from the sheets we wrap potato clippings in." He pulled himself closer to her and stared directly into her face. "How are you, Maudie?"

"Oh, don't worry about me. How are you?"

"As well as can be expected. I haven't turned into an animal yet. You got my letter, I hope?"

"Yes. And you mine?"

He nodded. "Thank you. I think I read it more avidly than the ones you sent me during the war. There's so much less to do here. And our Rosalinde is really going to England!"

157

"She should be visiting your mother on her way, even as we speak."

"It will be better for her." He sniffed.

"Have you seen a lawyer?"

She noticed him wince when he shook his head. "I put in a request but, so far, nothing doing."

"No formal charge, just a general arrest."

"They took all our possessions, identification, everything. Have they, uh, been back?"

"Yes, but everything's been taken care of."

"Walter—"

"Yes!"

Like their stone surrounding, an impermeable if invisible wall sprang up between them, and the desultory conversation limped on, each of them more focused on what each decided must be left unsaid than on the niggardly and guarded words they uttered. They could not recall ever having had a more difficult conversation between each other, one so fraught with potholes and dead ends and sharp turns and landmines.

Context is everything.

Chapter Ten
PAST

Maud appeared at his door without notice, rushing into Carl's diminutive apartment, and squeezed his hand hard.

"Carl, we've got to talk," she urged. "Something terrible's happened."

They went outside and walked down the street.

"I got a letter from Aunt Mary," she began. "Uncle Hugh is sick. He might have to have an operation."

"That's awful." He tried to sound sympathetic, but, frankly, he had something else on his mind that he had to tell her.

"She's saying they can't travel here for the wedding."

"Maybe we should postpone things," Carl suggested, realizing they were the last words he wanted to say, or Maud wanted to hear.

"She asks if we could have the wedding in England."

"Oh."

"She says they could have it in their church, and the reception in their home."

"Hmm."

"I was afraid something like this would happen!"

"What do you think we should do?"

"Oh!" she groaned. "This is the worst thing that could have happened!"

"You never wanted to go back there," Carl empathized.

"Never!"

"Hmm." They walked. "You love them still?" he said.

"Absolutely! They raised me. They're the only family I really have. I could never get married without them."

"Yes. I understand. This is hard."

"Your parents... do you think they'd be all right with going to England for the wedding?"

"For a short trip, yes, I think so."

"As short as possible!"

"We can go ask them right now. I think they're home."

They changed direction.

"Now," Carl confessed, "I've got some bad news that I have to tell you."

She stopped and turned toward him, pulling him back with her hand.

"Carl, what's happened?"

"I received a letter from the Prussian court."

Her expression turned from shock to grave concern. "A letter?"

"A summons."

"Summons!" People stared at her outburst. Carl took her elbow.

"Let's keep walking."

After half a block, he admitted, "It seems an article I've written has ruffled the feathers of the, uh, military authorities."

"Carl! What did you say?"

"It was an article commenting on one of the military trials in Erfurt. A soldier was convicted for getting drunk and causing a brawl."

"Yes?"

"Well, I merely commented on the apparent injustice of the sentence. It was too strict, virtually medieval. Why should civilian law be so different from military law? It seems there's a double standard, and one that is not conducive to military recruitment, not that I care a fig for that. What do they do in countries like Switzerland, where they have a citizen militia? I doubt they have separate laws for soldiers."

She stopped him in his tracks once again, her fingers like pincers on his hand. "Carl," she demanded, her worried eyes inches from his, "what did you write?"

"I simply wrote that the judges had done their duty."

"No, Carl! That wouldn't've gotten you a court summons."

"That the law is cruel."

"Carl!"

"And—"

"Yes?"

"That military justice is not only blind, but deaf."

"No, you didn't!"

He hoped she didn't notice as he suppressed an involuntary laugh. "That she has a heart made of iron."

Maud snapped her mouth shut and looked around. They were near a park. She took his hand and led him to a bench. They sat down, and she shoved her face up to his again, eyes to eyes, squeezing his fingers in a kneading, pulsating motion.

"Carl, you have to realize one thing."

"Yes, dearest."

"If you marry me, you're no longer writing just for yourself. You're writing for me as well."

"I understand."

"I'm not sure you do. I'm even more vulnerable than you. I'm a foreigner here, and I'm a woman."

He sighed. "You're right. I'm sorry."

"Carl, what if you're arrested?"

"I'll probably just be fined."

"Carl, are you even listening? What if you can't get work? What if you're exiled from the country?"

"I should have known better, Maud. I apologize."

"Well, you might as well realize it. Just remember that every time you sign your name to a piece, you're really signing mine to it as well."

"I've never really considered it that way before."

"Well, that's the way it is."

"It's going to take some getting used to, but I'll try."

She shook her head again. "No, Carl. Trying isn't good enough. You're going to have to change."

"I love you, Maud."

"If you're going to marry me, you're going to have to stop antagonizing the Prussian brass."

"Right."

"You can't go around insulting the Kaiser and his people."

"I'm his people. We're his people."

"Carl, what happens when I become pregnant?"

His eyes were wide. Things were connecting for him for the first time.

"That's right, Carl. Your child becomes a target just like you and I do. So you can start imagining a third signature under everything you're writing."

He felt overwhelmed in a flash. A pain in his head. All he could do was nod, gravely.

"Carl, you need to promise me right now."

"I promise. I'll remember."

"And one more thing, Carl."

He looked at her with a new form of dread.

"We have to be open with each other from now on. If you're thinking of putting your neck in the noose, you have to come to me first."

"I will."

"There will be no secrets between us." Their eyes were locked.

"Yes, but you should remember something as well."

"And that is?"

"You were arrested once."

She swallowed. "Yes, but I'm talking about now. From this point on."

"I know."

She mussed his hair and smiled. After a few seconds, they stood in unison and continued their way.

****

When she appeared at the guest room door of her guardians' home in Lambeth, Maud's eyes were red from crying. The door was half opened, and Rosalie and Gustav were sitting in easy chairs inside. Maud stumbled in, her hand over her mouth. Rosalie jumped up and approached her, and Maud collapsed against her. Gustav jumped up as well, led both of them to the chairs, and then closed the bedroom door.

"They attacked me," Maud cried. "They tried to get me to leave Carl, to not marry him." She couldn't go on. Rosalie left her chair, carefully knelt down before her. Gustav went over to the bed, took a glass of water off the nightstand and brought it to Maud, who drank.

"Take your time," said Rosalie comfortingly. After some deep breaths, Maud nodded. "Why don't you start from the beginning, slowly?"

"They asked me to stay home instead of going with Carl to visit Mr. Angell, and I did."

"Yes."

"I thought it was something to do with Uncle Hugh, that he was feeling worse, so I wanted to stay. But when I went to see him, after saying good-bye to Carl, he said, no, that he was actually feeling a little better. Then Aunt Mary came in, and they started in on me."

"What do you mean?"

"Rosalie, they said I'm throwing my life away!"

163

"By marrying Carl?"

"By marrying Carl, by leaving England, by staying in Germany..."

"They love you. They wanted you to come back home to England. To raise a family near them. Their hearts are br—"

"No! This isn't about that. Allen's people must have gotten to them. They have completely changed from the way they were before. Before they were supportive, they understood what I was saying, now—"

She broke down again, her head slumping down. Rosalie and Gustav exchanged looks.

Staring at the floor and shaking her head slowly from side to side, Maud whispered, "I can't stay here tonight. We have to leave. I can't sleep under this roof."

"Of course, Dear, if that's the way you feel."

"We'll find a hotel," said Gustav, "and go back to Germany tomorrow."

Still shaking her head, Maud said, "I just can't believe this happened to them. Maybe this whole thing was a ploy to just get me to come here, maybe Uncle Hugh isn't really sick at all."

Rosalie looked at her husband. "Gustav, should we be scared?"

He shook his head. "I don't think so. But perhaps we should pack our bags, just in case."

"Rosalie, will you come with me to my room?"

"Yes, of course."

"I'll pack my things," said Gustav. "When do you expect Carl to return?"

"Hopefully, before dark."

The three of them exchanged looks.

"Okay. Let's go."

****

Carl was let in by a butler and led down a hallway. At first, he had felt so good about the fact that he had followed through on his idea to contact Norman Angell. At second thought, the pilgrimage seemed a harebrained notion, but then he'd mentioned it to Maud, and she thought it would be a good thing; she wanted to join him and meet, talk to the man who she had studied so long, who had, in a way, brought the two of them together. When the letter from Angell had arrived, and he seemed to welcome them with open arms, they'd finalized their travel and wedding plans with his availability in mind. Carl was disappointed, however, that Maud had been unable to join him at the last minute.

He was let into a study where the man, then in his forties, was working at a long table that had been arranged as a desk, piled with texts and papers. Angell got up at once and went to shake Carl's hand. As they greeted each other, Angell noticed Carl's battered copy of *The Great Illusion*.

"Oh! Wonderful, you've brought it." He took hold of the book and flipped through it.

"My goodness! So many notes!" He laughed.

"They're all singing your praises, Sir," joked Carl.

"Please call me Norman," the host said. "Here, let's sit down."

"Maud is very sorry she couldn't join me. She is a real advocate of your work."

"I expect with the wedding, she is quite busy."

"Yes, Sir, uh, Norman."

"I can't tell you how pleased I am to be sitting here talking with a fellow pacifist from Germany, and a young one. You are just the sort of spirit that we need in the movement. By the way, your English is very good."

"Thank you, and thanks to Maud. What are you working on now, if I may ask?"

"My piece on the Balkan War is just out, so I'm addressing issues that arise regarding that. But," he swept his arm toward the table, "my present project is a work on political internationalism."

"Sounds fascinating."

"Well, it's the direction we have to go in if we are going to lead the way. There isn't one pacifist movement yet; there are dozens, and, sometimes, I feel like we are imitating the inhabitants of the Tower of Babble. It's not just that pacifists come from different countries and speak different languages, but they have different principles and different goals. They have different ways of going about and doing things, and the in-fighting can be brutal. They make different assumptions, and often those assumptions are hidden from them. One can either try to dig them out, or one can try to start afresh, try to come at it as scientifically as the subject allows. After all, science is the universal language.

"So I'm attempting to pinpoint first principles that everyone can accept, and then argue deductively from them. The *archai*, as Aristotle called them so long ago, as a way to avoid the problems, the *aporiai*, in his terminology, that can only divide us. But it may take a long time. There's an impasse around each corner. It's like some diabolical maze. The sense of the permanence of political boundaries is so damned entrenched and inveterate, that, sometimes, I feel I'm preaching to a blank wall. That's why I have such high hopes in your generation. There's a lot of education that's going to have to be done."

"I'd appreciate anything you can tell me to help me be more effective in my work."

"Of course." Angell rose, poured water into glasses, and gave one to Carl. He sat back down. "First, Carl, people must have the basic functions of government drilled into them so well that no politician can shake them: safety and well-being, material and moral. If government can't place these within reach of every citizen, then it's misgovernment and should be replaced."

"Start with fundamentals."

"Oh, yes. And then it must become clear to people that military power is irrelevant to the promotion of safety and well-being. Preparations should not be for war but *against* war."

Carl nodded and sipped. It was a warm afternoon. Behind the desk, a window let in a soft breeze.

"Spend as much time as you need on *why* this is the case. For most people, this is the hardest step to take, due to a variety of factors: distrust, religion, passion, simple poor decision-making. But, most of all, I think, if we can help people see the obsolescence of national borders, that will be the key to progress. The economic stage we have reached in Europe means that companies are economic rivals, not states. Political and economic units do not coincide."

"That is a powerful idea."

"Actions of political authorities that are designed to control economic activity without taking the limitations of political jurisdiction into account are necessarily irrelevant. But try to tell that to a politician, a Churchill, for instance. He immediately feels his *raison d'etre* is being undermined. The governors have come to believe that government is for them, not the other way around."

"He really has made himself into England's answer to von Tirpitz, hasn't he?"

"Precisely! It's all about naval power for them."

"And the taxes to pay for it."

"Right! It's all part of that old, moldy thinking that sucked us into the Crimean conflict and almost into the Balkans. And on the side of Turkey, the worst example of the old, primitive form of governing! Thank God we finally had the courage to break some treaties for once. But I'm preaching here to the choir. Tell me about yourself."

And Carl talked about his court case, his recent articles, his concerns. As he talked, he noticed items on the walls and shelves, and he asked about them: there was a diploma from the Lycee de St. Omer; there was an old photo "from his wandering years" of a much younger Norman wearing chaps and a cowboy hat, working as a cowpuncher in California, where he'd also planted grapevines, dug ditches, prospected, homesteaded, and written journalism; a framed article he'd written in *Éclair* about the Dreyfus case; a similarly framed title page of his pamphlet, *Europe's Optical Illusion*, the first version of the text Carl had carried with him. Nearly two hours later, they made their farewells, Angell wishing him well on his marriage and court case, and directing a servant to drive Carl back to the train station.

But as soon as Carl found his seat on the train, a man, about his age, came and sat facing him. Carl looked at him. Was this someone he'd seen before? He looked out the window at the landscape flying by, but soon the man gestured toward Carl's book.

"I see you're reading Angell," the stranger said.

"I just talked with the man."

"What do you think?"

"One of the finest afternoons I've ever spent. If only the rest of humanity were half as rational."

"Well, I think it's all bloody daft."

"Really! How so?"

"You're German, aren't you?"

"Is my accent that bad?"

"Yes. But imagine being like Angell and trusting your stinking Kaiser with his phony overtures to peace!"

"You're not going to bother me by insulting Wilhelm," Carl clarified. "I'm not patriotic."

"No. As a matter of fact, your Kaiser has charged you with a crime, hasn't he?"

Carl sat up in his seat. "You seem to know quite a lot about me."

"Too much, if you ask me."

"I see. You've been following me since I left the home of Maud's guardians this morning, haven't you?"

"It wasn't hard. If you're a German spy, you're a bloody lousy one."

"And you're Allen, aren't you?"

"I won't deny it."

"Do you enjoy stalking the fiancé of your ex?"

"Let's just call it reconnaissance."

"As you wish. But back to Angell: can you articulate your position more clearly than by simply taking a swipe at William II?"

"Gladly. Let's begin with the vagaries of utopianism. Your Angell has constructed an artificial form of morality out of the romantic novels and called it truth. It's a husk of delusions lacking a kernel, and it is flattering to the secret pride that lurks in its converts."

"Isn't all morality artificial? Oh, I see, your Darwinism flows from the wilderness into society. We're all just creatures of nature."

"Where the law of tooth and claw reigns."

"The glorification of war. Is your time in the maritime service satisfying the lust?"

"I hate war just as much as you or Angell do, or Maud, for that matter. And what I'm doing by serving is the best antidote to suffering it."

"Rather than solving our problems before we get there."

"Angell, like all pacifist utopians, wants us to leap from the burning building and straight into the abyss."

"Instead of…?"

"Instead of taking the fire escape."

"I'll have to remember that one." Carl opened his book and pulled out a pencil stub. "Let me write that one down."

"While you're at it, here's another: those who beat their swords into plowshares will plow for those who don't."

"Brilliant," Carl commented while jotting. "And don't bother telling me the one about Quakers. But can you, in fact, articulate arguments, or just aphorisms?"

Here, their back-and-forth picked up its pace.

"Why has your country been able to build its fleet? Because of the reparations you took from France."

"We squandered that like Timon his fortune. Angell writes all about it."

"Only at the beginning. Then Germany got smart with monetary reform, and you were able to increase your military power without straining the masses. Your standard of living improved."

"Not *my* power. I want nothing of it."

"Face it: Your near parity with England is due to your defeating of France. Thus, came your empire."

"The reparations created a trade imbalance that actually hurt the German economy. France produced cheaper goods while inflation exploded across its border. This also in Angell."

"The importation of raw materials doesn't hurt the importing country that can use them in manufacture. Coal from Belgium."

"Just don't become dependent upon those imports."

"Even after Great Britain lessened its use of force and coercion on its colonies, other countries benefitted from continuing to do so: Spain, Portugal, France, the Dutch, Belgium."

"The changes in your colonial policies are, themselves, the result of failed coercive tactics. They don't last."

"I know," Allen said sarcastically, then aped the supposed soft voice of a pacifist. "It's not the way human beings relate to one another naturally."

"You're starting to bore me."

"Why do you want to ruin Maud's life?"

"You're insane!"

"She belongs in England. It makes no sense for her to live in your country."

"Thankfully, she's the one to make that decision, not you."

"You're a cad, a Boche cad, like your Kaiser. Carl the cad."

Carl stood up. Allen rose, face to face with him. Their noses were almost touching. Carl could see himself in Allen's pupils.

"Really, Fritz," the latter whispered, aspirating into Carl's face. "Pacifists should control their passions."

Passengers on both sides of them sprang up, held them back and got between them. Simultaneously, the train started to lose speed. Everyone leaned symmetrically in a kind of bizarre choreography.

"All right," said one man. "Enough of this!"

"Who started it?" asked another.

"This fellow's been trying to pick a fight with this one since he came on board," vouched a third.

Allen pointed at Carl. "This Kraut's a German spy!"

"You're blotto!" said the second man.

The train's whistle pealed shrilly as it slowed down further, coming into a station.

"Then off with you!" said the first, grabbing Allen by the collar and shoving him toward the door. When the train stopped, Allen exited, turning once to scowl at Carl through the window before vanishing into the crowd.

In the best English he could summon, Carl thanked the three men for getting involved.

"Don't mention it," said one.

Another said, "My grandpap's German."

The third hung back and whispered to Carl, "I'm a barrister, and he had a sorry argument. You may be a spy, you may be an enemy, you might even be Satan incarnate. But he bloody well should present an argument that holds a spit of water." Then he, too, went off. Carl straightened his suit and sat down.

****

Before he stepped off his train, Carl reassessed his lively afternoon: while its pleasantry had diminished, its memorability had increased. Meeting Maud's former beau was the low point; his *tete-a-tete* with Angell was the high, but coming across the three British strangers who helped him was a close second. He also decided that he would not mention his encounter with Allen.

But he was quite unprepared for what he found when he arrived at Hugh and Mary's. Maud had already called an old friend, who arrived with a car. When he walked up the path, he found the four of them waiting for him and sitting on their luggage.

They explained what had happened and started to load the car. But all of a sudden, Mary ran out toward them, wailing, running after Maud to apologize.

"I'm so sorry," she cried. "I only meant the best for you. I can't believe I made such a mistake. But I only had the best intentions."

When she tried to hug Maud, she, at first, resisted. But then she saw her Uncle Hugh coming towards her, tapping with his cane, weeping, and she started to sob, melting into her aunt's supplicating arms. After a good ten minutes of cathartic lacrimation, the seven of them went back into the house, carrying the suitcases.

The Man Without a Party

Maud and Carl were married the next day at old St. Agnes Church, as scheduled. The weather was overcast. The bride wore white.

Chapter Eleven
PRESENT

The week after his transfer to Sonnenberg Concentration Camp, Carl and some others were marshaled one night out of their cells and holding rooms and into the courtyard. There, they watched in the light of hissing torches as two inmates were made to dig pits. The guards shouted at them to dig better, harder, deeper, not to let up, and then all were informed that the duo were digging their own graves.

Carl watched the men, listened to them grunt with each effort, and tried in the flickering flames to tell who they were. Then he gasped as he started recognizing one of them: the man gritted fractured teeth, but it was his strange beardlessness that helped Carl to identify him. Carl searched in the uncertain light, saw the crude swastika branded onto the shaved scalp, and then he knew the man to be Erich Muhsam. Muhsam! He had heard the famous anarchist and poet was there, had picked up the bits of information that helped identify him, and now he heard the name spoken about, some men covering their faces, moaning, "Erich, ah, Erich!"

Now the commandant appeared. He screamed at the men, "Dig harder! Faster, you pigs!" Then, to the guards standing around, "Count the good shovelfuls only! One minute to live for each of those. Do you hear that, Jew pig! You get nothing for the lousy digs! Only for the good ones! We will decide!" The guards started counting, at different rates for each man. The metal ricocheted off the deadpan. "No! Not that one! Not enough dirt!" crowed the commandant as he strutted around the edge of the pit. "No! He's slacking! Start over! Start over!"

174

After a while, he seemed unsatisfied with the proceedings and went toward the men. "Shout him on! Yell something! No, not something good! Call out to him what a Jew bastard he is! What a swine!" He swung at them with his cane. "Yes! That's right! Keep it up!"

"Jew!"

"Swine!"

"Traitor!"

"Criminal!"

When there was enough yelling that Carl felt he could do so, he yelled, "Genius!" He waited to see if there were a reaction from the guards, then inserted more exclamations among the others.

"Poet!"

"Executioner!"

"Hero!"

"Pervert!"

"Artist!"

"Lunatic!"

"Journalist!"

"Leftist scum!"

"Leader!"

"Judas!"

"Author of *Judas*!"

"Revolutionist!"

"Revolutionist!"

The fluttering torchlights, still hissing their acrid smoke, showed the two gradually descending as the pits grew deeper.

In the morning, before they had anything to eat, the men were brought out again to witness the execution. Muhsam and the other man were made to lie heads down in the dirt, each outstretched in his own grave, and two guards reached down with a rifle trained on the head of each prostrate man. Between the graves stood the commandant, facing the assembled prisoners.

"You will now see the execution of justice, a long-due, National Socialist justice that will make up for the weak, sickly attempts of the Social Democratic kind that only resulted in further offences against our country. Our intention in having you witness this act is that you will benefit from it; that, unlike these two incorrigibles, you will redirect your concerns away from where they have been, away from undermining the strength of our folk, away from tearing apart the unity our Party is achieving. For, if you take advantage of our discipline and change into wholesome members of our society, you may someday look back upon these sorry criminals and say that here, on the occasion of their deaths, you first felt the throes of a new life and, over time, were reborn to the spirit of Our Leader." Here, he nodded toward guards who held shovels over the dirt piles made the night before. These two men commenced heaving soil onto the backs of the condemned, who winced and wept openly with each deposit. Several of those gathered to witness started weeping as well. Carl did his best to jam a lid on his emotions.

"On the count of three!" the commandant directed to the riflemen.

"One!"

Several prisoners looked away. "No! Turn and look! You must learn from their deaths, or die as well!" They turned back to look. "Two!"

Now there were wailings from the pits and from the on-lookers.

"Three!"

Both triggers were pulled; there were two clicks, but other than that, nothing. The condemned men cried louder. Carl now felt a dam burst behind his eyes, and the tears flowed liberally.

The commandant stepped closer to the group, standing between the two holes. He produced a long series of exaggerated nods.

"I could be laughing right now," he said. "But then you might think that this event was no more than a joke to me. That would be a mistake! There is no joke. I am deadly earnest. These executions are not cancelled; they are merely postponed. These open graves will remain here. These two are indeed dead men. But I will allow them to live temporarily, not only so that they can better prepare themselves for where they are going, but as examples to you criminals so that you may prepare yourselves for where you are going. Will you end up in a pit like them, or will it be back into German society with you, so that you can atone for your crimes by helping us build a new power, a new people?

"You must look at your stay here not only as a punishment, but as a rehabilitation. You have been given the rare opportunity to benefit from an early, earthly Purgatory, a chance to pay for your sins before you die. To clean your souls. You may think that the suffering you experience here is harsh, but far more severe will be that cosmic suffering you will undergo in the afterlife for the sins you have committed against your Fatherland. Yes! You will learn to be grateful for each blow, each bruise.

"I have no great hope in you. Faith I have in Our Leader, and that faith induces me to hope that here, we, myself and these soldiers here, can achieve a miracle and send you back out there to do penance for your sins. For this, I have a little hope."

And he did an about face and marched off.

As they were directed by the guards, the prisoners helped the two out of their holes; they were too paralyzed to climb out on their own.

Carl could not remember ever seeing either one of them again.

****

The punch that cracked his tooth hadn't even been meant for him. It hadn't been meant for anyone, in particular; just the cuff of the habitual variety, to hurry on the sluggish group, but one that had found a target on Carl's cheek that caught the molar in just the right way to split it. Carl, his eyes watering with a red tinge as if washed over with diluted blood, had kept moving, afraid for another blow like the first, even accelerating in the hope of getting out of harm's way. Later, over the course of the day's work, the tooth had come fully apart, and, once he'd spat the shard out into the dirt, the jagged edge of the snaggletooth remainder had cut into the flesh of the inside of his cheek.

And this was why, day's work done, he went into the infirmary and told the man there that he had a dental problem.

"Dental problem? I'll give you a dental problem!" and, swinging his fists, he had chased Carl from the building.

"Keep your filthy mouth shut, and see if that helps!" screamed the man at Carl's back.

And in the darkness of Carl's mouth, each of his other teeth awaited its turn.

****

Maud decided it was time to go. Carl wasn't even in Berlin anymore; they'd sent him somewhere near Kustrin, far away. The apartment would be let to others as early as tomorrow. She had found a home for the cat, given items away to neighbors, some to dispose of, some, like Carl's things, to those she trusted most for safekeeping, and others she had packed in her suitcase. There it lay, on the floor near the entrance to the apartment, open and uncloseable, piled as it was with things she needed.

The Man Without a Party

She stared at it from the couch. The noise from the street seemed far away, the building was quiet, and the clock, not a keeper, was ticking with muted defiance on the mantel. Maud sat motionless, staring at the sum of her life.

She was exhausted. Her limbs felt leaden and her spine ached. The closing of her eyes worked like a switch, capturing her in a flow of memories. Her first meetings with Carl. Who was she, where was that girl? Why had she gone away? She didn't know the answer, but the one she flashed on was the war; always the war; the war took everything: Carl, her younger self, their early life together.

The realization was like a slap in the face: there was no returning to square one. The crushing military and collective, communal defeat, unprepared for because of all the government's deceit and lies of omission; then the revolution, a shining flash before becoming intermittent, a stop-and-go birth that left a deformed creature for the country to deal with; the counter-revolution, hidden, subterranean, bitter, vengeful, apparently causeless; Carl speaking before a crowd, Carl moving her to the capital, Carl vanishing into his work. Inflation; inflation upon inflation; the mockery of the subversion of values, further eroding whatever social gains had been made, making life senseless, ridiculous. Maud lost herself, now as then, in the many turnings: her traumatic reaction to the bloody putsch, her difficult childbirth, the tender, squalling tyranny of the baby, the inquisitive toddler, the headstrong child. Carl, suddenly helpless in his shocked paternity. That cruel division of nature's labors, defining her role.

Then, the final, ultimate global economic debacle and the return of National Socialism from the dead.

She threw herself off the couch to jettison her reverie, bent over and placed both hands on the piled clothes, and shoved with all her might: it gave an inch. She stepped on top of it: another

179

inch. She sat on it: no air left to expel. Giving up, she pulled from the stack the one thing of Carl's she had kept, a thin suitcoat, and brought it back to the couch. Wrapping herself in it, she lay down again. His tobacco-dominated scent made her close her eyes again to more clearly engulf herself in her husband's presence.

She went back again to their early years together. They had loved each other so much! The euphoria of romance had, at least in their case, struggled against time's erosion valiantly and long. But how long can bodies sustain the lightning bolt turmoil? The nascent thrill had run its course; the weight of life had curved the lovers' soaring trajectory back down to earth. Incrementally, the shady bastion they had built up around their vulnerable coupling had dwindled piece by piece; each, alone, had successfully detached from the beautiful ruin, rather than cling to the fading, youthful myth. And yet, they had landed on their feet, facing each other, wrapped in a new kind of love! The fraying mystery had done its job, had gotten them thus far in spite—in defiance, even—of the shambles of what was going on around them, and their honeymoon years were jettisoned like a no longer needed daydream. Without voicing their deeply felt symptoms, each had passed, in lonely isolation but in steadfast parallel, through a mazy process of disorientation, embarrassment, disillusionment, loss and pain and maturation and illumination. Each was wiser than each had been, *un peu triste peut-etre,* yet more aware and grounded.

Together, they didn't pick over the details of the separately experienced ordeal; they each took it all as a private, internal matter. If, individually, they picked over some shards of the shattered fantasy, they didn't share them with each other. And, grateful all over again for each other, they had recovered, regained some equilibrium. And then...

She thought of the baby at her breast, Rosalinde's first sounds, her first tantrums and smiles, the gradations of solid food and babbling and reaching and turning, kicking and crawling, taking steps and dropping on her bottom, the child's involuntary giggling, first words, toys and birthdays, playmates, school, running and jumping, her first books and pictures. She remembered watching her, not quite three, trying to tie the laces of her father's shoes by wrapping the one around the other. Maybe one more wrap would work the magic!

Surely the actual happenings of their family life had served them as barriers to the harsh chaos of outside, fighting at least, however futilely, against the crushing tide of inexorable meaninglessness? Surely doing what they had done to make their lives together was to do the work of living, experience and feel its whizzing moments, and even try to fix them as a kind of foundation for their… their betweenness before they slipped away into the surrounding fog?

Did she have the strength to write the last chapters of her story, at least set its tone? They had been, were still, a family! Rosalinde was growing into womanhood! There was much to be thankful for!

She wiped away the dampness on her cheeks with a sleeve of his coat. The building was silent. She could hear the pulsation in her ears.

When she got up again, sometime later in the slanting sunlight full of motes, she succeeded in closing the suitcase but could not lift it. After dragging it a few inches toward the door, she flopped it over on its side again and reopened it. What else to remove? When she gave up, she returned to the couch and, exhausted with her fruitless efforts, fell asleep under Carl's coat.

She sat bolt upright. It was dark in the room. Lights from the street cast her silhouette on the floor before her. Was someone there in the apartment? She'd had a dream. A nightmare!

She stood up and pushed the switch: no lights. She found a candle on the sill, lit it, and went through the rooms, into the bathroom: she was alone. Dropping her drawers and lifting her skirt, she sat on the toilet. Shivering, she pulled Carl's coat closer around her, a cape in the cold. Her breath materialized in the dark air between her and the burning wick.

The dream had to do with Hansel and Gretel. It had started with the presentation Rosalinde's class had made to the parents before the holidays. What level had she been then? Six? Wearing a cap with an elongated bill, she had played the duck at the end that leads the two back over the pond and safely home.

But she, Maud, and Carl had been in the dream. He had played the kindly father, Maud the mean stepmother and—oh dear!—the witch. The boy who'd been Hansel in the play was still there, but Rosalinde had been Gretel.

Maud had woken up right when Rosalinde was trying to push her into the oven. Dreams!

When had their relationship begun to sour? Maud left the bathroom and brought the candle back into the parlor. She set it down on the floor, blew it out, and lay down again.

Carl had told her that what she called Rosalinde's willfulness was the natural, healthy development of will, but Maud, feeling she knew more than he about what lay ahead, had been more active in trying to counter, re-direct that will. At least at the start. When had she first become challenged by Rosalinde, threatened by her?

Carl's increasing absence due to work hadn't helped. It had spilled over into Maud's relationship with her daughter by putting them both in the same position, missing Carl. And, with the shared lack, a greater weight had been placed on their relationship, a weight that Maud, in her aim to just get through each day, had done her best to ignore. The double tug-of-war, 'I want my parent' and 'I want my way' had exacerbated things, and Maud, understanding the tangle better now in hindsight, wondered if her present awareness would have helped things back then. How does one make the inevitable breaking-away less painful? She thought of her own upbringing and shuddered.

Puberty! Like childbirth in its forced intimacy, its messiness, its rupture, but drawn out in years, and wrestled with publicly. And she couldn't deny the looming reality of Germany's terrible disasters, their effect on their family life. But then she caught herself. Once again, was their present suffering trying to write its own version of their past? She didn't have to give into it! Hadn't the three of them, even in their struggles, experienced happiness? Weren't the struggles themselves part of a rich fabric of abundant lives?

When Rosalinde was ten, her class had gone to Humperdinck's opera, and Maud had been a chaperone. While she hadn't been able to sit with her daughter, Maud had enjoyed sitting a few rows behind her, had watched her chatting with classmates and reacting to the opera, especially Gretel's scenes. She saw when, during the fight over the strawberries, Rosalinde exchanged some playful shoves with the boy next to her; then she straightened, craning her neck, so as not to miss a bit the angels standing guard over the sleeping children; and—here Maud thought she saw the peak of interest on the part of Rosalinde— again when the witch was pushed into the oven. Conversely, Maud was surprised that her daughter didn't seem to show much interest in the gingerbread children or all the music and singing.

She fell back asleep, this time nodding off while the song "We Are Safe" kept running through her mind.

The rapping at the door awoke her. It was mid-morning.

"Mrs. Ossietzky!"

She recognized the voice. She stumbled over to the door and opened it. It was Mrs. Hunicke again.

"They've sent Carl away."

"Yes. I know. They've reopened that old prison on the Polish border." Then the old woman noticed the suitcase on the floor.

"You're leaving! I'm so glad I caught you before you left! Where are you going?"

It was a conversation that had to wait while Maud went into the bathroom and threw water on her face. Hunicke waited, taking stock of the apartment. When Maud came back, they tended to the suitcase.

"Do you have a pillowcase?"

"Yes." Maud pointed to the bedroom. Hunicke was already on her way. When she came back, she had an empty pillowcase and started stuffing it.

"I want you to come with me," Hedwig said. "We have room."

She handed the full bag to Maud, closed the suitcase and picked it up. They were on their way down the stairs.

"Have you had something to eat?" She asked when they were out on the street.

"Not yet. You woke me."

"We'll be there soon."

But halfway down the avenue, they encountered a marching group of brownshirts, stopping traffic, brandishing banners emblazoned with their sacred swastika. Maud froze when she saw them. Hedwig had to turn back to her when she realized she was no longer being followed. She assessed the look on Maud's face, took hold of her forearm and, making sure they made eye contact on the busy boulevard, directed the harried woman in how to act.

"When they pass, do what I do."

Hedwig waited for those around her to raise their right arms in the Roman salute, then she imitated them physically if not orally. She made sure Maud followed suit. They stood like statues until the soldiers started to turn the corner. Both women breathed a sigh of relief and continued their trek in the opposite direction from the marchers. But then Maud's progress was stopped again, this time by a commotion behind them.

The Man Without a Party

At the corner, a brownshirt was punching a man in a suit. Maud brought her hand to her throat; she thought of Carl and was paralyzed. Her anxiety took over.

Hedwig came back to her again.

"Probably a Jehovah," she explained. "Or a foreigner. Some have been told by their governments they don't have to salute. Let's go." She took Maud's arm and turned away from the scene.

But there was no going. Hedwig looked at Maud's face and immediately grew concerned.

"Mrs. von Ossietzky."

No response. Maud was staring at the businessman down on the diamond-shaped stones.

"Here," said Hedwig. "Let's go in here and have something to eat. Finally, she got Maud to move. They went inside the restaurant and sat down. Hedwig ordered eggs for Maud, but had the waiter bring rolls and coffee right away. She put her hand on Maud's and patted it.

"Take your time, Dear. Everything will be all right." Maud just stared at her, disheveled, still wearing her husband's coat. Hedwig's mind was racing. She sensed Maud was thinking of her husband. She started to think that finding a place in her home for Maud wasn't sufficient; she started thinking about a sanatorium.

****

The voice came over the radio:

"A number of erring counter-revolutionary fellow Germans detained in protective custody have now been concentrated into camps on the model of those conceived for Indians in the United States, the better to embark upon their re-education and re-entry into German society. Well-tried and tested party members, forming ranks in the rationally organized security and administrative apparatus of each camp, are developing those to be regenerated over the course of internment into an organism such as the proper battalions of the old army would observe with pride. Amazing what has been created in a few months out of the long-neglected complex of buildings by the well-directed work of political malcontents! Newly trained joiners, carpenters, plumbers, masons, and ditch-diggers have created a veritable home and blossoming school for themselves. Needless to say, it is more than beams and pipes that they have joined together. Yes, a home!

"All are welcome to bear witness to the practical and healthy sleeping quarters, simple but wholesome canteens, light and pleasant showers, rejuvenating care in the adequate sick bays, kitchens that would not disgrace a good hotel; in a word, hygienically flawless provisions for basic human needs. Thus begins the rehabilitation of beggars and vagabonds, incorrigible Bolshevist rascals, semi-animal loners, brutal criminals and anarchic rioters, whose sly, false and insidious features struggle desperately against the straight and narrow path and call for somewhat draconian measures, else the generous efforts of the new German state to retrieve them from the gates of perdition would all be rendered fruitless.

"Bear witness to the high and dry, well-ventilated rooms, the three-tier sleeping berths, the straw mattresses and pillows of coarse gray cotton, the neatly folded blankets; herein commences the recovery of the most atavistic renegade, the most recalcitrant stirrer-up of strife. Do not think that such ne'er-do-wells originate from the working class, in spite of what detractors of our state may claim. These members of the ranks of future builders of German culture have seeped from the Communist and Social Democratic sewage, a poisonous and noisome river of waste that stems from the November criminals and shirkers from the time of war.

"To refute, once and for all, mendacious reports written by hidden subversives, here follows an authentic account from one of the inmates who has already blossomed back into the ranks of law-abiding citizens: 'During the whole time of my detention in the concentration camp, I was not, nor did I see any individuals maltreated in the least. I was never deprived of breakfast or of receiving a visit. Warm midday meals, identical to those served soldiers, were conveyed in field kitchens to those toiling in the fresh air, sometimes out of camp on behalf of the local community. On the contrary, the treatment of methodical inculcation by everyone concerned was always thoroughly good and even respectful, directed whole-heartedly toward the moral and social reformation of those in dire need thereof. In fact, I sincerely thank the commandant and his assistants for their care for my good treatment and everything else. Furthermore, I hereby undertake to refrain from any political activity hostile to the state of our Leader, in spite of the efforts of people without good heads who are making my life difficult once again.'"

In Sonnenburg, the prisoners were lined up in the yard to listen to the announcement. After that, the new guard had them practice the Roman salute to Hitler, counting out one hundred times.

****

Maud brushed off the sanatorium suggestion, but, after three days at Hunicke's, she was ready to listen. And, when Hedwig told her that she was acquainted with the facility, that it was inexpensive, and that she knew the doctor who ran it, Maud started weighing her options. The last straw was when Hedwig said Mrs. Ebert, the widow of the former President of the German Republic, was a patient there; almost all of Maud's misgivings melted away.

Hedwig walked her to the facility the next afternoon and checked her in. Maud seemed to bond at once with Dr. Wolpert. And the man had a surprise for them: he decided there would be no charge if Maud would give him lessons in English.

Speaking in broken English, Dr. Wolpert asked Maud about her childhood. Since he already knew what she had been through more recently with her husband's problems, she had been surprised by the question. Why should her childhood matter now? But still, he had insisted.

"Your childhood is the basis of everything!" he had proclaimed.

So she did her best to comply, thinking of her reveries more in the vein of opportunities for the man to practice his English listening skills.

****

The new guard, Ohnesorge, shoved Carl up against the wall of a barracks late one afternoon as the men were returning from work.

"Ah, it is the nobleman I heard about!" Ohnesorge taunted. Two other guards were behind him. Prisoners passed by on their ways to their blockhouse, the latrine, the place where they bartered, wherever they could go during their free time, even the early queue for the soup line. "The writer who poisoned innocent citizens with his godless drivel! Where are you from?" The question was accompanied with a push that bounced Carl off the wall again.

"Hamburg."

"Hamburg! I should have guessed it! The breeding ground for Marxist pigs! Repeat: 'I am a Marxist swine from Hamburg.'"

"'I am a Marxist swine from Hamburg.'"

"'Who poisoned the German people.'"

"'Who poisoned the German people.'"

Carl was surprised that the guards weren't stopping the prisoners, weren't ordering them to stand and watch; often, such demonstrations were made to edify the others. One didn't waste such opportunities for elucidation as this. But maybe they didn't know what to expect from the new man. He was strange, even among them.

Ohnesorge changed the look on his face to an expression of astonishment. He turned toward his fellow guards.

"I've just found Wessel's killer!" he shouted over his shoulder. His companions nodded, not knowing what to make of the comment, but the prisoners kept passing by, heads down. "Here he is! Horst Wessel's murderer!" He grabbed Carl's shirt and shook him. "This is the man who poured poison into Germans' ears for so long and stirred them on to destroy our hero." He kicked Carl in the shin. "Sing the song! Sing the song, I say."

Ohnesorge started to sing, nodding his head in exhibition, shoving Carl to the beat of the song.

" *'Raise the flag! Close the ranks!*
Quickly march with measured step—'"

Carl sang along:

" *'Veterans injured by the Reds*
Quickly march with measured step.'"

" *'Horst Wessel fell, but others rise—'*" Ohnesorge continued. Carl followed suit, " *'Inspired by the hero's death.'*"

"Again!"

Carl started the song over.

****

Maud had never met Mrs. Ebert before, but she knew what she looked like from seeing her in many photographs, standing next to her husband. So, when she saw her in the sitting room of the sanatorium, reading a magazine, her dilemma was how to approach her.

She had long known that, as far as Carl was concerned, Friedrich Ebert had represented everything that was wrong about the Social Democratic Party: secret compromises with the military, short-sightedness, weakness, betrayal of democracy. In short, Ebert, and men like him, could be blamed for the downfall of the Republic. She also knew that Carl had expressed his views in print about the man for years, and that, therefore, it was highly unlikely that Mrs. Ebert was not aware of all this.

The woman, Louise was her name, looked peaceful enough. A couple of decades older than Maud, she had weathered much, but she still was not without some beauty. At a loss, Maud even toyed with the idea of not revealing her name, or of using an alias. She had no idea how, as Mrs. von Ossietzky, she would be received by the woman. Oh, Carl! She chewed her lip and approached the former first lady of the country.

"Mrs. Ebert, I…I'm Mrs. Oss-…Oss-…Oss-…."

The magazine dropped to her lap, and Mrs. Ebert looked up, shock on her face and then recognition; all with the calmness of someone who had once been in a position of substance. Then, slowly getting to her feet, the expression went in a different direction, a deeper recognition; it seemed to register the victimizing bite of time's passage, the loss of better days, and the woman, reaching both arms out toward Maud, burst into tears.

The magic of human nature did the same to Maud. They pulled away, examined each other like long lost relatives, and hugged again.

At the second separation, brave smiles flashed, quickly extinguished; during the third embrace, Louise whispered into Maud's ear, "We must find a quiet place to talk," meaning, "more privacy," and, handkerchiefs dabbing eyes, they went out into the small but vacant yard behind the facility, holding hands, the magazine left on the floor.

"We have much in common," Louise started after they had found a bench. "I just sent off a petition to Hindenburg. You see, they have my son, Frederick Junior, the Gestapo does." She stifled a sob.

Maud was nodding. They held each other's hands, leaning toward each other.

"Have you seen Mr. Ossietzky?"

"Just twice. Carl is doing as well as can be expected. I have the feeling he's not telling me everything, you know, to spare me."

"It's so stupid!" the woman raged. "Evil! Just having been a Social Democrat is enough to get you arrested. My son wasn't doing anything. Totally blameless!"

"Perhaps Hindenburg—"

"I have very little faith in him!" she decreed. "Especially after everything that has happened. Even if he started to have a pang of conscience for what is being done to his country, the Nazis would be able to blackmail him over the East-help matter. That's one thing my husband made sure to stay away from. Any kind of bribery, corruption. Politics drove him to an early grave, but he stayed clean."

"Your other children—?"

"I was doing my best to keep them together, when I got so run down that I had to come out here. Dr. Wolpert thinks…"

Unable to go on, she grabbed her nose in an effort to keep her emotions inside. Maud patted her knee.

"My daughter's in England," she shared. "But I can't leave Carl here by himself."

"Of course not! They're beasts! Sadists are running our prisons today."

Finally, they were silent. Passions spent, each felt exhausted.

"I'm going to have a lie-down," said Louise. "The doctor warned me to be careful." She stood up and, recovering herself with an effort, extended her hand. "I am so glad we connected. Are you free for dinner?"

Maud took her hand and nodded.

"Good. I'll see you then!"

Watching the woman return to the building, she wondered if she herself had the energy to dine with Mrs. Ebert.

****

Carl was shoved from behind. He kept balance, but a second shove sent him sprawling headfirst into the dirt. He was kicked before he could get up. He turned to face his attacker: that infernal Ohnesorge again.

The man stood over him. This time, he was unattended. There were no onlookers.

"Ah! It's the writer scum! Prisoner Von!" More kicks. How did the man know where Carl hurt the most? Then came a stomp on Carl's thigh; the pain was immediate and searing, causing his eyesight to waver; the crack was audible.

The guard walked on, humming the anthem, *"Germany, Germany over all!"* If you had cared to ask Ohnesorge what he had just done, do you think he would have been able to provide a reliable account?

Carl struggled up, but the pain was too great. Black spots swam across his vision when he tried to put weight on the leg. He started crawling toward the infirmary, begging his body to remain conscious and dragging the useless leg behind him.

****

"You've told me about your husband," said Dr. Wolpert. "You've told me about your daughter. And you've told me about the three of you as a family."

"Yes," Maud answered, the two of them facing each other as they sat in the psychiatrist's office.

"Can you tell me about the first time in your life you remember having a sense of family? Way back?"

She froze, head rearing back as if she'd just stepped barefoot on a pebble. "Oh. Oh. Oh." The sound of turning deep inside.

She didn't intend for the statement to sound oracular: "My first trip here, to Germany."

"How old were you?"

"Twenty."

The doctor squinted at her. "So not earlier? Not in India?"

She shook her head. "I was very young when my parents died. I have no memory of them. Then, nurses took care of me in Grandpa's huge home. Amahs. Then they sent me to the monastery school. It was awful."

"Why?"

"Everything was about saints. When I asked to put a photograph of my mother on the wall above my bed, they, the nuns, said no, because she wasn't a saint. When I asked how she could become one, they laughed and frowned at the same time."

"Not very saintly on their part. But in England?" Wolpert prodded.

"Aunt was so strict—what we now call 'Victorian', only as criticism. Everything had to be done a certain way. I wasn't even allowed to sit in a chair, just straight-backed stools. Until I was eighteen! For posture. If I slouched, I would never find a husband, which is what everything was about for her."

"I see. But what was so special about your trip to Germany?"

"Christmas!" she beamed. "Not like a British Christmas. At Sophie's home, there were children, and even the servants were involved. All the waiting, the suspense! I'd never seen a tree decorated like that before. She had sixteen-year-old brothers, twins, from the cadet school, and a six-year-old brother as well. So much excitement. The singing, everything had more meaning because of their excitement.

"And they even gave me gifts! Things they had made. That's how I first got into sewing and knitting: to pay them back for the things they made for me. And wood-working. I was so proud of the glove box I made and decorated. And I was developing myself in other ways, too, by tutoring English and Bridge."

"I want to ask you to try to do something."

"Okay…"

"Close your eyes. Now try to feel the way you felt back then, back during that time in your life at Sophie's during Christmas. Take your time."

She laid her head back on the antimacassar. Soon, her jaw dropped and her mouth opened.

"Tell me how you feel."

"Warm inside. Like a tingling. Young again. A feeling of together. Love. I feel loved."

"Okay. Now open your eyes. How do you feel now?"

"Much better, Doctor. Thank you."

"Now, if you can do that for a memory going back decades, certainly you can do that for all the times with your husband and daughter that you wish to return to."

"Of course!"

"They won't bring your loved ones back, but, as we've seen, they can have a like effect."

****

The Man Without a Party

Why is there pain? Carl thought, lying in the bed after the medical school dropout had set the fracture. It seemed much a useless thing, worse than useless, even.

Unable to sleep, he gazed up at the blank ceiling above him. The classical dichotomy between pleasure and pain, or rather their placements at opposite ends of the continuum connected by indifferent sensations, probably had an evolutionary explanation better than the ones tradition handed down. But what was it, other than the difficult general claim that there had to be some benefit for survival in the perception of pain? Death catalyzed evolution, but was pain's advantage lost in the twine of its rope? Did you need to start with unicellular animals, and work your way up the complex tree? Forget that! Leave it for scientists.

And was the increasing, unfolding complexity of the resultant beings simply a quantitative expansion in what pain meant, or a qualitative one as well? How would one unravel the tangled threads? Since his injury, he'd kept thinking of the story about Epictetus, chiding his slaveowner who was torturing his leg, "I told you it would break if you kept doing that!" Only a Stoic sage and a slave as well could speak that way about his own body, as *not* being his own, whole or part. Probing his still problematic snaggletooth, he wondered how far away this was from Shakespeare's lines, favorites of Maud:

"For there was never yet philosopher
That could endure the toothache patiently."

So much for the consolations of philosophy! He remembered someone paraphrasing Leibniz, who evidently queried the opposite: why *wasn't* there pain? The rationalists couldn't fathom the point of pain, so either explained it away as a relative thing—Spinoza—or concluded with Leibniz that it was the normal condition of living things. Could it help one to have that viewpoint? It seemed to make perfect sense for Carl where he was, but it certainly didn't lessen his suffering.

And, slipping off at last to sleep, he wondered how many more of these reflections would be granted him, with the way things were going, before he lacked even these wretched and futile thoughts, before the flame finally flickered out.

How many levels of hell can one pass through before he loses count?

****

Maud noticed that Dr. Wolpert had started entering the sanatorium from the back, and that there were furtive whisperings among the staff. Then, one morning, she looked out the front windows and saw a small crowd. Finally, when the doctor arrived a few days later, staggering through the back door with a bloody gash on his head, the secret came out: anti-Semites had targeted Wolpert, a Jew, and his facility, with the intent of shutting it down.

Wolpert called together his staff and those patients who were available and told them he had been endeavoring to find a replacement for himself from his Gentile colleagues, but he had been unsuccessful. The sanatorium would have to close. Weeping, he said that upsetting his patients had been the last thing he'd wanted to do. He promised to keep the facility staffed until the last patients had been able to find new accommodations, but he himself would not return.

Before he was finished, Maud had already made a decision: she would take up Edith Jacobson's offer and stay for a while with her in her London flat. That way she could see Rosalinde. She would be away from Carl, but she could make connections abroad with people who might be able to help Carl, and, even if that failed, at least she could visit their daughter.

The question was, did she have it in her to go back to England?

The Man Without a Party

****

And the citizens couldn't read comprehensive reports about the March 6 general elections, the last in Germany until 1946, in which, in spite of the coercive powers of the state, the Nazis received less than 44% of the vote—they needed the votes of their coalition partner, the National Party, to reach 52%. Nor could they study new Parliamentary laws overthrowing state governments or enabling Hitler himself to fashion and finalize legislation, thus creating his legal dictatorship. It would have been hard for the citizens of Germany to ask whether democracy had brought about its own demise, since all eighty-one Communist Party delegates to Parliament had been secretly arrested, and some Social Democrats had been prevented from attending the session on March 23 in the Kroll Opera House. Nor could they encounter in print negative responses to the Nazi Party's nationwide boycott of Jewish-owned businesses. Nor were they able to inform themselves about decrees excluding Jews and political opponents from civil service jobs and disbarring non-Aryan lawyers.

Not content with preventing dissenting views from being printed, the Nazi Party, now the only legal party in Germany, organized book burning rallies throughout the country, rallies against un-German publications. Issues of *The Worldstage* are liberally represented in the conflagrations. What would they burn next?

There was a deafening silence about mandates for the forced sterilization of the disabled, Gypsies, blacks and non-socials. There was no opportunity for enlightened consensus formation regarding media organizations that exclude Jews from employment. Laws stipulating that farms cannot be bequeathed to Germans with Jewish or black ancestors since 1800 could not be discussed by German citizens in any intelligent or engaged manner.

The state-ordered blackout on 'bad' information recalled the public silence about Imperial losses during the war.

And so, since they weren't able to read about such matters in an informed way, Joe wasn't able to look across the table at Mark and say, "Aren't we a democracy? I just read somewhere that the abolition of state sovereignty and federalism has nothing to do with making justice for all uniform, or unifying our country under democratic principles, or even strengthening Germany against its foes, but that it has everything to do with Hitler's complete usurpation of power over us under the semblance of parliamentary enactments."

And Mark wasn't able to reply, "That would match with what I came across in my paper concerning racial cleansing through the marginalizing of minorities in this country, even to the extent of castrating Romas and darkies and even people who just don't care to participate in all the Nazi rigmarole."

"What do you think of that?"

"It stinks! What are we going to do about it?"

Instead, the citizens of Germany read the following, from an article by Dr. Achim Gercke:

"Allowing free development and equality for the Jews has led to an 'unfree' situation of exploited competition, and to a handing over of important positions within the German people to those of a foreign race... The legal measures that have just been issued by the government are cleansing actions that adroitly respond to Judah's declaration of war... a people's community is a community of blood... All proposals that include a permanent presence... of the Jews in Germany do not solve the Jewish Question, for they do not eliminate the Jews from Germany... If the Jews are able to exploit their host peoples forever, they will remain a constant source of the open, destructive flame of Bolshevism… a danger to racial unity."

Or this, from the *German National Catechism, for young Germans in school and work* by Werner May:

"While the German people were fighting a life and death battle during the World War, the Jew incited people at home and seduced them into treason. The November Revolution of 1918 that brought about Germany's collapse was the work of the Jew… His lackeys in leading positions in the Realm persecuted the National Socialist movement, bringing the fighters for a new Germany before judges and throwing them into prison. He corrupted Germans through bad books and mocked true literature and German music, replacing it with un-Germanic music. Everywhere, his influence was destructive… No German man may take a Jewish woman as his wife, and no German girl may marry a Jew. Those who do that exclude themselves from the community of the German people… France… has accepted large numbers of blacks into its army. It has given them the same political rights as the whites. Thus it can happen that black officers command whites. Blacks and Moroccans fought against Germany in the World War. After the war, blacks raped German women and girls in the Rhineland. Germans—never forget that!… You are born into your people, my child, of a German mother. Your father is a German. And you belong to the German people just as every part of your body belongs to you. You are a link in a great chain, a part of the whole. Alone, you are nothing, but when you live for your people, you are everything. Your people's destiny is your destiny… The history of your people is great and glorious, and you can be proud of it. The days of betrayal and the years of shame that Germany had to endure between 1918 and 1933 are a warning to you. You must work and create for the resurrection of your Fatherland."

Chapter Twelve
PAST

Maud, Carl, Rosalie, and Gustav left England the next day. They said farewell in Ostend, with the newlyweds spending a few days on the beach in De Panne while the others returned home. After an idyllic *lune de miel*, Maud and Carl moved into his apartment to start their life together.

When Carl was moving their luggage inside, he saw Maud surreptitiously stuff an envelope from the small stack of mail into the pocket of her skirt. Something stirred inside him, and, after placing the bags on the bed, he returned to the front room to hug her. Before she knew it, he had the envelope, which he saw was addressed to him, and was opening it.

She squealed and reached to grab it, but he held it over her head, reading.

"Aha!" he shouted, shaking his head. "So you paid my fine behind my back."

"Of course I did, Darling. You weren't going to do it."

"And forfeit the opportunity of an eye-witness account of my time in one of the Kaiser's jails? It could have been the article that launched my journalistic career."

"Or destroyed it!"

"You've obviously never heard of Henry David Thoreau."

"Who?"

"The American! *Civil Disobedience*?"

She shook her head, still reaching for the letter. "No, but I've read *De Profundis* and *The Ballad*, and they're pitiful when you compare them to what came before."

"Maud, when I married you I didn't know you could be so sneaky. Behind my back!"

Smiling, she was reaching behind his back now, where he had the government missive. She snatched it away from him and read through it. He placed his arms around her.

"You need to know, for a journalist, that getting a jail summons is like winning an award."

"You promised me: no secrets."

"Look who's talking! And anyway, this all happened before I made the promise. Now I'll probably never know what it's like to be a prisoner."

Dropping the letter to the floor, she placed her arms around him, reaching under the arms that were encircling her.

Nose to nose, eyes blurred by proximity, they kissed.

"That was just about being the Kaiser's prisoner. You're still my captive." She pulled him down to the sofa, sat on his lap, and they kissed as the seconds ticked away.

"Should I carry you into the bedroom?"

"No. Here."

****

When he and Maud reached his parents' apartment, they hurried inside. Rosalie was collapsed in a chair, forehead leaning on a hand that was leaning on a table. They'd thought it was about the Kaiser's announcement of war, but they weren't quite right. She hadn't seen Gustav for hours, and was worried. Carl asked her about some of the locales he might have been, then, leaving Maud with his mother, he went to look.

It was after dark when he found the hall where the Social Democrats were holding their meeting. When he entered the room, he was hit with a wall of sound. Watching the backs of the heads of the men standing in the crowd in front of him, he slowly filtered the noise into units and clusters. Moving up, he made out the voice of the speaker in the front of the room. Still looking to identify Gustav's head, he listened to the speaker.

"Yes, the fuckers have betrayed us. But they've only started. Get ready, friends and comrades! You will be singled out for your opposition to the war, isolated because you are right in rejecting this absurd decree of the Kaiser and his generals. Saving the West from Czarist barbarism? Who do they think they are kidding? They want annexations and indemnities! This is no war for the working man! We must band together as at no time before, turn the tables on our traitorous leaders, expose and isolate them. They have grown so comfortable with the status quo, with their positions and their pensions, that they have forgotten the principles that separated us long ago from the violent terrorists of the first generation of our movement.

"We social democrats have always prided ourselves with our non-violent approach to political affairs. But our leaders claim they are not without their pretexts. We see the tail between their legs! The assassination of Jaures has sent them scampering like hares for cover. If the French can silence their greatest voice, what can happen to the German functionary who steps out of line?

"But if we would not take up arms against our capitalist oppressors before, we will certainly not take up weapons to kill fellow workers now on the behalf of our true foes! No, that is the last thing we would choose to do. And it is morally treasonous for Ebert and his minions to think they could persuade us to do so. I say, if they give you a gun, turn it on them!"

Cheering! There was Gustav, leaping up and down among those in the front. Carl threaded up to him and placed a hand on his shoulder. Gustav swung his head toward Carl, who saw, in his stepfather's face, an expression he'd never seen there before, anger, rage even, a wildness in the red-tinged eyes. Without a nod of recognition, Gustav turned back to the speaker's platform where another man had taken the former's place.

"The question now is," said the new man, raising his arms, "what do we do? I am calling for strikes, for peace marches, for door-to-door canvassing to spread the word. The people need to see that there is an alternative to the Kaiser's bloodlust. He will not draft us into his war machine! Down with the war! (Hooray!) Down with the war allocations! (Hooray!) Down with Ebert and the politicians! (Hooray!) Down with the conscription of German workers! (Hooray!) Down with the Kaiser's military government! (Hooray!)

"We will start in the morning at nine o'clock right here and march. Tonight, I will send word to Stuttgart, to Essen, to Jena, to Mannheim. We will link our resistance to theirs and let Berlin know, let the whole nation know, that our movement is united. Our craven leaders have given us the opportunity to take the initiative, to take matters into our own hands. Where they lack leadership, we in Hamburg will provide it. We can stop this accursed madness. We must start here and now, small and united as one, and we will build up our strength and numbers as we move toward Berlin. Comrades! I will see you here tomorrow morning!"

Cheering. As the meeting was breaking up, Gustav was shaking hands and saying goodbyes to those around him. Carl followed him out of the building. Once they were on the street, Carl could hear that his stepfather was mumbling; he strained to understand the series of incoherent phrasings. He got closer to see if he could make anything out. Slowly, as they separated from the others in the raucous crowd, some words started making sense. And Carl noticed the smell of beer on Gustav's breath.

"I should have known," he kept repeating. "The rejection of the mass strike... marginalizing Bebel... everything subordinated to winning seats… fucking chauvinism! They've been moving in this direction for a decade!"

"Mom's very worried about you."

"I'm very worried about me! And I'm far down on the list! *Mais, j'accuse moi-meme, mon fils*! Yet, even if I'd seen it all in advance, even if I'd registered their backsliding and revisions, what could I have done? What could we have done? The only one who's standing up to the traitors is the young Liebknecht, and his own party is actually reprimanding him for it."

"So," Carl asked, "you think it's too late to accomplish anything?"

Gustav stopped, grabbed Carl by the shoulders, stared directly into his face. "You should have stayed in England," Gustav said.

Carl suppressed a snort. Was Gustav drunk? Had he gone crazy?

"I'm serious!" Gustav assured him. "Carl, I'm probably too old for the officers to sink their claws into me, but you, those bastards are going to want to turn you into cannon fodder."

"Let them try!"

Gustav hugged his son, then pushed him away as if to get a good look at him, as if Carl were going off to war at once. Then he turned away and continued walking. The street was full of people celebrating, shouting, singing patriotic songs. Guns were being let off. Had the entire country gone mad?

"I'll write to Switzerland," Gustav was mumbling again. "They'll take you and Maud in. I still have some friends there."

"Really, Father!"

"I'm serious! Your wife is British! She'll be seen as the enemy."

"She speaks German better than most Germans. And her name in von Ossietzky."

At that time, back in the apartment, Rosalie was saying to Maud, "Everything is coming apart. I can't believe this is happening."

"I know it. It's terrible."

"The prospect of Christians fighting Christians in our day and age. I just don't understand how this can happen."

"And the way the question of war is dividing the German people."

"You should have seen Gustav before he left! Like never before! He's such a peaceful, quiet man. I thought he was going to break something."

"I can't believe what's happened to women. The suffragists are backing the war in all countries. Support for votes; they are willing to make a deal to have their husbands, sons, fathers, and brothers die."

"All I know is, if something should happen to either Gustav or Carl—"

She stopped.

"I'm sorry," said Rosalie. "I shouldn't have said that."

Maud rested a hand on her mother-in-law's. "It's perfectly natural. I feel the same way. Carl is the center of my life. But, really, you don't think they'd take Gustav—"

"It would destroy me, Maud."

"And me, too."

They heard steps. Rosalie jumped up, met the two men at the door, and hugged both as if they'd been away for years. The four sat around the small table in the kitchen.

"I'm sorry I upset you," said Gustav to Rosalie. It looked like he was coming back to himself. "It was very selfish of me to take off like that, but I had to see what the others were thinking."

Rosalie nodded, holding his hands.

"What will happen?" asked Maud.

"This is something we've never seen before," said Gustav. "Questionable alliances are leading nations into the unthinkable, like leaves drawn into a vortex."

"Who could ever want this?" asked Carl.

"Certainly not the farmers," said Rosalie. "Their harvest is already started."

"The competition between countries has truly become an international affair," Gustav stated. "Worker solidarity across borders has been broken by imperialist power. It's the triumph of chauvinism, plain and simple."

"Our lives are no longer our own," Carl sighed.

"They never were, Carl," said Gustav. He squeezed his son's shoulder, staring deeply into his eyes. "They were just on loan from the Kaiser," Gustav scowled. "He's taken them back now."

Rosalie suppressed a yawn. "We all need to sleep. Tomorrow will come too soon."

When Carl and Maud left, Rosalie hugged them both tightly. She whispered in Maud's ear: "I'm so glad you're part of this family."

But three days later, when Maud was drawing cash from her bank, something on the withdrawal receipt stopped her; she returned to the teller.

"There must be some mistake," she said. "This amount is too small. My parents' trust releases funds to my account every month."

The man in the window suppressed a pitying smile. He gestured to a sign next to him in explanation. "Haven't you heard? There's going to be a war. England won't be sending you any money from now on. The governments of all belligerent countries have frozen the funds of their enemies."

Maud's knees buckled; she grabbed onto counter in front of her as it shifted before her eyes.

"What you have left in your account here in Germany is all the British government will allow you to keep."

"But when will more funds be released?"

"When the war's over?" The man shrugged.

She walked unsteadily out of the bank, careful to stay near something she could grab onto if necessary.

****

One morning in September, Carl was walking down the street when he noticed a commotion in front on the office of the German Peace Society. He inched through the crowd and went inside. The large window looking out of the street had been smashed.

Otto was sweeping up the glass, while two older men were packing things in crates. Saying a quick hello, he commenced to helping the latter. When he saw the duo were quietly, grimly carrying the crates upstairs, he fell in without comment and did the same. Upstairs, there was an empty room looking out on the back of the building where they were stacking the crates. When three men, apparently large movers, appeared and started carrying the furniture upstairs, Carl decided to take a break with Otto and the two older men. They sat on the shady pavement in the small courtyard behind the building, a world apart from the street, with a single lime tree that turned it into a bower. Otto passed out sandwiches and beer.

"What a mess in there!" he said.

"It could have been much worse," said the younger of the two strangers.

"Oh, yes. At least they didn't enter the room and vandalize it."

"No. Everything's intact," Otto commented.

"Where's Fritz?" Carl asked him.

Otto turned to the two men, saying, "This is the gentleman I told you about."

One extended a hand to Carl. "Hellmut," he said, smiling. "I've read your work."

"Ludwig," said the other, shaking Carl's hand. "You write well, and, of course, we approved of your ideas."

"Wait!" said Carl in disbelief. "You're—"

"Quidde," said the elder.

"I'm Gerlach," said the younger.

"My goodness!" gushed Carl. "It's, it's an honor to meet you both."

"I especially liked your application essay," said Hellmut von Gerlach. "Impromptu and all."

Carl chewed; his swallow took a long time going down. "Well, yes," he admitted, "but I've thought about these things for a long time."

"That was as clear as everything you wrote."

"It's bad news about Fritz," said Otto. "They wasted no time drafting him, and he fell the night of the attack on Liege back in August. I've been meaning to inform you."

The four men sat quietly. Carl stopped chewing and swallowed hard. All of a sudden, he wasn't hungry anymore. Gerlach sighed, "Poor Fritz. It didn't take him long to die."

"It didn't take them long to kill him," corrected Quidde. "Just wait. They'll make an example of you two as well, as soon as they get a chance to put you in the front line to get mowed down."

"You mean they knew he was a pacifist?"

"Oh, yes."

"I hate to say it," said Hellmut, "but you men are marked. We would be too, if we were young enough."

"They may get us yet," said Ludwig. "We're as vulnerable as glass."

Gerlach grunted.

"I'm sure I'll be called up soon," said Otto. "In spite of my Quaker background."

"Well," said Carl, "I'm happy to say I flunked my physical. 'Unfit for service at present time.' A variety of ailments, weaknesses; evidently my heart is weak. My family was ecstatic with my lack of fitness, but I'm still liable to be called up at any time."

"Oh, yes. And defend the stained honor of Germany."

Gerlach guffawed. "*The Manifesto of 93*. What rubbish!"

"With aching hearts, our troops were obliged to set Louvain aflame as a punishment for the treachery of its inhabitants," the older man droned in mockery of the declaration.

"Citizens lay in ambush," Hellmut paraphrased in the same manner, "mutilating our wounded compatriots, murdering, in cold blood, German doctors doing Samaritan work…"

"…We must decidedly refuse to buy a German defeat at the cost of saving a work of art…"

"…We did not trespass on Belgium, since England and France had already resolved to trespass on it, and it would have been suicidal not to have pre-empted them…"

"…Hordes of wild Mongolians and negroes, incited to rape, robbery, and riot over white civilization, have necessitated the preservation of German culture by a justified and disciplined German militarism…"

"…Lying is a poisonous weapon, false witness an affront to the sacred and holy legacy of our artists and philosophers…"

"…Kant, Goethe, and Beethoven beseech the entire civilized world to protect their hearths and homes…"

"I can't believe all the theologians," Otto broke in finally, "who thought it was acceptable to sign their names under all that filth. Harnack and Naumann, Father Albert and von Schlatter…"

"It's the artists who shocked me," said Carl ruefully, "Hauptmann and Liebermann, Eulenberg and Fulda, Reinhardt and Humperdinck, Sudermann and Klinger…"

"And the scientists," added Hellmut, "Planck and Roentgen and Ehrlich, Haber and Lenard, and Nernst…"

"And Haeckel!" included Carl with more ruefulness. "A scientist! He used to be a hero of mine."

"It's the philologists, the historians and the archaeologists that get to me," said Ludwig. "I'm still incredulous about Willamowitz. But not just him. I scratched my head about Theodor Wiegand, too, for a long time. And von Duhn and Wilhelm Dorpfeld. He followed up Schliemann's work on Troy, for goodness' sake! Why do that if you're going to support the destruction of art, and humans, elsewhere? *Why*?"

"At least Nicolai is trying to put together a counter list."

"Let's hope he gets a lot of signatories."

"Not in Germany, he won't," said Ludwig. "And they won't even bother asking us."

"The truth is," said Hellmut, "no section of civilization is immune to succumbing to barbarism under certain circumstances. The painter just knows beauty on a canvas; the scientist only seeks truth in a laboratory. But they trip themselves up as soon as they remove their smocks. Even the moralists have an Achilles' heel when it comes to their own morality."

"And where does that leave us?" asked Carl.

"Back where we started," judged Quidde. "The only war worth fighting is the war against war."

"Well," concluded Gerlach, standing. "Shall we finish this?"

The next evening, Otto showed up at Carl's apartment and offered him Fritz's job. Carl accepted.

Chapter Thirteen
PRESENT

And they didn't read about how, by banning Jews from the German Labor Front, the government had effectively denied them the chance for employment in Germany. They couldn't read objective accounts of the so-called "Night of Long Knives," a series of political murders soon perfunctorily declared legal by the Parliament, approved in judgments based on trumped-up accusations of a government takeover by the victims. Or that, after Hindenburg's death, Hitler abolished the Presidency and declared himself The Leader of the German Realm and People, not for the general welfare but in order to make all opposition illegal in his creation of a totalitarian state for himself. Or that Himmler had consolidated control of all German police forces, under the name of the Gestapo, in order to activate the tentacles of Hitler's spreading police state.

Instead, they might have read Himmler's speech to SS group leaders:

"If I assume the number of one or two million homosexuals, it is clear that about 7 or 8 or 10% of the men in Germany are homosexual. If this remains the case, it means that our nation will be destroyed by this plague. *Kaputt*!... We are a men-state and, with all the faults which this men-state has, we must staunchly hold on to it, for the constitution of the men-state is the better one... In the positions of the state and the economy, in which women are employed, no honest man will be able to claim that the position is gained purely on the basis of merit. For—be honest—there are only men here, therefore one can say it very calmly—in the moment when you choose a typist and you have two candidates before you, a very ugly 50-year-old one who types three hundred syllables, almost a genius in this field, and another who is 20 years old, racially sound, and pretty and who types only one hundred and fifty syllables, you will—I would have to misjudge you all completely—probably with earnest mien and a thousand moral justifications because the other is old and could easily get sick and whatever, take the pretty young 20-year old candidate who types fewer syllables. Well, one can laugh, for this is harmless and proves meaningless because, if she is pretty, she will soon get married; and besides, the position of stenographer is not crucial for the state; it now has others to choose from… Homosexuality, therefore, undoes in the state every merit, every basis for merit, and destroys the state in its foundations. That is not all: the homosexual is a thoroughly mentally-ill man. He is soft; he is in every crucial regard a coward. I believe that he can be brave here or there in war; in the field of civil courage, however, they are the most cowardly men that there are… the homosexual lies pathologically. He is not lying like a Jesuit… We will gather up all of these 17 to 18-year-old boys, except for those who are already spoiled, and bring them into a camp. We will try to make these boys reasonable again, something which, as I said, has already been done successfully in a large number of cases… I am of the conviction that the Roman emperors, who eradicated the first Christians, did exactly the same thing that we are doing with the communists. These Christians were, then, the worst yeast which the great city contained, the worst Jewish people, the worst Bolsheviks that there were… I am furthermore convinced that the way out for the few who do not want to yield to this homosexuality, especially for the country parsons, the majority of whom—more than 50%—I estimate to be gay, is to procure for themselves in confession the necessary married and single women; I assume that, in the monasteries, the homosexuality ranges from 90 or 95 to 100%... Gentlemen! A misguided sexuality brings about the craziest thing that the mind can imagine. To say they are animalistic is an insult to animals, for animals do not do such things. So, this question about properly guided sexuality is a question about life for every people."

His captive audience wondered at his ability to cover so many subjects. And what edifying reading for the youth of Germany, especially after that nasty Rohm affair!

****

What were the types of pain? Was there any point in asking the question? Did the exploration have a chance of leading one to a diminishing? It's easy to keep trying something, no matter how pointless, when it's your *idee fixe*.

Carl started with the pains in his head, the soreness between ear and temple where he'd been whacked by a guard the day before: a simple ache but also a sharpness, depending on how he held his head, as if a jagged piece of skull sliced directly into his gray matter like a shrapnel splinter. Then the headache behind his left eye, a piercing stab that might be related to the effects of the punch, but certainly a spatial contrast to the other, a menacing throb that made him want to pluck out the eye, as if that would help. The harsh, ubiquitous glow from the overcast worsened it; it helped to keep the lid closed, though it was amazing how much that reduced his depth perception. And then, this pain seemed to snake its way up into his sinuses, transforming itself as it did so into a burning, searing pain whenever the bone-chilling gusts off the permanently damp heath found an uncovered nostril to invade. He wrapped a cloth around his face and draped it over his nose.

And that punch to his head had also put a gash inside the soft tissue of the inside of his cheek, next to the jagged tooth. This was an internal bruise bringing with it its own cut, followed by the cry of the moist, flexible cells whose *raison d'etre*, to stay fused, had been violated. And the ripped flesh had previously covered the original tear, when the tooth had first been cracked. Though the body had done its best to heal, obeying its own drive toward equilibrium, the brutal reality of camp-life had overtaxed the powers of its natural tendencies. And, because of the meager diet, his self-healing body had less and less convalescent strength to draw on in its quest for maintaining wholeness.

His stomach, the dull, organic emptiness he carried around within him, gnawing without object, boring and pinching, the inner groan barely silenced after wolfing down the watery meal, and hunger's radiating stretch, tentacles that reached out through his core, as if to notify his limbs of the danger of caloric nothingness, messages of dire need, warnings of want, sharp siren calls to forage, find whatever could be thrust into the orifice, crammed down the gullet.

His broken and healing and rebreaking and rehealing leg never left the horizons of his thought, conscious or subconscious, sleeping or awake, its numbness and pins and needles, its refusals to work, the straining and then the piercing, searing rebreak, a bolt of light that brought your focus back to the first break and the original spot, the I-told-you-sos and the I-can't-fix-it-if-you-are-going-to-keep-doing-thats, new swellings flaring out over the old, the newly care-worn nerves, the renewed self-reminders of caution, the vigilant nights and the reawakenings of pain shooting through the cursed limbs.

And finally, everything came inescapably back to the Hunger, now no longer merely the singular wail of the stomach but a deadening weakness that encompassed all, his being itself, his essence; a negative aura, the ruthless creeping diminishing of self, of connection, of care, because they all took too much energy, because they took any energy at all. Its image was the wretched deposit of his shriveled paunch, not a real bowel movement anymore but, in a place where dysentery meant death, a success if only he escaped soiling his trousers before finding a squatting-place.

And heaven forbid his sore throat should grow into a full-blown infection, or that he catch his death of a cold!

****

Georg Bernhard and Berthold Jacob walked together down the street in Paris. It was April 29, 1934, and Jacob, who strode with a sheaf of papers under his arm, had traveled that morning from Strasbourg to help Bernhard fill out the forms necessary to nominate Carl von Ossietzky for the Nobel Peace Prize for 1935. They carried no hope for a successful selection for their candidate, but they intended that the mere nomination would have an international effect that could be manipulated in such a way that Carl's continued detainment in Esterwegen Concentration Camp would reach a critical point in which the German government would be induced to free him. Their ultimate goal was to have Carl and Maud emigrate from the accursed country and re-unite with Rosalinde.

Each of the men carried a price on his head back at home. Each knew that, had they not escaped the clutches of the Nazis, they would be inmates in a concentration camp like Carl, or worse. Since the beginning of last year, many such as they had materialized in countries around the world. "There but for fortune go…"

At last, they stood at the bottom of the steps to the Swedish Embassy. They stopped and looked at each other.

"Well, shall we go through with this?" asked Georg.

"Absolutely!"

They trudged up the stairs. Inside, they finally found the right person to whom to deliver the papers. After the man perused them, he said that everything seemed to be in order and told the duo they would be notified of any developments.

Then he said, "So, who's this von Ossietzky?"

Bert turned toward Georg and said, "There. You owe me a cognac."

"Let's go find a bar," the other replied. "If help is going to be on the way for the poor man, we obviously have quite a crusade to map out."

****

He wasn't curious, and he no longer knew it.
He wasn't witty, and he no longer knew it.
He wasn't clever, and he no longer knew it.
He wasn't loving, and he no longer knew it.
He lost his aggressiveness, and he didn't miss it.
He lost his tact, and he didn't try to recover it.
He became suspicious, and he didn't know it.
He became resentful, and he didn't realize it.
He grew in a kind of lethargic guile, and it didn't embarrass him.
He felt envy and didn't hide it.

And, though he experienced a vague feeling of a general loss, an awareness of something missing, he couldn't be bothered with it. It was like words you don't use anymore.

Richard Tres

****

Ernst Toller, one of the many artistic, intellectual or political exiles from Germany—He checked all the Nazis' boxes!—caused quite a commotion when he arrived unexpectedly at the Badeles School in Hampshire, England, and asked to see Rosalinde von Ossietzky. The school's founder, John Haden Badley, devout follower of Montessori, Pestalozzi, Frobel and Dewey, in his last year as headmaster, descended from his office to meet the guest.

Toller had been asked by Maud, since he was already in England, to look in on her daughter. Badley sent for Rosalinde and gave the playwright a quick tour while they waited for the girl. As he strolled through the rooms, Toller asked about her; Badley asked about her father.

When Toller saw Rosalinde, he was shocked. Badley left them together, and they found an empty room to sit and chat.

Rosalinde was dressed head-to-toe in black. After she responded briefly to all Toller's questions with careful positives, Toller, astute in matters of disguise, smelled a rat; the teen was putting up a front, trying to brush him off. Rather than deterred, the man was challenged to break through her protective barrier. How many times had he seen people wearing costumes, people who hurt, people who feared? It had been his lifelong vocation to pierce the veil, poke a gaping hole through the walls, and then to write about what he saw.

The problem was, how to do so in this case, what tact to use. Each human, he had learned, was *sui generis*, whatever science claimed about the matter. And adolescents were a different matter entirely; their armor metamorphosed into eggshell as soon as it was punctured, and the ego vanished further into an inner clam. And, with her situation, Rosalinde was no ordinary

218

teenager. He decided to talk about himself, even though she had barely asked about him.

"I'm putting together one of my plays for a Manchester production," he started. "Manchester's not London, and London's not Berlin, but exiles like us can't be picky." He tried to notice something, anything, a chink in the hardened masonry. Nothing. She simply nodded, a tragic-romantic heroine worthy in her innocent beauty of Byron, Shelley, Goethe.

"*Rake Out the Fires*," he went on. "From a few years ago. Oh, and I'm working on an autobiography. Wish I'd kept a journal when I was your age. It would have saved me a lot of trouble now. I'm racking my brains to recall things I probably never thought I'd be able to get out of my mind, back in the day." He waited with baited breath, then, "Do you keep one?"

A journal? She shook her head. One would think the sadness would finally brim over, the dam would open up, just a crack. She sighed.

"Do you know who Mary Baker Eddy was?" he asked, shifting subjects. No, by headshake. "An American religious figure. Another piece I'm planning. Are you at all religious?"

Another headshake.

"Your mother wrote the Society of Friends is helping out with… everything."

Nothing! Not charity, not mother. The castle must not be breached!

"A collaboration," he said. "We're planning five acts."

"You certainly keep busy!" This was delivered in adult triumph, but it was something, finally! Would she drop her guard?

"One has to, I find. Otherwise, black depression takes over."

She looked up and finally engaged. "You're depressed?"

"How can I not be? I've lost family and friends, country, means, language, and audience; what else is there?"

Head back down. Homer's 'he wished the earth would open up and….'

"And you may have heard things weren't running too smoothly for me before the Nazis took over."

Her swallow seemed to get caught on the way down: an abortive gulp. He pushed ahead with what he hoped was the key that would open the chest.

"Oh, and I'm also working up my old prison poems for publication."

This remark did it; she thought of her father. Her face froze, she pursed her lips till they purpled, and the mask cracked into a dozen pieces, each one seeming to dart in a different direction. Children didn't cry like adults, and adolescents were unique in sharing the features of a middle ground between full cloudburst and controlled collapse. Here, the child vied with the adult. The struggle showed how teens had their own, special kind of conflicts, defeats, and dignity.

Rosalinde strove to conceal her wounds by dropping her head face-first, as if struck by lightning, onto the fabric between them, using the sofa to muffle her cries and otherwise do what the beautifully resistant and fragile veil now failed to do. Suddenly maskless, her black hair spilling over the cushions, she actually seemed to try to descend into them. Toller comforted her by placing a hand on her shoulders, but he left her to pass through the stages from outbreak to melting, to hysteria, to anger, to embarrassment, to catharsis, and to subsidence before, relieved in finding his handkerchief clean, he offered it to her.

She took it as a desperate curtain, still insistent that he not see her face. He said—what were words? He lied, telling her he was sorry if anything he'd said caused her to… *E misera!*

She had snuggled against him, nestled her head on his shoulder and gave into another wave of emotion. He patted her hair, encouraged her, felt his own sadness, strangely, as if at arm's length.

"Oh, I'm *so* unhappy!"

When she could talk enough to put sentences together, they determined that, though not perfect, the situation of the school and the influence of the Quakers were not to blame. She had been driven from home and family, plunged into an alien world at a particularly sensitive time in her life, when vulnerability enveloped her like skin, when, without agreement from her, without consultation or warning, she was already losing her childhood. The even greater loss of her parents, and her sense of their sufferings, weighed especially on her soul. The one thing she knew was that she could not go back to Germany. Never.

This was all Toller had to go on, and he grasped at it.

"Am I right in thinking that a change of scene, a—?"

"Yes!"

"I have friends here, connections. I will explore."

"Thank you!" She had pulled away, dabbing around her eyes with his handkerchief.

"Do I have your permission to write to your mother, just to say—?"

She shook her head as if a bug had flown at her face. "No one here must know!" The jaw jutted out in a defiant statement of burgeoning identity, a phoenix rising from the ashes of her internal conflagration. Toller was more than impressed; he saw a new, aggressive person forging through the features of Carl and Maud. He felt privileged to be present at a birthing. The thirteen-year-old is the mother of the grown-up; and so is the twenty-three-year-old, with all the points of process in between.

For, he realized, this wasn't the only stage, this wasn't the end of Rosalinde's transitions. There had been, would be, dozens of unrepeatable unmaskings over the next decade for her, each time the chick persistently pecking her way through the no-longer-useful shell.

"Here at the school?"

"Right!"

"Of course. I'll say nothing." He didn't know if he were going to have to go back on his word. Badley should be told something. But he said, "Just to your mother."

Over the next weeks he talked to friends, then wrote his suggestion to Maud: the school at Dartington Hall. A change of scene might make all the difference for the girl. In addition, the school had been recommended by Lord Russell, and, even more importantly, it took charity cases.

****

When Carl woke up, the guard was urinating on him; the warm, noxious piss splattered on his chest and sent droplets, golden in the sun, over his face to rouse him. Also, the man must have kicked him while he was down, because his leg hurt more than it usually did. The other prisoners were standing around, loiterers dumbly watching the spectacle.

He must have fainted on the way back to camp after work; the guard had simply been an opportunist in emptying his bladder.

The man was shouting at the men standing around. "I hereby... remake thee, 562... transforming you... into... my piss!" Then, crowing over the heads of the bystanders, "Digestion is a necessary function of the People!"

Finishing, he shook himself off. Carl slowly got to his feet, making sure his hind end was closest to the guard so, in case he was kicked again, it wouldn't be in the head. Above all, one must protect one's head. Things were spinning around for him bad enough as it was.

"Come on, admit it, 562! You must be a damned kike."

"I was baptized at St. Nikolai's," Carl replied. He couldn't decide whether to pull his reeking pajama uniform closer to his body in the stiff breeze.

"Really! With a beak like that? And your stink? You smell like a Jew."

Carl exchanged looks with his fellow prisoners. He did not hold it against them if they thought, 'Better he than me.' Tomorrow it would be one of them.

He would have felt the same if one of them stood where he was. If? When!

"Then why do you act like them?"

The question hovered in the air like a dank and noxious fog.

****

Maud stepped off from the train car and put her feet onto the concrete platform. It was the first time she had touched the ground of England since 1913. At the time, she had vowed never to return.

She looked around at the passersby, then stared at her feet on the pavement. She was back. But what did she feel? Dread. Angst. She put one foot in front of the other.

An ever-chic Edith Jacobsohn welcomed her into her chic apartment and settled her in an extra bedroom. Part of Maud's anxiety left her when she dropped her suitcase on the floor. They hugged and sat at tea, and Edith smoked and talked in her allusive manner, spinning elliptical sentiments in the air along with the smoke trails of her exhalations.

"So you'll just be here for a brief visit? No more Germany for me. I sold my company to Maschler, but we'll see how much money one Jew can spirit out of that wretched country now in aid of another. I was damned lucky the man had some British bank accounts he could make available in partial payment. Now he can have Dr. Doolittle and Winnie the Pooh and whatever Kastner produces for kids with his Emil and the detectives."

"What about *The Worldstage?*" Maud asked.

"What indeed! I fear we've each become its bereft vestals, Maud. Sorry. The paper's defunct in Germany, of course," Edith replied, then took a long drag on her cigarette, letting the smoke out as she continued to speak. *"C'est fini.* Walter's in Czechoslovakia doing his best to resuscitate it. I hear Kurt Hiller is out of his concentration camp and is helping him in the cause, but I can't be any aid to them there. The Schiffer family funds have saved the paper before, but Daddy Max's trees are long gone. Cut down and turned into buildings or fuel or pulp or whatever. Maybe some issues can be printed and smuggled into Germany. Who knows? Not that it'll help your husband, though I've written to my uncle Judge Eugen and my cousins the Cassirers about him. So we'll see. I know you're hard up. You're welcome to stay here as long as my meager reserves hold out. But that's the great unknown. My next plan is to see what publisher might need my translation skills, then to see what Jewish aid groups can offer me in my plight."

The next day, Maud had gone to see a solicitor she remembered in order to look into her chances of drawing funds from the blocked inheritance. The prospect wasn't good.

When she visited the Quaker school, she was impressed. The grounds were expansive and well kept, the buildings solid, the faculty friendly. And Rosalinde seemed to be doing fine, considering the circumstances, though most of her statements had been monosyllabic and non-committal.

Rosalinde told Maud nothing about Toller's visit. In fact, Rosalinde told her very little.

"How are you getting along, my dear?"

"Fine."

"Are they feeding you things that you can eat? The British don't have much of a grasp of the appetite."

"You're British."

"Yes, but—"

"The food's fine, Mother."

"And your studies. Do you find yourself well prepared?"

"Mother, you really don't have to worry about me. Everything's fine here."

Maud was at a loss. The relationship was already strained enough, communication was sufficiently difficult without all that had happened to them. What could she say? 'Your father and I miss you so much.' Ridiculous! There was nothing normal about their predicament, and normality had been a regular thicket.

"How's Father?"

"As well as," here she was, already tearing up, "can be expected." She stopped, then said the wooden words: "He sends his love, of course."

Maud felt her daughter's eyes on her as she fought off the whimper and wiped her nose. Cold eyes, observing! She sought desperately for something.

"His friends are doing everything they can to get him out."

"Is there much of a chance?"

"Well, they are actually trying to start an international push by nominating him for the Stockholm peace award, the one Stresemann and Quidde and Angell have won."

The girl suddenly came alive. "That's wonderful, Mama! Is there anything I can do to help?"

On the verge of brushing her daughter's question aside, Maud caught herself. What was the harm? "There's a woman in Paris who's coordinating everything. I can get you her address, if you like."

"Wonderful! I'll have all my friends write letters. And their friends. And families too."

225

"Well, of course, Dear, if that's what you'd like to do."
"We'll show that Hitler!"
"Not so loud, Dear."

Chapter Fourteen
PAST

Looking over Carl's file, filled with arguments, appeals, and deliberations relating both to Carl's pacifism and his tenuous health, a functionary in the massive Prussian military bureaucracy decided that the war effort would get more out of the sickly peacemonger in a work regiment than in combat, and stamped the levee papers accordingly, for limited service. In so doing, the nameless clerk most likely saved Ossietzky's life many times over.

Some months thereafter, sitting with other newly-minted rookies on their way to France, Carl was looking out the window of the train car, but, instead of watching his country pass, he was focused on the dream he'd had the night before which, like so many of his other dreams over the last six weeks, had been obsessively centered around their drill sergeant, Major Engebreth, and around the many ways the dreamer killed him.

Last night's dream had dramatized a diabolical Carl, luring the major toward the equestrian exercise arena adjacent to the stables. He enticed him with the promise of a beautiful woman, someone who, evidently, had wandered into the male-exclusive encampment. But when Carl succeeded in trapping Engebreth in the corralled oval, he'd quickly clubbed the man with a stick of wood, which had suddenly materialized in Carl's right hand, and down went the officious, pusillanimous, chauvinist, anal, ogrish, petty, oleaginous, stertorous, semi-literate, smelly homunculus onto the freshly raked sand of the exhibition grounds. Quickly, not a second to waste, Carl had freed the stout horses from their stalls and started them circling around the periphery, making sure that they never missed a chance to trample the wretch into a bloody nothingness.

Truth be told, Carl felt bad about the dream. The therapists could talk all they wanted about wish-fulfillment; Carl would staunchly maintain that he'd felt no pleasure in the nightmare. And he refrained from going as far as the others, who at least spoke about their vengeful hopes for the sergeant-major's precipitous and violent demise. One trainee had even spoken of finding a way to infect Engebreth's allegedly roving wife with a form of venereal disease. Carl kept his nocturnal dramas to himself; after all, he was a public pacifist; he shouldn't even be having these thoughts, albeit subconscious. But while he felt bad, he still found himself automatically ranking the most recent dream among the others, comparing and contrasting it with them for its creativity, suspense, intricacy, propriety and, yes, viciousness.

As it was related to Carl's recent punishment, the cleaning of the stables, for a multitude of nebulous infractions—slovenliness? Tell that to Rosalie, or Maud, for that matter!—the dream ranked high under the criterion of propriety but surely no higher than the one of Carl pushing the worthy victim into subterranean stench of a full latrine and calling an assembly to enjoy the vociferous fecal drowning; this had to be just as notable in that category, coming as it did right after his unwarranted selection for latrine maintenance—revet, prop, level, heighten, chamfer, fill in. And the gem about Carl's hammering of the man straight into the ground and then pulling him out like a nasty weed with a gardening claw was just as gory, yielding plenty of colorful imagery satisfying in guilty reflection. Carl had blown the man up on many occasions, using a panoply of bombs with great skill: grenades, trench mortars, shrapnel, stick—his personal favorite—gassed him; poisoned him with the thin gruel the cooker called soup; rendered Engebreth a captivating and complex lacework during an impressive rifle practice; and even stooping to decapitate him with an exploding cigar, a gift banded with a scarlet ribbon and tagged with the note, "From an admirer, unknown."

Ah, comparisons are odious!

Carl grew drowsy; his heavy eyelids began to droop; his head started swaying in circular fashion with the contrasting motions of the train as it both surged forward and remained on the uneven tracks. He was dreaming again.

****

Less than a week after his arrival in France, Carl was called into the orderlies' station. His commander, Lieutenant Muller, called him into his office. He shoved some papers across his desk toward Carl.

"You recognize this, Soldier?"

"A letter to my wife, Sir."

"'Letter,' bullshit!" the man exploded. Muller drew a monocle from its holster and affixed it around his eye, glaring at Carl as if seeing him for the first time. "This is an article you've written about your training. Unacceptable! You can't send this in our mail! We know all about you, Ossietzky! You want to publish this in some pacifist rag."

"No, Sir. Just my reminiscences, Sir. For my wife to read. Respectfully speaking, Sir."

"Well, you can't send crap like this in the German mail!"

"I'm sorry, Sir."

"And she's British!"

"Only by background, Sir."

"You want to spend the rest of your life in a military prison?"

"I apologize, Sir. It won't happen again."

"You're damn right it won't!" Muller's mustache quivered. Then, with finality worthy of the stage, "Dismissed!"

Carl made sure to gather the pages before leaving the blockhouse; he hoped to get them to Gerlach or Quidde during his next leave. As long as they weren't still in prison for speaking out against the Kaiser's war.

****

The next time he had a quiet moment and sat down to write to Maud, he thought and thought. His appointment to a labor company had solved the problem of carrying weapons. But, frankly, his issue wasn't there; it started way back. And he truly accepted the power of the self-defensive reflex, a philosophical apriorism going back, at least, to the ancient Greek Stoics. If he needed to kill in order to defend himself, there was no problem there: he would. To get back to Maud still breathing and in one piece, he'd commit all the crimes he'd fantastically performed on Engebreth, and more. No, Carl's issue was the network of forces putting him here, the purposefulness of brute force overpowering the quiet intentionality of reason; that was his real enemy. And that power was simultaneously nowhere and all around him. But how to combat it? And how not to get sucked into its hurricane vortex?

He had deliberately decided to immerse himself in everything his fellow soldiers were immersed in, but without allowing himself to be tainted. He had full faith in the stance he had taken; his rejection of the 'all' of war was the viewpoint he wanted. But how to keep that perspective, when all around you was chaos? How to see what was in full view in front of your very eyes, when that deep-seated reflex told you it was safer to be blind?

Long before his draft, he'd grown sickened by the way the enemy was seen at home: the animal, the evil incarnate, the 'must-be-annihilated.' All he had to do was think about Maud, and he was cured of that ubiquitous folly. Humans are humans. But now he was able to see how the German soldiers were treated by their own officers, their own Supreme Command, their own Kaiser and country: the pig-sty trenches, the cannon fodder, the blood and guts and brains, mere matter to be inhumed, mere tools of strategy right or wrong, sensible or insane. In other words, what significant difference stood between the way friend was treated from foe?

He recalled something Fr. Anton had said to Rosalie, something he'd retained from childhood: "It's the man who hears, not the ear." But if that was true, it was true of both enemy and self as well. And, if so, why were he and his comrades mere amputatable appendages, infinitely expendable? And, while he'd known this was embedded inherently in the very concept of the military, cognitively, it was quite another manner to overhear officers speaking unself-consciously to this effect in easy earshot to the expendables. When they looked at them, at the rank-and-file soldier, did his leaders think of them, palpably, as so many instruments to hand, so many monotonous and replaceable pieces of a whole that functioned on quite another level of meaning from its parts? Ants in the anthill, bees in the beehive. Did those leaders fear fraternizing, not with the enemy, but with their own men, lest they fall into the trap of humanizing them? Did the analogy work: German soldier to German leader as enemy soldier to German soldier?

He stared at the empty page in his hands. In order to survive this war, he had to find another way to write.

****

Carl was told by a messenger to report to the new orderly station at once.

"Shit!"

He left those with whom he was working on latrine duty and went to the makeshift blockhouse on the side of a nearest hill, facing away from the front. After being told to wait outside, he was met at the door by Lieutenant Muller, who seemed relieved to escape the stifling interior, leading Carl to a table in the shade of a tree at the hilltop. Muller sat and motioned Carl to do the same. He pulled out some papers and shoved them toward Carl, who recognized them at once.

"Did you write this?"

"Yes, Sir. Just for my wife. I can explain—"

Muller read, "'Over-Lieutenant Oberg became enraged with his batman, clubbing him over the ears for over-salting his ceremonial eggs...'"

"To entertain my wife a little. To save her worrying—"

"'When we entered the enemy's trenches,'" Muller continued, "'we found that they had been vacated during the preliminary barrage. And that we were lost in the darkness of early dawn, our leader bewildered in the labyrinth worthy of Daedalus himself, as the OL remarked later. He wished he'd paid better attention in class when compasses were explained, for Dante in his wild wood, as OL pointed out later, was never so forlorn as we.'"

"Sir, it helped me to deal with..."

"'It helped you to deal with'?" Muller mocked.

"I meant no disre—"

"And did you happen to have any particular officer in mind when you, Ossietzky, gave Oberg a moustache—"

Carl couldn't help staring in shock at Muller's walrus. "Oh, no, Sir. Absolutely not—"

"You're quite sure?"

Carl was vigorously shaking his head no. "It's just my way of, of having some fun. A meaningless detail. I fully apologize."

"The censors, you understand. It's not their job to have a sense of humor."

"Never again, Sir." Carl imagined the court-martial, the weeks in solitary in a sweltering blockhouse.

"Maybe another way."

"Sir?"

"This would be harmless enough if you just changed the names to French or British."

Carl could only stare.

"Write this drivel about the enemy, Ossietzky!"

"Ah! I see, Sir!"

"Make them the targets of your satire. I guarantee the censors will have no problem."

"Thank you, Sir!"

But Carl wasn't even to the bottom of the hill before he was questioning his commander's suggestion. While he was convinced that all military behavior was wrong-headed, foolish and destructive, he was not motivated to make fun of the soldiers of the Entente to the benefit of Germany. And his pacifism coincided with an outright internationalism that saw no point in favoring one form of militarism over another. The point was to get others to see beyond nationality! The downfall of his satirizing strategy created for him, as a loving correspondent with Maud, not only a problem to be solved but, as a serious writer, a rhetorical challenge to be overcome.

****

Dear Maud, my Dearest Love,

I hope all is well. We continue to hold body and soul together somehow. Lately, my comrades and I have been working in trench maintenance, sinking shafts, making or remaking dugouts, setting concrete posts, facing walls with sheets of corrugated metal, and laying out drainage. All this while nearby bombs make their drumroll, machine guns rattle, and carbines pop.

Around the meal table, old timers tell entertaining tales of the enemy. I don't know how they gather their information, but it seems authentic. Many stories they tell center on a French officer, quite the 'heroic' type, at least in his own mind, a Lieutenant Ledebec. He served as a gendarme during peacetime and advocates a risky, sportive devilry and romantic luck that astounds. An autodidact, he certainly would have been a Renaissance man had he enjoyed wealth, class, and family. In the trench, when his fellows yawn with boredom or complain of discomfort, our lieutenant studies plant and insect life in the chalk or clay or gravel before his eyes, reflecting on its difference or similarity with human life or, better yet, discovering fossils of starfish and mussels and opining a marine past for the wasteland of the present.

Moving on, he expanded his studious explorations to the local varieties of louse and rats, distinguishing the latter not by length of tail, color or size, but by temperaments, wit and gastronomic preferences. It was in regard to the rodents that Ledebec managed to gain recognition from his superiors in a most ingenious way. He led a raid that succeeded in forestalling an enemy attack. Let me tell you how this event unfolded.

One afternoon, while his men decried the current rat infestation, which had plagued their fitful attempts to rest, befouled their habitations and diminished their food supplies, Ledebec challenged them to stem their violent passions in the direction of a hunt for the infernal critters. They took up his challenge and in no time the sharpshooters had the rats on the run, with hardly any soldiers injured in the percussive melee. So well did the men triumph in putting the rodents to flight that a veritable exodus ensued, which found its way into the enemies' trenches.

The Man Without a Party

The terrified rats so terrified the foe who, by chance, were on the verge of attack, that the enemy took flight, chased from the front by the onslaught of the diminutive quadrupeds. Ledebec's men followed this up and took their opponents' trenches, where they found ample evidence of an offensive. This occurrence resulted in official recognition for the lieutenant from his regimental commander, an accomplishment not at all diminished by the former's claim that he "owed it all to the rats."

All love to you, Maudie my love. Will let you know as soon as I get word of leave.

Your utter slave in love, Carl.

****

"Ossietzky in trouble again!" the messenger shouted.

Carl swore, dropped his shovel, and took off for the orderly station, all the time razzed by his companions.

"They want to know if they can print your story about the Frenchman," started Muller.

"Sir, you know I'm a pacifist."

"So?"

"I absolutely refuse to do anything more for the war effort than I'm forced to!"

"Yes."

"Then how can you possibly expect me to go against my principles by concurring—"

"Now, wait a minute. You wrote the piece."

"Yes. But for private enjoyment. Not for propaganda!"

"I remind you to watch your tone, Soldier."

"Sorry, Sir."

"I don't give a damn whether you say yes or no. I'm just conveying the proposal."

"You've been very understanding, Sir."

"You know, pleasing these people could be beneficial in making things, uh, more comfortable for you, Ossietzky. Perhaps they'd let one of your articles pass."

"I can't go down that path, Sir."

"How is it I had a feeling you'd answer that way?"

"Anything else, Sir?"

"You're dismissed. Wait! Do you draw? You know, cartoons?"

Carl just shook his head and, after saluting, walked away.

Once again, before he'd reached the bottom of the hill, he'd begun to analyze his quick rejection of Muller's insinuations. But on what grounds? What was the line he couldn't cross? He stared out over no-man's land, watching men scamper about, wondering. Other people had, or lacked, other lines they wouldn't cross in other endeavors. Where did they take form, these boundaries not to be crossed? Were they the effects of shallow training, like the drills Sergeant-Major Engebreth had forced upon them? And did these moralizing demarcations constitute the essence of the ethical, all else simply decorative trappings?

As he returned to his work squad, Carl was somewhat surprised at himself to suddenly find that there were subjects that the humorizing of which did not help heal, much less please him; which, no matter how witty and comic and burlesque the treatment, soured on the palette, struck the wrong chords, even rebelled at the sophomoric tone of the hilarity, denying the desired release and escape. The operations of gas bombing and flame-throwers he simply could not parody; he felt physically unable, incapable. He had seen the bloated faces and swollen lips, the bristling beards and moustaches in tragic similarity the puffing wind-gods on old maps.

Also, the violence done to horses was off limits to his mimetic manipulations; he'd seen the beautiful creatures panicked by detonations, racing aimlessly, grotesquely injured, one, he couldn't help from recalling, scratching forward on forelegs, dragging itself with a fractured spine. And, increasingly, the ever-younger soldiers had virtually sworn him to silence on their entry into victimhood; he had seen them marching to annihilation, wandering into death, oblivious to the concept of cover, deaf to the screeches of projectiles, blind to the trajectories of bombs, illiterates for whom the misreading of the moment meant instant destruction.

The longer he stayed in the war-zone, the more he seemed to run out of usable material for his pencil.

****

Dear Maud,

I love you and miss you so. I pray all is well. Lately we have been felling trees in a forest above the plain of combat, so you have little to fear in my case.

"Have I written to you about Lieutenant Ledebec's most recent, and most harrowing, adventure? The French Supreme Command had sent orders for a precipitate attack upon one zone, but these messages had been misinterpreted at the regimental HQs to be an attack on another. When, however, the dispatch reached the divisional HQ, it was understood to be a call for a general retreat. This, of course, was questioned, and subsequently re-interpreted to be a specific retreat in Ledebec's section, which, when it arrived finally at the front, was, once again, mistakenly but undeniably read as a command to attack—a meaning which, when rationally reconstructed, was not far from its original intent, although in an entirely different sector. I hope I haven't confused you, Dear.

At any rate, after a fiery speech in which he quoted Napoleon himself, Ledebec led a passionate raid on the target at the crack

237

of dawn, without any preliminary barrage. The suddenness of the attack caught the enemy unawares, at first, but they regrouped and flushed out their French attackers with a fresh phalanx that would have impressed Alexander himself. Men were cut down all around Ledebec, and he led the remnants in a full retreat. Under a withering fire, they leaped into a large shell-hole, in which they found several stretchers. In a moment of brilliant elan, Ledebec ordered his men, some to lie on the stretchers, others to carry them, and all to race backwards toward their own lines in an attempt to trick their enemy. This they attempted to do, with as much poise as possible, although some bearers were cut down, either by the wily enemy or by confused friendly fire, though there were always more to pick up the fallen stretchers and faux-wounded and press valiantly onward—or backward, if you will. Diving at last into their trenches, the supposed casualties shocked their comrades when, at once, they took up arms and defended their positions.

An amazing exploit, I'm sure you'll agree, Maud!

All my love!

Your Eros (Carl)

****

He awoke in the night suddenly. He'd been dreaming of an ill Gustav, a dream in which they had retraced the walk through the Hamburg wharves they'd taken years before, but, when they had crossed the bridge where the river split, the sick man had tried to throw himself over the parapet. Carl had exerted his last ounce of strength to hold him back while Gustav had pleaded to let him go, then cursed him.

They'd both collapsed, sitting on the pavement, breathless and exhausted.

"I'm only a burden to your mother!"

"You're the only one she has to hold onto."

"I'm only bringing her down!"

"Nonsense!"

"Carl, I'm dying! It'll only get worse for both of us."

"Dad, she wants to take care of you."

It took ten minutes for Carl to clear his mind of the nightmare. Then he couldn't help but lie awake in his bunk and think. Now he could see only the front that stretched below him every morning when he left his tent, the terrible front of war, bleak with ingrained, inveterate suffering. It struck him that the inescapable circularity seemed to be obvious only to him: the men going into battle were told that patriotism was the highest virtue, the Fatherland the highest ideal, an honor to die for; and those same men were told at the burials of their comrades that the deaths of their comrades made that Fatherland meaningful and worthy of their death-defying patriotism; and thus the burden weighed ever heavier on the men.

****

Dearest Maud,

I hope all is well, and if the total devotion of my thought toward you ensures it, then you are, even if I'm far away.

"Lately we have been disinfecting the trenches, a horrible but necessary chore, and I have a terrible headache from the chemicals, the worst in my life, but the job is finally over, thankfully, at least for a few days. Goodbye, vermin!

An interesting story I've heard recently, Maud, from our garrulous old-timers, had to do with issues surrounding the commingling of nations among the Entente. Once again, our narrators do not say how they came across their material, nor do I understand how the enmities between the French and Scottish originated. The fact that France has required other countries to

Richard Tres

come to its aid certainly has been a cause for tension on both sides, helped and helpers. French soldiers are well aware that they would have been bled dry had they been left to fend for themselves, and those coming from elsewhere would, no doubt, have been happier staying at home. Perhaps the French retort that at least they freed themselves of monarchy, and maybe some taunt is thrown about the uniqueness of the Scots' attire, although I hear that this is a matter of patriotic fervor every bit as much as the French fighting for their own soil.

At any rate, the story goes on that, at a tavern safely behind the lines, soldiers from each land were enjoying hospitality when one of the Frenchmen, having had too much to drink, started to make fun of the 'kilties,' as they are called. The tense back-and-forth told the hosts that they would soon have a destructive altercation on their hands if they didn't intervene, and so the most vociferous were tossed from the establishment, and a relative order prevailed. Each side, however, talked of revenge.

So, in the dark of night, after a skirmish particularly costly to the Scots, a few Frenchmen stealthily stripped the corpses of their kilts and proceeded to scatter them in areas considered off limits, especially around a building occupied by French women and known for surreptitious after-hours fraternizing. Subsequently, several groups of Scots, all of them members of the Black Watch, were interviewed by their superiors. Night guards were posted around the building in question.

You might have thought that the French were happy with this turn of events, but they weren't. For, inadvertently, they had also brought it to pass that they too were kept from visiting the popular spot. All of a sudden, the men felt like they were fighting on two fronts.

Now, one of the women there had many admirers, but she herself was particularly enamored of a member of the Indian army. This handsome Gorkha youth, of Nepalese extraction, was

240

The Man Without a Party

far and away Rene's favorite, in her eyes dashing both with and without his Indian uniform, and in spite of the guard, the lucky man was still able to sneak into the ménage and enjoy the ample gifts of his belle.

However, this state of affairs could not go on forever. The Gorkha participated in an extremely violent engagement in which his commander was slain. Evidently, when Gorkhas lose their leader, they have only one thing on their mind: attack. Forgetting all else, including their own safety, they rush forward en masse with their rifles ready at hand and, a weapon even more trusted by this race, their Bowie knives. I don't know how many of the enemy were killed before the last Gorkha fell, but every last one fought till his death, and their corpses littered the enemy trench. After the corpses were further disfigured, they were tossed over the rampart into no man's land, where the rats and birds had their turn. Before long, with gullets and chests exposed, the cadavers looked like a flock of plucked and sleeping turkeys.

Within a few days, her lover's absence told upon Rene. With her companions, she formed a plan as a result of which one of the Scots guards was lucky enough to be lured inside the abode of Eros, where, while he was busy, his boots, kilt and tartan were passed along to Rene, who donned them at once and set forth to the front line under cover of the dark. No sooner had she arrived when the sector she had happened upon came under attack by the Germans who, in a raid, were looking to kidnap a soldier for information. They never discovered that the prisoner they carried away was female, totally lacking in the intelligence they sought before, on their way back to their side, they were all cut down, including the heroic Rene.

In the morning, the amorous Scots guard made his way, naked, back to his camp, with some clever explaining to do.

Maud, I hope this silly story helps you pass the time, as it did me.

241

I think of you every moment.
Love, Carl

Carl was very undecided about sending this last composition to his dear wife. The last thing he wanted was to upset her. Thinking it over during a free and relatively quiet afternoon in the canteen, he shared it with some of his comrades in the hope of receiving some helpful advice. Before he knew it, the proposed missive was being passed around and opinions were coming at him like shrapnel from every direction. More than that, the men were looking at him as if he were suddenly a stranger, an alien, an enemy.

'Where did he get the idea?' one asked. 'Why did he write it, and what was the point?' put in another. 'Why couldn't he just write a normal letter to his wife, talking about the suffering and the boredom and the danger of their condition?' asked Johann, a thoughtful soldier. 'It wasn't hard staying away from the stuff the censors would nab you for. What was wrong with their own story, and what did this concoction have to do with their own experience of the war?' Worse still, 'what kind of wife did he have, such that she might like reading about Gorkhas and Scots, rather than a normal letter about good German soldiers?' added an even more pensive soldier, nicknamed 'Freud.'

More particularly, 'did they actually have such women as Rene on the other side?' a naïve adolescent wondered. Many of them had already fraternized with French women in the areas occupied by Germany, and they were not like Rene. 'Did he want to make his wife jealous?' a devoutly married man asked, looking worried. 'Didn't he think she was being faithful to him in his absence? And take out the interracial love theme!' advised a purity-in-blood-and-soil fanatic pan-German. The opinions seemed to be endless. 'Omit the references to carrion animals at the end!' 'Have the Indian die another way to break Rene's heart, like dysentery, or that strange new influenza that seemed so lethal.' 'And the kilts,' pointed out a graduate of a university: 'they had no point in the story. Were they supposed to just be a prop or, worse still, a symbol?'

Needless to say, Carl had more input that he ever could desire. He felt all this flood of response made it even harder for him to form a single decision. Part of him wanted to tear up the letter or, better still, burn it in a bonfire. Even Muller—during a lull in the shelling's percussive background *tutti*—showed up and threw in his two marks: 'Send it off to the propaganda magazine for German soldiers. Maybe they could use it.' But that wasn't the worst thing that happened.

Three soldiers, Potato, Amorph and Ajax sat at a table and passed it among themselves, grunting and shaking their heads. All of a sudden, Ajax leapt to his feet, knocking over his chair, drew out his Mauser, pointed it at the papers and pulled the trigger. Everyone in the canteen jumped at the explosion, hushed and stared, craning their necks in a flock toward the scene of the action. Potato had stuck his head forward so far that his eyes were just inches from the hole in the middle of the script, from the blackened edges of which smoke and the smell of cordite emanated to prickle the nostrils. Amorph, a dumbfounded expression on his face that surpassed everyone else's for its clueless, bovine quality, jumped up and looked along the barrel of the gun and the extended arm up to the head of the man, who still scowled at his innocuous target.

After a few moments of utter silence, Sergeant Muller broke the *tableau vivant* and approached Ajax, carefully removed the pistol from his inert hand, and escorted him silently from the room. Slowly, incrementally, the men came alive again, finished their beers, realized they had other things they had forgotten to do, and vacated the premises. Someone, on leaving, deposited the letter, such as it was, in front of Carl, who actually looked, from his frozen expression, as if he had drawn into a shell—this was his nickname among his fellow soldiers. Soon only one other man remained, a taciturn soldier who went to the table that had received the shot from Ajax's gun. He studied the hole in it and picked at the floor underneath until he had extricated the bullet. Then he came over to Carl's table, sat down across from him, and set the spent alloy on the wounded parchment between them. The drumroll of shelling on the horizon re-commenced, along with a menacing *pizzicato* of machine guns close-by; the lull was over.

'Red' was his nickname, given to him because he had been transferred from the Eastern front after the German-Soviet treaty, and, as with many of those soldiers, justly or not, it was assumed they had been tainted by their brush with the Bolsheviks. Carl did not know him well, and had seen no evidence of radical ideas, but had only noticed a sort of ponderousness to the stranger's movements along with a concomitant layer of weariness. Red scratched an ear and looked at Carl, and that glaze of heavy fatigue in his eyes seemed to spread toward our hero.

"You surprised me," Red finally offered.

Carl just looked at him.

"Not because of your being a writer. I already knew that. I've read some of your stuff."

Carl, in his overwhelmed state, could only open his hands as if to say, "And?"

"It's that you seem to have abandoned your pacifist tenets, or at least become ambivalent to them."

'*At least this was something different!*' Carl thought. If only he had more patience to listen to it! But too much had happened for him to receive the man's comment *aequo animo*. As if with a life of their own, his own words had passed the barrier of his teeth before he had considered them properly:

"Why should a communist care about what a pacifist thinks?"

Red smiled and nodded. Feeling a pain inside, Carl winced.

"I'm sorry," Carl added quickly. "That wasn't fair."

"Not at all," Red responded. "The question applies to me just as much as my moniker."

"But," Carl insisted, grimacing, "I spoke without knowing."

"Oh, I was a radical long before the Kaiser sent me to Russia. The war there just helped me hone my views to a fine point. If I thought it would advance the cause of the worker, I'd blow Muller's brains out, all the officers, yours too. Soldiers, turn your weapons on your officers! Trotsky says. But, in the present case, what would that accomplish? My death! The proletariat in Germany needs organization, not more shedding of blood."

"Well!" Carl seemed to be taking the man in whole for the first time.

"But to go back to your question," Red went on, shifting into a more comfortable position in his seat, "there's no reason why Marxists should ignore the views of pacifists, social democrats, or anarchists any more than they should ignore what capitalists think and say and do."

"I suppose so. My rather pedestrian explanation for what I've written is that it helps me deal with the utter hell of being here, a way to detach. A *pharmakon psukhake*, as our Greek teacher would have said back in the classroom."

Red gestured toward the papers. "But you've romanticized war. Isn't that a mortal sin for people like you?"

"Ah," Carl granted. "That's where my wife comes in. An even simpler explanation. I suppose the whole point is to soften it all up for her. Rhetorical effect. I heard it was an old Marxist strategy."

Red chuckled, shaking his head. "I thought that might be the answer. You have a reprieve this time. Just don't let the Alfred Frieds of the world see what you've done. They'll cast you from their cult out into the desert."

Carl laughed, scrunched the papers up in his hand—the bullet clattered back to the tabletop—and, after shaking his fist with them, he stuffed his boot with the offending missive.

"How about another beer?" Carl asked.

Red nodded. When Carl came back with the drinks, he asked, "So you'd kill me? Like some rat in no-man's-land?"

Red brought his right hand up in the shape of a gun. He pointed his index finger at Carl's forehead and pretended to pull a trigger. Carl noticed he was missing the tips of two fingers. "But not like a rat," he allowed. "Like a man."

Between sips, Carl asked, "And would you really try to shoot our leaders?"

"I told you under what conditions. Put bluntly, I have the courage of my convictions. That's why communists can only be pacifists in a relative sense. Brest-Litovsk won't last forever and, realize, it doesn't apply to the Whites. They're all targets, and the sooner dead, the better. But yes, if those bastards give you a gun, use it on them. Just don't be an unprincipled opportunist about it. It only messes things up in the long run. You know, for workers down the road."

"And do you really think about it when people like Muller are around?"

"Shooting them? At first, I did, but one grows used to carrying a weapon, and the novelty wears off, as I'm sure even you yourself have noticed, for all your peacemaking. The great 'if' is whether it can be scientifically shown that using that gun advances the cause of the proletariat one iota. That doesn't mean never, but it is a tough bridge to cross. A huge and forbidding *caveat*: let the shooter beware. But you, Saint Ossietzky, do you think about *not* using your weapon every time you have it in your possession?"

"Nope!" Carl replied, smiling. "I'm not one of *those*. I'll do whatever I can to get back home to Maud in one piece. What I want to stop are the things that get us this far. The mentality of belligerence."

"Good luck."

"Yeah. Well, I guess we'll both need all we can get of that."

"The shame is depending on mere luck to make the world a better place."

"Our condition."

"Not mine, if I can help it. By the way, where did your wife get that name?"

"British India. She says it's Tennyson's doing. Her aunt calls her Matilda. You're from…?"

"Saxony. Chemnitz. Factoryland, where labor issues are absorbed with Mother's milk."

"My father was, still *is*, I suppose, an old-style Social Democrat. Back in the day, he would have loved airing out his viewpoints with you, Red. But… by the way, what's your name?"

"Krause. Simon."

"Well, Simon," Carl explained, "when the party leadership supported our belligerent Kaiser, it just about killed my stepfather. Gustav's never been the same. I owe a lot to him, poor man. He saved my mother from total devastation after my father's death."

"It destroyed his party," Simon commented. "But finally, a true left has a chance to develop." He finished his beer, then added, in undertone: "If we can ever get our leaders out of prison."

"Good luck."

Two days later, Carl rewrote the entire letter and sent it off to Maud, altering the ending: Rene and her paramour escaped via a nocturnal ride on a stolen observation balloon.

****

When he arrived at home on leave, Carl went with Maud to his parents'. Gustav was ill with influenza. He lay sweating in bed; Carl held his hand. After a while, Rosalie and Maud left the bedroom; Carl heard them whispering in the kitchen.

The sick man shifted a little. When he finally took in Carl in his uniform, the eyes widened as if in fear.

"Father," Carl spoke gently.

Gustav struggled to speak. Son brought a glass of water to his lips. He sipped a bit, coughed, and started to form sounds, syllables.

"Carl. I…" The voice had become mainly aspirations. He tried clear his throat.

Carl swabbed the damp forehead with a rag.

"I…was…angry." Gustav paused, sighed with pain and effort.

"Yes, Father?"

"…statue…"

"You don't have to talk," answered Carl. "Rest." More water to open the congested passage.

"…Hau…Hau…Haupt…mahhhnn."

"Yes? Gerhardt Hauptmann, Father?"

A pause from the monumental effort.

"You took me to his play when I was a child." Carl tried to provide the words so that all Gustav needed to do was nod.

"…wrecked…I wrecked it."

"You wrecked it?"

"…angry…" He raised his hand, scratched the air in front of Carl's tunic.

"My uniform? You're angry at my uniform."

The old man frowned, gave his head an impatient toss. Carl leaned closer, waited.

Gustav was asleep.

All of a sudden, Carl felt a great weariness; he'd been traveling all night to get to Hamburg. He shuffled back to the kitchen and dropped into a chair.

"He was delirious," sighed Carl. "Mumbling something about being angry."

"Oh, yes," said Rosalie. Carl had never seen her eyes looking so exhausted. How she had aged! "He keeps talking about being angry at some Hauptmann statue and wrecking it."

"Was he working on something before he took sick?"

"Nothing here. And very little at all since the war came."

The next morning, Carl visited his parents' again; his father was sleeping soundly. Carl stayed awhile, then decided to go to Gustav's workshop. Nothing but rubbish on the floor in Gustav's area. Carl wandered around the open space. Finally, he brushed dust off the seat of an old chair and sat, staring at the pile of rubbish. Then he noticed some markings on the wood floor. He stood up, found a broom, and gently swept the dust and debris away. Several chalk drawings materialized at his feet, fragmented studies of anatomy, evidently male, some features distorted: broken limbs, a head smashed in. Carl started picking pieces out of the rubbish heap and looking for a matching drawing. There was a spot for just about every piece of stone above a certain size. He sat back down and looked at the shards of the aesthetic puzzle in front of him.

Before long, he rummaged in a drawer, found some scraps of paper and a stub of pencil, and started copying the lines of chalk, integrating the markings as much as possible into a semi-sensible whole: a man stooping forward at the waist, head bowed, apparently wearing a helmet with one side caved in; one arm with compound fracture, the other a stump; one leg, bent oddly, trailing the other. It would have been difficult, if not impossible, to keep such a statue balanced.

He wondered what this had to do with the dramatist Hauptmann, but then he remembered Gustav had told him, years before, that the playwright had tried to become a sculptor but had given up when his statue of a soldier had collapsed. What if, Carl asked himself, Gustav had tried to make intentional what had been an accident for Hauptmann? Carl tried again at assembling the broken pieces, but they never made up more than a jumbled mess. A far cry from the finished, symmetrical works Gustav was known for.

But still, was it in some way intended, the mess? Or was it just the result of his illness? Of his depressive state brought on by the political situation and the war? On the field of battle, Carl had seen so many men, soldiers, pitilessly torn apart, brutally dismembered, mercilessly broken up into fragments like these. Deliberately or not, Gustav had produced something that echoed every soldier's nightmares. But had he actually been trying to make a statue of what war does to men?

While puzzling over the mystery, Carl found an empty wooden box. He set the papers on the bottom, then carefully deposited the broken pieces in it. He left the box on his father's worktable. He decided that, although he was aware of artists who could have produced such a disturbing work, Gustav would have had to totally change his style, his entire artistic identity, to do so.

The next day, Gustav slid in and out of consciousness; he passed during the night. Carl stayed for the funeral, then returned to his regiment. He joined them in working on defensive fortifications that were part of what the soldiers were calling the Kriemhilde Line. With their proximity to the Argonne Forest, there was much talk of the newly arrived Americans, brought into the fray largely because of the dogged continuance of von Tirpitz' unlimited submarine attacks on neutral shipping. Had the tide of the war changed? Carl stared across the no-man's land toward the new and fresh enemy.

Dear Maud,

Hope all is well. Father's passing lies heavily upon me. I shall never stop feeling grateful to him for what he did for me and my mother. I think of the three of you every chance I get.

Many soldiers have fallen in the fighting for the Argonne Forest, but, according to the old-timers, an American soldier is glad not to be one of them. A Texan, named Casanova for his prowess with women, was saved from certain death, and I'll relate to you how it happened, along with the strange aftermath. He was hit in the head by a piece of shrapnel, but, luckily for him, the jagged projectile failed to pierce his helmet. Unluckily for him, however, the blow knocked him out cold, and he fell forward, lying spread-eagled in the dirt. Worse for him, his injury occurred at a critical moment in the conflict when a sudden barrage allowed those fleeing to take cover and then chase their foe. The Americans fled in retreat around and over Casanova until one of them, a giant from the state of Georgia, tripped over him and noticed some movement from the injured comrade. The giant, named Marcus, tossed Casanova over his shoulder like a pillow and, bullets whizzing past his ears, trudged back to his line in safety with his groggy burden flopping behind him.

As soon as he recovered consciousness, the Texan became obsessed with his oversized savior. He refrained from going as far as making himself a slave to the out-sized man, Marcus Giddes, but his obsession focused itself in one direction: to help his benefactor benefit from his own success with the ladies. Casanova—who seemed utterly incapable of wasting his time in executing sexual affairs—already had three girlfriends in tandem: a farm girl in one village, a barmaid in another, and a schoolteacher in a third. Casanova had Marcus meet all three and, playing Cupid, offered them to his newfound friend. The triple rejection stung, but, undeterred if somewhat insulted, the beneficiary pressed on in his mission. How could the man be so selective? What Casanova didn't know—would the knowledge have just challenged him more?—was that Marcus was not only a virgin but pathologically shy with women and prudishly embarrassed by the very presence of his private parts, much more any forces that lurked beneath them. Casanova, in truth, had been saved by his opposite.

Things went on in this fashion until Marcus, in a rare fit of rage after a skirmish with many American losses, slugged a stone wall and bruised his hand badly. Reluctantly, he went behind the line to a field hospital and immediately fell madly in love with one of the British nurses. Head over heels, he started composing passionate though chaste verses to his beloved. Edith was flattered with the attentions from her otherwise tongue-tied admirer, even if she realized the poems left much to be desired. And although usually she was no cold fish, and not infrequently unwilling to reciprocate the attentions of her virile patients during her rounds at night in order to ameliorate their condition, truth be told, she was a little frightened of the behemoth.

So when Casanova came to visit, it was easy, if painful, for Marcus to see that the Texan could easily have a fourth lover if he wanted; Rather uncharacteristically, Casanova refrained on this occasion. But, when he saw how easily Edith's head had been turned, Marcus was quietly outraged; not only had she fallen into disfavor in his eyes, but now Casanova was unwittingly transformed into a vicious schemer intent upon defiling the immaculate purity of ideal womankind.

Back at the front, Marcus' officers noticed an untoward change in him, a surliness which they decided to rehabilitate with the assignment of menial tasks; one was latrine duty. Marcus and his partner dug a new latrine, replaced the straddling boards

The Man Without a Party

from the old pit—now brimming with sewage—to the new, and commenced to fill in the former with rocks. When these were hard to find, the partner suggested they just cover the stinking hole with dirt; this they did. It was only later that Marcus realized the potential repercussions of their laziness.

Later, in the dark of night, after a festive time at one of the hospitable villages, as Casanova made his way back to camp, Marcus lay waiting. He met his friend and pretended to be on his way to the latrine. Casanova said he would join him, But the suddenly crafty Marcus led him to the old pit, not the new, and, when there, knocked Casanova on the head. The amorous youth fell headlong into the sucking, excremental quicksand of the old latrine with barely a sound and sank like a stone; one might even say, facetiously of course, that he had found a new home. Marcus returned to his tent and, the next day, acted just as startled as his comrades when Casanova was absent for roll call. Had the confirmed lover of women deserted with some damsel? And Marcus looked just as shocked as they when, some days later, Casanova's boot was noticed sticking out of the muck, now hardened by evaporation. The formerly simple Southerner proceeded to feign grief, putting on quite a show for all to see, especially those officers assigned to investigate the death.

Dear Maud, I apologize for the improprieties I have taken in articulating this noxious tale. Please forgive me.

All my love, Carl

He sent the letter off without consulting his mates. Three days later, Carl stepped on a piece of shrapnel; it went through his boot. After the accident, he was transported to a field hospital. Then he was granted leave for healing when the wound became infected.

****

Carl was even more glad than usual to get away from the deteriorating situation and the sour morale at the front. After a week of convalescence, though, he was already back on a train to the front. He was asleep, his head rolling around on the seatback when the train came to a sudden, screeching halt. Everyone in the car jumped up and looked at the windows: the blackness of night. Someone craned out a head.

"There's flames up ahead!"

Carl climbed out with some others and walked toward the fire up the tracks. Sparks from what appeared to be a bonfire straight ahead showered the dark sky. As they approached, the soldiers saw it was a stack of railroad ties that was burning; they had been laid directly across the tracks. Armed men stood around, silhouetted by the flames. Illuminated faces awaited them.

One of their group passed along what had been heard: "You hear that? The war is over!"

"Armistice? You're crazy!"

Finally, the matter was clarified: the men up ahead were deserters.

"They say they won't let the train advance!"

After some shouts and grumbling, someone blurted, "They want us to be lined up and shot just like them!"

Carl pictured himself before a firing squad. He pushed forward and stood with the men in front facing the others.

"Will you write us a note so we have something to show for why we didn't go back?"

Scornful laughter.

"Comrades!" shouted one of the deserters. "There's no joke! We'll shoot you if you try to go on."

"To hell with the Kaiser's war!" yelled another.

Yet another raised his rifle and screamed, "We're through dying for Luddendorf!"

Behind him, a piece of wood emitted some gas with a pop. Several men jumped. This time, uneasy laughter.

"Fuck the monarchy!"

"Down with Hindenburg and the Kaiser!"

A voice from behind Carl, "Well, the train's kaputt! The engineers have gone off!"

Carl turned and walked back to the train; he'd heard enough. He retrieved his bag and started walking along the tracks to the station they'd just passed. He soon found that he was joined by others. At the first town, there was turmoil. Soldiers were pouring in, all accommodations already taken. He slept in a park with others. The next day, there was a stream of men, trudging along the tracks. Carl joined them. When they finally found a train going east, they saw it was full and overflowing, with some soldiers sitting on the tops of cars.

He kept walking, and the crowd kept growing. Three days later, he was home in Hamburg again.

Chapter Fifteen
PRESENT

And they didn't read that when, on April 4, 1933, the Apostolic Nuncio to Germany, Cesare Orsenigo, received a missive from Pope Pius XI requesting he "look into whether and how it might be possible to become involved" in helping victims of Nazi persecution, he replied that any intervention was inadvisable because it would be seen as "a protest against that government's law." Nor could they read about the turmoil caused by Hitler's imposition of Nazi Ludwig Muller as Bishop of the newly formed Realm Church, the government's attempt to coordinate all 28 regional Protestant sects in the country, with the intent, among other things, of dejudifying the bible by jettisoning the Old Testament from it. Nor could they read how former U-boat captain Martin Niemoller joined Karl Barth, Hans Ehrenburg and Dietrich Bonhoeffer in founding the Confessing Church, in opposition to the Nazification of Germany's Protestantism, or how Karl Fritz, outspoken editor of *The Straight Path*, a Catholic paper, was arrested and hustled off to Dachau, where he soon died. Nor that the Catholic politician, Erich Klausener, was assassinated on the Night of the Long Knives after criticizing Nazi repression; or that his assassin was promoted to Assault Unit Leader in the SS.

Ironically, though publication of an anti-Realm Church petition by Confessing Church pastors and laity was suppressed in Germany, it somehow found its way to foreign presses. As a result, the Gestapo decided to investigate this act as national treason and sent Dr. Friedrich Weissler, one of its authors—and a Jew baptized into the Protestant Church as a child—to Sachsenhausen, where he died within days of his arrival.

****

Maud visited Rosalinde just before she left England. The visit was difficult from the very beginning. When she suggested they walk the grounds, Rosalinde said something that made Maud's chest tighten.

"Mother, I'm missing class!"

Maud stood, trying to unlock her jaw. 'Be the adult,' she coached herself.

"Rosa, I'm going back home. I don't know when we'll see each other again."

"You don't understand!" Rosalinde exclaimed. "I'm making a presentation to the class. They're waiting for me!"

Dramatically sighing, Maud stared up at the ceiling of the foyer of the building. All Maud could do was stare.

"It's a play, Mother," her daughter went on. "I'm in charge."

Maud, still speechless, raised her arm toward the adjoining room. "Can we at least sit in here and talk for a bit?"

Rosalinde heaved another sigh. When her mother took a step toward the room, she stomped around her and preceded her through the doorway.

When they sat, Maud said, "Honey, I'm so glad to hear of what you're doing here!"

It didn't work. The girl folded her arms and snapped her lips shut.

"What's the play?"

"It's a German one. I picked it."

"That's wonderful, Rosa."

The reply was *sotto voce*, with the speaker's eyes averted, climbing the wall: "Oh, stop pretending to care!"

257

Maud felt punched in the heart. Should she ignore the outrageous comment? But before she could answer her own question, she burst into tears.

Rosalinde let her cry, staring at the top of her mother's head with an expression, not of empathy, regret or guilt, but of scorn, as if Maud's crying were a pretense to prolong Rosalinde's absence form class. Then the girl got an idea.

As Maud dabbed her eyes with a handkerchief, Rosalinde said, "I'm using something you did to me in a scene."

Maud sniffed. "Something I did to you?"

"When you hit me on the arm with a hanger."

"I hit—?"

"Don't deny it, Mother. You hit me right here." She raised her left arm and squeezed it above the elbow. "I had a welt for a week."

Maud stared in horror at the person to whom she had given birth. She shook her head as if to clear her brain. Then, making a decision, she threw the handkerchief into her purse and got up from the chair. She walked out of the room and out of the building.

Rosalinde stood and took a step toward her, then stopped. She watched her mother depart. Then, slowly, she turned toward the stairway and started up the stairs.

She hadn't had time enough to tell her mother that she had cast herself in the role of the character wielding the weapon.

Maud left England for the last time the next day.

****

Stepping gingerly in their wood-soled shoes, they were marched out to the edge of the peat field. It seemed as endless as the overcast sky. When they arrived, they were handed shovels and told to dig.

And so they would dig the peat. And dig. And dig.
But would the digging crush them?
Would the stinking peat bury them?
Crowned with wispy fog, the bog stretched to the horizon.
And they started digging.

****

When his play had closed, Toller decided he had to visit
Ossietzky's daughter at the new school. He had bad news for her:
he couldn't continue helping to pay for her tuition. Things for
him were going as well as could be expected but, if funds didn't
start coming from elsewhere, he would be pinched. Belatedly, he
decided he'd donated too much to the cause in Spain. It wasn't
going so well there, either.

Rosalinde, walking between classes, happened to see him
stepping out of the car he had borrowed. She ran from the
window and met him at the entrance. They found a room and sat.

"How are things?"

"Much better, thank you. I have friends here."

"Wonderful," said Ernst, feeling a pain inside; she would have
to leave them.

"And wait till you hear this, Mr. Toller: the German class is
putting on one of your plays. Just selections, but—"

"You're taking German here?"

"No, but others are. The teacher asked me to assist with the
class. And then I suggested this play—"

"Really? How did you know about it?"

She shifted her shoulders awkwardly. "I've been reading your
writings."

"I'm flattered! Which one are you, uh, doing?"

"*Blind Goddess*. The teacher let me pick."

"That's…" Toller fairly choked. "That's ambitious!"

"We're just starting small, like little skits in the classroom."

"Well, I'll have to talk to my agent," he joked. "Royalties, you know."

The girl looked down. "Oh, I didn't know."

He patted her hand. "Miss von Ossietzky, I'm only joking."

Her excitement immediately returned. She'd been just as primed for quick elation as for sudden disappointment. Adolescent moods!

"Maybe we will make some money with it," she went on. "We could present it to the parents and families, the community—"

"As I say, I'm quite flattered."

He knew, with the reference to money, that this was the time to bring up the bad news, but he saw something that drew his attention.

"What's that in your hand?"

She held up a lump of metal. "Oh, it's just my good luck charm."

He took it. "I've seen this before."

"It was… is, Dad's. I brought it when I left Germany."

Toller turned it over in his hands and laughed. It was an ashtray, still covered in soot, in the shape of a frog, jaws opened grotesquely wide enough to receive not only ashes and matches and butts, but the burning ends of cigarettes and cigars as well. "It even smells of your father!" He didn't need to bring it any closer to his nose to make that determination. "Now I know why I was suspecting you of sneaking smokes behind buildings!"

She laughed and took back the memento. "No, not me!"

"Did you have this with you the first time I visited?"

Rosalinde nodded. "It was the only thing small enough for me to pack that I wanted."

He kept turning the object over in his hands. "Yes," he said, looking at the piece of metal as if to assess it, "your father is truly an amazing man!"

As soon as the words were out of his mouth, he panicked: he couldn't remember whether he'd used past or present tense. Had he said *was*? He stared at the girl to see her reaction. She was just nodding with a serious look, and he decided he had not committed the *faux pas*. But, damn! That he couldn't remember for sure what he had said a second ago! The aging brain was already misfiring! Who had said it: 'Of all the things to befall a man, growing old was the most unexpected'?

After a while, Toller rose and said, "Well, I should let you get back to your German studies." They hugged at the door, then he added, "I need to say a few words to your headmaster. You go on back, now, and I'll visit soon."

Thanking him for everything, she planted a kiss on his cheek and ran up the long staircase. Toller went to go begging on the girl's behalf with the man in charge. He was mentally making a list of British *vip*s he knew to support his petition.

Chapter Sixteen
PAST

"Why are you hungry? *Why are you hungry?*" Carl shouted from a raised platform over the heads of the small crowd assembled in Hayns Park in Hamburg. "We Germans have been deceived! Our faithful leaders have led us astray. Oh, how far astray! But you can mislead through simple incompetence; that is a straightforward fault. Citizens, we were lied to! Mendacity is a devious moral vice and an intentional misdeed. They told us we were justified to attack our neighbors. They ordered us to invade neutral Belgium. And why? 'A presence on the sea was needed to deny England its nefarious stranglehold on the throat of German shipping.' But did this despicable lie allow Germany to perpetrate war crimes on non-belligerents?

"They gave us many reasons. Von Tirpitz had built his fleet. But, Citizens, what good was it? After the Jutland fiasco, the expensive armada languished in port, useless, the shiny ships worth millions of your hard-earned marks rusting away. We have heard already from the sailors of Kiel what they had to do to prevent their insane commanders' suicide mission: a vain and self-destructive attempt to rationalize the expenditure of so many funds, so much of our sweat and labor and hunger. To keep the Imperial regatta out of the hands of our nefarious enemies! Your sacrifices, Citizens! Your country's taxes at work! Those ships are why you had your kohlrabi and rutabaga winters! The Germans on the home front have bitterly learned how to perfect turnip cuisine!

"But finally, it's not about the blunders of a Kaiser or a von Tirpitz, a Hindenburg or a Luddendorf. We all have blundered!

War itself is the greatest of all blunders. And that is why I say these sailors showed more sense, and much more courage, by denying their maniacal superiors their death wish. They rebelled against their rebellious superiors, and how were they rewarded? *They* were branded the traitors, not their commanders! They, who had languished for years with the superfluous fleet, they realized the suicidal folly of the orders they'd been given, and they were punished for doing the right thing. No reward for the heroes, my countrymen! Yet instead, they inadvertently ignited a movement that still spreads, from sea through countryside to the cities, on its way to Berlin!

"And where have our belligerent leaders gone? Where is the Kaiser? Absconded to a foreign country with his corrupt and degenerate family! Where is Hindenburg? The man whose birthday you celebrated by offering up your silverware, your jewelry? Where is Ludendorff, who somehow was given dictatorial power over all of us? Where are the murderers of our youth, the ones who put us through so much suffering, who have ruined Germany and its name before all the world? Under what slimy rock do they hide, cringing from your worthy revenge?

"But I am not here to stir you up for revenge, fellow Citizens, no matter how just that vengeance would be. Yes, even though I might have fallen in battle with my comrades, I harbor no desire to lash out against the perpetrators. Yes, I stood in the line of fire for God, king and country, but I know that violence breeds violence. I stand here before you calling on a new time to begin, a new age to dawn in our hearts, one that buries the sword forever and defuses the bomb for once and for all. Let the ships of war rust, Citizens! Instead of learning war, let us learn peace. Too, too many have died not to try a new and different path.

"Let us study the ways of peace, fellow Citizens. And yet, I remember that we wanted peace before. What happened? Our Kaiser pledged himself to peace. But how? With hollow pledges,

Countrymen. While he pledged peace, he prepared for war. Just like our neighbors, we readied ourselves for war. The tragic, foolhardy, and costly contradiction was seen by many, both here and abroad, but the abolitionists of war and weapons were scoffed at, called fools, disregarded, even jailed. Will that happen again, Citizens? Or will we listen, finally, and, at last, will we hearken to the eternal wisdom of the evangelists of peace? Before, the warmongers had their way. We see their results! But will we let them have their way again?"

The first time Carl gave this speech, pensive silence; the second, some nasty heckling; the third, he was pelted with smut. And, driven off the dais and out of the park, he was never able to finish the fourth recitation. From that point on, the former soldier had to be wary of where he went and who was behind him. He put in his hours at the Hamburg office of the German Peace Society and published articles articulating the nurturing of a peace mentality.

But then, something had changed. Sailors from Kiel had started to appear on the streets and parks, and they had given their own speeches and posted their own notices. Carl noticed the sailors accompanying police on patrol, assisting in the accommodating and provisioning of other returning soldiers, distributing food. After listening to one of the speeches from a sailor, a raw outburst that reminded him of 'Red' Krause, Carl asked if he could add some words and was invited up the steps. He looked down on the group of about thirty and delivered the talk he had before, updating his message to include recent developments in the city. Before he had finished, he was interrupted by a voice from below.

But it wasn't a heckler; it was the very man who had given way to him. The sailor, standing in the crowd, turned among them and yelled, "This is the typical speech of a pacifist! Join in with him, and, the next time there is a hard decision to make, you will be caving in like him!" He made his way back up the stairs and stood next to Carl.

"This man will never defend you when you are attacked by your enemies! When you look for someone to protect you, you won't find him!"

"That's not true!" Carl shouted back. "But there are other solutions than violence. We've both just seen…"

And so it went on, back and forth, with the dispute between the sailor and Carl punctuated by shouts from the crowd. After a while, the audience started breaking up. Carl shook hands with the man and invited him to visit the Peace Society office.

That night, as he lay in bed, he kept Maud awake, going over the encounter.

"Isn't it interesting!" she said at last. "How ironic!"

"What do you mean?"

"No one attacked you from the other side."

"What? Say that again."

She laughed. "You didn't have any hecklers from the right."

"My God! You're right! I hadn't even noticed."

"Maybe a change of direction has finally come."

They lay for a while, staring up into the darkness above them. Then Maud, more quietly this time, asked, "What would you do?"

Carl yawned. "When?"

"If members of your peace group *were* attacked?"

Carl sniffed. "I'd defend them, of course! And myself. I'm not a 'Saint Francis' pacifist, and, besides, I've just spent over a year learning about how to handle weapons in defense of myself and my comrades."

"But," she went on, suddenly seeming very awake, "what if it was the police who were doing the attacking? Your former 'comrades.'"

He snorted. "Maud, the police aren't my comrades."

"Okay. The 'Red Guards,' then? People you wouldn't expect to attack you, but people with some authority."

Carl gritted his teeth in the dark. "Okay. What would *you* do?"

"If I had a gun, I'd shoot, of course," she replied. "I'm a suffragist first, a pacifist second. And, while it would take a lot to make me a militant suffragist, I wouldn't categorically rule violence out just based on principles. You see, I suppose that, at some point, I'd be willing to die, and kill, to win for my sex the power they should have always had, the power it looks like we might finally get in this disgusting country, if this revolution gets anywhere. I always try to keep in mind the wisdom of the Wife of Bath.

"So," she continued, "my peaceful ex-warrior, have you thought about what you'd do if, not the enemy, but the new powers that are stepping up went after your pacifists? Would you fight against them in the streets? It's one thing to oppose the Kaiser on paper and in court and then find a way to survive his bloodthirsty machinations. But it would be quite another if, as it's looking, Germans finally gain democracy and *actually chose* to wage war, against its perceived enemies, intestine or external. How would *that* affect your stance?" This last thrust came right before a luxurious, operatic yawn. "Oh, I'm so fatigued!"

Carl's speechlessness was like a slap in the face to him; he had become so voluble lately, even glib. He kept staring toward the hidden ceiling, desperately trying to form a response. Finally, after fifteen minutes, he whispered, "Maud?

"Maud?" he repeated. Eyes closed, his wife was breathing the breath of the angelic dreamer. In asking him one question, his wife had given him a bundle.

Germany would have a new government; the victorious countries were demanding it before negotiating any treaty, before ending their lethal blockade. But what kind of government? How radical would the changes be?

Would he approve of the results?

What role would he, should he, Carl, take beyond his present one?

How far would the government move left?

What would the conservatives and moderates do? Who would take the lead, and how would the followers follow?

Would the people take over? Would there be war trials? Generals in the dock? If so, who would the judges be? Certainly not the Kaiser's chosen! But how could the imperial judges be removed? And if the imperial courts were abolished, what would they be replaced by?

How would law and order be redefined?

A new constitution would have to be written!

Would a people's court rule, as in the French Revolution? Or with soviets of workers, like the Bolsheviks?

It occurred to him that Caesar never died in acts one or five of the play. How would anyone know *when* a revolution had ended?

And if the officers went to prison, what would happen to the army? Carl pictured Muller behind bars, squinting through his monocle, mustache quivering. The man had been fair to him, almost paternal. At the time, Carl had thoroughly disapproved of him; now, he knew, things could have been quite different. How far had the man gone in actually protecting Carl?

What role would the Entente have? Would they simply take over? What would they do to the military, the Prussian core of the German state?

But if the army wasn't dismantled, how could a new government succeed? What would happen to Germany's unique, imbalanced relation of the states and electorate? All these impasses would have to somehow be worked out! It was as if an abyss had opened before Carl. Every whisker on his face seemed to stand out from the others; he could feel each one.

The Germans had been led to expect annexations. Now, to the west, France would do its best to have its way, especially with the industrial cities. To the east, there were virtually no borders anymore. What would be done with Poland, where many Germans lived? Where would Russia end? How could a country exist without frontiers?

What would happen to the Kaiser's schools and teachers? Education! Suddenly, he felt a wave pass through his body. Maybe this was where Carl could act, to *counter*-act the Kaiser's pedagogy of military imperialism. The tail had been wagging the dog long enough. Pacifism would be strongest when it started with the teaching and molding of children. No one was born a belligerent; it was a learned trait. And, if it was learned, a change in the process of acculturation would hopefully change the finished product.

How…?

The next day, he and Maud both noticed the appearance of red flags, of red armbands on the patrolling sailors and soldiers, more speakers, more posters denouncing monarchy and militarism. And the sea tide seemed to strengthen each day. 'Red guards,' they were called. They infiltrated the administration of the city. Evidently, other cities had anticipated Hamburg in the movement left. A sheet printed on red paper was disseminated listing other places: Hanover, Bremen, Lubeck.

But as Carl worked on his next speech and article, he noticed another change around him: when things broke down, the movement toward repair slowed; foodstuffs were slower appearing; distribution lagged. People started to complain.

****

"The road to a new democratic republic is long," shouted Carl, "and as we here in Hamburg are already seeing, it will be rocky as well." It was a cold morning in a city park, where the usual thirty or so had gathered in the crisp, clear air. "Our logistical problems will be exacerbated while we grow accustomed to new modes of doing things, in everyday matters and deeper, more profound ones, like how we go about communicating with each other.

"Those opposed to a republic have already started their attack, both verbal and, especially in Berlin, violent. As there is absolutely no excuse for violence, I will confine myself to refuting false *claims* coming from the reaction. They have said and, no doubt, will continue to repeat, that this unfamiliar mode of government has been foisted upon us, that the only way of rule appropriate to Germans is authoritarian. It is not enough for me to say in response that we have heard the post-1870 message of imperialism; it has spoken; we have seen its tragic results.

"But to simply focus on our present injuries would allow the all-too-ready historians of empire to revise our liberal tradition and obliterate the, yes, specifically-German yearning for freedom, a yearning we hear in the emancipating words of Luther, Leibniz, Kant and Hegel, the searching, soaring strains of Goethe, Schiller, Schubert and Beethoven, as well as in the scientific breakthroughs of Copernicus, Kepler, Planck, Einstein, Herschel, Helmholtz, Hertz and so on, Germans of genius who have loosened all mankind from the shackles of ignorance. Our culture, our traditions, are not merely political, and they are certainly not exclusively military. The message of German modernism is defiantly and spiritually liberating.

"And we don't have to look that far back to find the roots of our healthy radicalism. Were the strikes in January foisted upon us from without or within?"

"Within!"

"Have the many mass demonstrations since then been fomented by foreigners?"

"NO!"

"Was the naval mutiny in Kiel caused by alien influence?"

"NO!"

"No, Citizens! Our starving multitudes have been driven by their own leaders to say at last, 'Enough!'

"And so, when we see our defeated soldiers returning, when we see the members of foreign armies in our occupied zones, we must make a special effort to realize that it is the culture of war that was foisted upon us by imperial leaders, that the rule of weapons was something imposed and imported from within by a truculent Prussian state no more genuinely German than Agamemnon's regime typifies what is best about the ancient Greece of Socrates, Plato and Aristotle, or the Crusades the Beatitudes of Christ. Regrettably, I myself was a soldier once, serving at the front at the command of our Kaiser, and I saw how my comrades were dehumanized long before the enemy appeared on the horizon. I am here to tell you that all soldiers are victims."

Here, Carl gestured to a woman in the growing crowd. He beckoned her forward. She came to the front line carrying a child.

"Can you see this infant? A beautiful baby! Now, if you will, imagine this child wearing a soldier's uniform. A ridiculous image! But why? My countrymen! No one is born a soldier! They are made! But how? That is the question we have to answer, Citizens! What is it that turns this blessed and peaceful baby into a human who wants to kill his brother? What evil magic can transform the sacred and innocent into the dangerous and destructive? Some might answer: the social virtue of patriotism itself. I want to resist this conclusion. Perhaps there are two kinds of patriotism. For, long before the virtue of patriotism has metamorphosed into a lethal machine of war, certain propagandistic processes have been at work.

"In order for the infant to become a soldier, patriotism itself must be twisted into such an ugly shape by militaristic lies that it would not recognize itself in a mirror. Healthy, peaceful patriotism would shrink back from that twisted image engendered by the war press. People will tell you that love of country and willingness to kill are one and the same, but don't let them get away with it. No, Citizens! Democracy has not been foisted upon us. But something else has: the condition of living in the shadow of the Prussian sword. Whether our new government lives or dies depends on our leaders' abilities in lifting this darkly decorated shade from over us. Rather than work against this endeavor, let us support them in accomplishing this enlightening and democratic task. Thank you for your attention."

He received applause, but the grumblings continued. Windows were smashed. A food distribution center was broken into and ransacked. Police accompanied by Red Guards were attacked with rocks. And when firefighters did not appear soon enough at a blaze, demonstrators marched to the station in protest.

****

Late one afternoon, he arrived home to find Maud sitting on the couch with Sophie. They were both crying.

"What is it?" he asked.

"The funeral," Maud replied. When she saw his blank look, she added, more sharply, "Sophie's friend, Ellen! I told you this morning."

"Yes! Yes! I'm so sorry."

"It was so sad," wept Sophie, dabbing her eyes.

"She leaves four children," Maud explained.

"Hans is in no condition to care for them properly," Sophie asserted.

They were looking at snapshots from a program. They made room for Carl between them on the couch.

"She's young," said Carl.

"Just 29."

"I forgot. What did she—"

"The influenza."

A beautiful family.

"Wait!"

"What is it?"

"I know this man," said Carl.

"I don't think you've met—"

"I'm sure of it. But where?"

"He's quite famous. Perhaps—"

"That's it! I remember now. A talk I was giving at the beginning of the war, long before they took me. I was being heckled by a man in uniform. He was yelling that I didn't know anything of what I was talking about because I wasn't a soldier. I'd heard that sort of garbage before. but people were starting to walk away when this man, here in the picture, spoke out. He was also in uniform, with insignia, and shouted that no, I was right in everything I said."

Carl smoothed over the image with his thumb.

"What happened?" asked Sophie.

"It saved my talk. They argued for a while, people came back, more joined in, and this man hounded the heckler away. That's the last I saw of them, walking off and arguing with each other."

"He's Hans Paasche, the son of the vice-president!"

"I never got to thank him."

"Well, he was just released from a sanatorium in Berlin where they stuck him for opposing the war while in uniform."

"Yes, I know about the Paasches. I just didn't know it was this man."

"The revolutionaries freed him, and he started leading a workers' council, much to his father's dismay, I'm sure."

"But evidently he was too radical for some," Maud added. "Wanted a people's court to go after the military leaders, so the moderates sent him packing. And then Ellen became sick."

****

"How can we raise our children so they don't become killing machines?" Carl asked the crowd in the park. "How will we help the next generation to embrace the coming democracy, to support it and to build it, to love it and to reject what its detractors are saying?"

He stared at the faces below him. Had he started a thought in them?

"If you will, for just a moment, close your eyes. What do you see? A blank. The newborn has been called a blank slate, a *tabula rasa*. How does that innocent and needy blankness become a victimized victimizer who marches jack-booted over the mangled corpses of comrade and foe alike? If we could locate and identify the turning points, perhaps we could change them. Citizens, perhaps we could educate the young to face conflict in a different way, to resolve it, to transform it. So that the child of peace can become the man of peace."

He paused and knew that he was lost. He stuffed the script in the pocket of his jacket, and he decided he would do something he had promised himself he would never do: speak unscripted.

"I apologize, Citizens, but I've decided that I can't go on without speaking on the recent events in Berlin. You all know about them, and they touch upon my subject too closely for me to ignore them here and now. What does the raising of children have to do with what has happened in our capital? I shall try to say.

"They have killed the leaders of our third revolution. Should I say 'executed'? 'Murdered'? I'll leave that for you to decide.

273

The Social Democrats have slain the communists Liebknecht and Luxembourg. To protect democracy, they claim, they turned artillery upon sailors who carried white flags, asking for their back pay. But what was so unacceptable about the workers' and soldiers' and sailors' councils? Who decided they suddenly had to be disenfranchised, destroyed? Why was the movement of the people curtailed in this shameful, bloody way? Has Ebert made a backroom deal with von Hindenburg and the other war criminals? Why has Scheidemann betrayed his own proclamation of a German republic? How could Noske, a Social Democrat, gun down other Social Democrats and turn his artillery on the naval heroes of Kiel?

"So many dead. So many questions. How far have we strayed from the euphoria of November? How long do our leaders think the people can continue to be deceived?"

"Save you energy, Mate!" someone yelled.

Carl waited, caught his breath.

"I know you mean well," the voice went on, "but you don't know what's happened yet. So save your breath."

Just when he saw the man who was shouting at him, another voice burst forth. "He's trying to tell you about the capitulation of the Red Guards here in Hamburg."

Carl turned his head toward the new voice.

"What are you saying?" Carl asked.

"It's all over here. They've given power back to the bureaucrats, the Kaiser's men."

Carl practically screamed. "Don't tell me they're bringing the Kaiser back!"

"Not that bad. It's just that these radicals don't know shit about getting things done. So they've given up. The revolution in Hamburg has failed without a drop of blood."

Carl opened his mouth, closed it, and looked around.

"I suggest we march to the assembly hall and ask some questions."

"I'm with you!"

About half the crowd took off toward the center of the city. When they got there, they found the doors locked. The motley group broke up.

If the revolution was an unfolding blossom, Carl speculated on his way home, its flower had shriveled on the stem. Seeds of progress had fallen on the soil of defeatism; the barely germinated plant had withered in its infancy.

At home, there was a letter on the German Peace Society letterhead waiting for him:

> *Dear Mr. Ossietzky:*
>
> *We at the German Peace Society have been impressed from the start with your brilliant and tireless work for pacifism in general and the GPS in particular. Your speeches and articles from Hamburg have made waves throughout the country and, now, at this crucial time, we are calling you to come to the capital and take up work as the Secretary of the GPS. Berlin needs you at this critical juncture.*
>
> *Sincerely,*
> *Ludwig Quidde*
> *President, GPS"*

Richard Tres

Chapter Seventeen
PRESENT

With very little to read that might contradict Hitler's words, in 1933, the German people heard The Leader say, *"You are not second-class, even if the world wishes it so a thousand times over. You are not of lesser value, of lesser significance. German people, remember what you are, remember your past and the accomplishments of your fathers, of your very own generation! Forget fourteen years of disintegration, and rise to two thousand years of German history! We have called out to you this way, my fellow-countrymen throughout Germany, from the first day onwards to instill in all of you this conviction from a feeling of inner solidarity: Germans! You are a strong people if you will yourself to be strong! The millions who are demonstrating in Germany today will return home with a feeling of a newly won inner power and unity. I know, my comrades, that tomorrow your tread will be firmer again than it was yesterday. For all of us feel it: today it may be possible to rape the nation, to put it in chains— but it is no longer possible to break or humiliate it! Thus it is also our desire, on this day, to fortify the confidence not only in yourself, German people, no, but the confidence in your government, too, which feels bound to you, which belongs to you, which fights with you for your life, which has no other purpose but to make you, German people, free and happy once more."*

There were no criticisms of these words in print for the German people to read, nor of his action on the day after he said these words, when all trade unions were banned, replaced by the government-controlled German Workers' Front.

276

The Man Without a Party

And a month later, in a speech at the University of Marburg, Vice-Chancellor Franz von Papen uttered the following: "The function of the press should be to inform the government where deficiencies have crept in, where corruption has settled, where serious mistakes are being made, where unsuitable men are in the wrong positions, and where transgressions are committed against the spirit of the German revolution. An anonymous or secret news service, no matter how well organized, can never be a substitute for this responsibility of the press... If other countries claim that freedom has died in Germany, then the openness of my remarks should instruct them that the German government can afford to allow a discussion of the burning questions of the nation." Unfortunately, the soon-to-resign Vice-Chancellor over-spoke concerning the "openness" of his speech, as it was almost entirely suppressed from print, and very few Germans encountered it. If public discourse in the country wasn't moribund, it was virtually bankrupt.

****

As the prisoners marched toward their task, they carried spades on their shoulders like rifles and sang.

"Soldiers of the moor we are
Lifting shovels for the peat.
Soldiers of the moor we are
Lifting shovels for the peat."

Carl had never heard the dirge before. He looked at the man next to him. "It was made by men from a nearby camp," the man explained, "after singing *The International* was forbidden. And *The Marseillaise*."

"Whichever way the eye can see
Only peat and heath can flourish,

Not one bird sits in a tree,
Nothing for the oak to nourish.

"Here upon this barren marsh
Stands the place we call our nest,
Fenced in wire barbed and harsh,
Far from joy and far from jest.

"Marching columns in the morn,
Toward the moor we start our toil,
Branded by the sun, forlorn
But hoping we can find home soil.

"And instead we have a guard
To show us we will lose our life
If we venture from this yard
Attempting to return to wife.

"And yet for us there's no complaining
We hope one day to gladly sing,
'On the moor we're done with straining,
Coming home is everything!'"

Carl found himself singing along to the refrain.

"Soldiers of the moor we are
Lifting shovels for the peat.
Soldiers of the moor we are
Lifting shovels for the peat."

But then Carl noticed something and asked, "Why are the guards singing?"

"They must think they're moor soldiers too."

Carl smirked.

"Or maybe they just like the song," the man added.

And then the men started to sing in chorus over, and over, until they arrived at the worksite.

****

Sophie opened the door.

"You made it!" she shouted. Maud dropped her suitcases and they immediately hugged, a long embrace, during which they had time to cry and recover.

Sophie carried the bags inside her home, the one she'd grown up in, and they sat in the parlor, spending the next three hours catching up on life.

But Sophie didn't tell Maud everything.

****

Every few months, on an afternoon after their back-breaking labor on the marsh, the five or six Jehovah's Witnesses in the camp were rounded up and marched to the HQ. Being 'voluntary' inmates due to their religious beliefs, they were each encouraged to sign a recantation.

Whoever signed could go free.

Over the time Carl had been at Esterwegen, two had signed.

One particular afternoon, when they came out of the building, the JWs were in a different sort of mood, lighter, uncharacteristic. They smilingly pushed each other, exhibiting a rare kind of jovial scorn, like close team members joshing each other as they left the field of play.

Carl was in the small group that faced them to see what was up. He was always curious about the JWs, having worked hard at understanding why they refused to participate in military service, and yet were not pacifists, like him.

"Gregor wanted to sign," one offered.

"I'd had enough of this place!" Gregor exclaimed.

"Did you sign?"

He shook his head but didn't say anything.

"Why not?"

"Horst threw a fit!"

"You got mad?" one asked, turning to Horst. The JWs laughed at the question.

"No! He literally threw a fit!"

"He started rolling around on the floor, moaning and spitting." The speaker tried to imitate what Horst had done to save the soul of his brother in faith. Horst grinned mischievously.

"On purpose?"

Horst put his index finger to his lips.

"Doesn't deception go against your religious tenets?"

"It was an act of spiritual courage."

"A divine madness!"

"So what happened?"

"Gregor ended up not signing!"

All eyes veered back to the would-be apostate, who avoided them, staring sheepishly at the edges of shadows on the ground.

"Why not?"

"I don't know," he replied at last. "With all the commotion, I just didn't."

"Maybe next time."

"No. My brother has saved me for eternity."

"We'll see."

"Never!" Gregor shouted. Then, turning to his savior, he patted him on the shoulder. "Thank you, Horst, you rascal."

Before the little group broke up, someone asked, "Say, why doesn't that one hang with you guys ever?" He pointed to a prisoner who was always mustered together with the JWs, but who had separated from them as soon as they left the HQ.

"He's not one of us," was the answer. "The Nazis don't know the difference." The *tete-a-tete* broke up. Carl remained standing there alone, watching the man who had been indicated. What was he, then?

****

They were made to construct dolls for the children in the nearby town. This was after a full day of work out on the peat.

They would take a couple of sticks from the pile, thread the yarn around where they crossed, and continue wrapping the clew around the sticks, as they had been instructed to do, double-wrapping for the head and hands and feet, before tying off. Then the crude doll was tossed on the finished pile, and the process was started over.

They made hundreds. Most of them vanished into the towns surrounding Esterwegen. But many were still left behind, and the prisoners started finding them hanging everywhere, placed in front of windows of their barracks so that they found them each morning, or dangling in the latrine, or along the fences of the compound. Evidently, the guards were having fun with them, posting them during the nights, trying to endow the figures with symbolic values at the expense of the men. Hanging was always on the horizon.

It didn't stop there. Some guards tied strings to them, making necklaces, and flung them over the necks of the inmates, evidently at random, as if to brand the wearer, or mark him for a death that waited around the corner.

And then, one day, Carl saw something that made him immediately retch and vomit. Nothing had changed. But when he

281

looked up at one moment and saw the dolls, strung up in a row against the sunlight, he saw them as children, hanging.

He had to force himself not to run over to the fence where they dangled and pull them all down. He would have been shot, cut down by one of the tower guards before he'd freed half of dozen.

And so, at the camp, death went on, in one form or another.

Chapter Eighteen
PAST

Quidde introduced Carl to the GPS members attending their meeting in Berlin the evening of February 21, 1920. The duo was upon a stage with Ludwig at the podium and Carl sitting at a table to the side. Smiling, Carl nodded to the audience of around fifty. He was busily recording the proceedings.

"The main agendum for this meeting," Quidde went on, "is our preparation for next month's conference in Switzerland, the first international peace conference since the war.

"So much has happened since those dark days when the world was literally torn apart by raving belligerents. And while we can't say that all is sunshine now, we hope that the violence and bloodshed are passed, and we remain confident in our goals and principles.

"One might feel at a loss in assessing the events of the last year. To me, it's rather like sifting through ashes after a fire, hoping to come across something valuable that has survived the conflagration. Maybe pacifists are the only ones to look for a silver lining in the darkest storm clouds, but this is something we must do!

"And strange to say, after the vertiginous fall of the German Empire, the valuables are there to be treasured. The Kaiser is gone! And, at least formally, we enjoy a republican mode of government at last. Germany has finally turned the corner and joined the countries of the modern world in granting enfranchisement to its citizens!

"Though much has been accomplished, there still is much work left to be done in this area as well…"

Carl was scribbling feverishly. Although he had a copy of Quidde's speech in front of him, he wanted to get down the setting, the reception of the words; and Ludwig was not unknown for launching into off-the-cuff remarks. But, suddenly, all was stopped by some incoherent shouting in the midst of the crowd. Carl looked up just in time to see scuffling, arms flailing.

"It's all a load of shit!" one of the fighters screamed.

"Get them out!" another yelled. It was Gerlach's voice. "They can't break up our meeting!"

Punches were landing; thuds mixed with groans. There was a surge of men toward the fracas, a pile-on with a life of its own, and slowly relative order resumed as the three troublemakers were pushed toward the door of the meeting room and shoved out onto the street. Others were attending to the one man still on the ground—Carl could see it was Gerlach, bleeding from the head and evidently unconscious—and to another, this one standing, a man about his own age but a little taller. He had marks on his face and was rubbing bruised and bloody knuckles.

"Good job, E. J.!" someone yelled. "You drove them away from Hellmut!"

Quidde had joined others bent over Gerlach, trying to revive him. "Carl!" he called over his shoulder. "There's a tavern next door! Fetch some spirits and damp cloths!" But when there was no response from Carl, several turned to look toward the stage. Carl wasn't there to receive the order; he'd already left the room. Someone else went next door.

Outside, Carl raced down the dark street after the three men who'd caused the scene. Two were far ahead of him, but he was gaining on the other, who appeared winded. Carl grabbed the collar of the man's coat and yanked. They both fell to the ground, gasping. Carl shouted into the ear of the man he was holding as the other two sped away.

"Who?"

"In the bar," the stranger panted. "They bought us drinks if we promised to start a brawl."

"Why? *Why*!"

The man shook his head. Carl turned away from him, leaving him to escape, and hurried back toward the bar. He stuck his head in and yelled, "Whoever shouldn't be here when the cops come better leave now!" Then he went back out and hid behind the arch of the door. When two men rushed out, Carl did something that surprised him every time he recalled it: he leaped on the man closest to him and, grabbing him around the neck, jammed the thumb of his other hand in the man's back.

"I'll pull the trigger if you don't tell me who sent you!" he yelled in the man's ear. His companion was already gone. The one Carl held, larger than he, started dragging him. He jabbed his thumb deeper into the flesh of the man's back, between the ribcage and the spine.

"WHO!"

"The NPP! The NPP!" spat the man.

Carl cursed and shoved him as hard as he could.

"Next time," Carl yelled back, "our guards will blow your fucking heads off!" The man ran way. Carl waited for the footsteps to fade, then went back into the meeting room.

Gerlach, still on the ground, was sitting up. Like a cornerman, Quidde held a wet towel to the swelling cuts on his face. Others were still uprighting overturned chairs and cleaning up the mess. Everyone looked dazed.

"They were NPP men," Carl informed them. "Or at least sent from them." He went back to his table and started writing: "The National People's Party sent men..." He looked up, thinking. He didn't want to forget any details. There was an article here somewhere, his first to offer as a Berliner.

"Most of the Free Corps come from the National People's Party," said the one who'd fought them off of Gerlach. Then, as

285

if to sum up the whole fracas in its entirety, he added, referring to the party's leaders, "Delbruck and Helfferich." He kept pacing, shaking his head.

Quidde came over to Carl, who was looking at his notes.

"I don't want any of this in the press," he said in an undertone, though the others could hear him. Carl stared at him in amazement.

"Ludwig, we must get this out."

Quidde shook his head no.

"It will be to the Society's advantage," Carl said, "if people can read about what's been done to us here."

"Not if the powers that be decide it's too dangerous for us to meet at all." This from Quidde, louder, though still measured. Then, as he turned away, in an undertone: "Or if people decide it's too dangerous to attend our meetings."

"But we've been attacked!" Carl said in pleading tones.

"Maybe later. Not at this time. I'll let you know when."

"But you said I could go on with my writing!"

"Not about this!"

People were staring at the two on the stage. Ludwig realized he'd gone too far, spoken too loudly. He bent over and patted Carl's shoulder. Carl forced himself not to shrug the hand away.

"Not all GPS matters," the older man said, almost in a whisper now. "I'll tell you when and what."

In order to avoid saying something he'd regret, Carl stuck a cigarette in his mouth and fired it up. He took a long drag and exhaled in an interminable, theatrical hiss.

The difficult moment somehow finally passed.

The remnants of the meeting were breaking up, several volunteering to escort Gerlach, who 'categorically' refused medical attention. When Carl departed, he made a point of distancing himself from Q.

The Man Without a Party

Halfway down the block, he noticed there was someone behind him. He turned around.

"Do you go by E. J.?" Carl asked.

"Sure," said the man who'd come to Gerlach's aid. "Or Emil. Or Gumbel. Just don't call me Julius."

Carl laughed. "Okay." When they shook hands, Carl noticed a wince on EJ's face in the half-light of the gas lamps.

"Oops. Sorry, I forgot about your bruises."

"It's okay. I don't think anything's broken."

"On you, at least. You have quite a right hook."

"Not bad for a teacher, I guess."

"Well, I bet the guys you hit are going to feel it for a while."

"Hope so!"

"What do you teach?"

"Math."

"Einstein! With fists!"

"Hardly. I'm no world-class theoretical physicist."

"Do you specialize in a branch of math?"

"Barely a branch, but it's new. Statistics."

"Impressive. A pacifist mathematician who can box."

"I'm actually hoping to publish something about what's going on in the courts."

"You mean about the Social-Democrats not replacing the Kaiser's judges?"

"More specifically, about their damn verdicts exonerating perpetrators on the right who claim they were motivated to hurt others because of patriotism."

"Sounds far afield from your expertise."

"That's just the point. I'm quantifying the cases so you can easily see the disparity between the treatment of those on the right and those on the left. I call it 'political death.'"

"'Quantifying.' 'The New Objectivity!'"

"Down with mere Expressionism!"

"Unscientific! Back to Galileo."

"One of my heroes. It's all about application, and it starts with the killing of Liebknecht and Luxemburg."

"Yes!"

"Also, my best friend was murdered."

"God! I'm so sorry!"

"This killing on both sides has got to stop!" EJ's shout echoed off the brick buildings and came back to them.

"I couldn't agree more," said Carl, feeling somewhat lame with the comment.

Then, confidentially: "Carl, he shouldn't have yelled at you like that. It was shitty of him."

"Quidde? Aw, the old fart, I owe him a lot. But, you have to admit, for all that he's despised the Kaiser over the years, there are unfortunate similarities. Imperial fossils!"

They came to a corner where their directions split.

"I won't try to shake your hand."

EJ laughed. "Keep up with your writing."

"Thanks. Good luck on your, uh, applications."

****

Two days later, Carl visited Gerlach. The man looked worse. He lay back on a couch with a damp towel over his bandaged face.

"How are you doing, Hellmut?"

The answer was a grunt.

"Has a doctor seen you?"

A slight nod side-to-side.

"Can I get one for you?"

"M-more coffee, please."

"Of course!"

"Not so loud!"

"Sorry," Carl whispered.

Carl jumped up and took the empty cup into the kitchen. Gerlach's wife, Hedwig, was there, and she sent him back to sit with her husband, then appeared with two steaming cups and some pain medicine for her husband to take. When she left, going off to the back part of the large house, Gerlach sat up slowly and said, "I hear you and Q locked horns."

Carl was sheepish. "Yes. My fault."

"Not at all. I just wish I had been more *compos mentis*, enough to take your side. Q is like many people who ration out respect based on how much you check him; you might as well know that if you're going to be working with him. In fact, he probably thinks even more highly of you in the aftermath of your spat."

He tossed some pills into his mouth and swallowed them down with the brew. "At any rate," he continued, "go ahead and write your article about the meeting and the dust-up. We'll find a way to publish it somewhere, anonymously, if we have to." He drank some more. "Hell, I'll co-write it with you and take any blame. Just don't make me look bad."

They laughed, Gerlach ending in a wince.

"Thanks. Are you sure there's nothing I can do to help?"

"Hedwig's enjoying being a nurse. And the von Gerlachs are hard-headed. My grandfather was police chief of Berlin, you know."

"I didn't."

"Anyway," he whispered, "this knock isn't as bad as the one I got coming back from Poland."

"I heard about that," said Carl, drinking the coffee. Hellmut took the cigarette that was offered.

"Not the whole story," the older man said, leaning forward to use Carl's match. "That's because I wasn't telling anyone." He looked around as he took a drag, making sure no one else could hear him. "But I'm telling you now because you're going to need to be very much on your toes, the more you get wrapped up in this mess of things."

Carl lowered his voice. "What happened?"

"I was coming home from Poland, and I had to switch trains at the border. I made the mistake of wandering too far from the station while I was waiting for mine to come along. Bored, I guess. Anyway, a guy drew a gun on me."

"Thief?"

"You tell me. He didn't seem too interested in what money I was carrying."

"What did he want?"

"To kill me."

"Hellmut!"

"Ssshhh!"

They stopped, looked around, sipped.

"He fired twice; two misfires. I tried to fight him off, but that's when he clobbered me right here." He pointed to his forehead where he still had a scab. "Hedwig thinks I fell."

"An assassin!"

"Quiet, please. A *de facto* pistol-whipper. I'd been shooting my mouth off a little too much, I guess, dragging the monarchists through the mud where they belong, and somebody wanted to silence me."

Carl whistled. "And now this!"

"It's all derailed me somewhat from my work about the mess in Poland, and I only hope I can get back to it before the bottom falls in."

"What did you learn from your trip?"

"Well, you know that after the war the Entente Cordiale was pressing the Poles to attack the Red Army. But Pilsudski refused." Sighing, Gerlach sat up and leaned over the table in front of the sofa. As he talked, he picked up items, a book, an empty glass, a pill container, an extra towel, and juxtaposed them to illustrate his words. "Now they're on the verge of allying themselves with the Ukrainians to fight the Bolsheviks. To make both countries independent, just like the Estonians and Latvians have done. But that's only part of the mess.

"In addition to the troops of the Allied mission, you have *in loco* German troops withdrawn since armistice from Byelorussia and Ukraine, headed by Count von der Goltz, White Russians under Yudenitch and Rodzianko, and this crazy Prince Lieven leading Russians we've released from internment, all of them sucked into this vortex. It's like a powder keg ready to go off any second."

"What would you like to see happen?"

"I want what the Poles want for themselves."

"And for our country not to get involved."

"A disaster!"

"Do you think the Reds will invade?"

"Another disaster! And even worse would be any success for the Whites."

"Why is that?"

"Haven't you heard? The Whites not only want to bring back the Romanovs, but they also want to join with the German monarchists and get the Hohenzollerns back on the throne over here."

"It would be as if the revolution had never taken place, politically speaking."

"Can you believe it? Talk about turning back the clock!"

At this point, Hedwig returned to the room, sweeping in to end Carl's visit so her husband could take a nap. Carl was amused to notice how the man, caught in a moment of anger, seemed to deflate before his eyes under the woman's mastery, and magically the man's nation-assessing thoughts scampered back into the bandaged head. He sagged down onto the couch, swathing his forehead again, and Mrs. Gerlach picked up the blanket that had fallen to the floor and draped it over him up to his chin. Hellmut, closing his eyes, said no more, and Hedwig saw Carl to the door, thanking him for the visit.

****

When Carl shook hands with Klepper, the editor of The *Sentinel*, he felt like a wire stretched to the breaking point. He pushed the just-typed article across the desk and tried to slow his lungs, still thinking of the scene he'd had with Maud, who hadn't wanted him to go out again during the fighting on the streets of Berlin.

Before coming to Berlin, he'd gotten an agreement from Quidde that he could continue, and even expand, his journalism while he was working for the Peace Society. He'd initiated a daily fact sheet of pacifist-related items already, but he was already feeling that the job of a secretary was not for him long-term: too confining, especially under Q's scrutiny. Yet the new canvas of Berlin beckoned him to dip his brush and start composing.

So when the Ehrhardt Brigade had refused Minister of Defense Noske's demand to dissolve itself now that the revolution and civil conflict seemed over, and paramilitary's armed members, capped in swastika-swathed helmets, had marched in protest into Berlin on the 13th of March, 1920, Carl had sought the scoop that would lead to the story introducing him to a new readership on the big stage of the capital. And, through an old war acquaintance, the scoop had come.

Now, Carl had finished the article and presented to an editor. The two men sat on either side of the desk, and Carl expressed his gratitude for the meeting.

"Well, we won't be publishing anything while the strike goes on, of course," Klepper explained, gesturing to the candles burning on his desk. Since the beginning of the general strike, which had started from Berlin and spread, there had been no power, water, gas, mass transit, and no local papers.

"Of course," said Carl. "I understand."

Klepper looked at the first page and smiled. Still looking down, he asked, "You write the cabinet met at four the morning of the 13ᵗʰ?"

"Yes."

"How do you know?"

"An informer."

Klepper rolled his tongue along his cheek and turned the page. "And the meeting broke up at 6:15?"

"They had to hurry away. General von Seekt ruled out protecting the Parliament building against the Free Corps brigade because he refused to fire on German soldiers."

"How can you verify this?"

"My source is an acquaintance of Noske's aide."

This time, Klepper's smile was more like a wince.

"And Noske told this aide that he was considering suicide?"

"That was before the Social-Democrat leaders escaped to Dresden."

Turning the page.

"And the National People's Party refused to form a provisional government?"

"They thought General Luttwitz was rushing things. They wanted more time."

"But they changed their minds?"

"The Berlin police informed them that arrest warrants had already been issued for them. There was no time."

"Kapp, Ludendorff, and Pabst?"

"Yes." Carl's voice fluttered like a feather.

"You're aware that the latter is implicated—"

"Pabst has been linked to the murders of Liebknecht and Luxemburg."

A nod. More reading, turning of pages. Then Klepper sat up straighter.

"You don't confine yourself to factual claims. These are predictions."

"That is the strongest part of the article." Carl waved his arm expansively toward the desk. "Why would Noske's aide lie about what will happen? The Social-Democrats agreed to negotiate with the putschists."

"And the Social-Democrats consented to the disbanding of the National Assembly?" The editor looked up. "That's the most democratic part of the new government."

"The parties on the right fear the National Assembly will become permanent and replace the Parliament. With Soviets."

Klepper read on about the proposed compromises. "Amnesty?"

"For the leaders of the putsch. If they resign."

"New elections?"

"In June."

"The Army will be left free to arrange its own affairs?"

"No war criminals. A state within a state. But the Free Corps will be dissolved."

"Workers must end the strike and lay down their weapons?"

"That's why we're hearing the firing squads in the city garrison. The leftist leaders are already being executed as belligerents."

Now Klepper squirmed in his chair. "Is there *anything* the Social-Democrats said no to?"

"Only Luttwitz's appointment as Supreme Commander. I say that." Carl stood up and pointed on the sheet.

"But he gets a full pension!"

"And cash and a false passport, if he wants them."

"And, von Ossietzky," said Klepper, pushing himself away from the desk, "do you expect me to believe all this?"

"No. I expect you to believe that an acquaintance of an acquaintance reported all this, and that I transcribed it accurately. And I hope you'll print it in The *Sentinel.*"

He pushed the papers back toward Carl. "Sorry."

Carl's jaw dropped. "But…?"

"I applaud your—uh, fervor, but the connection's too tenuous. Iffy."

"Even as a hearsay report?"

Klepper snickered. "Can you tell me your source?"

Eyes wide, Carl felt the ground give way beneath him. Was the man going to report him to the authorities, that is, the new authorities? Was he a turncoat?"

"You know I can't do that."

"And I can't stick my neck out for a green novice from Hamburg whose delivering hearsay to me."

"But your paper is supposed to be based on leftist principles!"

"We are, along with strong journalistic ones, I assure you."

"But certainly, in the present political climate—"

"'The climate' makes me even more cautious than before. Can you promise me my head won't roll with yours?"

Carl was speechless. Dumbfounded.

"Look," said Klepper in appeasement. "I like your writing. You have a spark, and I'll be glad to look at your work in the future… if there is one. But this... now…" The editor gestured helplessly.

"A crisis!" Carl shouted. "The people need to know!"

Klepper laughed, shaking his head.

"To know? And you will tell them? Oh, the wisdom of youth!"

Carl hated the man now.

"Look," Klepper relented, leaning forward. "No offense, but, a long time ago, I realized I really knew very few things. I'm not a total skeptic, but I think a methodical skepticism isn't just Cartesian; it's downright healthy. Two plus two equals four, and this chair I'm sitting on is real, and statements that approach these are better than those that don't. But after that, what's true? What the churches say? Each one still thinks God is on its side! Science? But don't I have to be a scientist to really know, then? And don't scientists disagree? And even if there's a consensus, for how long is it true? Didn't Hegel himself point out that factual claims of time only last a minute? I'm sorry, Mr. Ossietzky, but *ipse dixit*s just don't cut it in this field."

Carl stood up, taking the article. "I'll go to someone else," he said, half to himself.

"As you wish." Klepper stood and extended his hand. "No hard feelings?" He waited, then dropped his hand. "Ouch! Now I know how Ebert felt."

"I'll go to one of your competitors." Carl turned and left the office.

But before Carl got around to selling the piece elsewhere, he was shocked one afternoon to come home and find Maud, dressed only in a shift, curled up in bed and sobbing. He ran to her.

"Maud! What's happened?"

"Oh, it was awful!"

He brought her a glass of schnapps; this she choked on, and it was several minutes before she could talk.

"I went down to the Brandenburg Gate, just for a stroll. But then I heard marching. It was that damned Ehrhardt's Brigade leaving the city. The putsch has failed."

"That's wonderful! It means the strikers have won!"

"Listen to me, Carl! Some people on the other side of the street started laughing at them. Others tried to shush them, but they wouldn't be shushed. Then there were some pops." She broke down again. Carl caressed her forehead. He'd never felt her skin so stiff, so furrowed. He massaged it to soften the ridges.

"I hid behind the news kiosk there on the corner." Her lungs were in spasms, one of her nostrils collapsing with the forced intake of breath.

"Take your time, Honey."

"Carl, some of the soldiers stopped and took aim at the crowd with the hecklers! They started firing! Indiscriminately!"

"My God!"

"They took aim like it was target practice!"

"Then what?"

She took a deep breath. "At least a dozen people fell. When the troops had passed, we ran across the street to see what we could do. Blood everywhere! Screams! Oh, God! It was so horrible!" She wept some more. Carl scanned her face; her expression darkened.

"God, Carl! If I'd been on the other side of the street, I could have been killed!"

He stayed with her, comforting her until her spasms diminished and she fell asleep. Then he got up from his knees and went into the parlor. He sat in the stuffed chair and grabbed his notebook. He would add what she'd told him to his article. Or perhaps start a new one.

It was three days before she could leave the apartment. Over the telephone, Sophie had convinced her that she needed to face her fears. Suddenly, she jumped up from the couch and exclaimed, "What? Am I going to avoid that patch of sidewalk for the rest of my life! That's ridiculous!" She ran into the bedroom and got dressed. "Carl, will you go with me?" The question had the tone of a child in it.

"Of course," he said, as comfortingly as he could. They threw on their coats.

Downstairs, on the street, there was a sharp wind whisking up the canyon of buildings. They walked toward the Brandenburg Gate, clinging close to each other. Block after block, she seemed to tense up more. He whispered gentle encouragement in her ear. Five more blocks, four, three. They ignored everyone else. Then they stopped.

The patches on the sidewalk had been scrubbed, but she could still see some telltale stains of red; she still remembered, vividly, exactly where they had been. He let her stare as long as she wanted. Then, she seemed to deliberately break her gaze away. He guided her across the street toward the kiosk. But when they got there, he did a double take. A stack of fresh *Berlin Sentinel*s caught his eye.

"Where did these come from?" he asked the woman in the cubicle. The strike was still going on.

"They had those printed out of town and trucked in," she explained. "A special edition."

Carl's stomach was churning as he glanced at the headlines. He handed the woman some change and grabbed an issue, folding it under his arm; he didn't want to try to read it here.

"Shall we go back?" he whispered into Maud's ear. She nodded. "You're doing wonderfully," he praised, and they headed back down the windy boulevard. She seemed to gain strength with each step.

Back in their apartment, after reading the paper, each article an expansion of a different item he'd shared with Klepper, he burned it in the stove and chalked the theft up to experience: a hard lesson. Other than that, there was nothing to be done. Klepper was a piece of shit; that was a Cartesian fact. And here was another one: a shit with a very good memory.

****

Metal doors clattering. Click-clacking over track connections.

The Man Without a Party

Shuddering with its push-pull start, the swaying train car was already full of tobacco smoke and the din of male voices. They sat on benches that faced each other in pairs. Conversations took place in every configuration possible: shoulder-to-shoulder, face-to-face, back-to-back and over-the-shoulder, as well as across aisles. Some were even communicating from one end of the car to the other with piercing, sarcastic shouts.

The mood was very different from that in the car Carl had just left. He'd held out longer than most in the car that the women had chosen to settle in, and, as the men had filed out, leaving their significant others to chat together, Carl had stayed with Maud and Sophie as if to make a point, not because he had anything more in particular to say to them. He just didn't like giving into the assumptions lurking behind the consensual segregation of the genders.

But Maud had answered his raised eyebrows with a quick nod, and he'd made his way from what was now, virtually, the women's car. The last thing he heard as he left was weeping.

They were all going to a memorial for Hans Paasche, who'd been shot and killed on his property by unofficial soldiers of the Weimar state.

In spite of the sadness of the occasion, the "men's" car sounded unaware, doggedly oblivious to the tragedy of the journey, and Carl had to admit he welcomed the different mood in spite of its impropriety. In a way, this was the very reason he had been so excited to come to Berlin: he had craved the greater, broader conviviality it offered, its style and cosmopolitan *esprit*, the banter and the wit.

Gerlach, sitting next to Quidde, motioned him over, and, as Carl approached them, he noticed two standing men arguing at the far end of the car; or rather, one man was yelling at another, the latter holding a sheet of paper. Carl also noticed, before he sat down, that several flasks were being passed around. After sitting, he particularly noticed two men across the aisle who, although they were not whispering, almost touched foreheads as they conversed.

"Hiller and Tucholsky," said Quidde in explanation, seeing the direction of Carl's gaze. "Weighty matters."

Carl nodded. There was a yell from the far end, and Carl looked up just in time to see the shorter of the two standing men snatch the paper from the other's hands, wad it up and throw it in his face, before stomping from the car.

Everyone's head had turned toward the commotion. Hiller stood and started clapping, but the man who'd been hit simply shook his head and began to walk down the aisle across the length of the car.

"Jacobsohn and Harden," explained Gerlach. Carl knew of them; both were editor-writers somewhat notorious for libelous articles.

"Harden is the uncle-in-law of Paasche," Gerlach added.

"I know," said Carl. "Poor Ellen's uncle."

"He wanted to read something at the memorial," explained Jacobsohn before sitting down across the aisle. "I simply disapproved, and he flew off the handle, as he does. Paper bullets."

"You should have let him, Siegfried," said Tucholsky.

"He can do as he likes," Jacobsohn replied. "I simply gave him my editorial opinion."

"I know what that feels like," quipped Tucholsky, to the roar of laughter.

Hiller stood up and shouted in falsetto toward the door Harden had just slammed: "Max! You can read what you like!" There was more laughter.

"What did he want to say?" Tucholsky asked Jacobsohn.

"Much too much, and all of it inappropriate for the context. Good Lord! As far as we know, the Paasche children will be there."

"I doubt it," said Quidde. "I'd be surprised if much of either family shows."

"I hope you're right," said Siegfried. "But, just in case, a little restraint is in order."

Tucholsky handed Jacobsohn some sheets of paper. "Here, Siegfried," he said with a sigh. "Then you'd better read my poem before I cause any trouble at the ceremony." A few men chuckled quietly.

"Poor Max," sighed Hiller as he sat back down. "He has so much to atone for."

"You probably know about Eulenburg," Quidde said *sotto voce* to Carl. "Before the war—"

"Prince Philip Eulenburg was William's confidant," Carl interposed. "A stabilizing influence on the Kaiser. That is, until—"

"Eulenburg was charged with pederasty and withdrew from public life," finished Gerlach.

"Which some think made William unhinged and led to the war," Carl offered.

"Well," Gerlach went on, "Harden was the one who outed Eulenburg."

"Oh."

"A lot to carry on his shoulders, looking back," said Quidde, peeling a bit of tobacco from his upper lip before re-inserting his cigarette into his mouth. Carl nodded thoughtfully, his eyes roaming along the scuffed wooden flooring of the coach.

The three of them spent the rest of the trip discussing GPS matters. But when they rolled into their station and everyone stood up, Carl pulled a notebook from his jacket pocket and pretended to be deep in thought. He nodded to the others as they

301

left, saying he would catch up with them. Then, when the car was empty, he returned the notebook to his pocket, stood up, and walked over to the place he thought he'd seen Harden's paper vanish. There it was, still wadded up, against the wall.

Carl stuffed it into a pocket of his trousers and went to find Maud and Sophie.

At the memorial, which took place under a leaden overcast on a grassy swale at Woodland Peace, the estate of the Paasches, Carl couldn't get his mind off the un-uniformed armed men who stood guard under the ring of pines along the perimeter of the property. Protection? For who from what? What did they think was going to happen? What were they trying to prove? There was already talk about an investigation of the paramilitaries' claim that they were searching for a weapons cache and communist fugitives, as well as about the way Paasche died. He had tried to run, the perpetrators had insisted, although others present disagreed.

At a certain point in the ceremony, Carl broke away from his musing about the armed men—would they suddenly open fire on the mourners they surrounded?—and refocused as Kurt Tucholsky approached the podium. The man had interested him perhaps more than any other German writer. A biting, sarcastic satirist who used several *noms de plume*, he also wrote novels, poetry, and cabaret songs. In order to increase sales of his first book, he'd served free schnapps to anyone who bought a copy. Carl strained to hear his poem about Paasche that may have passed Jacobsohn's perusal:

"Another one. Tradition.

Pacifist as treasonous prey.
Victim in a bathing suit,
Net fishing with his kids.

The Man Without a Party

How many men were needed
To save the state from one?
Who did he run from and why?

He hated war, so kill him.
Pretend you're back in Flanders.
What were the weapons? Newspapers!

Shrug your shoulders, Government!
Turn your heads away, Citizens!
Close your eyes, Judges!"

Many nervous looks were exchanged. Would the infantry start firing? The moment passed. A minister took Kurt's place, and Carl's gaze went back to the circle of grim riflemen.

Sophie collapsed halfway through the ceremony. Carl and Maud took her back to the Paasche home, where she lay on a bench on the porch until she could move on. Then, before the others, they headed back to the station.

After leaving Sophie at her stop, they returned to Berlin. As soon as they arrived home, Maud went into the bathroom. Carl noticed the paper in his pocket, pulled it out, and sat in the stuffed chair. He smoothed out the sheet and read what Max Harden had written:

Woodland War

We will not raise a glass to you,
O Commander.
You would not approve.
You hunted down big game, but
we will not celebrate your life

by tasting roasted flesh. You
won in battle but preferred
to pacify unpraised, unvictorious,
to succor the defeated and the injured
and change bloodthirsty minds.

In the morning light, Lukanga Mukara
saw the ugly truth we missed about
ourselves: our obsessions with winning,
with killing, with guns and uniforms,
reparations, annexations and empire,
empire, empire! Our sins, my sins,
your sins, sins and guilt. And yes, shame.

Suddenly, he heard Maud vomiting in the bathroom and rushed to the door.

"Maud! Are you all right?"

More retching. "I'll be okay," she croaked.

She had insisted on wolfing down a sausage drowned in mustard and sauerkraut in the station. Carl supposed it was food poisoning.

"Is there anything I can do?" His hand was on the doorknob.

"No." Her voice was a creak. Then, "I'll let you know if I need anything."

He waited a minute, then returned to the sofa.

Advocating peace, you found new enemies,
father, father-in-law, me! And Count Nikolai and
a staff of spies who imprisoned you
in a padded cell till revolution, crazed,
ran rampant in the streets. They freed you
to lead once again, then kicked you out
because you wanted trials for the officers…

Once again, back home, you aided
the injured refugees, the hunted. This
was your death sentence. It took sixty
to gun you down with children watching.

What country will they grow up in?

He stared out the window to register what the flow of words had done to him. But then he jumped up, his reflection cut short by Maud's heaving again.

It turned out not to be the food at the station. With flushed face, Maud told Carl three days later that he was going to be a father.

****

Quidde thought Carl was acting selfishly. Sure, he had been offered a new position at the *People's Paper*. Sure, Carl had wanted to be a writer 'all his life,' and this was his dream job. Sure, he was grateful to Ludwig for bringing him and Maud to Berlin, the center of so much, and, sure, he would always be a pacifist and spread the gospel of pacifism, especially as understood by the GPS. But Quidde and the GPS had gone out of their way to hire him when they could have chosen so many worthy and needy others, making him secretary of the entire, sprawling network of the Society, with branches that had connected him to the international movement. Did von Ossietzky realize how much he owed them? Quidde had expected him to stay on for at least a year! And he seemed to be settling into the work, especially with the innovation of the daily sheet. Yes, the climate here in the capital was extremely volatile; things were happening right and left, new things each day. Berlin culture was blossoming under the Republic, however shaky it was, especially after abolishment of censorship. But that didn't mean one should have one's head swirling like a weather vane and yield to the first temptation.

He knew Gerlach thought differently: let the young man take flight. Wish him the best and give him your blessing. It wasn't the loss of a good pacifist, but the spreading of the message. Diasporas were good! And had Gerlach actually said that Carl would work as a fighter battling against the enemy? Such language!

The Cause was everything. One subsumed oneself to the Cause, in the Cause. One sacrificed oneself to move it along. Excelsior! He, Ludwig, only had to look at himself to see the benefits, the wholesomeness of immersing oneself in the great endeavor to save the world. How selfish he himself had been in his salad days! Pacifism had saved him from turning old as a crabbed medievalist. What nonsense to dedicate one's life to the dead past! If one wasn't working for the Cause, what was one doing? Wasting time, wasting one's life! Letting the forces of evil make matters worse and worse!

Carl had complained to him about the in-fighting in the peace movement, apparently seeing only its incongruity. "If pacifists couldn't agree with each other, how could they expect the unconverted to join them?" a disillusioned Carl had asked in his inexperience. Such things were to be expected in the crucible of progress! You can't have a world movement without some disunity. That was part of the process; that was what you worked through. Goodness! They had pacifists from India, China, Argentina! People had such different backgrounds! The issue of language itself almost turned one into an Esperantist. Almost.

But one works through it all. What if their forerunners had let discord defeat them? So much had been accomplished already! Conflicts were stepping stones to greater understanding.

Everything was an opportunity for teaching and learning. It was dialectic.

Quidde wasn't sure he'd ever be able to forgive Carl for the betrayal. Still, it was a hard road. Look at what happened to Gumbel's apartment during the putsch; lucky he was in Switzerland at the time.

Many were called, but few…

Diaspora, indeed!

Chapter Nineteen
PRESENT

And they didn't read balanced evaluations of Hitler's March 16, 1935, announcement of German rearmament in violation of the Treaty of Versailles. While the official pronouncement was hardly a surprise, the citizens of Germany were not afforded astute print analyses of the causes, motivations, and repercussions of the significance of the timing of the speech or its actual content. In addition, there were no challenging articles published in Germany linking the growing anti-Semite legislation of the Nazi regime to earlier laws from that year forbidding German non-Aryans, including Jews, from displaying or carrying the German flag and preventing them from serving in the German armed forces. Also, legislation was passed banning organizations connected to Jehovah's Witnesses due to the religion's stance against pledging allegiance to any temporal armed forces. And the anti-homosexual Paragraph 175 was expanded to promote the systematic persecution of male homosexuals.

As a result, discussion of citizens took place in a severely damaged and deformed public sphere. It would have been bad enough if that sphere had been barren, sterile, and empty. Worse yet, it was full of poison, toxins of words and noxious germs of lethal speech, corrosive language that gnawed at the fragile moral compass of their brains.

****

The Man Without a Party

They had drained a great deal of the seasonal overflow from the peat swamp and were now told to dig pits into the paludal plain when, on that overcast day, a businessman came out from the direction of the town and, holding the cuffs of his suit trousers above the top of his boots, trudged carefully through the muck right up to their guard, informing him in a strange accent that he was the mayor and had chosen a time when townspeople were less likely to notice his absence, as they did not like to be reminded that there was such a work camp so close to where they lived.

The guard tried to convince the man that there was nothing to be embarrassed about in that.

"These men—" he gestured.

"That's not why I came out here," interrupted the mayor. At this point, Carl and the other prisoners slowed their digging and exchanged glances. Would they get a break in their work while the two were busy? The prisoners, wary, kept digging for the time being, watching the threatening hippo whip in the guard's hand. They didn't want any trouble; Carl's ever-present headache was already making him nauseous.

The mayor walked the guard up to the edge of the pit.

"What you're doing is wrong!" he shouted into the crisp gusts. "This is not the way to go about it!"

He pointed down into the peat field that had been drained. The guard looked as well.

"All you succeeded in doing is lower the ground level where you have drained. The water is gone, and now the peat has dropped."

The guard was nodding. "But now you can harvest the peat more easily."

"That's not the point!" the man yelled. "The next rainy season this will all fill up, and what will have happened?"

The guard shrugged.

"The water will be deeper! That's the opposite of what we wanted!"

Helplessly, the guard stretched his arms out, a carbine in one hand and the whip in the other. "I'm just following orders, Sir."

"'Just following orders,'" the townsman mimicked. The prisoners acted like they hadn't heard. Carl even moved further away from the two.

Suddenly, a large white bird flew out of the grass, almost under his feet. It scared him so much he could feel the hairs on the back of his neck, and he became faint again. No, he told himself. Not a good time to faint. There never was, but this would be a particularly bad one. The guard, he would be more upset than usual after the brow-beating he was getting within earshot of the men.

All heads turned uniformly, as if in mute and respectful salutation, as the large bird lifted up and kicked off the ground, battering the resisting air with determined wings, rising into its transparent medium of choice, attuned to it, and rhythmically pounded away.

Shuffling his raw feet in the wooden shoes, Carl turned back toward the ground, using the edges of his sleeves to protect the raw skin of his hands. He made a show of digging, bending down, but then he saw what the bird—egret? heron?—had been after.

Under the clump of grass, a large turtle lay on its back. Carl was sure it must be dead, as the shell was partly empty. The predatory bird, with a beak like a scythe, had feasted on the turtle's insides through the openings for the legs, especially the hind ones. The bloody stomach lay plundered a few inches from the useless carapace.

But then something happened that made him jump like the bird he'd flushed: the head and forelegs started to move. Bizarrely, the vital organs must not have been consumed or destroyed and, helplessly, the creature continued to writhe, endeavoring to turn itself upright. The upside-down head stretched back and forth, like a man whose cravat was too tight. Other than equilibrium, what could it accomplish by flipping its shell? Its wounds had to be lethal.

In his shock, Carl shifted position again, wanting to get away from the disgusting thing. Suppressing dry heaves, settling down his own innards. His head throbbed. Weak, he continued digging in the place he had left. The sky above him seemed to reel and sparkle, the edges of his vision frayed, and he pleaded with himself not to faint. Just keep punching the spade into the soggy earth.

The men were still arguing, now over whether the correct word was peat or sphagnum. Neither one was paying any attention to the prisoners; in fact, Carl hadn't seen the townsman even cast a glance at any of the diggers. They didn't exist for him.

Carl stood to relieve the strain on his lower back, looked at the other prisoners; he wanted to tell them about the turtle. He considered going back and taking another look, and, disoriented and confused, he was having a hard time explaining to himself why the incident was having its effect upon him, why he had become fixated on it.

Lurching back down, he bit into the mud with the tooth of the blade.

****

The Gestapo men surrounded Captain Schneider as he left the police station. One of the men told him to come along with them. Every muscle in his body seemed to tighten, and he put up no resistance. As they walked, he put his head down, thinking of the times when he had stared at such a one as he now was, a suspect, their quarry, and he avoided the stares of passersby.

311

They took him down to a room in the basement of a quiet building. They sat him at a table, closed the door and let him wait alone, in silence.

After ten minutes, a man with a face full of scars entered the room and shut the door behind him. They both hailed The Leader. Then the man sat down across from Captain Schneider.

"We're all very curious about you, Captain Schneider," started the man.

"Why is that?"

The man seemed to stretch with his thinking. Like a snake in the sun, Schneider thought.

"Usually when we come across someone who is up to something, we find, after little investigation, that they are, uh, erring in any of a number of ways. But you are different."

"I don't know what you are talking about."

"Undoubtedly. You aren't dealing with the black market."

"No."

"You seem to have no mistresses."

"No."

"You're not a boozer or an addict."

"No."

"You don't gamble."

"Never."

"You contribute to the Party."

"Yes."

"Your wife's background is clear enough."

"Of course!"

"A clean slate. Apparently."

"I hope so, Sir."

"And so why are you harboring the wife of a notorious enemy of the state in your home?"

Schneider froze.

"Can you say that again, please?"

The Man Without a Party

Carl spiraled downward over the next weeks. Consciousness thinned out to near-nothingness. The last thought to evaporate was the question he always made himself ready to ask a guard, yet never uttered: When you torturers see the final vanishing of human essence, do you recognize yourselves?

And that, too, was finally gone. It was over. He was done for. How should he kill himself? That was the only problem. The mental image of an empty noose whispered to him, tantalized, and taunted.

But just when he felt that he was at his end, that he had hit ultimate rock-bottom, that death would be better, and he considered various modes of exit he'd already seen used— touching the high-power fence seemed simplest to him— something happened to revive his spirits, if not his flesh and bones. Someone arrived at the camp, and the spirit of the camp changed almost immediately, as if by a kind of osmosis.

"Do you know who's here?" one prisoner would ask another. "It's Finck!"

Even the guards seemed to be excited; already they were diverted from their usual hands-on *modus operandi*.

The new prisoner's arrival, unanticipated, created an anticipation of its own.

"Have you seen him?"

"Have you talked to him?"

"What did he say?"

And so, although it didn't take long before a performance was announced, expectation made the wait longer for both prisoners and guards than the few days measured by the clock. It was a rare fine day on the Emsland heath when, after the men returned from work, they were told to assemble in the yard.

By habit, they lined up in their squads for roll call, but then were told to sit in the dirt. After chairs were placed behind them, the camp's officers took seats and prisoner Werner Finck took the make-shift stage. Carl, sitting cross-legged next to Julius, hadn't noticed what direction the man had come from. And looking up while meditating on his aching, rag-wrapped feet and wooden shoes, he heard the comedian's voice.

Finck started talking even before he was at the spot front and center of his audience.

"Well, what a wonderful day we have out here in hell's anteroom, the Devil's foyer, Satan's vestibule!" There were already laughs, to which the accomplished vaudevillian immediately reacted. "Ah! I see some of you are yet alive! The wonders do not cease! Yes, I was told this was the den of hardened criminals, and now it is confirmed. I see them all seated behind these poor wretches in the front." Here he gestured to the SS officers and the guards standing in a ring around them. After a nervous pause, the Nazis erupted with laughter, officers first. The prisoners looked behind them, making sure the comments were well received before joining in.

"Well, Folks, my name is Werner Finck and, in case you've never heard of me, I'm on vacation here from my regular job at The Catacomb in Berlin. Our Leader has given me a respite from intellectual labors and sent me to this wonderful spa on the Dutch border to serve as an emissary of saturnalian goodwill. Not that I am at all political; in fact, I did my best to recommend worthy friends like Hans Platte, Robert Deppe and Rudolf Stemmle, but nothing doing! I was the popular, the popular, the popular..."

"Choice!" the officers shouted.

"Thank you! Yes, 'choice.' The word had escaped me from lack of use. But I am in no way daunted by my task. You see, when we worked at The Catacomb cabaret, which is now temporarily closed down for repairs, we were always worried that some of our paltry attempts at that healing balm called humor would be taken amiss. But now, as I stand among you, I find that I am no longer a prey to such concerns. See, I'm already arrested! Ha!

"Wow! This is a tough crowd. Can I have a little life from you? There we go! That's a start. I was only hearing mouse farts before. As I say, I am not, like you all are, a political person. I mean, politics! Give me a break! What are those? Or is it singular? Who the hell knows, even? But I did, awhile back, try to start my own party. I don't know if you heard of it: the Comic Bones Party. It didn't go well. You see, comics are individualists, and individualists don't like to join groups, especially groups whose standards are so low that they will accept comics!

"But I hear we are all National Socialists now, so that is good. Having one party is good for the unity of a nation. At least that's what I'm told." Finck had started strolling along the perimeter of the crowd and came to a stop next to an officer who was writing on a pad of paper. He looked down at it. "Are you writing this down?" he asked. "There are critics everywhere! I hope I'm not talking too fast. Should I slow down? Did I really say that? Brilliant! What wonderful calligraphy you have! No wonder there are so many medals on your chest!" Flashing his disarming grin, Finck turned and came back to the front of the crowd.

"Speaking of medals," he continued as he went, "I hear Goring and Goebbels are vying for the largest collection. When Goebbels saw an arrow on Goring's chest, he asked what it was for. 'Direction,' Goring answered, and turned around and, sure enough, the back of his tunic was covered with more medals! But Goebbels had the last laugh. He said, 'I have more than that.' 'Where?' asked Goring. 'On my pajamas!'

"Ah! That's better. Keep it up, and they'll have to rename this camp 'Camp Chuckles.' Did I tell you I'm not a political person? By the way, why did the man have a sock in his mouth? That's right! He was making a political statement! I have lots more of these just like that one! What's that? 'Stop it, please?' How hospitable of you! The Gestapo disapproved of me, too. In fact, they disapproved of me more than I disapproved of them!

"It's been heart-warming seeing everyone working out on the moors. Peat! Ah, don't you love it? The smell, the aroma, the stench! I've never seen so many frogs. I hear it's because you prisoners are having sex with them. It's created a new breed of frog, one that only croaks from the left side of its mouth. But I tried to have sex with one of the frogs, you know, when I was feeling a little homesick for my sweetie, Kathe Dorsch. It didn't end well. The frog said she's telling Kathe what I did!

"Thank you! Thank you! Laughter is so healing, especially for the comedian. All the bruises inflicted on you hurt less bad. Yes, I've had a hard life. My father was an apothecary, so I grew up knowing all about drugs. But when I discovered the best drug of all was humor, I decided to take my show on the road. I called it 'The Good Soldier Shuts Up'! And look where it brought me! The edge of the world's shithole!

"Doesn't the sun ever shine out here? Quick. Why did the birds stop flying? Too many planes in the sky! Okay, okay, sorry. I'll retire that groaner. Everyone's a critic these days. Say? Do they release a lot of men from here out back into society? A few? Well, did you hear the one about the prisoner who was released and was telling his friend how wonderful the camps are? 'Of course,' he said, 'breakfast in bed; coffee or hot chocolate; soup, meat and dessert for lunch; games, coffee and cakes in the afternoon; nap, then movie after dinner.' 'Strange,' his friend remarked. 'That's not how Meyer described it.' 'That's why Meyer's been re-arrested' was the answer.

"Well, it is wonderful seeing the unanimity we have today in Germany. I was talking to a girl who said her father belonged to the SA, her older brother to the SS, her younger brother to the

316

Hitler Youth, her mother to the NS, and she herself to the BDM. I asked her if she ever saw her family members and she said, 'Sure we do! Every year at the Nuremburg Rally!'

"Well, I think I'll call it a day with a new version of an old story, one I told when I first started my career. Early in Our Leader's career, when he was still just Mr. Hitler, he was crossing a small bridge on the outskirts of Munich when he saw, at the far end of the span, three goats, each wearing very prominent horns. Undaunted, our future hero proceeded to high-step it across until, looking into the faces of the ruminating beasts, especially into their characteristically unsettling eyes, he paused and considered what he should do. Was it worth the danger to continue, or should he backtrack and detour down to the next bridge?

"While thus engaged, he noticed the goats clopping toward him, each staring at him with particular malevolence. Not wanting to be rammed, he stepped up on the parapet in the hope that they would simply pass by him. This they did not; instead, they halted at his feet and looked up diabolically at him, continuing to work their jaws, munching molars in a manner that, to Mr. Hitler, seemed downright mocking. When they reared up and threatened to topple him off the bridge, our man heroically turned his back, looked for a deep pocket in the diminutive river, and, holding his nose over his toothbrush moustache, leaped.

"Unscathed, Mr. Hitler waded over to the shore and stood, fully dressed and shod, in a foot of water. When he looked up, he was unable to see the beasts. As he was stepping out of the water, one of his acquaintances saw him and asked what he was doing.

"Our fearless Leader replied, 'I'm avoiding the only three creatures on earth who appear to dislike me.' No joke!" And with a wave of his arm, Finck walked off, to great cheering, laughter and applause.

With the crowd jumping up and clapping, Carl looked back down at his legs and feet. He'd been laughing so hard that the legs of his trousers, his bandaged feet and hammered clogs were speckled with gobbets of his blood. He'd coughed up his lungs. More embarrassed than hurt or scared, he quickly rubbed over the clots and blotches with dirt while the others gave Finck a standing ovation.

Finck was released on July 7, 1935, after six weeks at Camp Chuckles. A government car came specially to fetch him. Rumor was that his girlfriend had prevailed upon Goring to over-rule Goebbels and secure his manumission, and that, as he stepped into the car, he had said, shaking his head in emphasis, "Thanks, Martha, wherever you are!"

The next day, the camp was in a weird state, neither here nor there. People were quiet, rerunning the tape of Finck's antics. They were quiet the next day, but the mood had become morose. By the third day, Camp Suffering was back to its nightmare normal. They had only woken up for a short time.

****

When Kurt Singer saw the envelope from England, he lifted it from the stack. When he saw that "Ossietzky" had been written above the stamped "Dartington Hall" return address, he slit it open immediately.

Dear Mr. Singer,
I heard of the biography you have written about my father. I would like to ask you for a copy, but, unfortunately, I cannot afford it.
Sincerely,
Rosalinde von Ossietzky
although I usually don't like to use the 'von'

He showed it to his wife at once, and they exchanged looks of shock. Singer had put together his little book as a way to support the campaign for the Nobel Prize for Ossietzky.

He himself had had to escape from Germany when Hitler came to power, settling with Hilde in Stockholm.

While Hilde went to find a box to mail the book, Kurt sat down and started to compose the response.

The three of them started corresponding, then Kurt and Hilde, each in their mid-twenties, decided to make the offer. They would sponsor Rosalinde to come to Sweden, and if no other home were offered, they would take her in for the rest of her minority. When Rosa, who was worried about her future in England since Toller had run out of money, accepted their offer, they commenced looking for a school for her.

And Rosalinde made Sweden her home for the rest of her life.

Chapter Twenty
PAST

"Are you kidding me?" Carl protested. "I love my wife."

"Then why don't you go home?" Vetter challenged.

"My mother is there with one of Maud's friends to help out with the baby."

"And?"

"Too many women!"

"So it's not just your wife you're avoiding. Women in general."

"Carl laughed. "There's no room, Karl."

"Not even to sleep? You look like death warmed over."

"Especially not to sleep; that's the problem. There's another female there now."

"Your own baby daughter!"

"Precisely. Rosalinde has a knack for squalling as soon as I close my eyes. It's uncanny."

"Well, you don't seem to be doing much sleeping here. All you do is work."

"I'll take that as a compliment."

"Burnout is not helpful for our paper."

"Karl, I'll get home. Just as soon as I finish this review. Working at home is even more impossible than sleeping there."

"'More impossible'? See what I mean? Your brain's going."

Carl laughed again. "I'll plow through this. Don't worry."

"Damn, Ossi! You were stamped hard at birth."

"Not again, Karl! You know I don't go in for Schopenhauer: 'the Will is all.'"

"Of course you don't! Because he's so right about you."

"The man was right about himself, that I'll grant him. For him, Will has nothing to do with character; it was all about getting back at Hegel for taking all his students. All he succeeded in doing was pushing Nietzsche off a cliff."

"Maybe your rationalism is just a form of Will."

"Oil and water: you can't mix them. The difference between Apollo and Dionysus is not a matter of degree."

"Passion penetrates sentiment, no matter how refined."

"Sure, and the *id* undermines the *ego*. You can believe that Freudian nonsense if you want. After all, you're the boss. Maybe it explains you as well."

"*Touche*! Go ahead. Explain how I'm more a creature of Schopenhauer than you are."

"The way you run your staff. Talk about burnout! Why do you run them so hard?" Carl asked, a bit ruffled. "The way you squeeze every bit of energy out of them. Downright Prussian! As if they exist just to do your bidding."

"Now that *I'll* take as a compliment. An editor has to crack the whip. Discipline starts at the top."

"And if he does as you do, his second in command has to go around mediating, holding hands and drying eyes, counseling, putting out fires you've started. *Ergo*, Ossi slaving away in the wee hours to tell the reading public about Jean Paurel's *Don Giovanni, Don Carlos* at the People's Theater, Moliere and Mahler and *Le Marseillaise*, sung by Chaliapin."

"And don't think for a moment I discount all that you do. You're a perfect number two and a brilliant writer. I laughed for a half an hour at your criticism of Paurel: he of the 'once melodious larynx.'"

"You didn't think I went too far? An editor is supposed to edit."

"Not at all. You're very censorious of yourself. I wish your colleagues were half as circumspect of their own work. Wretched Pygmalions, all of them."

"And I was just talking about aesthetic pieces. No wonder my political work is suffering."

"We're all under the gun here. That's life."

"Exactly. And life doesn't need an *advocatus diaboli* in its obsession to maximize human toil. It does quite well without Karl Vetter's help, thank you."

"Well, I see your counseling doesn't limit itself only to my staff. I tell you, Carl, if I had more money, I'd give you a raise. I swear."

"You're wrong again, Boss, if you think I'm talking about compensation. I'm talking about having the peace of mind to be able do a good job for you."

Carl paused briefly, then took his plea to the edge of what he thought he could get away with without being fired: "And now you're planning to start a new political party."

"Imagine how it will increase interest in what we have to say," Karl said. "And other papers will have to respond to ours, or else their coverage of the next election won't be complete. Brilliant, if I do say so myself."

"As if twenty parties aren't enough for a country of sixty million."

"And, Carl, you know darn well not one of those parties represents our people competently, much less with conviction. The Social Democrats crumble with each challenge from the right, and the left: reparations, occupation, inflation, rearmament..."

"And your party is going to solve those problems!"

"How many coalitions have failed since the founding of the Republic? Half a dozen a year? Germany needs a unifying principle, a truly republican party. If it had one, those problems would have already been solved."

"You're not afraid of crushing your employees with a campaign on top of everything else? Stacking Mt. Pelion on Ossa..."

"Our country is facing severe crises, Carl. I just want to help."

Carl sighed. "I know your intentions are good, Karl. It's just that things are so fucking complicated."

"Well, I'm done," said Vetter, standing up. "I, for one, am going to get some sleep before sunrise." He patted Carl on the shoulder on his way out.

Carl managed to make his way home just as dawn was breaking. Maud was nursing the baby in the bedroom, Rosalie was in the kitchen preparing bottles, and Sophie was cleaning up things in the parlor. She motioned Carl toward her and delivered her warning with a whisper.

"A hard night. Your mom is going home this morning since I'm here. I'm sure you'll want to walk her to the station. But before you do, you'd better check in with Maud. She's been fuming about your not coming home last night."

Carl removed his shoes and, aching with a new, vulnerable sensitivity, went on tiptoe into the bedroom. In the half-light, he could see Maud sitting up on the bed, propped up with pillows, the baby at her breast: a sanctum of immediate intimacy that always left him stunned. He kissed them both on the tops of their heads, feeling the baby's throbbing pulse against his lips.

"Hi, Honey," he said as gently as he could. "Sorry I couldn't make it home earlier. Vetter wanted to talk, and one thing led to another."

"I'm too tired to get mad," she said, visibly controlling her voice.

"Sophie told me about your night."

There were dark crescents under her eyes. Her jaw was set.

The birth had been hard for mother and baby, with hours of difficult and erratic contractions leading to a tear. Three days later, Maud had her gall bladder removed by emergency surgery due to its decay during her pregnancy. At least this is how Carl understood it, when he had to explain what had happened. At any rate, convalescence had been longer and more complicated as a result. Rosalie and Sophie had stepped in and done a wonderful job coordinating visits to help out, and they had, in fact, built a relationship between them. But still, things were hard day-to-day. Four months along, Maud was still struggling to cope, languishing often in a dazed, sleep-deprived state.

"This, too, shall pass," Carl intoned.

Sometimes, she wanted to just slap him. She made her voice husky to mock him and said, "Everything will turn out."

Blessedly, they both found themselves snickering; the baby stirred. Maud suddenly placed her hand over the place where her stitches were. The look of unease faded slowly. He noticed a prescription on her night table, put it in his pocket. "After I drop Mom off, I'll take this to the druggist. Anything else for me to pick up?" She shook her head and closed her eyes, sighing.

Carl kissed them both again on the same spots, wondering at the comforting scent that surrounded them both; he called it the 'lullaby perfume.' He left the room with gratitude for the meaningful burden that had been placed upon him and with awe at the easy majesty motherhood had conferred on Maud. Impressively powerful before, now she could redirect the actions and emotions of others with the mere closure of eyelids or the down-turning of the mouth; her impact on him was regal, something uncanny that penetrated his skin and churned his insides, a fulfilling, glowing warmth that coupled itself with a vague, distant foreboding, like the feel in the gut of a marathoner at the start of the race.

'What had he signed up for?' greeted 'Thank you for giving me a purposeful life!' on the stairs and, in passing one another, became one and the same, not Janus-faced, but truly indistinguishable in the fatiguing quotidian fullness. It was all a mystery they loved talking to one another about, partly, perhaps, because they knew they would never solve it. He had shared with her, speaking with a mirthful silliness, which she appreciated even when she couldn't express it, about his recurrent daydream: Carl as Equimaux setting forth on the hunt that would either kill him or feed them for the long winter.

"Nanook go slay polar bear," he would announce sometimes in departing when they were alone. "Rotting seal is in the larder if someone has pangs. Ugh!" She was thankful for his lightness even when the stitches hurt.

Rosalie was ready; he picked up her light suitcase, and they went out onto the street.

"I didn't notice you limping," he said.

"Oh, these shoes."

"Too tight?"

"No. Just old feet! How's your foot?"

"Oh, you mean the one with the—"

"Yes!"

"Oh, fine. I just feel like I have a pebble in my shoe all the time. How are things at the rectory?" After Gustav's death, she had started working there, cleaning up after the two priests in the oversize building, and, after Carl's departure as a soldier, she'd moved in.

"Busy, busy, busy. It never stops. No end to the chores. But I guess I like the bustle; it keeps me on my toes."

"Don't work too hard, Mother," Carl cautioned. "Are the priests hard to live with?"

"I rarely see them. Just their smelly clothes and dishes. The earthly weight of saints lies heavy on their servants!"

325

Richard Tres

Carl, surprised at the aphorism, looked at her profile as they walked. The aging woman, formerly so insufferably pious, had mellowed and now chuckled with her son at her spontaneous remark.

He kept waiting for his mother to offer him unsolicited, scolding advice: 'Be there more for your wife,' or, 'You have a family now; act like it!' but, as they approached the waiting train, all she said was, "I know you're doing your best."

He helped her to her seat and set the suitcase next to her so she wouldn't have to deal with the overhead shelves. He stayed with her until the last second and then, under the ear-splitting whistle, she said in his ear, "Call me when you need me." He could read in her wet eyes and wrinkled smile the unspoken gratitude: 'Thanks for making me a grandmother, Son!'

****

Gretta was counting people off with her pencil. Staff members were slowly moving into Vetter's office, the only one in the complex large enough to hold them all. They treaded past his desk, foraging from the spread of sliced bread, charcuterie, cheese, and beverages available.

"Thirteen," she asserted; then, with tongue-in-cheek fanfare: "Let the *Berlin People's Press* bi-weekly lunch meeting for the date of January 24, 1924, commence!"

"Thank you, Mrs. Siedenfaden," said Vetter. He looked around at the writers who found spots to sit or stand.

"I thought we had sixteen on staff," said someone.

"Three are on assignment," Gretta informed.

"Aren't we all?" The question was ignored.

"And the thirteen sat down to break bread together," someone reflected.

326

"And plan their workload" said Vetter. "Let's start with…" He scanned the room, pointed.

"I'm looking into the anniversary of Rathenau's assassination," said Otterbeck. "What different regions and voting blocks are doing to remember him."

"Or not doing," Vetter added.

"Right."

"Are you including international responses? I would."

Otterbeck writing. "Will do."

"Don't forget linkages to Paasche," added Carl, "Karl Gareis, Erzberger, Scheidemann, Max Harden, Felix Fechenbach and all the work Gumbel continues to put out."

"And Landauer and Jogisches. That'll all be in the pyramid I'm constructing."

"Are you trying to gain access to any of those charged, to interview them? Some of them have regret. I heard one of the men involved in the Rathenau shooting melted when he got a letter from the victim's mother. Techow, I think, is the name."

More jotting of notes. "Thanks. Great idea."

"Good," said Vetter. "Keep us posted. Inflation?"

"Last time," the reporter who covered economy said, "I focused on the effects on people with fixed income, the impact on the middle class and general mores. This time, I'm interviewing bank tellers and other financial workers to determine how the plummeting of the mark is affecting their work."

"Very good. Sticking with the human, but from another angle."

"Right. That's on top of updating the statistics, government responses, the black market, fallout for reparations and Versailles, plus foreign relations."

"Especially with France and the U. S."

"Oh, yes."

"You're plate's full. That's why…" Here, Vetter stood up. "That's why I wanted to call on everyone here to help you." He looked around the room meaningfully. "None of us has been through this before; no one living has. We're not economists; we can only interview them, and we're finding many don't know their asses from a hole in the ground, or, even worse, they have reasons for being less than candid. We're dealing with a beast that keeps generating new sides, facets and angles. Hercules could drop a boulder on the Hydra, but we are limited to analyzing each new head as it pops up.

"Value is redefined twice daily for us," the editor went on. "What other society has this? Okay, Austria and Hungary, and we can learn from their ordeal and draw contrasts, but we're not there. Our situation is unique in history and, as journalists, our double burden is that we must write what we observe while we are going through it; we must examine our own turmoil. Our feelings are included in our subject. Trying to maintain that double consciousness is our unblinking job, and that's why I'm calling on all of us to help Richard. In doing our job, and doing it so well, let's not leave out our own human element."

"We're reporting on the sinking of the *Titanic* while going down with it."

"There," Vetter commented. "Does that formulation suffice?" He sat back down. "And since we're on the topic of economics, how's our 'goods for ads' program going?"

"Foodstuffs continue to be delivered Wednesdays," Gretta announced.

"So stock up, Folks! Sorry, bad joke. But it's to your advantage that we're doing this, and we all extremely fortunate that we're in a business where we can; most can't. Gretta continues to keep accounts and subtracts your acquisitions in lieu of full pay. Not easy when the balance of your account has to be continually updated due to the bizarre inflationary fluctuations."

There was spontaneous applause for Mrs. Seidenfaden.

"We're all very grateful that you're doing this for us, Mr. Vetter," she said.

"I'm glad we can; we're a family here. And I use the program myself. By the way," he waved at the desk, "that's where this spread comes from." He turned to another man. "How about our other source of goods?"

"My brother tells me he could use some more night-time volunteers to patrol his farmland and ward off people scavenging. The situation's only getting worse."

Three hands went up.

"Coordinate with Fred. Volunteers get first pick of produce."

"Why don't we just hire people to do this? It's loss of sleep!"

"We will if we have to. But the more we can avoid using money, the cheaper it gets to survive. Barter is smarter. Politics?"

"Nothing to report!" a young man named Jurgen yelled. Everyone laughed. "In fact, too much to go into," he added at lower volume. "Let me fill you in after the meeting, Boss."

"Excellent. And anyone who has input for him, make sure you relay it. We need all eyes and ears open and collaborating." He looked down at his list, then up. "French in the Ruhr?"

"I haven't heard from my regular contact in a week," Jurgen added. "I'm starting to get concerned. He's a target for both the separatists and the vigilantes, but they haven't found a body yet. At least not his."

"How long did it take to find Luxemburg's?"

Whoever blurted it out regretted it immediately. A moment of grim silence to absorb what they were all facing.

"Moving on. Ossi, any updates on the international peace movement or the arts?"

"It appears my old pacifist buddy, Gerlach, is backing the Social Democrats now. The incongruity is so inexplicable, I might have an article on what's behind it and a critique of his thought process. Also, in arts, I'm planning a treatment of indirect censorship on people like Grosz and Heartfield that goes against Article 118, and, of course, the reviews of shows."

"The Gerlach comment brings up what I saved till last so it wouldn't dominate: our elections in a couple months. I want to thank you all for your passion and efforts for our new Republican Party, and I urge you not to fade in your energies as we approach the finish line. Carl and I will be terribly busy with speech-making these last few weeks. Then we'll all be able to take a breather. Until then, I beg you all to re-double your efforts as we attempt to become part of the next coalition. Thank you from the bottom of my heart. Now let's get to it!"

As the meeting broke up, Carl heard a whisper, "And the thirteen were led to the slaughter."

****

During an introductory scene, in which a young woman comes to an island to visit a factory for the making of anthropomorphic automata, the idea was made that, while the cheapness of the machines' products was driving people out of work, in a short time all goods would be so inexpensive that humans would be free to do whatever they wanted; Carl was reminded of a passage in Wilde.

He'd stepped into the theater at the last minute on a whim and paid for entrance with his piece of coal. Now he jotted notes in the dark as he watched: 'living dolls,' 'laboring larvae,' 'Conrad Veidt never takes a break.'

In the next act, it's ten years later and births of humans have declined, since they're not needed. The circle is vicious, because humans keep demanding the construction of more 'robots,' as they are called, in order to further increase their leisure; as a result, the desire to beget children increasingly diminishes. When the young woman, Helena, discovers these things, she is shocked and, in despair, burns the formula for making the robots. As the scene ends, news comes to the island that the robots, suddenly sentient and vengeful, are revolting and plan to kill all the parasitical humans.

During intermission, Carl stationed himself at a far end of the bar and savored a coffee while writing in his notebook: 'capitalist overproduction of artificial people/workers,' 'sense of self awakens,' 'doomed to extinction since the secret of fabrication irretrievably gone.' He studied the program: '*Rossumovi's Universal Robots* by Karel Capek. Translated from the Czech language. 1920.' The robots had only been differentiated from the human in the first scene by their mechanical movements, monotone affects, and blank stares. In the second, unlike the humans, the robots had worn white blouses belted with a sash and pinned with a metal number. Carl had never before witnessed such a play; shades of H. G. Wells and Jules Verne.

He wanted to think more about prototypes—Tucholsky's favorite, Lucian?—but his attention was drawn to the other end of the bar by the sounds of two pompous voices arguing with each other. When he looked, he could hardly believe his eyes: there were three officers in imperial uniform, who looked like they had just stepped out of their field headquarters. Carl did his best not to gawk, quickly looking back down at his scribblings, but he was amazed at how his ears automatically tapered their range, as if instinctually blocking out the audio wall in the background lobby chatter and zeroing in on the voices nearby. He pretended to continue composing his ideas, writing, 'imperial powers turn androids into soldiers,' then surrounding the clause with an aimless pencil scratch. Surreptitiously, he raised his eyes

331

toward the immense mirror behind to bustling bartenders, angling his view to get a better look at the officers.

"If what you're saying about the factory chief is right," said one, "then who are the robots?" He was bald; no, all three were bald as billiard balls. But this one had a sinuous growth of gray spreading above his upper lip, reaching like ivy in both directions.

"They're not robots. They're *robotski.*"

"Bolsheviks?"

"Who else?"

"Why, the men in the trenches, of course!" the other countered, self-consciously drawing an index finger along a scar in front of his ear. Old saber wound from a student duel? It didn't seem fresh to Carl; the old man must've been fingering it for a long time. Embarrassment or pride?

"General, when will you stop reliving the war? Are you insinuating that our soldiers were exploited?"

"I don't think that way, but…"

"Yes?"

"Others do!"

"Ah, the back-stabbers! Have you been listening to them? That's your problem."

The defeated man looked up, re-fixing his monocle. Carl dropped his head, doodling vigorously.

"What do you think?" Carl heard the verbal victor ask the third veteran. "You've been uncharacteristically silent." In the dynamic of these three, the question was a formal challenge. *En garde!*

The quiet one was in the middle of taking snuff. "Precipitate attacks," He finally answered, speaking in a sharper voice than the others, "are, by definition, ill-advised. I prefer to withhold my opinion of the play's significance until I've finished watching it."

The other two exchanged looks, as if they had been offended. Then all three went back to their seats in onerous silence.

During the second half of the futuristic play, robots attack and kill all of the humans, except for the engineer, old Alquist, whom they pardon because, like them, he worked with his hands. Also, they keep him to plan the construction of more buildings. Over the years, the engineer tries to recreate the robot formula, to no avail. He attempts this by dissecting and studying the insides of the robots, an operation he loathes. Meanwhile, two robots fall in love with each other. When the engineer threatens to dissect now one, now another, each offers to die for the beloved. In astonishment, the engineer hands over control of the world to these two, and the curtain falls.

Hoping to catch the men in conversation once more, Carl hurried back to the bar and stationed himself again at the seat on the end. Sure enough, they returned and ordered more schnapps.

"Well, what do you know! I'm bowled over."

"I was expecting a replay of the immolation scene from Wagner, but the author gave us a twist."

"The Book of Genesis!"

"Okay, General, will you finally tell us who you think the robots are?"

The uncommitted veteran rolled a cigar between his lips to dampen the end, then lit it elaborately. "Do you remember Bismarck's test of von Moltke?"

"The two cigars?"

"Yes, one Cuban—"

"And the other inferior, of no special provenance."

"And Bismarck watched 'the Elder' inspecting them before choosing."

"And he inferred from this that his general was confident of victory."

"Precisely. But which cigar did he choose?"

"The Havana. But what does that say about the machines?"

"Nothing. But it says something about how I differ from you two."

"Indeed!"

"The robots are serfs," The reticent figure claimed while puffing furiously. "Inferior entities. I looked it up at home. That's what 'robots' means in Czech. And I have a feeling these serfs are even rather Czech, in spite of the claim to universality in the title, and that there's a lot of Masaryk and Benes and a bit of Germanophobia underneath it all."

The other two men were sputtering, and Carl had to admit he was dumbfounded.

"Well!" exclaimed one of them "You've missed your profession when you entered the military."

"What's a young man to do?"

****

Carl couldn't remember the last time he was this drunk. He didn't like getting drunk anyway; he didn't even like getting tipsy—it seemed an affront and offense to the work he'd put into developing the meager cognitive powers he claimed to possess. A waste of rationality. Overdrinking was unnatural, senseless— literally. He wasn't going to go as far as the abstaining Paasche had, and he wouldn't think of legislating for others, but why would you toil so hard to think clearly, and then just hand over willingly all your accomplishments to your irrational self to violate and abuse? If someone had forced you to do so, you'd protest, wouldn't you? So why do it to yourself? Carl shook his head vehemently.

Besides, people do things when they're drunk that they simply would never do when they were sober, and then regretted it later. Suddenly, he realized that was the reason why he'd gotten so drunk tonight: to balance the stupidity he'd shown all these months while he thought he was so salubriously sober. As it turned out, he and Vetter had been acting like drunken men, thinking they'd make an impact on the political situation. And worse, they dragged the staff of the *People's Paper* along with them.

Forty thousand votes! That was the fact that kept punching his ego! Forty thousand! The fledgling, stillborn Republican Party had not earned one member of Parliament! In spite of the ready-made party organ, the *People's Paper*, they'd only been able to garner forty thousand votes in a nation of sixty million! How could they have led themselves, and others, so far astray? How could they have failed so badly in reading the political climate? And what did this say about their lack of political acumen, not just as journalists, but as engaged citizens?

The damage to their newspaper would be irreparable.

But then, done for the moment with flaying himself and Vetter, his anger turned toward the electorate. How could they have made such poor choices? Like Gerlach, caving into the *status quo*. Fools! The public!

Footsteps on the stairs. The door to Vetter's office opened.

"I'm here," said Carl.

"My God!" came Vetter's voice. "Can I turn on the light?"

"Just the one on your desk, preferably."

Vetter stepped over to his desk and switched on the lamp; it cast its beam down on the desktop, a mellow light beyond its shade. He squinted across the room at Carl, who slouched in the stuffed chair.

"I wondered where you'd gone."

"I couldn't stand it there anymore at the bar. Too many sad faces."

"Yeah." Vetter sat at his desk, head bent as if he were studying the grain of the wood. "People can't think straight because of the inflation. And the inflation's because the government just keeps printing money. And they keep printing money to pay off the workers, who don't work because of the passive resistance policy against the French. And the French are doing what they're doing because of the Treaty, and our non-compliance, and the war, and the guilt."

"Like Count Harry said," Carl responded, "most Germans would agree to the reparations if they didn't think it was all going to French rearmament. It's a vicious circle."

"I suppose I'll recover from this. Someday." Vetter continued to pick at the wood with a fingernail.

Carl tried to comprehend what had happened to them. "I think I finally understand something of what my stepfather was going through when his Social Democrats split over support for the war. At the time, I didn't understand why he was so crushed. Now, I think I do: something he totally identified with had committed suicide. He kept trying and failing to understand how and why it could have happened. The sense of losing the ground he stood on never left him.

"And I thought I was going through the same thing when I left the GPS, but I was wrong. I'd just changed my mind about what to do in my life. I was still a pacifist; I just didn't want to work inside the movement anymore. It was too demoralizing. But I was ready to move on; he wasn't.

"But this is different, Karl. I've lost some of the ground I used to be able to walk on. Someone tore up the flooring, and I'm having to watch out where I step.

"Maybe someday I'll recover some faith in the German citizen again. Maybe not. I don't know. I can't see when or how it would happen; I'm lost there."

Vetter was watching him and nodding.

"Yeah," he said. "I doubt I'll continue with the paper. I know you won't, but I'm not worried about you. You'll continue writing, find another paper, another editor. That's all you need to keep going, Carl. That and your family.

"But I am worried about some of our colleagues. If this paper folds, and it probably will, unless I can sell it to someone, I don't know if these youngsters will land on their feet. We all seemed to come together for a moment in time. We were a 'we.' That's a rare thing, as the world goes about its business. It hardly ever happens. And then it's shot to hell. What did it all mean? Some of these folks'll never recover. They'll try to find the same thing elsewhere, Geist or *esprit* or whatever you want to call it, but, mostly, they'll just find business as usual."

Vetter went on, "But you'd laugh if you knew the one I'm most worried about: Willy."

"The messenger boy?"

"They just took him to the hospital. He broke his foot jumping in the way of a tram in front of the bar. It could have been worse."

"On purpose?"

"We're everything to him. I'd just explained to him that we wouldn't be needing him so much anymore. He couldn't get it out of his head that the campaign would go on forever, that the election didn't have anything to do with our campaign. When he finally seemed to understand, I guess he became a little suicidal. And the booze they'd given him didn't help. Before we knew it, he'd run out into the street."

"Just broke his foot?"

"Yeah. George and Gretta walked him to the hospital.

Carl started crying. Not a lot; just tears. Immediately he stood up, hoping movement would stop the flow. He staggered toward the door and went down the stairs.

To hell with goodbyes.

He wanted to find the hospital and visit the boy. He wanted to talk to him, comfort him, tell him everything would be all right in a while. It would just take time.

He kept looking, wandering, hoping it would become light. When it became light, he would be able to find his way.

Chapter Twenty-One
PRESENT

And they didn't read about the evils of the Nuremburg Laws, enacted in September of 1935, condemning romantic relationships between Jews and German Gentiles, criminalizing the hiring of German Gentile females under 45 in Jewish households, and forbidding German citizenship to any but those of pure German blood. They could not access trenchant critiques of the causes, motivations and repercussions of the new laws.

They could not read balanced or critical analyses of these laws, because the only papers that would have published such articles had been banned by the government of the Realm. The papers that remained trumpeted the regime's successes and parroted its every move.

****

They were trudging back from the swamp. It was a march they had performed twice daily hundreds of times, feet aching in the wooden clogs, arms and hands and joints screaming from their worthless effort. But, this time, the trip was somehow different.

Carl, who had been pushing himself unsuccessfully to talk to the man who wasn't "one of us," according to the Jehovah's Witness, saw him up ahead.

"I heard the Jehovah's talking about you," he forced himself to say after sidling up to him. No response.

"They say you belong to a religion." Nothing. "But that you don't believe the soul's immortal."

"That's bullshit!" another prisoner butt in.

339

"What?" asked a fourth, who had been beaten in the head by some guards three days before and wasn't used to being deaf yet. "What did you say?"

"It can't be a religion, then!" yelled the one who'd barged in.

"It's a hard point," Carl conceded, still wanting to hear the mystery man say something. "How can a religion not believe in the afterlife?"

They kept walking.

"We..." the man said in a croaking voice, then stopped.

"What do you call yourselves?" Carl asked with a soft voice, hoping to entice an answer he could chew on.

"Christadelphians."

"Christadumbasses! Yer a fucking bunch of idiots!" blasted the interloper, who hurried forward, as if to rid himself of some stinking nuisance.

"What? What did he say?"

A guard had caught up with them. "What I don't like is the way the camp has changed," stated the guard. Evidently, he was reacting to the departed man's polemical fervor. He thought he was picking up the thread of some conversation.

Carl was shocked. He almost stopped in his tracks, but then recovered and, opting not to ignore the remark, asked, "What do you mean?"

"You're not supposed to be talking to us!" the deaf man informed the guard. He was still hot about being beaten. All he'd done to merit it was to be a little slow getting into the delousing vat. He hated that chemical smell!

"Shut up!" shrieked the guard, who shook a fist. "Or we'll do it again!"

The deaf man hurried away from them.

Then, to Carl and the stranger, the guard continued, going back to his original, more even and controlled voice, "I mean,

I'm one of the older guards here, and this camp has really gone downhill lately."

Now Carl felt he had to pursue this, whatever it was. "Can you explain?" he persisted. "I still don't know what you mean."

"Aw, hell, you're just a bunch of eastern Jews and criminals now," he explained. "You used to be mainly politicals, reds and such, a bunch of eggheads but, you know, a decent sort. Your values were all screwed up, but at least you had them."

Carl didn't thank the man. "And now?" he prodded.

"It's a thieves' den, and worse! They're all organized, the hardened ones, and they're starting to cause trouble with the others. You know, taking over."

They were back at the camp. The stranger had disappeared already.

Carl couldn't fathom what was going on with the guard, but something made him want to prolong the moment.

The guard lit a cigarette for himself and then offered one to Carl. Carl saw in his eyes that he had considered apologizing for not offering it at once, but overruled the notion. Carl took the cigarette, planning to trade it later for bread—he was no longer interested in smoking—but the guard took the cigarette back when he realized what Carl was up to.

"You know," the guard continued, blowing smoke and shaking the hand with the cigarette, "there's no, there's no…"

"Solidarity."

"There's no solidarity among the prisoners anymore," the guard went on. "You guys used to have some, and it kinda made coming to work less nerve-wracking, but now you've lost it. Everyone's out for themselves, it seems. It was never fun coming here, but at least it was different. I'm, I've never worked in a prison before, see, so I'm not as used to the criminal element, and, you know, the Jews are Jews, especially the ones pouring in from the East. I don't like the mood. A bunch of hard-nosed

341

bastards, each one out for himself. Why don't you guys do something about it, you politicals?" Then he shook his head. "I guess your numbers are down, and all, and they outnumber you. It would be hard for you to take it all back."

"Perhaps you need a change." Carl hardly believed he was suggesting a career move to the man, but the words seemed to roll out of his mouth on their own.

"I need a change!" concluded the man in agreement. It was a revelation.

They were silent. Then Carl quietly suggested, "You guards are different, too." What was he saying!

"Hm." The guard finished his draw on the cigarette with finesse, lifting his chin abruptly. "How so?"

"At first, you were brutal. Then, you got more organized and tried to educate us. When that didn't work, you went back to—"

"But that's just my point!" he exploded, stabbing the air between them with the smoking cigarette. "That's exactly what I'm saying. It's because you prisoners have changed that we've changed. Convicts and kikes! There's hardly any here just like you anymore." He puffed.

Finally, Carl asked, "Aren't you afraid you'll be in trouble for talking to me like this?"

"Naw." He shrugged, chuckling. "I'd just say I was trying to bribe you to rat on someone. You're the one who better watch out." He looked right and left, miming furtiveness. "The Capos will probably think you're a stool-pigeon," he whispered in mock caution. Then, tossing the butt to the ground, he walked away. A prisoner immediately swept in and carefully retrieved the still-smoking cigarette.

The next week, the guard was awarded with a transfer.

****

Robert confronted Sophie about Maud. Why had she misled him? Why was Ossietzky's wife living in their house under an assumed name?

He had waited until Maud had gone out for her afternoon walk.

"Are you trying to get us killed?"

"She is my friend!"

"And you didn't even tell me who she is? You lied to me! 'Mrs. Kohl'!"

"I didn't want you to worry."

"Sophia! The Gestapo interrogated me yesterday! We might be in grave trouble!"

"Well, do we have to put her out on the street? I am her last friend."

The captain ran his fingers through his hair. "No," he said. "At least not yet. I have an idea, and the man said I could give it a try."

They hear Maud at the front door.

"What do I have to do?" she asked anxiously.

"Don't tell her I know," he whispered.

****

Ernst Toller was coming to Sweden to see one man: Kurt Tucholsky. But it seemed impossible to find him. Toller had heard Tucholsky was in a bad way, thoroughly paranoid, thinking Hitler had sent assassins to liquidate him, and the upshot was that the ones who wanted to help him couldn't locate their would-be beneficiary.

That's why Toller contacted Kurt Singer, the man who had been instrumental in discovering a place for Ossietzky's daughter.

"I heard he's holed out in Hindas, thoroughly spooked," said Singer. "He won't let anyone see him. I suggest you just show up and hope he lets you in. Do you need a car?"

Toller drove up to Hindas the next day and found the house without much trouble. He walked right up to it and banged on the door. A woman answered, another right behind her. Recognizing him, they stared at each other, and then jointly decided to let him wait in Kurt's study.

Ten minutes passed, the ticking of a clock on the wall the only sound. Toller picked up a volume of Heine, leafed through it, set it back where he got it, and looked at papers scattered across the desk. Scribblings: creativity in embryo.

Finally, Tucholsky rushed in, breathless.

"Toller! You found me!"

Tucholsky, nicknamed 'Chubby' for as long as Toller had known him, looked bloated, apoplectic.

"Kurt. I hear you're unwell."

"Who told you? How did you find me?"

"Hello to you too!" Toller sat down. "Relax and talk to your old comrade!"

Tucholsky spread his arms as if to display his wretchedness. "As you see, the demons have descended at last!"

"I don't know. It looks to me like you should be comfortable here."

"Perhaps if I tried harder, is that what you mean? Rather paradoxical, don't you think?"

"Surely something can be done for you."

"My good man, everything is being done for me. Didn't you see the nice ladies? Everything, and nothing helps. My paradise is positively immersed in poison. We're in a hothouse fit for *les fleurs du mal*."

As he talked, he paced the room.

"That man, Singer," Toller suggested. "Can't he find you a doctor, a… psychologist?"

Tucholsky, stopping to look out the window, shrugged. "My writing used to transport me," he said, turning toward Toller to grin bitterly. "It had salvific powers. But, it seems," he tapped on a chair, "I've run out of viable aliases." He waved an arm over his desk.

"Go to America!"

"I just might."

"Escape from this wretched Europe, if you must."

"We've discussed it many times."

"Or better yet, come with me to Spain!"

"Are you crazier than I am?"

"We're finally putting on a fight in Spain, Kurt. It will invigorate you. Breathe life into you."

"I wouldn't last a day! My nerves can't even handle the monotony of Sweden, Ernst."

"It might revitalize you, my friend. In Spain, we're finally making a stand against fascism."

Tucholsky scoffed, stuffing his hands in his pockets. "Do you really think they'd have use for me?"

"For everyone! That's the point, Kurt."

"And what will you do?"

Ernst lit a cigarette. "I already gave them my money. Hopefully, they'll let me fight in the brigades against Franco."

"Yes, you were always a fighter."

"Fighting made a writer out of me. Maybe it'll happen again. When they threw me in prison, after the Munich soviet, I became inspired. Produced my best work. Since then, my most inspiring workplaces have all been the size of a cell." He gestured to the spacious room. "I'd drown in here."

"I'm the opposite. Confinement strangles me. The walls close in."

"Yes, I suppose we are opposites."

"That's why I left Germany in the first place, you know. After Jacobsohn's death, when Edith made me editor of *The Worldstage*. But I had to stay put, there in Berlin. And then I found out that editors could be thrown into prison for something their rag printed, even if they didn't write it themselves. And so, when Jacob came to me with his articles…"

"Berthold? You mean you could have published them in *The Worldstage*?"

"I'm not proud of it! Yes, I sent him away. We had enough trouble on our hands. And that's—"

"That's why they were published in *The Other Germany*."

"And that's when I decided to resign. I knew I wasn't cut out for being an editor-in-chief. I'm a writer, dammit! So—"

"You returned to France."

Tucholsky lit a cigarette, hands shaking. "Everyone thought it was because of my love of Paris. It's true: *J'adore Paris*, but there was more to it than that."

"And Ossi took over the paper."

The clock ticked half a minute before their conversation continued.

"And now he's in a labor camp," Toller added.

"To think I criticized the man for not mentoring me like Siegfried had done!" Tears started streaming down Tucholsky's face. "Why did I still need a mentor? I thought he was too indulgent, too patronizing of me when he didn't critique my work. He just accepted it as is. I said he was too remote to be an editor. Now, he's suffering for my excesses!"

"He's suffering for all of us."

"He was the only one of us who understood what we were up against; that, after the press, the courts were our only recourse against the fascists. Remote? All the time, I was cowering behind him!" He covered his eyes with his hand and tried to wipe away the tears.

"Kurt, you have nothing to feel guilty about."

"Oh, I'm not done, Ernst!" He paused, looked at the flickering tip of his cigarette. "I considered coming back once. That was when Carl was already in jail. We were being tried for that notorious sentence I wrote, the one about soldiers being murderers; me, in absentia. I felt I should be there, stand there in the court with him, but I talked myself out of it. I just couldn't chance it."

The clock ticked.

"I'll always remember," Toller offered, "the leadership he provided when spearheading that unofficial inquiry into the Bloody May massacres. Not just his ability to deliver stirring speeches off-the-cuff, although that really surprised me, him being such a quiet person. But the way he interacted with the witnesses was so impressive to me, someone more inclined to use a cudgel than kid gloves.

"There's an art to asking questions," Toller went on after a drag on his cigarette, "not well practiced in our country, without casting suspicion on the person being questioned."

"The art Socrates tried to teach Athenians. Before they killed him."

"Hm. Yes, Ossi was good at that too, but I'm talking about a way of doing it that emphasizes a shared humanity, a kind of affective bridge that allows the other to step over his vulnerability and cross over, expose himself, as it were. He showed he was a master in the course of those terrible days, considering what we were up against.

"I must admit that I never thought we'd get much of a showing, or many witnesses willing to come forward, things being the way they were in Berlin in those days, but, as it turned out, we had to allot extra dates and venues to our inquiry because of the response. I don't have any other explanation for it, but I feel his role, the personal and honest interest he showed—you can't fake that sort of thing—and his call for justice in the matter, they were instrumental to our success."

"Before," Tucholsky responded, "I was relieved that I wasn't in the country at the time, but now you've made me feel half-regretful I wasn't there with you, in spite of the dangers you faced."

"Oh, we could have been bludgeoned, I suppose!" Toller drew on the cigarette again, but then seemed to shake himself. "You've written your letter to Oslo, I assume?"

"We all have. If only it gets him out of there."

"You know, his daughter's here in Sweden."

"I can't see her!"

Toller took a long drag on his cigarette. "I understand," he said at last.

Finally, Toller stood up and came over to him, holding out his hand.

"I'll write to you from Spain," he said, comfortingly.

They shook, Toller noting that the haunted look of the other had never left him during the entire visit.

Tucholsky did not see him to the door.

Before getting into the car, Toller told the women, "Get him on a ship to the U. S. The sooner the better!"

Toller ended up leaving Sweden without seeing Rosalinde, though he couldn't quite explain to himself why he didn't.

Singer kept Toller's brief visit to Sweden a secret from Rosalinde, but he couldn't manage to keep the news of what happened to Tucholsky from the lonely girl. Kurt Tucholsky took poison and succeeded in fleeing his demons on the first day of winter.

****

When Sophie came home from shopping, she felt the house was too quiet. She looked for Maud and ended up in her room. She immediately noticed one of her guest's suitcases was gone. When she saw the letter on the table, she froze. Maud had just told her of Edith Jacobsohn's suicide, hanging herself in her London apartment. *No!* With trembling hand, she lifted the page.

> *Sophie,*
>
> *I'm so sorry about this. I feel ashamed for not coming to you, but I couldn't.*
>
> *I'm going to Esterwegen to see if they'll let me see Carl over the holidays.*
>
> *I had to go. I know you're having family come, and I was looking forward to seeing them, but then I realized that I just couldn't. I didn't want to bring things down with my unhappiness. Especially with Carl by himself in that awful camp.*
>
> *I will be back in the new year. Thank you for everything, Sophie.*
>
> *Love, Maud*

Exhaling with some relief, Sophie folded the letter and stuffed it in her pocket. Then, just as she was turning to leave the room, she was drawn to a folded sheet of paper jutting out from under some books. She slipped it out and examined the writing: names, addresses. Berthold Jacob. Georg Bernhard. She would show them to Robert; they might be what he needed to appease the Gestapo.

****

Letters poured in at the Nobel institution. Thomas and Heinrich Mann, Ernest Hemingway, John Dewey, Upton Sinclair, Ludwig Marcuse, Ernst Toller, Harold Laski, Albert Einstein, Jane Addams, Samuel Eliot Morrison, Sidney Hook, Norman Angell, Gilbert Murray, J. B. Priestley, H. G. Wells, Bertrand Russell, Aldous Huxley, C. Day Lewis, Leonard and Virginia Woolf, Kurt Tucholsky, Romain Rolland, Leon Blum, Edouard Herriot, Arnold Zweig, Lion Feuchtwanger, Karl Barth, Helene Stocker, Karl Frahm. Things, at last, were starting to look uncharacteristically good. And then the great Norwegian author, Knut Hamsun, who himself as a child had suffered brutal torture when beaten and starved by his uncle, and bore life-long neurological ailments as a result, printed his polemical bombshell:

> *Has not von Ossietzky provoked his imprisonment? Has he not insulted, repeatedly and deliberately, the Will of the People, and their Party, National Socialism? Would it not be better for him to remain silent in this difficult time, when the entire world has made a devilish alliance against a great people? What does he want to do, demonstrate as a pacifist against rearmament, but only against German rearmament?*

> *Does this man prefer to watch his land be brought to its knees, enslaved by the French and English, at the mercy of their questionable goodwill? Would those countries, and their peoples, consider the same, were the tables turned?*

> *"How is it even being considered, that Carl von Ossietzky deserves our country's highest award?"*

This, along with a negative letter from King Haakon VII, and turmoil surrounding the resignation of several from the selection committee who were also members of his government, had an effect. On November 19, the announcement was given: there would be no Nobel Peace Prize awarded in 1935. There had been precedent for this: none had been awarded in 1932.

Hilde Walter, composing a circulating letter, commented tearfully that this decision was tantamount to a death sentence for Carl.

****

After checking into the hotel outside the concentration camp, Maud went straight to the headquarters. She was shown into the office of the Commandant at once.

It didn't take long.

After she introduced herself and made her request, with utmost politeness, to see Carl, the man said, "Take off your clothes!"

"Pardon me?"

"I want to see what I'm getting!"

When she had returned to the hotel, she told the man at the counter that she wanted to check out at once.

"So soon?"

"Yes!"

"Let's see." He was looking at his ledger. "Mrs. Keller?"

"No."

"Mrs. Feingold?"

"No!"

"Ah! You're Mrs. Weiss!"

"NO!" She stood on her tiptoes to try to read the upside-down writing.

"I'm sorry, Ma'am, but Commandant Didier has so many women checked in here to see him that I can't keep track."

She jabbed her index finger down on her name. "That one!"

She paid, gathered her things, and left, taking the first train out of Esterwegen. Where, she didn't know. She'd decide on the way.

Chapter Twenty-Two
PAST

"What time did you stagger in?" Maud asked, standing at the stove, after he'd padded into the kitchen in his robe and slippers and sat down at the table next to five-year-old Rosalinde.

"No staggering," he chuckled. Maud set a cup of coffee in front of him. "I just had two beers, one before and one during dinner. I don't like to get bloated."

"You don't like to get drunk," Maud responded. "It betrays your sacred reason. But why won't you tell us when you came home? You were as quiet as a mouse."

"Yeah, Daddy," Rosa challenged him as she sat before the remains of her pancake. "When did you come home?"

He put his head over the steam from the cup and inhaled. "Four."

"Oh, dear," commented Maud. "Carl, you're not a young man anymore. You'll be a wreck all day."

"Why?" he asked in panic. "What are we doing?" It was Saturday.

"I thought we'd take her to the park."

"Just give me some time. I'll be all right after some coffee and a cigarette."

Rosa wagged a finger at him. "You're not a young man, Daddy."

He patted his daughter on the top of her head.

Maud set a plate of eggs next to his coffee and sat down across from him with a plate of her own. "Well, tell us about it."

He sipped. "Oh, Maud, you would have loved it."

"How many were there?"

353

"About thirty. Almost all writers for Jacobsohn at some time or other. Six big tables in the basement under the pub."

"Mr. Jacobsohn must have been so happy."

"Beaming. Going from one guest to another. Some of them were surprises for him. People he hadn't seen for years. Ones who'd come a long way."

"The twentieth anniversary of a paper is a big thing."

"I wish spouses had been invited, but it would have been too many. But, Maud, the conversations!"

"Like what?"

"Arnheim, the psychologist. I had a great talk with him before dinner. He actually studies at the Imperial Palace among all the murals. He's writing his dissertation on how we read facial expressions! That and handwriting. Wertheimer has him doing lab work on penmanship and how we emote! And Siegfried's got him writing movie reviews!"

"You write about movies, Daddy."

"Not like Rudolf. He's always focused on what's left out of a camera shot, not just what's included. What the viewer adds that isn't really there."

Rosalinde yawned. "This is boring." Carl raised his eyebrows.

"*Catastrophe* doesn't think so," Maud countered, nodding toward the cat, which was staring up at the table avidly.

"Oh, she just wants tidbits," Rosa explained, getting up and leaving the room. Catastrophe soon followed her.

"Sounds very Kantian," said Maud. "What the mind brings to experience, and all that."

"Yes, especially with regard to grouping, patterns, symmetry, and such."

"Fascinating."

"I knew you'd think so. But that was just the beginning."

"What else?"

"During dinner, Ihering got into an argument with Lasker-Schuler. Someone must have had a piece dropped by Siegfried. 'We've all felt that,' said Elsa. 'Growing pains.'

'The analogy is faulty,' Ihering argued. 'You're implying that artists mature.'

'Yes!' she gushed. She talks just like her poetry.

'No,' he went on, 'art is a hit-or-miss, one-and-done lightning strike. No one is privileged to any kind of continuity when it comes to creation. He, or she, may never be moved to take up the brush again.'"

"I see," said Maud. "Was he being pompous when he said it?"

"I think he actually wanted to compliment poets like Elsa who can make a life out of it, but she took it as a challenge, like he was pontificating. We've all been there, when we've said something we didn't expect anyone to question. 'So artistic careers are freaks of nature,' Elsa paraphrased.

'If that's how you want to put it,' Ihering agreed. 'Although, I don't think nature has anything to do with it. I prefer to think the artist remakes himself with each new piece.'

'But isn't that just another way of saying the artist grows?' Elsa demanded.

'There's nothing to grow,' he answered her. 'You have a product. What's strange is that the producer also produces himself. The execution of each inspiration brings a new artistic identity.'"

"Wow!" Maud exclaimed. "That's an extremely dynamic conception of art. If he's right, it makes you wonder how anyone can sustain it."

"But listen. Ihering wasn't done. 'There's another problem with thinking in terms of artistic maturation,' he continued. 'In art, there's no authority. Growth implies there's naturally a right way and many wrong ones. But,' he says, 'there's nothing natural about artistic appreciation. That's why we have *de gustibus*.

Elsa,' he says, 'you're dragging the whole, heavy peripatetic apparatus of biology into the realm of taste. Inspiration isn't some acorn with the ambition of becoming an oak. What's Aristotle's ugly term? Entelechy. That's it. And don't bother saying catharsis is an Aristotelian concept; catharsis happens in the audience, not the artist.' Elsa opened her hands and shook her head, as if to say, 'I didn't mention it!' 'And, interestingly enough,' Ihering went on, 'the Stagirite stays away from entelechy in his own *Poetics*. He was smart enough to know a work of art's a different thing from coming-to-be-and-passing-away.'"

"My!" said Maud. "You certainly have quite a memory!"

"But Elsa wasn't giving up," said Carl, ignoring her remark. "By the way, at this point, there were no other conversations going on at our table. People were just eating and listening to the two of them. So, she says, 'Herbert, it's almost as if you're saying art has no standards whatsoever.'

"'No "almost,"' he replies. 'Art has only preference, like the choice of bread and meat on your plate. It's the rather fortuitous coincidence of the perceiver's preference with the artist's execution that brings about artistic success. It's not the empty platitudes of some officious Winckelmann, nor even the pronouncements of an enlightened Schiller.'

"Elsa looked around the table, hoping for some recognition in each face. Was anyone going to come to her aid? Did anyone agree with her, at this point? But still, she rallied; she wasn't done.

"'Often,' she said, 'we're brought back to the realization that our carriage is being pulled by a horse just at the moment he stops pulling it. We were lulled into a kind of dream state of perpetual motion. Then what happens? You're thrown forward for one last half-step as the harness continues its thrust, then you're snapped back when it readjusts to its normal spot on the horse's back.

There's no going forward without some equine power; that's a given. But something else is required: direction.'

"'I don't see your point,' said Ihering. 'My view isn't affected by some simple figure drawn from the field of locomotion.'

"Elsa tossed her napkin on the table. 'Someone please illuminate the man,' was all she said." Carl paused.

"Was she the only woman at the table?"

"She was the only woman in the room."

"No wonder! She must have felt terribly isolated."

"But then Kastner stood up and pointed at Siegfried. 'There he is!' he yells. '*Q. E. D.!* There's your charioteer, Elsa! Authority in the flesh! Our own Scipio Jacobsohn Africanus!' Everyone in the room could hear; people laughed. A few at our table applauded, especially Elsa, and then more from other tables. Of course, Siegfried didn't know what was being discussed at our table, but he offered a mock bow anyway, and took the moment, since he had everyone's attention, to tell us in English not to talk about the proverbial elephant in the room."

"Did he specify?"

"No, so no one knew what new disaster of German life he meant. I mean, at first, I thought it had to be me," Maud smirked at this, "but, as I found, so did some others."

"Hmmm."

"Then Tucholsky shouted that it was Siegfried himself, and everyone laughed."

"Was it?"

"Siegfried said no. Well, at our table, Ihering was having none of it; he wouldn't be diverted from his argument. He told Kastner an editor was merely an arbitrary imposition forced upon writers by the ownership. It had nothing essential to do with art. That's when some of us got up and started milling around again."

Maud stood up and carried her plate to the sink. Carl brought his and Rosa's, and they started rinsing the dishes, leaning against each other at the sink.

"But then," Carl went on, "I caught the tail-end of some talk that really put everything else in perspective. Sternberg was lecturing Lewinsohn and Goldschmidt about the inflation, so I stuck my head in to see what I could pick up. Eggebrecht had just left them; evidently Sternberg had just told him off. You see, Eggebrecht had just returned from Russia very disillusioned, and old Fritz had scolded him that he should be giving Lenin's regime more time to settle after their civil war. Alex had taken it as an insult and limped off. That's when I came up to them. He was telling Richard and Alfons that German big business had actually made out like bandits during the debacle of the mark, in spite of their complaining.

"I'd at least understood already that our inflation wasn't the result of other countries arbitrarily raising the value of their own currency. It was because of our own government flooding the country with marks to pay for reparations and to support the resistance during the Ruhr occupation. And I'd known of the whole slough of them, Krupps and Thyssen and Siemens and Farben, demanding old currency for payments while they doled out the new marks to their workers. But I hadn't realized the scope or the level of hypocrisy and scapegoating.; I hadn't connected the dots.

"Well, Sternberg connects all the dots. He said the industries increased profits exponentially. The higher the inflation, the more they benefitted. And the Dawes Commission was icing on the cake with their cheap loans."

"It's enough to turn your stomach," said Maud.

"Though Alfons maintained, it wasn't all to the bad. The factories were finally modernized."

The Man Without a Party

There was a sudden shout from the front room. Carl and Maud ran to the parlor. Rosalinde stood at the window, pointing. Her parents looked out; it was yet another military parade. But this one was different. Soldiers and sailors carried not one, but two flags: black-red-yellow and black-white-red: the colors of Weimar's Republic alongside of those for the Kaiser's Prussian Empire.

"Hindenburg got his way after all," Carl inferred.

"*L'elephant a chie dans la rue*," sighed Maud.

****

Later, they'd swung by the apartment of Rosa's friend to fetch her on their way to the park. And, after they'd spread out the blanket on the grass, Carl had promptly fallen asleep. He woke up twenty minutes later when the sun shifted on him. After a yawn and a stretch, he'd tossed the ball with the girls, then returned to Maud on the blanket.

"Nice nap?"

"Very."

"You kept saying something while you were asleep."

"Really?"

"Yes, like you were desperate to be heard. Something starting with an 'L.' 'Lee' something."

"'Lee'? Oh, maybe 'League of Nations.'"

Maud laughed. "You've got that on your mind? Carl, sometimes I feel sorry for you. You're absolutely driven."

"Oh, that's just what I wanted to say last night. At the dinner. After listening to Sternburg, I noticed that some were returning with fresh drinks to a table. Feuchtwanger and Mehring, first, then Muhsam, Zweig, Tucholsky, and others. They'd pushed the dishes toward the center and had their heads leaning forward, as if they didn't want to be overheard. So, of course, I had to join them. Guess what they were talking about!"

"Women!"

"Try again!"

"Their favorite cabaret."

"No!"

"Tell me!"

"They were trying to figure out what Jacobsohn's elephant was!"

"Of course they would!"

"They had several choices before I got there, and they kept going over them: Cassirer's suicide; Hitler in Hamburg; Hindenburg's anniversary; the boycott of Ludwig Marcuse. Let's see: Stresemann's Peace Prize nomination; Heisenburg's theory; France's departure from the Ruhr—"

"But some of these are good things!"

"Yes, and some were disqualified as being old news. What else?"

"The two flags, of course!"

"Yes, and the SS. And then, right when I was going to suggest Germany's entry into the League, someone said Baker's Banana Dance."

"I'm sure that got everyone laughing."

"Guess who said it."

"Oh, you're full of guesses!"

"You'll never guess."

"That's right! I won't even try."

"It was Jacobsohn himself! He'd snuck up behind us."

"Josephine Baker? She was his elephant?"

"That's what people wanted to find out when they realized it was Siegfried who'd said it. He said of course, but he had that twinkle in his eye. Some objected that he couldn't nominate, that he wasn't eligible because he was the 'authority' who'd started the whole elephant thing."

They heard Rosa and Lotte yelling; their ball had fallen into the pond. Carl went off to help them retrieve it, but, as he neared the water, he thought he heard someone singing the awful song about Luxemburg's corpse being fished out of the canal. He froze, then turned around to look, but failed to determine anywhere the voice could have come from. And then, as he turned back to help the girls, he found it difficult to approach the water any closer, like there was an invisible barrier. The girls were staring at him, wondering why he didn't do anything. Finally, with great effort, he was able to pick up a branch and retrieve the ball for them. But, after they ran off, he stood there at the shore, looking at the dark, placid water; there was definitely no more singing. By the time he got back to Maud, he'd brushed the incident aside as the result of his fatigue and refrained from mentioning it to her.

"So was anyone leaving the party by that time?" she asked.

He laughed, his mind coming back to the night before. "Yes, a few. Some actually decided to go to The Harlem to see this notorious banana dance. Siegfried kept arguing that he was an editor, not an authority, so he should be able to vote on the elephant. Then Kurt Hiller showed up at the party with people no one knew. He said he'd been hanging out at Hirschfeld's Center and couldn't get away. Hiller gave Siegfried a big hug, like he was drunk, and when they told him what the argument was about, he said he had just two things to say: All the suggestions comprised one big elephant, and Siegfried was more an *arbiter bibendi* than an authority.

"Anyway, I started roaming again and found myself talking to Polgar, the Austrian journalist Siegfried's trying to wean away from Vienna. I asked him about the coffee house scene there, and he had a lot to say, most of it negative."

"Really? Like what?"

"He said most of the good talk was in the past: Hofmannsthal, Schnitzler, Altenberg, Kraus, Broch and so many others, not just writers, mind you. But now, he said, wit was no longer good enough. 'A crisp aphorism might even draw the wrong kind of laughter,' he says, 'and wit has drawn so far inward that it has dried up its very wellsprings. Scientific truth is all the youngsters can talk about.'"

"They must not have much to say, then."

"Alfred, that's his name, he compared the new generation to scorpions stinging themselves. It's one of the reasons he's seriously contemplating moving to Berlin. Though, evidently, they're here too. Another crop of radical empiricists who think they have to go farther than their predecessors. Either a statement is a viable scientific hypothesis, or it's meaningless."

"What about culture, religion, politics?"

"Down the sinkhole!"

"What's the purpose of language?"

"Language can't be trusted. It's the Tower of Babel. It has to be saved with logic. He said one of them told him to imagine a meteor hitting Earth and destroying all life. 'Would that be a tragedy?' the man asked him."

"The worst tragedy ever," said Maud.

"'No,' the man told him. Because there'd be no one to experience it. No audience! You'd be equally correct in saying that it was a comedy! The only truths that exist beyond language are scientific ones, the ones that would still be true whether language existed or not. The temperature of water boiling at a certain altitude, for example. The successes of medicine, all of biology. That's why scientists could, for instance, predict the discovery of elements, because they were needed to fill out the periodic table."

"My goodness!" Maud enthused.

The Man Without a Party

That night, while urinating, Carl wondered why, after sex, it felt like a tourniquet had been applied to his bladder. He wished he'd gone to the bathroom before being with Maud. He wondered if women experienced the same, but he was too inhibited to ask her when he went back to the bed and nuzzled up against her. It had been quite a twenty-four hours. He'd never imagined that his place of work could be such a rich environment. So many fascinating people! And with the stability of his life, with Maud and Rosalinde, he wondered if he were as close to human bliss as he would ever be. If only the external world would accommodate…

He suddenly started chuckling.

"What is it, Carl?"

"I forgot to tell you, when I was finally heading to the door, there were Elsa and Herbert still at the same table, with a bunch of people sitting and standing around them. Evidently, Ihering thought he could settle everything by challenging her to a poetry contest, and he'd written one in imitation of her. Some had agreed to be judges, poets like Mehring and Tucholsky. But she said she'd never agreed to the contest, refused to write anything, was irate, and laughed at what he'd written. People tried to calm her down, get her to admit his offering wasn't too bad. I looked at it, and it actually was a pretty good pastiche of one of her early love poems, though I could see why she'd be offended by it."

"It sounds like she had an awful night. Do you remember the poem?"

"Oh, not really."

She pulled him closer. "Come on, you've remembered everything else from last night."

"Yeah, but it was late when I read it."

"Come on, Carl." She put her arms around his neck. "Make something up, like most of the things you've told me today."

"It's all true!"

"You used to write lots of poetry. What would you write, if you were writing a Lasker-Schuler love poem for me now?"

"God, I love you!"

"Nope. Not a poem."

"Really? You're going to do this?"

"Yes!" she said, kissing him on the mouth.

"You're a hard woman, Maud!"

She raised her eyebrows.

"I'll have to just paraphrase from what I remember he wrote."

"I'll settle for that." A peck on the tip of his nose.

"And don't expect rhyme or meter."

"*Vers libre* will do." This time, each cheek.

He groaned, massaging her back as he thought.

"*I reached for you with moonbeam arms…*"

The smile on her face was immediate. "Yes?"

"*Our eyes courting each other like stars…*"

"Wonderful! And?"

"*You'd like to drink my lips…*"

She kissed them.

His free hand explored. "*While I sought the snowy treasure of your chest…*"

"Oh, I see where this is going." But she didn't shy away.

"*But the world is torn apart…*"

"Do that again."

"*But the world is—*"

"No! What you did."

He complied. "*The butterflies have fled…*"

They shifted their bodies in unison.

"*My arteries are exposed,*
Toes seek a ground no longer there,

A seashell's cry…"

****

Rosalinde would remember watching her father work, smoking, pacing the floor of the parlor, paper in hand.

But she wouldn't remember this particular afternoon.

With her almost six-year-old brain, she would remember the levels of smoke drifting in the room behind him as he chugged along in the locomotive back-and-forth of his creative process.

But she wouldn't remember this particular day, late in 1926.

She would remember the tobacco, acrid and choking, the laurel-scented after-shave, the palpable earthiness emanating from the shoes he would kick off before crossing his legs and setting one foot above the other on the desktop that barely protruded from the closet, his makeshift office.

But she wouldn't remember this particular pack of cigarettes, or what article he was working on as he consumed them.

She would remember, warm to her touch, the human wrinkles in the shoe leather, its smoothness stretched and scuffed, when she set the pair under the stuffed chair so in his preoccupation he wouldn't trip on them.

How did he always seem to know exactly where to find them again?

She would remember the slanting daylight from the windows to the street, filtering through the interior haze to differentiate the strands of his hair, still furrowed by its last combing.

But she wouldn't remember the specific domestic twilight of this third of December.

She would remember the ringing of the telephone and his bouncing into the chair, silhouetted in front of the recessed trio of windows to take the work calls.

But she wouldn't remember this one call, the expanding darkness of his expression, his listening in grave silence, the way his eyes opened ever wider, as if the receiver were directly raising his eyelids.

And she wouldn't remember his abrupt departure, after leaping back into the shoes under the chair and running with them still untied out of the apartment, shouting to Maud that Siegfried Jacobsohn had just suffered a massive heart attack and leaving Rosalinde to rush and close the door behind him before the cat got out.

Chapter Twenty-Three
PRESENT

"I have something for you," Captain Robert Schneider told the man with the scars. He reached a sheet of paper across the table.

"This is helpful," said the man, "potentially speaking. Bernhard and Jacob. We've been wanting to locate these enemies of the state for some time."

"I hope now you can see my full desire to help you in this matter."

"I understand."

"And that at no point did I intend to hide Mrs. Ossietzky."

"And you think the woman met with these men?"

"I have no proof of that. My wife found these names and addresses in her room, and I copied them down."

"You did well."

"I am ready to put Mrs. Ossietzky out on the street, if you want. In spite of her old relationship with my wife."

"No, I don't think that's called for at this time."

Schneider nodded.

"But keep your eyes open, Captain. And if you notice anything else, come and inform us at once."

"Yes, Sir."

****

But who knows? Perhaps it was a boon that the peace award was not bestowed during the '35 calendar year. After all, during '36, Germany was hosting the summer Olympic Games, Hitler, at Goebbels' urging, having done an about face on the matter. Regardless, Carl did not die.

And, unexpectedly, Hamsun's vicious article had an ironic effect. It's strange, sometimes, how things turn out. The piece ended up saying more about the great author's fascism than anything about Carl and, in doing so, was a public embarrassment not only for Norway but for the Nobel institution and its Swedish home, as it had garlanded Hamsun the Nobel Laureate in literature for 1920. Letters in support of Carl kept arriving, doggedly, many more than the year before. For instance, close by from Norwegians Sverre Stostad, Sigrid Undset and Borge Olsen-Hagen, but also from all parts of the globe: Thomas Masaryk, Emmanuel Levy and William Hull, Sir Alfred Zimmern and Henri See, Genevieve Bianquis and Gaston Bachelard and Henri Levy-Brul, Leon Brunschvicg and Marius Moutet, Caroline Playne and Sir Arthur Salter, Franz Boas and Alfons Goldschmidt, Gugliemo Ferrero and Hans Oprecht, Louis Gustave Jean Marie de Brouckere and Frijda, Marie Jurneckova-Vorlova and Daudin, from one hundred and twenty-five members of the Swiss Parliament, thirty-five members of the Czechoslovakian Senate and thirty members of their Parliament, twenty-two members of the Dutch Parliament, one hundred and eleven members of the French Parliament and sixty-three of their senators and members of their National Assembly.

In the wake of this epistolary deluge, in 1936, the committee decided to award two prizes for peace; Carl's was retroactive, for 1935.

****

"Maud? Where have you been?" Sophie stood at her front door, staring at her bedraggled friend, who was barely lifting her suitcase from the ground. Maud stepped into the house and fairly

368

collapsed against her. Sophie took her to her room. Luckily, no one else was in the house.

She got Maud to lie down on top of the bed, pulled her shoes off, pulled a quilt onto her, and then went to fix tea. When she returned, Maud raised her eyelids and told her everything, wiping her eyes the whole time. Sophie sat next to her and held her hand.

Using a very soft voice, Sophie said, "They're beasts. And you did the right thing to leave at once, no matter how much you wanted to see Carl."

"Oh, Sophie! I felt so ashamed!"

"Even if you'd given yourself to him then and there, you would have had no guarantee that you would have ever seen Carl's face."

Maud whimpered into her palm.

"Let me tell you something," Sophie went on. "Earlier, Maudie, when you first came and we were catching up on things, I didn't tell you everything. You'll remember, after my studies, I sang for choirs."

"Yes," said Maud with a nod. "You were going professional."

"Well, I tried. And it didn't go so well. So, you know, I started singing in the cabarets. And dancing. And then, when the inflation hit, things got really hard."

"Sophie, you could have come to me!"

"Oh, didn't I think of that, Maudie! Many times! You were so busy with your family, so happy, you and Carl."

"We would have been glad to have you stay with us!"

"I didn't want to intrude." Then she clenched her teeth in admission. "Okay! Of course, in hindsight, I wish I had done so, but, Maudie, I was too ashamed." She swallowed hard, and then her voice dropped an octave. "And that was only the beginning."

Maud was holding her friend's hand tightly.

"I started going with men for money. Just to get along."

"Many women were reduced to what you did at that time!" Maud announced, full of righteous indignation.

Sophie put her hand over her mouth. "Once, standing on the sidewalk, when I was calling out to men, I even saw Carl walk by. Thank God, he didn't recognize me! And then, and then I got sick, and I was arrested."

"Oh, Sophie! We would have been happy—we could have helped you!"

"That's when I met Robert. Maudie, he literally pulled me from the gutter. I owe him everything."

****

"Ah, there you are! The *cause celebre*."

The second most powerful man in Germany had come to have a word with Carl. Elaborately uniformed, Hermann Wilhelm Goering sat in a white suit, barely fitting into an armed chair, and nodded his dismissal of the guard who had escorted Carl to the remote building in the camp; he waited for him to leave before he spoke.

Then the corn-kernel double-row of teeth presented themselves in a fixed grin.

"Well, Mr. Ossietzky, the wheel of fortune has turned once again."

Six feet away, Carl stood in the quiet room, staring speechlessly at the man he had been hustled over to see.

"And the turn of the *rota fortunae*," Goering continued, "has shown that some at the bottom are now on top, and some on top are now at the bottom."

Unbidden, Jacobsohn's words from long ago came back to him. He said, "The important thing, Sir, is that we become more human with each turning." Carl was as surprised as Goering to have his intact self, considering the circumstances and its long absence, flash up from the depths, remembered or newly realized. Triggered by what? The shock of seeing the despised creature, palpably before him? The Latin phrase?

"More human is it?" Goering roared with bemusement. "Well, we shall see. The reason I am here is to discuss with you this ridiculous matter of the wretched Swedish award."

Carl was silent.

"What is ridiculous is that these nobodies are trying to cause trouble for the German state."

"I am surprised that you have taken any trouble with people of no account."

The laugh again, a reflexive guffaw that shook Goering's ample chest. "You're right. I thoroughly agree. A few fools! However, as it turns out, some of these letter-writers have inexplicably gained a bit of brief fame, and governments are involved and, uh, you have, perhaps, heard of our plans to host these international athletes this year."

"The timing is unfortunate, Sir."

"As you say. And therefore, we feel it is your duty to decline the prize and to do so in writing in order to put the whole matter to rest."

Carl gave a pathetic shrug. "Such a document is not beyond the, uh, policy of the state apparatus to create entirely on its own."

"Of course, but the document would have more meaning if it came directly from you. In your handwriting. With your signature."

"Sir, I'm afraid I won't be able to comply."

"*And why is that?*"

"Simply," Carl answered, "because I am not moved to do so."

The hands gripped the armrests of the chair, and, in his ruminating silence, Goering was working his mouth, a kind of jaw-expanding churning, kneading with the pronounced overbite, puckering the *bon vivant* lips. It was as if the man's mandible possessed an ebullience of its own. He shut his eyes for a moment.

"One would think," Goering pointed out, repressing his anger with a facade of shallow restraint, "after all the trouble you've caused your fatherland, that you would consider it your duty to comply with the will of Our Leader."

"I would have thought," Carl opined, "that as an international award, the Stockholm prize would be seen as favorable to the state, a plume in Mr. Hitler's cap, like the Olympic Games."

"But you are an enemy of the state!" Goering exploded, striking the arm of his chair. "The award perversely attempts to celebrate that!"

Carl followed this up immediately. "All of which can be swept under the rug while the government shows its impartial willingness to let fools honor whom they will."

"The government is quite capable of manifesting its impartiality without your advice!" Goering shouted, his face suddenly beet-red. "Besides, that advice is impossible. Your position in this country—"

"Hitler was at first opposed to hosting the Games, I hear—"

"Don't interrupt!" boomed the voice. Goering had shot up to his feet, but it is a physical law, even in Einstein's universe—albeit only in terrestrial corners—that those entering a chair carefully should refrain from exiting them precipitously, and Goering's wide rump ensured that he brought the chair with him as he rose, a matter both men could not help but notice, each with a different sort of chagrin.

Goering shoved the chair down, slamming it against the floor so hard that it bounced.

"You were trouble even in the days of the Kaiser. You antagonized the Republic and those wretched Social Democrats. You even tried to undermine the development of my Air Force! And now Our Leader can't stand hearing your name mentioned."

Silently, Carl scrutinized the man, making a point of examining every feature of the jelly face, the posture that towered over him.

Then, Carl whispered, "You've had me tortured before. What prevents you from squeezing a signature from me?"

"You have been a thorn in the side of Germany for much too long!"

Already slumped, Carl bowed an inch forward, as if to accept a compliment.

"You should be dead!"

"It is an inconvenience for you, I understand."

The man, who was in control of the Free State of Prussia, of German defense and aviation, economics and the four-year plan, visibly regained control of himself, and ostentatiously returned to the nest of his seat.

"Von Ossietzky," Goering continued, exhaling shrilly through his nostrils, returning with great effort to measured tones, "listen to reason. We can release you. We can make life easier for you, and for your wife. Think of her."

"She has always made it clear that she valued my attachment to the principles I hold," Carl responded. "In fact, she would disapprove—"

"I'm not talking about that! Don't be so selfish! Think of her sense of well-being, her quality of life!"

"With all due respect, Sir, I find that a very strange remark, especially in her case. A large part of her motivation to leave her mother country and live here was her firm belief in the values of German culture. She will not allow me to betray them."

"You are incapable of reasoning with!"

"I apologize. Perhaps too many blows to the head." Here, Carl grinned wider than ever before in his life, exposing the broken ridges of his teeth, maniacally displaying them. He wanted Goering to behold all the truncated molars in the back of his mouth, each cracked canine, every bi-decapitated bicuspid and serrated incisor, and he held the grin until he saw the look of disgust on Goering's face melt into a strange, indescribable expression that, to Carl, seemed to have a tinge of fear.

"It's too late, Sir," Carl whispered. But he did not have time to say his next words: 'Once barbarism is embarked upon, there is no turning back.'

"Guard!" Goering's cheeks were shaking. The door opened. "Take him away!"

As the guard escorted him back to his barracks, Carl grew increasingly shocked at what he had said to Goering, at the resolve he had shown toward the man who held his life in his hands, who could snuff him out with the flick of a wrist. The 'Carl' that had burst forth, like the genie from the bottle, was swiftly fading away. Simultaneously, he heard a ringing in his ears and felt his strength ebb, his muscles weaken and his knees buckle, so that the guard had to help him stumbling along, half-carrying him the last steps over ground that felt like quicksand. Inside, his eyesight grew dim, and he collapsed on the floor. He had only awakened for a few minutes, and now, his body writhing spread-eagled on the filthy floor of the barracks, he was paying for the effort.

The following week, Carl delivered this statement to the head of Esterwegen CC:

"After much consideration, I have made the decision to accept the Nobel Peace Prize which has fallen to me. I cannot share the view put forward by the representatives of the Secret State Police that in doing so, I exclude myself from German society. The Nobel Peace Prize is not a sign of an internal political struggle, but of understanding between peoples. As a recipient of the prize, I will do my best to encourage this understanding, and, as a German, I will always bear in mind Germany's justifiable interests in Europe."

Although the government claimed they returned Carl's passport to him and gave him permission to leave the country in order to receive the prize, this was a double lie. Carl would never see the medal, much less hold it in his hands.

King Haakon VII of Sweden broke with tradition by refusing to attend the award ceremonies.

****

And they didn't read about Germany's reoccupation of the Rhineland, in violation of the Treaty of Versailles. They couldn't expose themselves to the critical analysis of the causes, motivations, and repercussions of the decision of the government to take this momentous step. Thus, they lacked the information and reasoning to help them weigh the facts and opinions, the implications and complications of their own government's actions, actions which would, in time, weigh heavily on all German citizens.

They could not benefit from balanced analyzes of decrees regulating and restricting 'the Gypsy plague,' or that, later, 'Gypsies' were arrested and incarcerated in concentration camps, or that, before the end of 1936, the same was done to Jehovah's Witnesses.

Instead, they read about German victories in the Berlin Olympic Games in *The People's Observer*.

****

It was his last day at Esterwegen. They were going to release him to Maud and, under Gestapo custody, put him into a Berlin hospital, a place where Maud could stay in a room next door to him.

Carl lay in the bed in the medical clinic and dozed on and off.

He was watching a nurse who, thinking she was concealed behind a screen, was filling a syringe. What was she filling it with? Who was it for?

Carl immediately became suspicious. He'd heard things, patients being injected...

He watched the woman carefully. She had just been speaking to one of the doctors. The man had given her a vial and had been talking to her in an abrupt, authoritative way, giving her orders. Then he had departed.

Carl tried to sit up. He looked around at the other patients, most of them asleep. He wanted to get out of the bed, but he felt so exhausted.

The nurse was walking down the ward with the syringe in her hand, needle pointed toward the ceiling. Who was she going to inject? She kept walking, getting closer. No! Surely not him! He was leaving! Why would he need...?

She came up to him, pulled back the sheet. He struggled with her, called out. She fought against him, bared his arm, stabbed the needle into the flesh of his left arm.

He fainted. Had he been dreaming?

Hours later, when he arrived at the hospital in Berlin, he had a raging fever, and his arm was throbbing, swollen and red. The orderly made him sit in a wheelchair, not for his comfort, but because they said he was walking too slow. Maud ignored his wave of a hand, a feeble attempt to keep her away in his contagious state; she bent over him, took his head in her hands, and planted tear-damp kisses all over his face, each one an impassioned plea to reconnect. And he felt each press of her lips as a call to awake, here on his forehead, here on each cheek, each eyelid, each eyebrow, each ear, on his chin, his nose, the edge of his scalp.

"Rosalinde...?"

"Not today," Maud said.

"Where…?"

"We'll talk later."

Then, jamming one foot under a wheel of the chair and the other flat on the ground, he demanded to walk on his ever-aching feet the last few steps to the door of the suite of rooms, his bedroom, Maud's, a tiny bath, a little breakfast-sitting room with a kitchenette, the home afforded the Nobel laureate, albeit uncrowned, and the likely recipient of nosey, prying foreign journalists: appearances counted for something in the international press.

Then, first things first: he directed Maud to tell the hospital authorities, in no uncertain terms, that the services of a chaplain would at no point be desired unless, perhaps, it was someone from the Christadelphians. "I still would like to talk to one of them," he had told her, "if there are any still around."

****

The nurse helped him to use the bathroom. When she left him to do his business, closing the door, he stripped and stared at himself in the mirror. An old scarecrow, the inversion of a shrunken tree, debarked and dead-fish pale, the rotten, shrunken fruit in its crotch; the image stared with horror back at him. He saw his face, grown preternaturally large because his skull could not shrivel like the rest of him, glistening with involuntary tears, and he sank with a groan against the sink, dropping his face to his gnarled and ragged hands.

****

They lay in bed in the dark, their bodies turned toward each other. Both were apprehensive, tentative, drained.

Maud was afraid of hugging him, drawing him toward her. They'd hugged before, of course; it had been the first thing they'd done after he'd been released: hugged and kissed; and several times since then. But this was the first time they'd lain together, the first time in four years, and she was afraid after so long: afraid of the unfamiliarity of the touch, afraid that it would feel so strangely different, afraid of intruding and, yes, afraid of Carl, this fragile man who had become alien to her, her husband who had changed so much. A man she had never expected to lie with again.

And Carl was afraid. He was afraid of offering the wretchedness of his broken body to the woman who seemed the same as he remembered her, just like the last time they had been together, early in 1933, February, it must have been. He was afraid of what his body couldn't do. Would he even be able to provide warmth for her? Would she be repulsed by the old man, the stick figure he had become?

He was afraid of her rejection.

"I can't," she said finally. "Down there."

He said nothing.

"It would be too painful," she explained. "I'm all dried up."

Sad and relieved, he held her to him. After a time, their bodies gave a *caritas* of warmth to each other.

****

When Maud returned to their rooms with a sack of groceries, items Carl had requested that the hospital didn't have—she was so glad he was getting some of his old tastes back!—she found him, still in robe, pajamas and slippers, looking at some papers. He looked up at her confusedly.

"Maudie, what's this?"

She came over to him and looked. "Oh, Honey, that's the only thing I still have from your papers. Don't let the orderly find it, or he might pass it off to the guards. Though what else they could do to us, I'm sure I don't know."

"Mine?"

She sat down and took the typewritten sheets. "Yes, Honey. Look. This was published in *The Worldstage* in early '31. I thought you would enjoy looking at your typings." She handed them back.

He read with a voice that crackled from disuse. "'Only in front of the cinerary urn of the Second German Empire, may old people hold their funeral ceremonies, and young people, in piety, air their hats.'" Carl looked up at her in bewilderment. "Maud, I don't understand."

"Keep reading, Dear."

He squinted back at the page. "'Too much of the mischief of the imperial era is still alive to treat her as a venerable past.'"

"Right. You were writing about the continued celebration of the Prussian victory over France. The irony of how in the Republic, January 18th was celebrated more than November 9th." She took the sheets again. "See? Earlier in the piece, you write that the Republic really should have started in '71, but the opportunity was missed, 'blown up,' you say here, 'by the foundation of the small German empire of the Hohenzollerns.' 'A no more than dynastic incidence,' you say a little above."

"I… see."

But it was obvious, and concerning to her, that he didn't. Persisting, and with some energy in her desire to bring her husband back, she went on, shaking her head at the pages to find another quote. "Here. See? You even say that 'the first republican generation bred Hitler with their mistakes and sins of omission and showers of optimism.' Do you see the connection you were drawing? I think it was brilliant, especially back then. It was the sort of brilliant analysis that you produced so often, Darling." She stood, handing the papers back and bending to kiss him on the top of the head.

He looked up at her. "Thank you, Maudie," he said, unsmilingly. But his upper lip quivered with tension, and he pursed both lips to control the tic. He had thought that the author of the essay, whoever it was, had desecrated the memory of his stepfather, long-dead Gustav. But now, after Maud's explication, he wasn't so sure. He looked back down and continued puzzling over the typewritten lines, trying to put the pages back into sequence. Wake up, he told himself, wake up.

He could hear Maud, back in the kitchen, busy with the groceries.

The feeling of having hurt Gustav came back, weighing on him.

He had to atone. There was a pencil on the table next to him. He forced open his shaking fingers, frozen in the grasp of a shovel handle, and threaded the pencil between them. With his other hand, he drew the sheets of paper toward him.

"*Father*," he wrote, "*I followed you…*" He stared at what he had written for a long time. Then his eyes were drawn to the sunlight of the window. A mangy, emaciated dog sniffing around some trash. A hospital truck rolling down a road, gears screeching. A flock of birds filtering frenetically through the trees, seeking sustenance among the branches, each moving separately and yet staying together somehow. He tried to find something else to write, but his mind wandered.

Then he scribbled, "*…into the fog.*"

Chapter Twenty-Four
PAST

On his way up, Carl met Ludwig Quidde coming down the stairs from the offices of *The Worldstage*.

"Professor Quidde! It's been so long! How are you?"

Carl looked up into the worried expression on the older man's face. "As well as can be expected," he said, stopping to face Carl, his feet on adjacent steps.

"Yes, I know! It gets worse and worse each day."

"Well, I just dropped an important piece of information off with the new editor, and I hope it sees the light of day, but I'm not confident."

"Oh! What seems to be the problem?"

Quidde leaned back against the wall and sighed, then shook his head. "Look, can we talk somewhere else?"

"Of course! I'm just going to drop this off. Can I meet you in the café downstairs in a few minutes?"

"All right."

"Good. Order a coffee for me, please."

Carl ran up the rest of the way and entered the room.

"Mrs. Hunicke, how are things?"

The secretary looked at Carl, then toward the editor's office, then back. "A little tense," she shared.

Pursing his lips to refrain from prying, Carl bent down and, with both his hands, placed his article on her desk. "Here's the piece that was due yesterday. Sorry it's a bit late."

"That's okay," she replied, picking up the sheets. "I think we'll still be able to find a spot for it."

"Good. Thanks." Then, innocently, putting both hands palm down on her desk and lowering his voice, "How's it going with Kurt?"

She glanced again at the editor's office. "He just closed his door," she answered. "Dr. Quidde was just in there with him."

"Uh-huh. Everything seem okay?"

"Not quite. I could definitely hear them arguing."

"Well," he said, straightening up, "I hope it smooths itself over."

"Yes."

Carl raced downstairs, thinking how he hated gossip before becoming a newspaper man.

In the coffee shop, he sat across from Quidde and sniffed the aroma emanating from the cup in front of him. He set his pack of cigarettes and box of matches down next to it.

"It's about von Seekt," Quidde started. "I sent him a letter, challenging him about the clandestine rearmament." He shook his head and set his teeth.

"Yes?" Carl sipped.

Quidde made a dismissive gesture with his hands and then took a piece of paper from the inside pocket of his coat. He unfolded it and handed it over to Carl. "This is the original of his response. I left a copy with Mr. Tucholsky."

Carl read. When he came to the last paragraph, he sat up straighter.

For a people, General von Seekt had written,

> *as maltreated internationally as the Germans, ideas of international pacifism are difficult to understand. But if, after the experiences of the Ruhr invasion and in a time when France daily tramples the Treaty of Versailles underfoot, there are still Germans who argue in favor of the execution of that treaty to the advantage of the French, then I can only call this the peak of national*

indignity. Incidentally, I want to warn you that, in case the question touched on in your letter should be publicly discussed, I should immediately act against you on the basis of my emergency powers, regardless of whether or not charges for high treason were subsequently lodged in court.

Carl whistled as he handed the letter back. "'The Sphinx' sounds anything but enigmatic here."

Q answered with a sniff.

Carl took a cigarette out of the packet and appeared to weigh it in his hand.

"What did Kurt say?"

"That he would have to think about it before *The Worldstage* printed it. He seemed very troubled."

"Hm. I see."

Quidde folded up the paper and returned it to his pocket. "Carl," he said, "this is the sort of thing Jacobsohn would have rushed to press."

"He thrived on this sort of exposure," Carl agreed. "It's a scoop, Ludwig, tantamount to acknowledgment and confession. Siegfried would have eaten it up and welcomed the litigation, come what may."

"Siegfried was litigious to a fault. It was free advertising for him."

"You don't often get chances like this. Would it help if I said something to Kurt?"

"Don't. The man has to work this sort of thing out for himself, if he's going to be editor-in-chief. If he doesn't print it, I'll get someone else to do so."

"Von Seekt's emergency powers are set to elapse in about a week."

"It won't wait that long, Carl," Quidde assured him. "As you say, it's a scoop, and scoops grow rotten overnight."

"Kurt is a writer before all else."

"Siegfried was a writer too, but an editor first."

Carl lit a match. "As you say, it's something Kurt needs to learn."

"Or not," said Quidde.

Still holding the unlit cigarette in his hand, Carl looked at his former mentor with a new level of admiration.

****

"Kurt! Why are you so upset?" Magnus was talking to Hiller at the former's sex clinic. He massaged the back of his friend's neck.

"Haven't you heard? Apparently, Edith Jacobsohn's gone insane!"

"Oh, Kurt! The poor woman is still in mourning for her husband's death. A sudden shock like that can take a lifetime to recover from."

"Magnus! She just named Ossietzky editor-in-chief of *The Worldstage*!"

"I thought she picked Tucholsky."

"Evidently, he's jumped ship for Paris again. Being the paper's Kaiser didn't appeal to Kurt after all. He's gone back to being French correspondent."

"So what's the problem?"

"Ossietzky is a terrible choice! He's no leader."

"Can't he be a leader without being a Kaiser *a la* Jacobsohn?"

"Magnus! Do you really see that tongue-tied stone filling Siegfried's shoes?"

"Once again, he doesn't have to be Jacobsohn to do an adequate job."

"Adequate! I give the paper six months before it folds."

"Or maybe he'll resign like Tucholsky, and the man who really wants the position can take over: Kurt Hiller."

Hiller had no comeback.

"Aha! I knew it! You're jealous. Let me call the masseur to loosen these knots in your shoulders."

****

After the third visitor to *The Worldstage* office left, Carl nodded to Walter and Hedwig and said he would be down in the café on the ground floor of the building if there was an emergency. Otherwise, he would be working there and, hopefully, getting more of his own writing done.

He settled himself at a table in the back, opened a new pack of cigarettes with his thumbnail, set it down next to the steaming coffee and his two notebooks, and looked out the window to the street at the other end of the room.

It had been several weeks since, after Tucholsky's abdication, Mrs. Jacobsohn had chosen Carl to run the paper, and he was slowly acclimating to the new position. He knew reviews would be mixed; she had warned him. It was one of the reasons why, while accepting her offer, he had stipulated that he wanted Kurt's name to remain on the flag, under his, as the co-editor. At least temporarily, during the transition, so others would see them as collaborators. A sort of editor *emeritus*. But would the ploy stifle criticism of the newbie? Hard to tell if it had.

And that wasn't the main problem, the one he was hoping to solve in coming downstairs: keeping up his own writing. He didn't want to slide into the role of a writer who just filled holes in the paper, writing snippets to plug a page or fill a gap in coverage. But he had to admit that his own writing had suffered with his promotion. And what had he expected?

It wasn't that he disliked the new position, he thought as he took a sip of the brew and lit a cigarette. He could see himself getting better at it day-by-day, and he even enjoyed the expanded responsibilities being a chief editor demanded. Frankly, he was ready for the fresh set of challenges. And, in spite of his different style from Siegfried, who'd mentored both him and so many others, he felt he still had something to offer, something that perhaps the paper's founder hadn't had. It would just take time for his own skills to materialize, for his own contributions to be noticed, for his own style to be appreciated.

He opened one of the notebooks. The evolving piece about the state of the Republic had come to a halt at the feet of Groener. He still hadn't decided how to take the man up, much less what words and phrases to use to express himself. At a loss, he turned to the second notebook. There, he found the following list of scratchings, added, obviously, in moments of haste to use later as spurs for more inspiration:

2/11/27: riot outside Pharus Hall between communists and National Socialists.

3/5: Bavaria lifts ban on Hitler speeches.

3/20: fight between NS and commun. at Lichterfeld Station.

4/1: Hugenberg buys over half of Ufa.

5/1 Hitler by-invite speech in Berlin concert hall.

5/5 Steel Helmet two-day conference 100,000 in Ber.

5/21: Lindbergh.

6/5: CP declares readiness to fight rt. wing militias.

6/12: Nuremburg soccer champs over Berlin.

6/19: Schmelling champ over Belgian.

6/22: Horse carriages banned Ber.

7/11: Goebbels' article: 'Germany a colony exploited by Jew. finance.'

7/18: Car race near Koln.
7/27: Weissmuller WR 800m. 10 min 22.2 sec.
8/10: 10,000 protest at U. S. embassy against Sacco &
Vanizetti conviction.

He couldn't, at the moment, think of any items to use, then line out, as was his habit. Closing the second notebook, he looked up, staring vacantly at the pedestrians passing outside the cafe. Connect the dots, Ossi! Militarism was always the underlying motif.

Groener, Groener, Groener… Then he pulled from his pocket the ragged slip of paper with the Dittman quote about Ebert's 11 p.m. telephone calls to the Supreme Headquarters; Groener was the general he would converse with each night. He wanted a phrase that would seal the secret connection between the two: the agreement, the *tete-a-tete*, the November calls, the November… Pact! He had it! The pencil started spinning across the page, as if of its own locomotion: *"In the Munich 'Backstabbing' trial, he played like a trump card* (Yay, Maudie!) *the November Pact between the People's Commissar Ebert and the Supreme Army Command, and then praised Ebert's…* Ebert's… *undaunting patriotism."*!

He took a long drag on the smoke, then a sip of the coffee. Through the haze, the passersby looked like ghostly automata: Rosmer's robots, unaware of the dangers all around them. Soulless statues. He picked up his pencil again.

"The leaders of the 'Back-Red-Gold' group have suggested the erection of a three-man memorial to Ebert, Erzberger and Rathenau; but the selection is not fortuitous. It would be better to propose a composition of two statues, Ebert and Groener, clasping their hands to cement the November Pact, a composition perhaps designed and executed by Mrs. Kollwitz." On second thought, he put a single horizontal line through the last absolute

phrase, leaving it still legible but giving it a thumbs-down that he could reconsider later.

Oh, there was Hedwig. They'd found him!

****

He recognized the voice at once: Kurt Hiller was sitting with someone around the corner from him in the café. Carl sat smoking, writing, and sipping coffee in his usual spot, the table in the back of the room, where he could flee from the hustle in *The Worldstage* offices upstairs.

Neither Carl nor Hiller could see each other from where they were sitting. Carl immediately realized that Kurt, an incisive writer long-valued by his paper, was talking about him.

"But do you think he really said it?" Hiller's anonymous interlocutor asked.

"Knowing Giese, I think it's possible," came the answer.

Carl stiffened. He and Hiller had, on occasion, clashed swords; it would be an understatement to say that they had never been close, especially once Carl had become editor-in-chief. He knew that Hiller was one of the many who were open in questioning Edith Jacobsohn's decision.

Hiller, an outspoken homosexual, was one of the most brilliant people Carl had ever met. In all his writing, he combined a valiant, devil-may-care message with a witty cleverness that was razor-sharp. Carl wondered if Hiller knew Carl was sitting within earshot but was pretending not to in order to gain a kind of blameless freedom for what he was saying. He wouldn't put it past him.

Regardless, Carl stubbed out his cigarette and listened attentively.

"What was Magnus' response?" asked the voice Carl couldn't place.

"He laughed, of course," said Hiller. Magnus had to be Hirschfeld, alternatively called 'the Einstein of Sex' and 'Aunt Magnesia,' the head of the Institute of Sexual Research and a cohort of Hiller in the crusade for homosexual rights. Carl wracked his brains to remember what he might have said about the eccentric doctor that could have upset Hiller, but he came up with nothing. He himself took very little issue with the movement, saw homosexuals as oppressed people, especially in Germany, and had written to that effect. But he also knew that he was quite capable of biting attempts at witticism that, infrequently, caused him a pang of remorse. Efforts in the area of sarcasm were actually integral to his writing process. What had he said, and was the matter anything he should be concerned about? Then he started hearing the clues.

"Did Ossietzky mean that Magnus was a Hegelian," Hiller wondered aloud, "because he thinks homosexuals are a third sex?"

"You mean, a kind of synthesis?"

"Yes."

"Which is where you and Hirschfeld's views diverge."

"Most diametrically," Hiller added. "Quite apart from my aversion to that atrocious three-step mechanism."

"Right."

"Or was he insinuating that Magnus has a tendency to plunge into things rather precipitously?"

The other man giggled. "Certainly possible!"

"Or worse, was he referring to Magnus' somewhat expansive girth?"

A gasp of surprise, followed by, "I've heard Ossietzky's no svelte abstainer himself!"

Avidly listening, Carl winced.

"Hm," Hiller mused. "'His leap into the dialectical pool turned into a bellyflop.' It's inscrutable!"

Now Carl was really at a loss. He couldn't remember ever saying, much less writing, the quote just attributed to him. Then he made a decision. Stuffing the papers he had been working on back into their folder, he got up and, after leaving money on the table, came around the corner.

"Did I really say that?" he asked.

The two men stared at him, as if caught.

"I'm sorry for eavesdropping; I acknowledge it's a habit of mine. But I usually remember things I say and write, and I'd be loath to hurt Magnus' feelings. He has enough fighting on his hands as it is. I'd much rather defend him against his enemies."

Hiller had recovered from his surprise. "That's what I was told. By him." He pointed to the man next to him, whom Carl still didn't recognize. Carl extended his hand.

"You have the advantage of knowing my name," he said.

They shook. "Schad. Christian. I apologize, Mr. Ossietzky, if this turns out to be mere baseless gossip. Karl Giese told me someone named Fronny told him you said it."

Carl looked at Hiller. "That's Turville-Petre," Kurt explained. "The archaeologist who hangs out at the Institute."

"Now, I really *am* confused," said Carl. "I don't remember ever meeting the man."

"Well, it wouldn't be the first time Fronny's made something up. The *bon viveur* may be a scientist, but he isn't immune to concocting fanciful theories and tales."

"Now wait," said Carl, beginning to be amused. "I'm not saying I didn't say it. Let's see: 'His leap into the dialectical pool... turned into a bellyflop.' It's even the sort of thing I could see myself being proud of coming up with. And I don't even reject your interpretations, although they can't all be accurate."

It was Hiller's turn to be amused. He was surprised and impressed with Carl's poise and willingness to banter and play with the situation. "Are you telling me you're not denying you said it?" he asked.

"For the purpose of mere speculation, yes. But I'm even more interested in hearing how you disagree with Hirschfeld."

"Oh, I can't stand that view of homosexuals!" Hiller exclaimed. "Magnus and I agree on so much, and we'd probably both become martyrs for the abolition of Paragraph 175, but this talk of a third sex sickens me! We've argued so much about this! If homosexuals are a third sex, then why are they so different from one another?"

"I see," said Carl.

"It is human to have these inclinations, and absolutely natural. I've clashed with so many on this."

"I know. I've enjoyed reading your work."

"'Unnatural'! If propagation is the natural goal of sex, then Nature itself sins whenever a seed fails to germinate."

"That's a good point," said Carl. "I'd assume that more seeds in Nature go ungerminated than otherwise. So which is more natural, after all?"

"And yet they call us freaks, decadents, perverts, pathological degenerates, criminals. Cambaceres knew better over a century ago."

"I don't know who that is," Carl admitted.

"One of the authors of Napoleon's Code, which decriminalized homosexuality."

"But made everyone guilty until proven innocent!" Schad threw in.

"Was Socrates morally decadent?" Hiller went on without the flutter of an eyelash. "Was Michelangelo a pervert? If we have been criminals, it is because of evil legislation! No wonder we commit suicide under the weight of persecution! Mentally weak! Neurotic! One needs to be courageous to face the inveterate hatred of each day!"

"I can't imagine what it's like," said Carl.

"Neither can I," said Schad.

"England, The U. S., Germany, Austria, even the German canton of Switzerland! By disallowing our freedom to be ourselves, they kill us. You don't need a gun to kill."

"And that is so well said," Carl added, "I am even reluctant to suggest that you are Hegelian in at least one way."

Hiller exhaled like a punctured balloon. "I hate the dialectic," he said. "It's too damn mechanical."

"Right. But didn't Hegel also say that the progress of freedom is one with the history of the world?"

"I won't disagree with that," said Hiller. "History is a great way for measuring all types of things. Logos chases after Eros."

Carl was impressed with Hiller's response. "Damn," he said, looking at his watch. "They're going to roast me when I get back upstairs." He stood up and shook hands. "Kurt, I can't wait for you to give us your next piece. Mr. Schad, great to meet you." Carl hurried away.

Maybe he's settling in, thought Mr. Hiller.

****

The Ossietzky family waited until the third day after the shooting before going out. The first day, May 1, 1929, they had not left the apartment; the second day, they'd visited others in the building; all three days, they had stayed away from windows facing the street—They'd heard someone looking out had been killed by police. Now, Saturday, Maud had resisted an outing; she wouldn't even let Carl leave to check things at work.

To her, it seemed like he'd been on the telephone the entire time. He'd chain-smoked and paced with an ear to the receiver, mainly listening, sometimes asking questions, rarely sharing new information, especially not that around thirty citizens died, hundreds injured, all by police. Once, he telephoned in an entire article to his secretary at *The World Stage*.

By Saturday morning, Rosalinde was stir-crazy; they all were. Maud finally surprised them both by saying they could go out that afternoon, and Carl surprised her by suggesting a puppet show he'd heard about.

The weather was fine; traffic on the avenues and sidewalks was bustling, as if the turmoil of the days before had never taken place. After a Pulcinella opening act and a marionette version of the Pied Piper, Carl sent Rosalinde jumping by asking if she would like to go backstage to meet the puppeteers.

"Are you doing a review?" Maud asked.

"It occurred to me that it might make a nice contrast, with everything else that's going on these days."

They followed the long, dark hallway to the performers' room. Carl introduced himself, and they gained entrance by his mentioning a mutual acquaintance. When he slipped one of the men some marks, the two puppeteers, already stripped down to slacks and t-shirts, turned their backs at once to their dressing table and found chairs for the Ossietzkys. By the time they'd sat down, the men, leaning against the counter, had pulled out two stick puppets who started a conversation with Rosalinde, who was immediately entranced. Maud was equally entranced with watching her daughter.

Carl, smoking, noticed the man closest to him was staring at his cigarette. He pulled out his pack again and lit one for him. The man stuck the cigarette in the corner of his mouth and continued his ventriloquism. Then, exhaling, he held it, cupped in the palm of his hand, behind his back.

Carl leaned forward and whispered toward his ear, "I heard you had a brother who was shot."

The puppeteer stiffened, continued speaking to Rosalinde and the other puppet—they were having an argument—then nodded to Carl.

"We're meeting at the Great Playhouse Wednesday from three on to start an inquiry into police actions," Carl went on. "No names. We just want justice done."

Did the man nod?

Only then did Carl see, in the streaked mirror, the look of full attention on Rosa's face. They were just stick figures, the men manipulating them were in full view, and yet the primitive animated marionettes were enough to draw the girl fully into the artifice. And as for her mother, he noticed that all that was needed to stamp a big smile on Maud's face was the look of fascination on her daughter. Carl was convinced that to tell the two members of the impromptu audience to look up and see the reality of their reflected selves would have been a heartless disappointment to them both, a violation of their simple fantasy in the dingy room, and this realization struck him as an epiphany no less fantastic.

Before they left, Rosalinde shook hands with the puppets, then squealed as one of the men pulled from under the skirt of his puppet an even smaller puppet, and handed it to her as a parting gift. Her beaming face seemed to triumph over the dark days and redeem a little of the needless bloodshed.

****

"We should be sponsoring the inquiry," the man said, stepping in front of Ossietzky as he left *The Worldstage* building.

Carl faced the man directly. He knew who he was but couldn't come up with the name. "What else is new?" Carl replied. "After the SDP and the trades unions, who but the CP? Well, you're welcome to take the initiative, though it's getting late. The panel's already bursting at the seams: Doblin, Gumbel, Litten, Mann—Heinrich, of course…"

"You won't accomplish anything."

"Just having the hearing is accomplishment itself. By the way, you're welcome to give witness to the panel, along with anyone else. We're non-denominational."

"You'll be shut down by the reactionaries."

"Are you offering protection?"

"Uh…"

"I accept. Unofficially, of course. If anyone asks, I'll deny it."

"I'm not in a position to—"

"That would definitely be a help. You have some fine boxers and wrestlers."

"I can't guarantee any—"

Carl placed a hand on the man's shoulder. "I'm ready to be surprised. Who knows? Thalmann may win some more votes. Now, Mr. Pieck," at last he pulled up the communist functionary's name, "I must hurry along. I'm already late for a meeting of the panelists at Mr. Apfel's office. Good day."

****

"We are here to provide a citizens' forum for all those wanting to speak concerning the events in this city over the first three days of the month last week," Carl began, standing at the table on the stage of the Grand Playhouse with the other panelists. The first meeting at Apfel's on the 15th had shown them they needed a larger venue. "A hearing for anyone who wants to be heard," he went on. "Other than that, there will be no speech-making, I assure you. The goal here isn't rhetorical. We are here for you to air your responses to what happened, to seek clarification as a means to justice. Because, without justice, wrongs cannot be addressed, improvements cannot be made, and healing cannot take place.

"Logistically, as you see, you can line up to my right, in the aisle that is monitored by citizens like you. You are welcome to give your name and say something about yourself, but no one is required to do so. Your public testimonies, whether anonymous or not, will be written down, and the results of our informal investigation published in *The Worldstage* and delivered to Parliament and Interior Minister Severing, in the hope that our report will be considered with a view to ensuring that such a senseless tragedy never, ever takes place again in our country. Basic public welfare simply demands a reconsideration of May 1st through 3rd. Yes, our government has already given blanket approval and support of police actions and summarily rejected charges made against the Berlin force and Chief Zorgiebel, but our questions, like the injuries and deaths of many, still remain. As a matter of fact, our government's response has made the necessity of our inquiry even more obvious. Let us proceed."

"You are an employee at Weiss Manufacturing. Can you tell us what happened to you?"

"I was coming home from work. Unlike others, we were not on strike. I don't belong to a party. Anyway, as I passed a police post, I was told to move on. I was already moving when I was hit on the head with a truncheon. When I stopped to complain, they arrested me. I spent the night in jail. And, when… once in the night, when…"

"Take your time."

The man choked a little, fought back tears. "I became thirsty. I asked for some water, and, and… they brought a bucket. Then they flipped me over and stuck my head in it. I thought, I thought they would drown me right then and there. Finally, they pulled my head out. One asked if I'd had enough to drink, and they laughed. Then they threw me back in the cell.

"In the morning, they released me without charges."

"He pointed a gun at me, the cop," said the war amputee, "and I looked into his face, and the look told me he was going to shoot and kill me, that I would die. But there was a shout, and he ran off with the other policeman. I was shaking too much to get up off the sidewalk. People finally helped me get up and get out of there."

"You are a doctor in the Wedding district."

"Yes. Schmincke. I'm a communist. It's the only place I'm allowed to work, and I'd never choose to work anywhere else."

"What do you have to report?"

"I gave dozens first aid and had them sent to the hospital at Buckrow. I am here to report that most of the wounds were shots to the back. People were peppered with bullets as they attempted to distance themselves from the police violence. It made no sense! Why shoot at fleeing citizens when it's your job to protect them?"

"Do you have anything more to say?"

Visibly upset at himself for getting off his track, Dr. Schmincke looked at his notes. "Yes. The police would shout, 'Street open! Road clear!' and then they would shoot into the crowd. I couldn't believe what I was seeing. The lousy fuckers!"

He stopped himself, seemed to force himself to become calm, breathing deeply. "I'm sorry. It's just so difficult to…"

"We understand. Anything else?"

Another glance at the notes. "I attended to a girl who'd been shot in the thigh. A poor schoolgirl! Her parents were there, totally distraught; her father was irate, incontrollable. He said that the shooter, the policeman, had apologized, had said he'd been aiming at a cyclist, as if that was an explanation for the suffering of his poor little girl."

"You are a former policeman."

"Retired. Thirteen years on the force."

"You are aware that Chief Zorgiebel has ordered his men to withhold information and forbidden them from testifying here?"

"How dare they withhold important information from citizens! That made me want to step forward even more."

"And that we have been accused of 'producing a comedy,' of 'desecrating the dead,' and serving as 'intellectual puppets of the Communist Party,' or worse, the 'Muskovite horror'?"

The man laughed in response, then said, "It's almost as if Zorgiebel had something to hide!"

"Have you heard anything about police casualties?"

"There were none. Absolutely zero. I still have connections with the force."

"Not one policeman killed?"

"Not even one injured. Quite 'an insurrection'!"

"And is that what you came here to tell us?"

"Yes. That, and to say that I don't think you should pursue culpability on the part of the rank and file police."

"Why not?"

"They were acting on orders from above."

"Can you be more specific?"

"Oh, I'm not saying that they were actually deployed to drive over citizens on the sidewalk, as happened, or that every bullet fired was directed by top officers. I'm sure some were acting on their own, but they were rogues. For the most part, what happened over those three days transpired from orders the police were given."

"To shoot and kill innocent citizens?"

"This can be shown!"

"How?"

"The blame can be placed at the top because of the shape, the structure of the police actions over the course of the three days. The city of Berlin was transformed into a war front; the escalation of police violence was according to plan. First day, cold water cannons, followed by mounted police, rubber truncheons and shooting on the second. Then, on the last, armored vehicles and flamethrowers. Machine gun salvos in the direction of Hermann Square. A bloodbath. However, at no point was there a matching increase of violence on the part of the citizens, and no rooftop snipers, as was claimed, in spite of police shooting at windows."

"The barricades?"

"Merely a defensive counter-measure to slow down the police attacks. Several individuals who goaded police, I later determined, were *agents provocateurs*, because I saw them chumming with officers. Otherwise, at no point did I witness any resistance to the police. Just hoots and whistles."

"Wouldn't you say that the police were under a great deal of stress?"

"Look. I tried to put myself in their shoes. But when I heard one tell another something, then I understood."

"What was that?"

"'We aren't allowed to smoke out the whole nest,' a policeman told another."

"But why would Zorgiebel order his men to open fire on unthreatening citizens?"

"The record shows that he has done this sort of thing before."

"Not on this level. And why would our government support him?"

"Why would the Minister of the Interior ban the march? The Kaiser himself would never have prohibited the May Day march. The truth is that the Social Democrats were afraid the communists would have a bigger parade. Why aren't they jealous, instead, of the gatherings of the National Socialists?"

"But that still doesn't explain what you're claiming: a quasi-military operation to take over the city!"

"Personally, I think it's practice."

"*Practice*?"

"For the future."

Waves of disgruntled chatter rolled over the crowd. The next thing the man said could barely be heard, and he was asked to repeat.

"Isn't it obvious? The Prussian military has turned the SDP into a machine of state oppression." Then, rising to his feet, he added, his voice teeming with indignation: "And the split they have caused between the party and the communists will never be mended. Never!" He stomped his foot on the last word.

Now, the audience broke into a seastorm of deep-throated outbursts.

"Thank you for coming here today, Sir."

Panelist Erich Muhsam called the meeting to be adjourned; it would be continued in two days, same time, same place.

****

As Carl was setting up for the affair two days later, Apfel rushed in with Toller close behind him. Both had flushed faces.

"Carl! Do you know what just happened? I was shoved against the wall and told to call off the meeting at once."

"I saw it happen," avowed Toller. "I got in between them and screamed at the man until he backed off."

"Who was he?"

"He claimed to be sent by Otto Wels himself."

Carl whistled.

"Then Pieck's men started approaching, and he ran off like the rat he was."

"Thank God for Pieck's big bruisers."

"The Social Democrats are becoming desperate."

"If he was telling the truth."

"And it validates the ex-cop's testimony."

"At least it would support it."

"My name is Siegfried Jacoby."

"Why have you come forward today?"

"I was on my way home from work at the library at Alexander Square, on the afternoon of Wednesday the third. As I crossed New King's Street in front of Tietz Department Store, I was hit from behind by a policeman with a baton. I went down onto the pavement immediately."

"Is that why you are using a crutch today?"

"No. I've been lame quite some time, since a car accident."

"You say you were crossing the street using your crutch?"

"Yes. And carrying a load of books to my apartment. After I was struck, they flew out from under my arm; it was a mess. The man in uniform hit me and passed on, chasing some others."

"How many times?"

"Three. On the skull, shoulder, and spine. I went straight to Buckrow. That is, after I found my glasses. Some people helped me up and gathered my things."

"You are a scholar?"

"Mathematician. I was secretary to Professor Einstein for several years."

"That must have been quite a job!"

"I want also to say that, it seemed to me, Jews were especially targeted by the police, and I am willing to sign an affidavit to that effect."

"Thank you very much for your witness, Mr. Jacoby."

Before closing the hearing, they showed a short filmstrip that a UFA cameraman had taken over the course of the three days. As the projector rattled, fuzzy black images shifted and showed people marching in rows, carrying flags, mouths opening in silent songs and shouts; the heads and backs of bystanders on the sidewalks, at once, more static and chaotic than those *en parade*; people running, some falling in their rush, chased and hosed with powerful streams of water; others walking with arms raised, led by uniformed riflemen; a man lying on pavement with a bleeding head-wound; people helping another to rise; armed police hiding behind the corner of a building. The last series of images, which provoked shouts of outrage from the audience, showed half a dozen policemen aiming rifles at the upper stories of facing buildings, smiling as they discharged their weapons, evidently at random, and laughing as they smoked. Then the strip abruptly cut off, and the lights went on again.

After asking the other panelists if they would like to speak in closing, Carl stepped forward to the middle of the stage. "I have been asked to make some remarks before we finish. In doing so, I apologize for contradicting the rule I laid down at the outset, that there would be no speeches, especially from self-proclaimed pundits. In giving into the requests for closure, I open myself reluctantly to the charge of hypocrisy. But one must prioritize!

"First, I would like to thank all who have attended this inquiry, especially those who have so courageously given witness. The results of our hearings will be sent to representatives of government in the hope that such unprovoked and needless carnage never takes place again in our country, and that the welfare of citizens is better safeguarded by those called to protect them as their solemn duty. I hear that Chief Zorgiebel has been sent to England, perhaps with the plan that there he can better learn how to take care of his charges.

"Detractors have compared our proceedings here in the Great Playhouse to a joke, a comedy like the ones so often performed here. At first, I was offended by this criticism, but then I recalled that Aeschylus himself used the Areopagus as a set for Orestes' trial, and that the Rock of Mars symbolized a place of justice for ancient Athenians, the place of trial for those charged with murder in the first degree, even if they were divinities. Perhaps our detractors were more correct than they knew, in spite of their scorn for shining a light on evident misdeeds.

"In summing up our testimonies, I find that if nothing else said here is true, at least it must be admitted that, given the professed duty of police to protect innocent members of society, gross incompetence and lack of planning before and during the May Days massacres have been shown at every level. But that is the least that should be reported, because it assumes that all their actions, from Severing and Zorgiebel and Gzresinski down, were well-intentioned, an assumption that is undermined unanimously not only by those bravely volunteering their witness, but by the fleeting screen images we have just viewed here.

"That said, the charge of incompetence, although more, much more than our own government has proclaimed, is woefully under target. Assumptions are odious; but what if, for the purpose of argument, we momentarily accept a claim of the defenders of the police? 'In defying the ban,' they say, 'the communists wanted martyrs for their cause.' If true, Chief Zorgiebel, you have given them what they wanted! Let us speculate on what might have happened had the march not been banned in the first place. Could the carnage have possibly been worse, Chief Zorgiebel? Would a Bolshevist takeover of Berlin have transpired? Hardly! Perhaps, instead, we Berliners would have witnessed the defiant and inviolable tradition of worker solidarity, the state prohibition of which was seen as a blatant provocation, a challenge to preserve this symbol of the liberation of the world by labor in the face of unjust and uncalled for federal decree.

"And where do we go from here? I hope that the foreboding of one of our witnesses is proven to be false, the fear that the present rupture within the workers' movement is irreparable. I hope, in reflecting that the classical definition of comedy tells us that good prevails, and that the heroic character succeeds against all odds, I hope, fellow-citizens of Berlin, that what we have done here can serve as a beginning of healing and a ground for the solid reconstruction of public welfare. Remember that it was St. Paul, a stranger to Greece, who challenged Athenian law in preaching a God of mercy from the top of the Areopagus. Let us all make common cause and, mercifully forgetting whatever our petty differences may be, let us come together in defense of our Republic against the forces of evil, which we know lurk so menacingly in the shadows throughout Germany.

"Health and well-being to us all, Citizens of Berlin!"

Most people had left by the time Carl started his walk home in the dark. After a few blocks, he heard muted voices behind him; he turned to look. It was Pieck's men, escorting him respectfully at a distance.

****

Several days later, as he walked toward *The Worldstage* offices, Carl heard a tapping up ahead, and drew, once again, the bemused conclusion that it was only after meeting a stranger that one started noticing them ubiquitously. He hurried to catch up and came abreast Siegfried Jacoby, who, head down, kept tapping along with his cane. After greeting the man, he thanked him for speaking at the hearing, but then he got down to what he really wanted to ask.

"Please tell me what it was like to work with Einstein!"

"Hmm," said Jacoby, limping on. "He slept at all hours, worked at all hours. Thinking tired him out, then sleeping gave him back his genius."

"Do you have any stories you can share?"

"For your publication? Man, go interview him personally!"

"No," said Carl. "I'm sorry. I was just wondering."

"Yes, that's what journalists do. Well, Einstein wonders with his violin just as readily as he wonders with his pencil, or the chalk at the chalkboard. He's quite disorganized and always single-minded. Quite a combination!"

They walked on.

"Can I ask under what conditions you left his service?"

"Only confidentially, Mr. Ossietzky!"

"You have my word of honor."

"Hmm." He stared at the sidewalk in front of him. "I saw something I wasn't meant to see."

"Oh."

"He argued a lot with his wife. You know, she's a scientist as well. Anyway, I objected to his treatment of her. Let's just say that he was, uh, overly physical. We agreed to part ways."

"I see."

He rapped the tip of the crutch against the concrete to accompany his pronouncement: "The greatest scientific discovery fails to redeem one iota a single bruise!"

Their eyes were locked as, all around them, the city of Berlin whirled and clamored in its course.

"Thank you," was all Carl could think to say.

They came to a corner where their paths diverged.

"And, Mr. Ossietzky…"

"Yes?"

"Not all ethical axioms are relative. Violence must stop!" The man turned away. Carl watched him, thinking he'd encountered the second SJ that he revered.

But he didn't have much time to ponder that. Walter was standing on the sidewalk outside *The Worldstage* offices, pacing in front of the café's windows and smoking a cigarette. Walter never smoked. Carl hailed him as he approached. Walter turned quickly, his features full of wrinkled concern.

"There are two cops upstairs waiting for you."

"Did they say what they wanted?"

"Just to talk to you."

Carl took Walter's cigarette and sucked on it. When he started to turn toward the stairs, Walter reached for his smoke. Carl kept it away from him.

"Nasty habit!" he said, then vanished into the building.

Officers Krebs and Felder asked him to go into one of the side offices. Krebs closed the door, and the three of them sat down. Felder handed Carl a letter. He opened it and read the following:

> *Citizen Carl von Ossietzky:*
>
> *This is to inform you that an investigation has been initiated against you by the Department of Justice of the Weimar Republic into allegations of espionage and treason in betrayal of the German state for publishing certain articles in your position as editor-in-chief of the periodical* The Worldstage *written by Walter Kreiser, formerly an aeroplane pilot in the German Air Force.*
>
> *Pending the results of this investigation, you will be informed of any official charges.*
>
> *Sincerely,*
> *Office of the Department of Justice,*
> *Weimar Republic of Germany*

Carl folded up the sheet and slapped the desk with it.

"Thank you, Officers, for bringing this—"

"Sign here," ordered Krebs, handing over a form.

As he signed, Carl said, "Let me ask both of you whether you notice any changes in yourselves when you get home after a long day."

Krebs and Felder exchanged looks, but they did not respond.

"When *I* make it home," Carl continued, "I usually heave a sigh as I take off my tie and coat. I kiss my wife and daughter, pat the cat, and gratefully descend into the most comfortable chair available. Do you get me, Gentlemen? I think about my day and consider the things I have done and the decisions I have made, understand? Can either of you relate to what I am saying?"

Another sharing of glances. Officer Felder nodded to Carl.

"Ah! You *do*! Because I was wondering if, or whether, just possibly, you got out of your uniform and maybe spotted yourself in a mirror and, kind of like I do—I ask just for my own curiosity—you evaluate the results of your day and reflect upon your place in the world, in German society. Follow?"

Another nod direct from Felder, without the exchange of glances with Krebs, though the latter sent the former a judgmental stare that would have been withering, had it been received.

"Good!" Carl went on. "I imagine getting out of a uniform would be especially liberating, though, I must say, sometimes I feel like this customary suit-wearing makes me feel like I'm in a dang uniform too. But you know what I mean, don't you?" Carl raised his eyes to the ceiling directly above him. "Kind of like when you look out at night, however rarely it might be, and wonder at the stars in the sky and, well, you sort of take stock of things, and your place in it all. See?" He pointed above him.

"Sometimes," nodded Felder, whispering in almost a gasp. Krebs knit his eyebrows and gave his colleague a sidelong glare.

"Right," said Carl. "Because, when you think about it, I'm not really this suit I'm wearing, am I? Just as you're not your officer's uniform, because, underneath it all, we're just more or less fellows trying to cope and make our way in life, and still, underneath *that*, we're each individuals, the accumulation of all that's come before us, souls or whatever, and *that's* what's really important, isn't it? Not the everyday muddle or the uniform or what's for dinner or what we made or what we owe. It's really what we *did* with the time we were given here, on this clod of earth whirling through space, what we did and why and all that."

Felder was nodding assent.

"Mr. Ossietzky," interjected an irritated Krebs, "we really must go—"

"That's precisely the point I'm trying to make, Officer Krebs! I mean, I know you have other duties to perform, and we're always rushing to the next thing, and all that, but I'm wondering if we consider enough *who* it is who's performing those duties, and why, and what they mean in the big picture—"

"We're not at liberty to discuss your case, if that's what you're trying to—"

"But my case *does* relate to you, doesn't it?" Carl interrupted. "We're fellow citizens," he maintained, doggedly tapping with an index finger the salutation of the letter. "Because you're not just a policeman, Officer Krebs, though I don't in any way mean to belittle your role. In fact, I think it's all the more significant that you're an enforcer of German law and not a baker, for instance, or a truck-driver, you see. You're actually *enforcing* the laws that they say in this letter I might have transgressed, you're protecting the state they say I might have injured."

"Mr. Ossietzky—"

"Whereas I feel that I was upholding the proper values and stated commitments of that state in its interactions with the other countries of the world, and challenging that state to abide by its treaties and promises and principles—"

"We really have to go, Mr. Ossietzky!"

Carl shot up in his chair and extended his hand. "Of course! What was I thinking? Sometimes I'm a lunatic! I get so side-tracked!" He shook their hands, Krebs' reluctantly raised, Felder's more willingly, combined as it was with a wider expression in the eyes than when the man had entered the room. Carl showed them out, making sure to pat Felder on the shoulder in farewell.

Karsch was coming up the stairs as the policemen went down. When he arrived at the top landing, Carl handed him the letter, saying, "Well, Walter, here's where it all starts!"

Later, joking with their colleagues in the bar, Bauer elicited scorn for his unprofessional behavior, and Krebs provoked guffaws by dubbing the incident, 'The case of the insufferable man who loved nothing so well as the sound of his own voice.' But still, in quiet, solitary moments, the episode lingered with the two of them with a heaviness that was surprising.

Chapter Twenty-Five
PRESENT

December 21, 1937: Rosalinde was sixteen years old today. Far away. In Sweden. Previously, Maud had explained to Carl their daughter's reasons for not returning to Germany, an inability, not an unwillingness, and she had explained it to him again, and again. Maud herself could relate, even if he couldn't. She had experienced the same paralyzing inhibition about England in her youth, still felt repulsion toward the country even now. But it wasn't that such psychological matters were inexplicable to Carl; he just couldn't help wishing Rosalinde were here, with him. Rosalie, back in Hamburg, too old to travel, ensconced in her quarters in the rectory that had been her home for so long; *that* he could both understand and accept. Carl couldn't travel either. Besides, they'd spoken by telephone several times. He just couldn't help wishing, craving to see and hold his daughter once again.

They had worked all morning on the telephone to make the connection to Sweden. Finally, it came through. Maud watched her husband's face take on a glow she hadn't seen in years as he heard Rosalinde's voice.

"Hello, my Dear Rosalinde! Happy birthday!"

"Hi, Daddy! How are you feeling?"

Carl stared at Maud. He was disconcerted by the scratchiness of his daughter's voice and hoped the connection was better at her end.

Maud misunderstood the look. She had directed him not to ask Rosalinde when she would be coming to Germany, but to let their daughter bring it up herself, and now she worried he would broach the question anyway.

"I'm good," he went on, louder. "Can you hear me all right?"

"Yes. You sound fine. Can you hear me?"

"Just barely. You sound raspy. Do you have a sore throat?"

Either no answer or one he couldn't hear.

"Tell me, what you are doing?" he went on, continuing to raise the volume. "How are your studies?"

"They are going well. I'm learning the language as fast as I can."

"What do they have you studying? The sagas, for goodness sake?"

"Almost. *Gosta Berling*."

"How exciting!"

"Daddy, I think I want to do something in the theater when I grow up."

"Wonderful! Acting or writing?"

"I don't know. Maybe both."

"Stay away from criticism!" he joked. "It's a racket!"

"Dad, when are they going to let you leave Germany?"

"They say they're working on the details."

"Your lawyers?"

"Oh, dear!" he sighed. "*They're* long gone. Scattered to the four winds." He had no idea where Max was, or the Kurts, Grossmann and Rosenfeld, or Alfred or Rudolf, those men he owed so much! All exiled by the swastika!

She said something he couldn't make out.

"I think we're losing you," he told her. "This damn line is a bad one." He handed the receiver to Maud so she could say something. She put it to her ear and said hello but, after a few moments of listening, she hung it up.

"What did she say?" asked Carl.

"I think she said she had a boyfriend."

"Really?"

"Then the line went dead."

Carl insisted on spending the next half hour trying to make another connection, then gave up. He'd gotten himself so worked up in his efforts at remaking the call that he had to go lie down.

****

February, 1938: Carl sat next to Maud and listened to the lawyer deliver his speech. For once, the prosecution was on his side, although he would rather there were no legal proceedings at all.

The other irony, most terrible in this case, was that the National Socialist government was pursuing redress for him, for Carl von Ossietzky, enemy of the Nazi state. It was in a courtroom festooned with banners brandishing swastikas that Carl was seeking justice! Technically, he had appeared as a Nazi witness! And why? What a mess!

The day had not started well: the headache, the nausea, the aches and pains, his fragile lungs with their congested, liquid purring. Before he'd dressed, Maud had made him step on the scales and, yes, his weight had dropped since last time. Then, he'd had to dress for court: the three-piece, everything; he was fatigued by the time he made it to the breakfast table.

And, to top it off, to find the room had been set up for photographs! Maud had been afraid to tell him in advance. He thought he'd heard something; it was the photographer and his assistant setting up. Why did the lights have to be so bright? And hot! He was sweating! Where was Werner Finck when you needed him to cheer you up?

He was supposed to *pose* while eating? Maybe Maud could, eating her toast, but not him. Nonsense! She could go ahead and eat, but he would wait till the men were gone. Crossing his legs, sitting on his hands, hands together. "Smile for the camera, Carl. Don't look so grumpy!" She didn't tell him what it hurt her to think: that his head looked gargantuan on his frail and diminished body.

And now this! The poor man on the witness stand probably wished he could vanish. Carl could relate!

Maud had met the man in the dock, a lawyer named Wannow, in a restaurant while Carl was in Esterwegen. He offered to help them, visited Carl, and Carl, confused, had given him power of attorney. Wannow had sent his secretary to fetch some of the prize money in Sweden and bring it back.

Then their friend, Hilde Walter, had been in financial straits. Maud authorized her to get some of the money to use for herself. Nothing doing! The Swedish Academy refused!

That's when they started to discover what Wannow was up to. It appeared that he had made purchases for himself, loans to friends, had even acquired a cinema in Charlottenburg, placing it in the name of his girlfriend's father!

And when Carl had complained to Wannow? The man had threatened to have him sent back to a concentration camp! That was when Carl had asked his friend and doctor, Dosquet, for help.

Now, Wannow faced a Gestapo investigation, orchestrated by a government that wished to appear impartial, even toward enemies of the state.

Could things get any crazier?

Yet, when the verdict came down, and the sentence of two years of hard labor was given to Wannow, Carl felt no better. He knew in his bones, in every fiber of his being, what the sentence meant. Besides, he and Maud would never see the money. It was irretrievable, already spent! When the handcuffed convict had been led past the prosecution table on his way to the penitentiary, Carl could only whisper toward the shocked convict, "I am sorry." If anyone in the world understood the meaning of the man's sentence, it was the litigant.

****

It was Carl von Ossietzky's last public appearance. A pulmonary hemorrhage took his life on the 4th of May. Official cause of death: meningitis.

Before his body was removed from the hospital, Maud waited for a moment when they were alone. She had a mission, and she had come prepared. First, she made the door ajar; then she unrolled the soft plaster from her oversized handbag and pressed it with loving fingers over his face. Last, she sat next to the bed, meditating on the hardening clay, peeking from time to time into the hallway for anyone who might happen by, while watching the clock on the wall as the plaster gradually set.

From time to time, she got up from her chair to replace the clay where it had loosened from the skin.

She had been right to move quickly and take her precautions. In order to prevent Carl's burial site from becoming a memorial, the Gestapo operated swiftly to have his corpse cremated and the ashes disposed of in an undisclosed location. They did not want Carl von Ossietzky yet again, now posthumously, to become a problem for the German state. However, as things turned out, their aims were frustrated in this case.

Final Chapter

Although she did putter around with a feather-duster on occasion, Rosalie was no longer capable of the sort of basement-to-attic cleaning she had performed at the rectory in a cycle of *perpetuum mobile* for so many years. And she only answered the door now and then when no one else was around, shuffling from the ground floor room the parish proffered her in recompense for her antediluvian contributions and also as a charity case in the parish.

When Maud and Rosalinde arrived, on that day late in 1945, as soon as they could after the war, they didn't even know if she were still alive or, if so, where exactly and in what condition. So, when they were led into the bedroom and saw the old woman hunched over in a stuffed chair, they went straight to the possibility that perhaps they had come at the critical moment and exchanged glances of shock and deep concern. As it turned out, Rosalie was just snoozing.

The novice priest left them to determine the matter, shutting the door quietly behind him. But the click of the catch was enough to raise Rosalie's head, and a smile appeared, as if predesigned to do so, before any other expression, or even before her myopic eyes settled on her relatives and registered who they were. Then the brows lifted and, with a look of pleased surprise Maud and Rosalinde found reminiscent of Carl, the old woman's face broke into a broad and steady grin.

"Well now, look at who has just walked in!"

"Hello, Grandma!" Rosalinde exclaimed, hugging the woman and seating herself at her feet. "How are you?"

Maud followed with a soft embrace and then sat down in a chair facing Rosalie.

"As well as an old bag can expect to be."

"You look wonderful, Rosalie," said Maud.

"Well, they take care of me around here just about as well as I took care of them back in the day," Rosalie proclaimed. "What more can you expect?" Then she emitted a laugh that melted her daughter-in-law and granddaughter.

"What are you looking at there?" asked Rosalinde, gesturing toward Rosalie's lap.

Rosalie looked down at the double frame of oval photographs that she had forgotten about.

"Oh! It's Carl and Carl Ignatius." She lifted the portraits and displayed them. Both men were taken in uniform. Rosalinde was handed the diptych and studied each pose, then passed it on to her mother.

"That is Daddy before the Great War!"

"On his way to France."

"And what is the story behind Grandpa's photograph?" Rosalinde asked about the man neither she nor her mother had ever met.

"He's on his way to France as well," said Rosalie.

"When?" asked Maud. "This is something I've never heard about."

"Well, he certainly didn't want to go," Rosalie answered. "They practically had to drag him, just like Carl. The Ossietzky men have lost whatever warfaring strain they might have once possessed. He was on his way to Paris with Bismarck, to pay them back for what Napoleon had done, I suppose."

"Did Grandpa ever talk about it?" asked Rosalinde.

"Hardly ever. It was long before I met him. As a matter of fact, there is only once that I ever remember him relating anything about the experience, and that wasn't to me. He thought

I couldn't hear what he was saying. I was in the kitchen, and he was out in the other room sharing stories with a friend, an invalid from the same war.

"When I caught on to what Carl Ignatius was saying, I snuck behind the doorway, the better to hear. I was eavesdropping!"

"What did he say?"

"It was awful! I wish I hadn't listened, and I certainly didn't ask him anything about the French affair afterwards. He was telling his friend about when they were clearing out a village, and the men found a girl hiding in a barn, just a young woman. She might have been in her teens, he said. The other men were going to start in on her, you know, and Carl Ignatius didn't approve." Rosalie snickered. "A lot of help he was for that poor girl! He said that the last thing he remembered, before waking up three days later on a stretcher in an ambulance wagon in Bismarck's returning troop train, with his head bandaged, was stepping forward between the girl and the men and raising his arm."

"My goodness!"

"Yes! And I never mentioned the incident to him, neither the anecdote nor the aftermath nor the conditions under which I learned about it. But it answered a question I'd had for quite some time, about a knob under his scalp that never went away and always gave me trouble when I tried to clip his hair. And the story was also significant for another reason."

"What was that?"

"It further confirmed for me the strong conviction I already had: that I'd married the right man, a man whose mettle had survived years of training in belligerence. Not that I hadn't received other offers, some of them good ones. You see…"

Epilogue: 12/3/1992

Rosalinde von Ossietzky-Palm was slowly escorted down the steps of the German Supreme Court in Karlsruhe. Her companion patiently halted as, half-way down, Rosalinde stopped to catch her breath and take in the panoramic view of the city. She noted the Palace on the left, the Technological Institute in the center, and Market Square to the right.

Democracy had returned to the country of her birth, as well as, at long last, a kind of unification. The Wall had amazingly, jubilantly, cathartically, finally come down. But, as she gazed, the set of her aged features was grim with disappointment.

The highest private and criminal court in the land had just upheld her father's '31 conviction for treason and espionage, decreeing, "the illegality of covertly conducted actions did not cancel out the principle of secrecy... Every citizen owes his Fatherland a duty of allegiance regarding information, and endeavors towards the enforcement of existing laws may be implemented only through the utilization of responsible state organs, and never by appealing to foreign governments." Thus, her lengthy appeal to re-open the proceedings and reverse the verdict, after sixty years that included the catastrophic rise and fall of Nazism, had come to an end, unless, that is, the stalwart nonagenarian wanted to raise the issue of constitutionality and, in doing so, embark on an even greater crusade to defend her father's reputation, a daunting prospect, toward which, she was obviously averse.

She was done. The septuagenarian had performed her duty to her parents, and more. And, as she surveyed the city landscape, she tried to fit defeat into a suitable context for her father's legacy. Once again, reality had shown that success wasn't the only point; whether one succeeded or failed was not the end. There was never a last word, only the presence or absence of a core conviction that humanity had a direction, and that direction was forward to collective, universal freedom and justice and equality. Anything else was deception and dodge. And when you realized that, and kept it before you in all you did, then you couldn't help but see your long-dead father as a shining star.

Yes, democracy had returned to Germany. Much had changed.

But what hadn't changed?

Acknowledgements:

I cannot thank my editor, literary agent or publisher, since I have none.

I am to blame for it all.

I would, however, like to thank our public library system, especially the LINK+ service, without which my readings would never have been afforded.

And did I tell you this is all for Janice?

CPSIA information can be obtained
at www.ICGtesting.com
Printed in the USA
FSHW011345150319
56307FS

9 781949 472